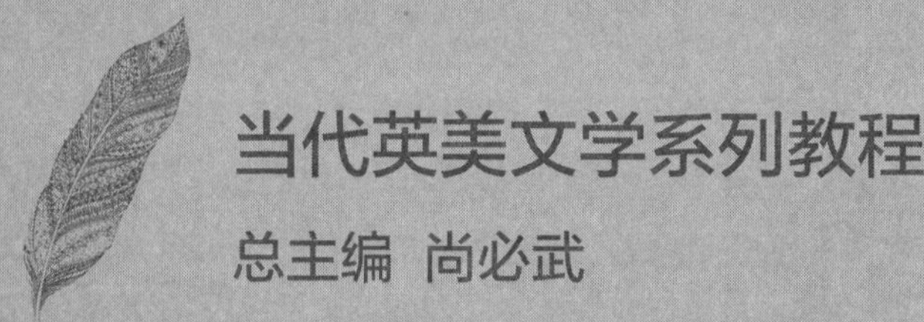

当代英美文学系列教程

总主编 尚必武

当代美国小说教程

A Coursebook on Contemporary American Novels

主编：陈　靓

编者：陈子幸　丁　艳　郝玉梅
井永洁　吴　叶　叶汶杰
袁　源　张晓雯　周小英

内容提要

本书为“当代英美文学系列教程”之一。本书的主要内容包括20世纪70年代以来的当代美国小说作品，以及当代美国小说创作和批评思想的阶段性特征和发展趋势。在小说作品的选择上，本书选择了不同类型和样式的小说，如科幻小说、族裔小说、女性小说等。每个门类下均选取数篇具有典型性的小说作品，并对其主题特色、历史背景以及相关文学特质进行介绍，凸显对文本敏锐的分析能力以及相关文学研究视角和理论知识的掌握。此外，本书介绍20世纪70年代以来，美国后现代主义语境下小说这一体裁中呈现的新创作手法、文学思潮和文体特征。本书适合国内高校英美文学专业的研究生、英美文学学者及文学爱好者使用。

图书在版编目(CIP)数据

当代美国小说教程/陈靓主编. —上海:上海交通大学出版社,2024. 9—(当代英美文学系列教程/尚必武总主编). —ISBN 978-7-313-31322-5

Ⅰ. I712. 074

中国国家版本馆CIP数据核字第2024NJ2899号

当代美国小说教程
DANGDAI MEIGUO XIAOSHUO JIAOCHENG

主　　编：陈　靓
出版发行：上海交通大学出版社　　地　　址：上海市番禺路951号
邮政编码：200030　　电　　话：021-64071208
印　　制：浙江天地海印刷有限公司　　经　　销：全国新华书店
开　　本：889mm×1194mm　1/16　　印　　张：15
字　　数：375千字
版　　次：2024年9月第1版　　印　　次：2024年9月第1次印刷
书　　号：ISBN 978-7-313-31322-5
定　　价：68.00元

Preface | 总序

2012年，国务院学位委员会第六届学科评议组在外国语言文学一级学科目录下设置了5大方向，即外国文学、语言学与应用语言学、翻译学、国别与区域研究、比较文学与跨文化研究。2020年起，教育部开始大力推进"新文科"建设，不仅发布了《新文科建设宣言》，还设立了"新文科研究与改革实践项目"，旨在进一步打破学科壁垒，促进学科的交叉融合，提升文科建设的内涵与质量。在这种背景下，外语研究生教育既迎来了机遇，同时又面临新的挑战，这就要求我们的研究生培养模式为适应这些变化而进行必要的改革与创新。在孙益、陈露茜、王晨看来，"研究生教育方针、教育路线的贯彻执行，研究生教育体制改革和教育思想的革新，研究生专业培养方案、培养计划的制定，研究生教学内容和教学方法的改革，最终都会反映和落实到研究生教材的建设上来。重视研究生教材建设工作，是提高高校研究生教学质量和保证教学改革成效的关键所在。"[①]从这种意义上说，教材建设是提高外语研究生教育的一个重要抓手。

就国内外语专业研究生教材而言，上海外语教育出版社推出的《高等院校英语语言文学专业研究生系列教材》占据了最主要的地位。该系列涵盖语言学、语言教学、文学理论、原著选读等多个领域，为我国的外语研究生培养做出了重要贡献。需要指出的是，同外语专业本科生教材建设相比，外语专业研究生教材建设显得明显滞后。很多高校的外语专业研究生课堂上所使用的教材基本上是原版引进教材或教师自编讲义。我们知道，"教材不仅是教师进行教学的基本工具，而且是学生获取知识、培养能力的重要手段。研究生教材是直接体现高等院校研究生教学内容和教学方法的知识载体，也是反映高等院校教学水平、科研水平及其成果的重要标志，优秀的研究生教材是提高研究生教学质量的重要保证。"[②]上海交通大学外国语学院历来重视教材建设，曾主编《研究生英语教程》《多维教程》《新视野大学英语》《21世纪大学英语》等多套本科和研究生层次的英语教材，在全国范围内产生了较大影响。

---

① 孙益、陈露茜、王晨：《高校研究生教材建设的国际经验与中国路径》，载《学位与研究生教育》2018年第2期，第72页。

② 同上。

为进一步加强和推动外语专业，尤其是英语专业英美文学方向的研究生教材建设，助力研究生培养从接受知识到创造知识的模式转变，在上海交通大学出版社的大力支持下，上海交通大学外国语学院发挥优势，携手复旦大学外文学院、上海外国语大学英语学院、北京科技大学外国语学院、东北师范大学外国语学院、中南财经政法大学外国语学院、山东师范大学外国语学院等兄弟单位，主编《当代英美文学系列教程》。本系列教材重点聚焦20世纪80年代以来的英美文学与文论，由《当代英国小说教程》《当代美国小说教程》《当代英国戏剧教程》《当代美国戏剧教程》《当代英国诗歌教程》《当代美国诗歌教程》《当代文学理论教程》《当代叙事理论教程》等8册构成。

本系列教材以问题意识为导向，围绕当代英美文学，尤其是21世纪英美文学的新类型、新材料、新视角、新话题，将文学作为一种直面问题、思考问题、应对问题、解决问题的重要途径和方式，从而发掘和彰显文学的能动性。在每册教材的导论部分，首先重点概述20世纪80年代以来的文学发展态势与特征，由此回答“当代起于何时”的问题，在此基础上简述教材内容所涉及的主要命题、思潮、样式、作家和作品，由此回答“新在哪里”的问题。本系列教材打破按照时间顺序来划分章节的惯例，转而以研究问题或文学样式来安排各章。例如，教材纳入了气候变化、新型战争、族裔流散、世界主义等问题与文学样式。在文学作品的选择标准上，教材以类型和样式的标准来分类，如气候变化文学、新型战争文学等。每个门类下均选取数篇具有典型性的作品，并对其主题特色、历史背景及其相关文学特质进行介绍，凸显对文本性敏锐的分析能力以及对相关文学研究视角及理论知识的掌握。除此之外，教材还有意识地呈现当代英美文学的新的创作手法、文学思潮和文体特征。教材的每章集中一种文学样式、类型、思潮或流派，选择2～3篇代表性作品，单篇选读篇幅在5 000～10 000词(英文)左右，每篇附有5 000字(中文)左右的分析导读以及若干思考题。教材对作家或理论家及其著作的选取，不求涵盖全部，而是以权威性、代表性和重要性为首要原则，兼顾年代、流派、思潮等因素。本系列教材适合国内高校外国文学尤其是英美文学专业的博士研究生、硕士研究生、高年级本科生、文学研究者与爱好者使用。

本系列教材在编写过程中得到了上海交通大学外国语学院、上海交通大学出版社以及国内外同行专家学者的关心、帮助与支持，特此谢忱！

尚必武

2023年3月

Foreword 前言

本教材将“当代”的时间限定在20世纪70年代至今这段时间。20世纪70年代，美国社会经历各种动荡，政治运动不断。作为反映社会现实的语言，在后现代主义的冲击下，在语言主体观上也面临巨大挑战。现实与语言这两大主体领域也在解构的浪潮下被不断重新整合。相应地，当代美国小说在写作策略、主题风格、文体特征等领域不断尝试创新，呈现出繁盛的发展态势。在后现代主义场域下被撕裂的语言使得对现实、身份、主体等传统领域的呈现具有了碎片化和不确定性等特点。阅读体验被高度个人化、主观化，更强调具体语境的特质场域。对小说的研究视角也涵盖语言本体、性别书写、族裔性、历史性、身份塑形、流散特质、创伤与记忆等诸多领域。在很多当代美国小说中，“现实”被割裂、模仿或重叠。而语言对它的呈现，以及作者、读者和作品的身份越发复杂地交织在一起，使得当代美国小说在创作风格、文学思想、文化社会背景等方面均有诸多新颖的突破。从小说的主题上看，性别书写和族裔书写中的身份意识在不断增强；由现代主义衍生而来的语言的游戏性和实验先锋理念也在不断强化，并在后现代主义的冲击下，发展态势愈演愈烈；从存在论的角度对人性、自我和暴力的思考依然持续；新科技以及大众媒体的浪潮下，文学的阅读、传播、跨媒介写作及其与文化话语的互动，构成了新时期美国小说的独特性。

就当代美国小说中语言层面的创新而言，20世纪70年代涌现的新生代作家有凯茜·艾克(Kathy Acker)。她在70年代集中推出了一系列作品，如《黑蜘蛛写黑蜘蛛孩子般的生活》(*Childlike Life of the Black Tarantula by the Black Tarantula*, 1973)、《我梦见我是一个狂热者：想象》(*I Dreamt I was a Maniac: Imagining*, 1974)和《图鲁斯·劳特莱克的成人生活》(*Adult Life of Toulouse Lautrec*, 1978)。聚焦于语言实验性的小说创作在叙述策略上有诸多探索，并将语言研究置于小说研究的中心位置。其间，雷蒙·费德曼(Raymond Federman)的《成双或成零》(*Double or Nothing*, 1971)，瓦特·埃比什(Walter Abish)的《字母非洲》(*Alphabetical Africa*, 1974)和唐纳德·巴塞尔姆(Donald Barthelme)的《亡父》(*The Dead Father*, 1975)均呈现类似特点。在小说的创作倾向上，以语言为本体论的观念在美国小说界也引发了争论。比较有名的是70年代晚期威廉·H.加斯(William H. Gass)和约翰·加德纳(John Gardner)之间的辩论,即作品应该被视为独立的语言存在,还是道德规训的载体?该意见分歧也是后现代主义在现实观层面的突破中必然要面临的障碍。70年代期间,传统现实主义的潮流和后现代先锋作品都在按照自己的脉络向前发展。前者以道·默斯曼(Dow Mossman)的《夏天的石头》(*The Stones of Summer*, 1972)为代表,而后者的后现代叙述策略在托马斯·品钦(Thomas Pynchon)的《万有引力之虹》(*Gravity's Rainbow*, 1973)和琼·狄迪恩(Joan Didion)的《祈祷书》(*A Book of Common Prayer*, 1977)等作品中得到了充分的展现。

两种文学潮流的发展也波及美国族裔文学领域,其中语言、权力和文化身份的互动成为当代美国族裔小说中身份构建的主要机制。例如菲利普·罗斯(Philip Roth)在1979年创作的《鬼作家》(*The Ghost Writer*)描述了动荡的文化背景下犹太裔美国人的身份探求问题。鲁道夫·安纳亚(Rudolpho Anaya)的《祝福我,乌蒂玛》(*Bless Me, Ultima*, 1972)则将神话和民谣等元素置于身份探求的过程当中。与此风格类似的是托妮·莫里森(Toni Morrison)在70年代创作的3部作品:《最蓝的眼睛》(*The Bluest Eyes*, 1970)、《苏拉》(*Sula*, 1972)和《所罗门之歌》(*Song of Solomon*, 1977),汤亭亭(Maxine Hong Kingston)的《女勇士》(*The Woman Warrior: Memories of a Girlhood among Ghosts*, 1976)也呈现了一定的魔幻现实主义色彩。少数族裔性特质中的传统身份元素,尤其是口述传统、神话传说、宇宙观及宗教元素成为少数族裔作家彰显身份的主要特质。大量的口述传统所包含的多声部叙述结构和对话性特质被吸收进小说的叙述结构中。此外,少数族裔传统文化中的超现实元素被融入到文本的现实构建中,呈现出鲜明的(后)现代主义现实景观。它们不仅从语言这个文学形式层面,同时也从现实景观的重塑这个文学内容层面推动了当代美国小说的创新。其中,美国印第安作家莱斯利·马蒙·西尔科(Leslie Marmon Silko)的《典仪》(*Ceremony*, 1977)以及詹姆斯·韦尔奇(James Welch)的《血色寒冬》(*Winter in the Blood*, 1974)就是典型代表。

身份构建是美国少数族裔小说的主旋律之一。20世纪80年代以来,少数族裔小说也努力在多元的文化语境下进行新的语言创作尝试和身份塑形。在"印第安文艺复兴""奇卡诺文艺复兴""亚裔美国文艺复兴"等族裔文艺发展浪潮的推动下,美国族裔小说在创作主题上从民族主义创作理念出发,开始进行带有超越族裔性的世界主义的创作尝试;在创作手法上也将自身的族裔文化叙述特质与西方的(后)现代写作技巧进行融合,更充分地展示了族裔作品在文本性上的独立主体性。

在当代美国族裔文学中,喜剧文学的元素频繁出现。喜剧风格作为美国小说发展中的核心元素之一，以其本土化特征从文学维度构建了美国独特的文化特质。它不仅有马克·吐温(Mark Twain)和华盛顿·欧文(Washington Irving)这样的白人作家作为奠基人，也可以在美国少数族裔的传统文化中找到强烈的共鸣。当代的美国少数族裔作品往往会运用传统文化中的幽默元素彰显族裔性特质，如印第安传统文化中的“恶作剧者”(Trickster)、犹太文化中的“贫民窟幽默”(Ghetto Humor)和黑人喜剧元素。二战之后盛行的“黑色幽默”(Black Humor)更是在新时期得到了进一步的拓展，作为解构性力量进入了族裔文学、女性文学和历史小说中。

同样，在当代美国女性小说中，女性的身份和主体性问题依然占据着创作与批评的主旋律。在创作主题上，女性小说和族裔、生态、科技元素有诸多交织；在创作策略上，作家们多以后现代主义和后结构主义的风格建构女性视域下的元小说语言和文本主体性。语言对现实的重塑功能在女性主义作家中也受到重视。她们通过探讨语言的性别化以及它作为男性权力的载体，在创作中将语言视为性别反抗的重要渠道。其中比较有代表性的作品是乔安娜·拉斯(Joanna Russ)的《女身男人》(*The Female Man*, 1975)。

“历史编纂元小说”的概念也同时在70年代兴起。在琳达·哈琴(Linda Hutcheon)的界定中，该类小说具有元小说的自反性认知，它们在叙述中建构历史的多重图景，同时也在质疑该图景的真实性，具有鲜明的后现代特质。小说家们开始深入思考语言与现实的关系，并创作了大量优秀作品，例如盖尔·琼斯(Gayl Jones)的《科里西多拉》(*Corregidora*, 1975)、华莱士·斯特格纳(Wallace Stegner)的《安息角》(*Angle of Repose*, 1971)、安妮·迪拉德(Annie Dillard)的《听客溪的朝圣》(*Pilgrim at Tinker Creek*, 1974)和汤姆·沃尔夫(Tom Wolfe)的《真材实料》(*The Right Stuff*, 1979)等。其中，E. L. 多克托罗(E. L. Doctorow)的《拉格泰姆时代》(*Ragtime*, 1975)影响力较大，以历史与虚构融合的方式呈现了多图景的社会画卷。在此期间的越南战争也进入了小说的题材范畴，迈克尔·赫尔(Michael Herr)的《新闻快报》(*Dispatches*, 1977)和蒂姆·奥布莱恩(Tim O'Brien)的《追寻卡西艾托》(*Going After Cacciato*, 1978)将自传、报道和历史叙述结合起来，以多棱镜的散射视角力图呈现越南战争的不同历史剪影。

美国建国以来，战争的硝烟一直伴随着美国的历史进程。70年代以来，美国政府陆续发动或参与各种地区冲突，包括入侵也门(1971)、格林纳达(1983)、洪都拉斯(1988)，空袭利比亚(1986)和南联盟(1999)，发动巴拿马战争(1989)、海湾战争(1991)、阿富汗战争(2001)、伊拉克战争(2003)和利比亚战争(2011)等。无尽的战争给美国社会带来了很大的冲击，也成为美国历代作家关注的重点主题之一。70年代具有代表性的战争小说有罗伯特·斯通(Robert Stone)的《亡命之徒》(*Soldiers*, 1974)、蒂姆·奥布莱恩的《追寻卡西艾托》和迈克尔·赫尔的《新闻快报》。这些作品从不同的视角审视了战争给美国的社会和民众带来的创伤，并以战争为题材开展了多种形式的文本创作尝试，在创作主题上对战争中的人类命运、难民、道德伦理、种族和性别歧视、心理创伤等问题进行了深入剖析，在创作风格上也经历了从现实主义到后现代主义的转变，以荒诞、碎片化和虚构等手法展示战争的非理性。新新闻主义(New Journalism)更是成为当代美国战争小说创作中对客观与想象描写的跨界性尝试。随着新闻媒体的网络化发展，新媒介中的影像、音频、图片等元素也进入了战争小说的叙事中，使得该文类的创作策略和审美标准也日趋多元化。

作为美国文学中的经典文类，哥特小说在美洲大陆上展现了别样的文本魅力和主题特质。它与美国的民族叙事互相交融。二战后，哥特小说在创作手法上充分吸收现代主义策略。伴随着城市化的进程，当代美国哥特小说在传统的边疆叙事之外，将创作视野拓展到族裔问题、都市犯罪、心理悬疑等领域，极大地丰富了作品的文本张力和主题内涵。

20 世纪 80 年代以来，美国社会的多元化发展大大拓宽了文学现实主义的视域，并触发了唐纳德·巴塞尔姆、约翰·巴思(John Barth)和罗伯特·库弗(Robert Coover)等人的元小说实验。与此同时，作为新新闻主义的开创人之一，汤姆·沃尔夫将外部的事实和描述与社会学的观察和集体想象融合在一起，将现实主义的异质性注入到他的作品创作中，其代表作有《名利之火》(*The Bonfire of the Vanities*, 1987)和《真正的男子汉》(*A Man in Full*, 1998)。一部分作家如安妮·泰勒(Anne Tyler)和理查德·罗素(Richard Russo)从关注地域环境的细节入手，呈现现实的复杂性；另一部分作家如拉丁裔美国作家卡洛斯·富恩特斯(Carlos Fuentes)从魔幻现实主义的视角将历史细节和地域特色与超自然和神话元素相融合。

在后现代风格下，语言通过变形、替换、消解、模仿或者嘲讽的方式建构不同版本的“现实”。而这种语言中的现实图景是现实的一个侧面，它与生活中的其他现实侧面一样真实。但同时期的美国小说家也在思考，受语言本身的范畴和性质所限，人们在语言所构建的现实中感知的存在有什么样的价值？它与现实生活中的存在有一种怎样的互动关系？这种关于语言与现实关系的后现代观思考在 70 年代开始升温，到了 80 年代，随着多元文化的盛行，开启了“经典的爆炸”，族裔文学、女性文学和同性恋文学纷纷从边缘走向中心。

在创作中，美国小说在叙述策略上融入了更多的先锋性语言技巧，从而在作品中塑造了各种形态复杂的“现实”景观，兼具连续性和断裂的特征，身份也开始从单一性转向多重性，从而构建了当代美国小说中丰富的异质性。受此影响，20 世纪 80 年代的美国小说具有了高度的语言自反性特点，即作家对语言本身有着高度的自觉性，对于语言在与身份、文化和历史等元素交织中所形成的文学进程中的自我定位保持旁观者的清醒。同时，在创作中，作家们开始越来越重视视觉元素的运用，例如约翰纳·德拉克(Johanna Drucker)和史蒂夫·托马苏拉(Steve Tomasula)的作品以视觉元素有效丰富了叙述的多层面。对视觉元素的运用在随后的美国小说的发展中被不断强化，并与背景和主题进行结合，呈现了丰富的互文性特质，代表性作品有迈克尔·查邦(Michael Chabon)的《卡瓦利与克雷的神奇冒险》(*The Amazing Adventures of Kavalier & Clay*, 2000)和乔纳森·勒瑟姆(Jonathan Lethem)的《孤独堡垒》(*The Fortress of Solitude*, 2003)等。

20世纪80年代中期以后，在科技的发展大潮中，人类自身的局限性开始逐渐显现，在高科技的背景下，人类身份的重新界定势在必行。美国小说界开始探讨人类身份与科技的互动问题，以及随之而来的人工智能对人类身份的挑战、克隆技术带来的伦理问题及基因变异导致的身份危机等。此外，因特网技术的发展开拓了虚拟现实的空间。如何看待人机互动所构建的现实？人类身份的未来和边界在哪里？这些问题无论在创作主题还是文本策略层面都给当代美国小说的创作带来了更多的思考，并进一步引发了“后人类”的范畴和主题探讨。在N.凯瑟琳·海尔斯(N. Katherine Hayles)的界定中，在后人类的理论范畴中，“身体存在和电脑仿真、自动化机制与生物有机体、机器人目的和人类目标这三个组别中没有本质的区别或绝对的界限。”[①]具有代表性的作品有雷德利·斯科特(Ridley Scott)的《银翼杀手》(*Blade Runner*, 1982)和威廉·福特·吉布森(William Ford Gibson)的《神经漫游者》(*Neuromancer*, 1984)。

在科技大潮下催生的当代美国科幻小说以“新浪潮运动”为创作方向，主题日趋多样化，并在创作上勇于尝试各种实验性语言策略，以超越现实的场景反观当下的性别、种族等社会问题。美国科幻文学在创作文类上分出女性科幻文学、军事科幻文学、赛博朋克、蒸汽朋克等分支，将关注的视线投向未来，通过虚拟体验来表达对当下和未来美国社会的生态、文化、政治等问题的思考。

1979年，哲学家让-弗朗索瓦·利奥塔(Jean-François Lyotard)在《后现代状况》(*The Postmodern Condition: A Report on Knowledge*)一书中对历史的宏大“元叙事”观提出了挑战，指出历史应该由诸多“微历史”组成。继而在80年代，在米歇尔·福柯(Michel Foucault)和后马克思主义历史观的基础上，“新历史主义”批评开始发声，以“历史的文本性”和“文本的历史性”概念消解了以往传统历史主义对“历史”和“文本”的同质性主体观，强调特定历史时期历史与文本的互动性与互相塑形。当代美国小说也多以历史事件并置的方式，以元小说的形式呈现历史的多面性，消解传统历史观中历史书写的客观和权威。

---

① Hayles, N. Katherine. *How We Became Posthuman: Virtual Bodies in Cybernetics, Literature, and Informatics*. Chicago: University of Chicago Press, 1999, p.3.

比较有代表性的是威廉·H.加斯的《隧道》(*The Tunnel*, 1995)和唐·德里罗(Don Delillo)的《地下世界》(*Underworld*, 1997)。这两部作品致力于在官方的历史叙述之下,展现被忽视的、交织互动在一起的历史碎片。它们组成了一股暗流,波涛汹涌,不时撞击着宏大历史叙事的冰层。在新历史主义者看来,只有充分挖掘暗流的能量,才能真正地展示历史的"真实"。加勒比小说家爱多尔德·格列森特(Edouard Glissant)曾将被官方历史的宏大叙事边缘化的历史描述为一种"非历史"(nonhistory)。它的特点是"(它)不可能像沉积物一样逐渐持续地堆积在一起……而是在一种包含冲击、矛盾、痛苦的否定和爆发性的力量的场域中汇聚起来"[①]。对于"非历史"的展示,需要有超越文化意识形态冲突各方的视野,以中立的姿态对被忽略的历史事件进行发掘、拼贴、想象和重构。随着后殖民批评理论在70年代的盛行,这种对"非历史"的展示策略尤为受到重视。

20世纪晚期的民权运动和自由言论运动推动了当代美国小说在族裔写作和性别写作领域的进展。美国政治文化对同性恋婚姻、合法堕胎等问题持续关注,学术界在性别理论和同性恋写作领域的研究不断深入,朱迪斯·巴特勒(Judith Butler)在《性别困境》(*Gender Trouble*, 1990)中提出性别是一种社会建构和操演的观点。关于"操演"的概念界定,巴特勒提出"性别通过一套持续的行为被营造出来,通过性别化的身体风格来认定"[②]。在女性写作的创作理念下,当代美国女性小说寻求从文本性的角度在作品的文体本身凸显女性特质,以建构其多元的性别身份。

21世纪早期,作为美国历史中的重要历史事件,"9·11"事件为美国的单极战略敲响了警钟,彻底改变了美国21世纪初10年的外交政策方向和政坛焦点,同时,也对美国社会和文化带来了强烈的集体创伤。很多小说家纷纷撰文,如琼·狄迪恩、蒂姆·奥布莱恩和乔伊思·卡罗尔·奥特兹(Joyce Carol Oates)等作家在《纽约时报》发文,表达了对逝者的哀悼,并描述了这场悲剧所带来的心理创伤。伊恩·麦克尤恩(Ian McEwan)曾哀叹称,自此以后"生活已无法回到从前",而且会"愈发恶劣"。[③] 2005到2007年的3年内,美国小说界发布了数量可观的作品,如麦克尤恩的《星期六》(*Saturday*, 2005)、乔纳森·萨弗兰·福尔(Jonathan Safran Foer)的《特别响,非常近》(*Extremely Loud and Incredibly Close*, 2005)、约翰·厄普代克(John Updike)的《恐怖分子》(*Terrorist*, 2006)、唐·德里罗的《坠落的人》(*Falling Man*, 2007)等。这些作品以"9·11"事件为主题,对当时的社会心理创伤

① Glissant, Edouard. *Caribbean Discourse: Selected Essays*. J. Michael Dash. trans. and intro. Charlottesville: University Press of Virginia, 1989, p.60.

② Butler, Judith. *Gender Trouble: Feminism and the Subversion of Identity* (2nd edn). New York: Routledge, 1999[orig. 1990], p.xv.

③ McEwan, Ian. "Beyond Belief." The Guardian, 2001 (September 12), G2:2.

和文化危机感进行了描述。该事件也成为美国当代文坛上一个独特的文化符号。与此同时，它也影响了美国社会的集体情感结构，并引发民众对种族问题、危机叙述、民族性和全球化背景下的文化冲突等问题的反思。

此外，随着全球生态环境日趋严峻，气候主题逐渐进入作家的创作视野中，并形成了如今流行的气候小说文类。21世纪以来，气候小说在美国读者群中的影响越发广泛，并引发公众对气候变化问题的普遍关注。它从生态的视角描述当今美国的社会问题，与科幻小说有一定的视域交集，同时与末日小说有较明显的差异。在气候小说中，生态问题被当作一个映射的原点，将作品的主题投射到经济发展、能源政策、种族冲突、环境正义及心理创伤等诸多领域，已成为当代美国小说中活跃且不可或缺的组成部分。

21世纪以来，在全球化的进程中，随着文化多元化的进一步深入，文化散播和移民趋势的增强使得内涵本就复杂的美国文化在民族身份的界定上受到更多挑战。如何在当代全球多元文化的背景下界定“美国性”？如何描述美国文化的“共同体结构”？如何看待当前美国少数族裔文化与主流文化的互动？似乎所有问题都可以归到对文化身份和个体身份的追问上。与文化发展紧密关联的当代美国小说也越发呈现出内部的异质性和多元化特征。尤其是在数字化时代，随着网络技术和信息技术的发展，数字和网络平台使得文本的创作和传播渠道日趋多元，意义的生成和延宕也被无限拉长，这不仅在作品内容上增加了如机器人等科幻创作元素，更是在文本形式和文本性上赋予了小说解读以更多的可能性。

综上，如何在传承与创新的视域中，重新审视当代美国小说与历史之间的互动，以及描述在互动中生成的新的文本性，这都将是文学研究者所关切的主题。本教材因篇幅所限，仅选取其中比较重要的8个主题进行呈现，涵盖科幻小说、气候小说、(后)“9·11”小说、族裔小说、女性小说、战争小说、喜剧小说和哥特小说。每个主题选取3～4部代表作品进行评述，以期对当代美国小说的发展做一个大致的轮廓勾勒和梳理。在教学设计上，本教材一方面尝试描绘当代美国小说发展的整体性视域，另一方面对特定主题进行针对性的文本特质阐释。每个主题中的不同小说之间也会有一定的互文性。在阅读的时候，读者可以从比较的视域进行汇通性解读。

Contents 目录

第一章
当代美国科幻小说

1970 年之后,“新浪潮”(New Wave)成为当代美国科幻小说的主流,转变了之前“黄金时代”的创作方向,从强调硬科学转向注重软科学,其聚焦点从科技的精确性转换到多重社会学观照。新浪潮作家强调文体实验和作品的文学价值,力图突破传统科幻小说的限制。

新浪潮科幻小说来源于 1964 年迈克尔·摩尔科克(Michael Moorcock)编辑的《新世界》(*New Worlds*)杂志。摩尔科克试图通过使用“新的文学技巧和表达方式”,利用该杂志实验新型的科幻文学。在该杂志的影响下,作家们开始尝试新的主题,比如以性别平等、性和种族为主题的女性主义科幻小说,以人工智能和半机械人等未来技术和黑色电影主题为特色的赛博朋克小说,还有以太空站、星际战争、银河帝国为背景的军事科幻小说等。

这个阶段的科幻小说创作主题丰富多样,一改“黄金时代”的硬科幻样式,更加注重社会和人性层面的思考。比较突出的特征如下:一、主题多样化和成熟化,开始对性别、种族和社会心理进行探讨;二、通过朋克系列小说,对科技的负面效果进行探讨;三、传统军事科幻小说重新崛起,对战争本质和儿童道德进行思考;四、通过对平行世界的描述,展现出对未来自然环境的担忧。新浪潮运动之后,随着科学技术的快速发展和互联网的普及,科幻小说呈现出更加多元化和多样化的发展态势。

第一节　新浪潮:从硬科学到软科学

无论是从主题还是形式上来说,20 世纪 20 年代到 20 世纪 50 年代的科幻黄金时代是比较保守的,探讨的主题集中在科学本身,用硬核的科学知识来解释未来科技,同时对未来抱有积极的态度,内容基本不涉及性或者暴力,甚至都不包含对未来的负面描写。它的处理方式也是直接和透明的,主要原因是那时候的读者大多是高中学历以下的普通大众而不是社会精英,所以过度深入的探讨将会导致失去大量读者。

但是在大洋彼岸法国新浪潮的影响下,美国本土的科幻小说开始在内容和创作风格上产生巨大的变革。在内容上,作家们能够更加自由地描述性、暴力和毒品。得益于新的评价系统,他们能够开始自由探索原来禁忌的话题,比如乔安娜·拉斯(Joanna Russ)的《女身男人》(*The Female Man*, 1975)和塞缪尔·R.德拉尼(Samuel R. Delany)的《达尔格伦》(*Dhalgren*, 1975)探讨性，威廉·福特·吉布森(William Ford Gibson)的《神经漫游者》(*Neuromancer*, 1984)探讨毒品文化，等等。除此之外，作家们对未来的态度也截然不同。如果把黄金时代比作乌托邦式的未来畅想，那么新浪潮则是对拥有美好未来的一种绝望和失落。核战争、冷战和越南战争是导致这种转变的主要因素。著名的多产科幻作家菲利普·K.迪克(Philip K. Dick)在《流吧！我的眼泪》(*Flow My Tears, The Policeman Said*, 1974)中就刻画了一个反乌托邦社会，一个在美国二次内战后由警察独裁统治的国家。同时在吉恩·沃尔夫(Gene Wolfe)的《新日之兀司》(*The Urth of the New Sun*, 1987)[①]中，外星人(或高度进化的人类)将一个白洞引入太阳以抵消黑洞的变暗效应，由此产生的全球变暖导致海平面上升，致使很多人丧生。

在创作风格上，新浪潮带来了形式、风格和美学方面的创新，涉及文学抱负和语言的实验性使用，其内容明显较少关注硬科幻的科学准确性或技术。例如，罗杰·泽拉兹尼(Roger Zelazny)在《致〈传道书〉的玫瑰》(*A Rose for Ecclesiastes*, 1963)中引入了众多的文学典故、复杂的独名模式、分层的含义和创新的主题。泽拉兹尼的作品，如《脸上的门，口中的灯》(*The Doors of His Face, The Lamps of His Mouth*, 1965)涉及文学的自我反思、有趣的词语搭配和新词。

总的来说，新浪潮在一定程度上是对科幻小说黄金时代的拒绝，是从硬科学到软科学的转变。阿尔吉斯·布德里斯(Algis Budrys)在1965年写道："20世纪40年代的'黄金时代'科幻小说中反复出现的特点——这暗示了纯粹的技术成就将解决所有问题，而且万幸的是所有问题都只是表面上的问题"[②]。新浪潮作家不是一个有组织的团体，但他们中的一些人觉得"纸浆"和"黄金时代"的比喻已经过时了，应该被抛弃。哈里·哈里森(Harry Harrison)总结了这一时期，他说"旧的障碍正在消失，低俗的禁忌正在被遗忘，新的主题和新的写作方式正在被探索"[③]。在这种趋势下，随着作者及读者的数量逐渐增加，题材的广度和深度逐渐扩大，语言和写作技巧日益复杂，文学性的意识不断加强，科幻小说也获得越来越多的关注。

第二节　新浪潮的蓬勃发展:科幻女性主义的崛起

20世纪70年代以来，性别和种族逐渐成为科幻小说的重要主题。塞缪尔·R.德拉尼是公认的重要美国科幻作家和文学评论家。他是黑人，同时也是同性恋者。由于身份的特殊，他被主流社会疏远，因此他想用科幻小说来对抗偏见和歧视。他的代表作之一《达尔格伦》成为了拥有百万销量的畅销书。他的《海卫一》(*Triton*, 1976)描述了一位经历性别转换的主人公在一个拥有极度社会和文化多样性的异托邦生活的故事。值得注意的是，德拉尼作为一位具有同性恋倾向的非裔美国人，他的出现打破了科幻文学界长期被白人男性统治的现象，在美国科幻文学史上具有重要的意义。

在这股探讨性别和性的潮流的推动下，厄休拉·勒古恩(Ursula K. Le Guin)逐渐从边缘地带进入

① 兀司指的是未来的地球。
② Budrys, Algis. "Galaxy Bookshelf." *Galaxy Science Fiction*, 1965, pp.186-194.
③ Aldiss, Brian Wilson & Harrison, Harry. *Decade the 1950's*. New York: St. Martin's Press, 1980.

科幻领域的中央舞台。在《黑暗的左手》(*The Left Hand of Darkness*, 1969)中,主角金力·艾(Genly Ai)是一名来自地球的男性,被派到一个陌生的星球去完成任务。他发现那个星球的居民既不是男性也不是女性,而是处于兼具两种性别的一种"无性"状态。而且在每个月一次的卡玛期(kemmer,指发情期),人们会随机进入男性化或女性化的状态,事后除非女方怀孕,否则又会再恢复完全的双性同体。这种对性别的探讨在她的后续作品《一无所有》(*The Dispossessed*, 1974)中又得到了进一步延伸。这部小说描述了两个截然不同的世界,一个是贫困但是人人平等的阿纳瑞斯星球(Anarres),另一个是富裕但极度不平等的乌拉斯星球(Urras)。小说在关注两个星球之间平衡的同时,也关注男性和女性之间的平衡。小说所描绘的无政府主义社会中的性自由和欲望、对身体的赞美以及道家思想都呈现出作者独特的女性主义意识。

其他作家比如乔安娜·拉斯也通过创作科幻小说来谈论女性主义话题。1972年,她在选集《再一次,危险的愿景》(*Again, Dangerous Visions*, 1972)中发表了短篇故事《当它变了》("When It Changed")。该故事描述了一个完全由女性构成的人类殖民地星球,其居民通过结合卵子来繁衍后代,因为所有的男性都死于30代人之前的瘟疫。当男宇航员来的时候,他们想找这些女性去生育后代以改善地球上目前的基因,却发现她们已经不再需要男性了。虽然男宇航员们声称地球上已男女平等,但他们的行为依旧透露出父系社会的高傲,这也导致了女性的极力反抗。然而拉斯并没有停止探索的脚步,她于1975年发布了《女身男人》。这部小说讲述了四位在不同时间和地点的平行宇宙中的女性的生活。第一位是乔安娜(Joanna),她生活在一个类似于20世纪70年代的美国社会。第二位是珍妮(Jeannine),1969年住在纽约市,她生活在一个大萧条从未结束、第二次世界大战从未发生过的世界里。她的世界陷入了永无止境的萧条,没有经历任何重大的女权运动。第三位是珍妮特(Janet),她的世界是一个只有女性的乌托邦星球,也就是《当它变了》里那个没有男性的世界。第四位是来自反乌托邦世界的杰尔(Jael),她在那里已经进行了40年的性别战争,男女通过互相交换孩子来生存。她们的世界互相交织在一起,都表达了各自对性别的观点,最后也回到了她们自己的世界。拉斯希望通过这种大胆的主题探讨,挑战读者心中根深蒂固的性别观念。

另一种性别探索能在小詹姆斯·蒂普垂(James Tiptree, Jr.)的作品中发现。小詹姆斯·蒂普垂是作者从1967年到去世一直使用的笔名。在此期间她的粉丝纷纷猜测她的真实身份。由于她的写作风格偏男性,外界一度认为她是男性。直到1977年,人们才知道蒂普垂是位女性,而她的真名为爱丽丝·布莱德利·谢尔登(Alice Bradley Sheldon)。她利用自己在军队和中央情报局的经历模仿了男性的口吻,成功地隐匿了自己的真实身份,使得读者更加欣赏其对性别主题的独特看法。在《男人看不见的女性》(*The Women Men Don't See*, 1973)中,作者就是用男性的视角去看待女性。该小说的标题本身就反映了谢尔登时代女性的隐形。正如弗朗西斯所说,"那是一个杰出的例子……颠覆性地使用类型小说来产生一个非常规的话语立场,即女权主义主题。"①

有关女性主义抵抗的小说也层出不穷,比如雪莉·斯图尔特·泰珀(Sheri Stewart Tepper)在1988年发表的《女性国家之门》(*The Gate to Women's Country*)。故事发生在一个被核战争摧毁300年后的社会,它已经朝着生态乌托邦的方向发展,发展出以小城市和低技术的当地农业为基础的可持续经

① Cranny-Francis, Anne. *Feminist Fiction*. New York: St. Martin's Press, 1990, p.30, p.33, p.38.

济。它还发展出一种母权制，妇女和儿童与少数男性仆人一起住在城墙内，而大多数男人则住在城外的战士营地。故事探索了生态女性主义主题。在小说中，暴力似乎是由生物学决定的：女性只选择非暴力个体进行繁殖，通过基因选择方式来筛选社会所需要的人。男性若具有一些性格特征，尤其是暴力特征，就会被彻底踢出社会管理层。这些人要么被送到城墙外当兵，要么在城墙内当女性的仆从。

在新浪潮的影响下，随着女性主义话题的升温，读者和学者们越来越重视这批原来游离于科幻边缘地带的作者，纷纷开始研究他们的著作，同时也更关注科幻小说的文学性，并对其思想性进行更加深入的思考。

第三节　后新浪潮时代：科幻小说的百家争鸣

到20世纪80年代，新浪潮运动就开始呈现出截然不同的趋势，作家们开始变得保守起来，科幻界有点回归早期的模样，就像是一种传统科幻的复兴。早期黄金时代的科幻小说不乏军事元素，在这个阶段越来越多相关主题作品的涌现使得军事科幻变成科幻文学的一个正式分支，比如洛伊斯·麦克马斯特·比约德(Lois McMaster Bujold)的沃尔科西根传奇系列(The Vorkosigan Saga, 1986)，还有那个年代最受关注的军事主题科幻小说，奥森·斯科特·卡德(Orson Scott Card)的《安德的游戏》(*Ender's Game*, 1985)等。

《安德的游戏》的背景设置在未来，人类已经掌握星际飞行技术，与外星生物“虫子”爆发了战争，人类获得了暂时的胜利。但为了防止虫族反击，人类训练天赋异禀的孩子，组成星际舰队去围剿外星种族。作者在小说里探讨了有关战争的道德问题以及利用孩子来达到某种社会目的的行为。就像《星球大战》系列电影一样，这部军事科幻小说是这个阶段非常独特的存在，它标志着传统科幻的重生和复兴，与70年代充满种族和性别伦理挣扎的潮流背道而驰。但是这不代表科幻又要回到黄金时代，这更像是传统科幻最后的荣光。因为随着互联网的出现，新浪潮运动逐渐衰落，赛博朋克(cyberpunk)、蒸汽朋克(steampunk)慢慢脱颖而出，成为当时科幻的主流创作方向。

在这个阶段，黑人女性科幻作家也开始崭露头角，最出名的就是奥克塔维娅·埃斯特尔·巴特勒(Octavia Estelle Butler)。她的成名作《血子》(*Bloodchild*, 1984)和异种三部曲(the Xenogenesis trilogy, 1987—1989)以一个外星星球为背景，描绘了人类难民与类似昆虫的外星人之间的复杂关系。这些外星人将人类留在保护区以保护他们，同时也将他们当作繁殖后代的宿主。人类与外星生物融合的创作理念打开了一扇新的大门，同时也获得了文学评论界的一致好评。美国书评家吉姆·米勒(Jim Miller)评论说：“奥克塔维娅·E.巴特勒的作品是最好的科幻小说。《〈血子〉和其他故事》让我们走出了人迹罕至的地方，并鼓励我们以不同的方式思考我们的生活方式，以及我们对待自己和彼此的方式。这使奥克塔维娅·E.巴特勒不仅是一位优秀的科幻小说作家，而且还是当今最有趣和最具创新性的政治作家之一。”①

---

① Miller, Jim. "The Technology Fix." *American Book Review* 17.3(1996): 28. Rpt. in *Contemporary Literary Criticism*. Jeffrey W. Hunter & Polly Vedder, eds., Vol.121.

此外，人类对环境的破坏也引起了科幻小说家的关注，环境问题开始成为科幻小说的重要主题。其中，最具有代表性的作家就是金·斯坦利·罗宾森(Kim Stanley Robinson)。他的许多小说和故事都有生态、文化和政治主题，并把科学家视作英雄。他获得了无数奖项，包括雨果奖、星云奖和世界奇幻奖。他的加利福尼亚三部曲(Three Californias, 1984—1990)描绘了加利福尼亚州的三种截然不同的未来发展方向，表达了他对科技发展与环境恶化关系的思考。他的代表作火星三部曲(Mars trilogy, 1992—1996)详细描述了人类对火星的殖民和改造。它侧重于描写火星上取得的平等主义、社会学和科学的进步以及地球所遭受的人口过剩和生态灾难问题。同时，罗宾森还非常热衷于或然性历史书写。在2002年发表的《大米和盐的岁月》(*The Years of Rice and Salt*)中，罗宾森设想了这样一种历史：黑死病致使欧洲99%的人丧生，而不是历史上所说的1/3人口；北美印第安人免于被屠杀；欧洲成为亚洲国家殖民的圣地。这种书写或然性历史的科幻小说反映了现代人对现状的不满，同时也表达了对未来美好生活的无限渴望。

然而科幻小说的主要关注点还是在未来。从20世纪80年代开始，伴随着电脑技术的高速发展，越来越多的科幻作家开始描绘互联网的未来。其中最出名的作品就是威廉·福特·吉布森的《神经漫游者》。这部小说让大众第一次看到了赛博空间、虚拟体验和编码记忆等超未来科技，开拓了一条全新的创作思路，即人与机器的结合。小说几乎包揽了科幻界的所有大奖，同时也是赛博朋克运动的开端，但是这种潮流是十分具有争议性的，支持者认为它是科幻的未来，反对者则责备它是一种对现实的不满和抱怨。就像新浪潮一样，它是对旧事物的一种叛逆，只不过这次叛逆对象是新浪潮本身。

在此之后，科幻小说的分支和类别就变得非常多样化，以至于很难去定义哪一个是主流。因为互联网带来各种信息，作家们的创作思路也层出不穷，作品不再拘泥于某个特定主题，比如赛博朋克流派的迈克尔·斯万维克(Michael Swanwick)的《真空花》(*Vacuum Flowers*, 1987)、迈克·雷斯尼克(Mike Resnick)的非洲乌托邦寓言故事《基里尼亚加》(*Kirinyaga*, 1988)和弗诺·文奇(Vernor Vinge)的太空歌剧《深渊上的火》(*A Fire upon the Deep*, 1992)。除此之外，安妮·麦卡芙瑞(Anne McCaffrey)的佩恩系列巧妙地将奇幻元素和科幻结合在一起，吸引了大量的科幻粉丝和奇幻作品爱好者。

科技的发展让许多科幻想法变成现实，越来越多的作品被搬上荧幕，其中最著名的当属星球大战系列(Star Wars)和星际迷航系列(Star Trek)，这也使科幻小说吸引了更多爱好者。如今科幻小说数量惊人，有些人甚至开始担忧科幻小说家将无物可写，但不断涌现的新作家和新想法告诉我们科幻的未来没有结束，探索的道路仍然在前方。

第四节　主要作家介绍与代表作品选读

一、厄休拉·勒古恩

(一) 厄休拉·勒古恩简介

厄休拉·勒古恩(Ursula K. Le Guin, 1929—2018)是美国最重要的科幻作家之一，是世界文坛上第一位同时斩获有着“科幻文学界的诺贝尔奖”之称的科幻文学领域国际最高奖项——雨果奖、星云奖这两项大奖的女性作家。同时,她也是一名奇幻文学作家与女性主义文学作家。勒古恩出身于学术家庭,父亲是人类学家,母亲是作家及心理学家,三位兄长都为学者。勒古恩年纪轻轻就开始写作,在11岁时便已向杂志社投稿。她1951年于哈佛大学取得学士学位,1952年于哥伦比亚大学取得硕士学位,后在大学任教。

勒古恩获得的奖项和荣誉不计其数。她是世界幻想文坛的传奇女王,在2016年被《纽约时报》誉为“美国当代最伟大的科幻小说家”。她获得过雨果奖、星云奖、轨迹奖、美国国家图书奖、世界奇幻奖等200多项世界文坛重量级大奖,更获得美国科幻和奇幻作家协会“大师”称号、《洛杉矶时报》“罗伯特·基尔希终身成就奖”等荣誉。2000年,她被美国国会图书馆列为作家与艺术家中的“在世传奇”。2014年,她获得美国文学杰出贡献奖。

勒古恩的科幻作品颇丰。她最重要的科幻小说之一《一无所有》讲述了阿纳瑞斯星球上的谢维克博士前往乌拉斯星球推广自己的一套乌托邦理论“奥多主义”的故事。这部小说重新界定了乌托邦小说的范畴和风格,同时斩获了雨果奖和星云奖两项世界大奖。她的另一部科幻小说《黑暗的左手》叙述了星际联盟使者金力·艾来到终年严寒的格森星试图说服星球上的国家加入联盟的故事。该小说因其对两性问题的全新思考、丰富的思想内涵和高度的文学成就被公认为“划时代的伟大作品”,同样荣获了雨果奖和星云奖。《世界之词乃森林》(*The Word for World is Forest*, 1972)讲述了人类在地球资源枯竭以后开始星际殖民与开发的故事,于1973年荣获雨果奖。她的《地海传说全集插图版》(*The Books of Earthsea: The Complete Illustrated Edition*)在第77届世界科幻大会上荣获2019年雨果奖最佳艺术书籍奖。

厄休拉·勒古恩的奇幻作品也有许多。她是“奇幻小说三巨头”之一。她的重要奇幻作品《地海传说》系列一举奠定她在西方奇幻文学领域的经典地位。该作品往往与另两部西方奇幻经典——托尔金的《魔戒》三部曲与刘易斯的《纳尼亚传奇》相提并论。《地海传说》系列借由奇幻冒险背景探讨了青少年成长的心路历程。

厄休拉·勒古恩不仅写科幻和奇幻小说,还出版了纪实小说、诗歌、散文、游记、文学评论、剧本和童书等,是美国文坛一位十分独特的女作家,也是当之无愧的科幻文学女王。

(二)《一无所有》简介

《一无所有》讲述了阿纳瑞斯星球的物理学家谢维克博士(Shevek)前往乌拉斯星球推广自己的一套名叫“奥多主义”(Odonism)的乌托邦理论的故事。小说展现了两个生活方式截然不同的文明社会,探讨了对于乌托邦的愿景与批判。

在小说里,宇宙中有两个星球——阿纳瑞斯星球和乌拉斯星球,它们互为卫星。阿纳瑞斯星球荒凉贫瘠、布满灰尘、人民朴素,而乌拉斯星球富饶无比、环境优美、人们光鲜亮丽。谢维克博士是阿纳瑞斯星球上的物理学家,他研究的“共时理论”可以发出安射波,这是一种跨星系的同步通信装置,可以使信息传播完全没有延时。

谢维克博士离开自己的家乡,前往乌拉斯星球推广自己的奥多主义理论。奥多主义社会是一种无政府主义社会，可看作一个乌托邦。在奥多主义社会，“没有一个明确的政府来维持秩序”[1]，那里没有政府、没有法律，人们几乎完全自由、不被压抑。但乌拉斯星球上的人并不接受谢维克的理论，他的奥多主义理论并没有受到重视，因此该理论在乌拉斯星球上的推广以失败告终。

谢维克最后回到了家乡阿纳瑞斯星球，把奥多主义理论交给了两个星球以外的另一个星球，保存到博物馆里。《一无所有》只是为读者展现和描写了两个星球上的两种不同文明，至于奥多主义是好是坏，小说的结局是开放式的，作者让读者自己去判断奥多主义是否是一个好的主义以及是否能实现。《一无所有》这部小说呈现了多个主题。

《一无所有》的主题之一为乌托邦主义。小说中的阿纳瑞斯星球可以被视作一个乌托邦，因为它的制度是基于人类的相互合作和相互团结而构建的。阿纳瑞斯星球没有法律、没有阶级、没有财产，一切属于每一个人。阿纳瑞斯星球的卫星乌拉斯星球则与之不同。在乌拉斯星球，人性建立在金钱和权力的基础之上。阿纳瑞斯星球的谢维克博士前往乌拉斯星球，想推广自己的乌托邦主义理论——奥多主义理论，但最终没有成功。小说的结局是开放式的，小说结尾指出奥多主义理论虽然在乌拉斯星球未能推广成功，但可能会在其他星球上适用。小说没有明确指出阿纳瑞斯星球和乌拉斯星球孰好孰坏，只是向读者描述和呈现了两个截然不同的星球以及两个星球上的两种不同文明。《一无所有》也并没有将阿纳瑞斯星球描绘成一个绝对完美的乌托邦，只是如小说副标题所展示的，这是“一个模棱两可的乌托邦”。

《一无所有》的主题之二为无政府主义和资本主义的对比。阿纳瑞斯社会是无政府主义社会，乌拉斯社会是资本主义社会，两者存在鲜明对比。阿纳瑞斯没有一个明确的政府，也没有成文的法律，维持阿纳瑞斯社会秩序的只是一套负责行政管理的网络系统，即生产分配协调处，它在所有从事生产工作的协会、联盟以及个人之间进行协调。它管的不是人，而是生产。人们没有任何形式的财产所有权，但人们拥有自由。小说主人公谢维克提出的奥多主义理论里的奥多主义社会也是一种无政府主义社会。

《一无所有》的主题之三为女性主义。小说在关注两个星球之间平衡的同时，也关注男性和女性之间的平衡。小说所描绘的无政府主义社会中的欲望和性自由、对身体的赞美以及道教思想都呈现出女性主义思想。比如，小说主人公谢维克所使用的语言体系中没有用于表达性关系中所有权的词汇或句子，因为他们认为一个男人说自己“拥有”一个女人是毫无意义的；又比如男女做爱中“性交”这个词的主语只能是复数，因为这是两个人一起做的事情，而不是一个人能做或者归一个人所有的事情。小说对于主人公所使用的语言体系的描述展现了作者的女性主义思想。但小说也呈现出一些反女性主义的思想。小说中的一部分情节提到女性不太能胜任创造性的脑力劳动，提出可以让女性去从事那些创造性不强的工作，从而让男性能够从繁琐且重复性强的事务中解放出来，去从事一些创新性的工作。小说中的某些片段里女性的社会角色似乎次于男性社会角色，呈现出一定的传统男权社会观念。

（三）作品选读：《一无所有》[2]

“Well, several of Dap’s friends—that nice composer, Salas, and some of the scruffy ones too. And real nuchnibi used to come through Round Valley when I was a kid. Only they cheated, I

[1] Le Guin, Ursula K. *The Dispossessed*. Agawam, MA: Millennium, 1999, p.182.
[2] Ibid., pp.293-297.

always thought. They told such lovely lies and stories, and told fortunes, everybody was glad to see them and keep them and feed them as long as they'd stay. But they never would stay long. But then people would just pick up and leave town, kids usually, some of them just hated farm work, and they'd just quit their posting and leave. People do that everywhere, all the time. They move on, looking for something better. You just don't call it refusing posting!"

"Why not?"

"What are you getting at?" Takver grumbled, retiring further under the blanket.

"Well, this. That we're ashamed to say we've refused a posting. That the social conscience completely dominates the individual conscience, instead of striking a balance with it. We don't cooperate—we obey. We fear being outcast, being called lazy, dysfunctional, egoizing. We fear our neighbor's opinion more than we respect our own freedom of choice. You don't believe me, Tak, but try, just try stepping over the line, just in imagination, and see how you feel. You realize then what Tirin is, and why he's a wreck, a lost soul. He is a criminal! We have created crime, just as the propertarians did. We force a man outside the sphere of our approval, and then condemn him for it. We've made laws, laws of conventional behavior, built walls all around ourselves, and we can't see them, because they're part of our thinking. Tir never did that. I knew him since we were ten years old. He never did it, he never could build walls. He was a natural rebel. He was a natural Odonian—a real one! He was a free man, and the rest of us, his brothers, drove him insane in punishment for his first free act."

"I don't think," Takver said, muffled in the bed, and defensively, "that Tir was a very strong person."

"No, he was extremely vulnerable."

There was a long silence.

"No wonder he haunts you," she said. "His play. Your book."

"But I'm luckier. A scientist can pretend that his work isn't himself, it's merely the impersonal truth. An artist can't hide behind the truth. He can't hide anywhere."

Takver watched him from the corner of her eye for some time, then turned over and sat up, pulling the blanket up around her shoulders. "Brr! It's cold... I was wrong, wasn't I, about the book. About letting Sabul cut it up and put his name on it. It seemed right. It seemed like setting the work before the workman, pride before vanity, community before ego, all that. But it wasn't really that at all, was it? It was a capitulation. A surrender to Sabul's authoritarianism."

"I don't know. It did get the thing printed."

"The right end, but the wrong means! I thought about it for a long time, at Rolny, Shev. I'll tell you what was wrong. I was pregnant. Pregnant women have no ethics. Only the most primitive kind of sacrifice impulse. To hell with the book, and the partnership, and the truth, if they threaten the precious fetus! It's a racial preservation drive, but it can work right against community; it's biological, not social. A man can be grateful he never gets into the grip of it. But he'd better realize than a woman can, and watch out for it. I think that's why the old archisms used women as property. Why did the women let them? Because they were pregnant all the time—because they were already possessed, enslaved!"

"All right, maybe, but our society, here, is a true community wherever it truly embodies Odo's ideas. It was a woman who made the Promise! What are you doing—indulging guilt feelings? Wallowing?" The word he used was not "wallowing," there being no animals on Anarres to make wallows; it was a compound, meaning literally "coating continually and thickly with excrement." The flexibility and precision of Pravic lent itself to the creation of vivid metaphors quite unforeseen by its inventors.

"Well, no. It was lovely, having Sadik! But I was wrong about the book."

"We were both wrong. We always go wrong together. You don't really think you made up my mind for me?"

"In that case I think I did."

"No. The fact is, neither of us made up our mind. Neither of us chose. We let Sabul choose for us. Our own, internalized Sabul—convention, moralism, fear of social ostracism, fear of being different, fear of being free! Well, never again. I learn slowly, but I learn."

"What are you going to do?" asked Takver, a thrill of agreeable excitement in her voice.

"Go to Abbenay with you and start a syndicate, a printing syndicate. Print the *Principles*, uncut. And whatever else we like. Bedap's *Sketch of Open Education in Science*, that the PDC wouldn't circulate. And Tirin's play. I owe him that. He taught me what prisons are, and who builds them. Those who build walls are their own prisoners. I'm going to go fulfill my proper function in the social organism. I'm going to go unbuild walls."

"It may get pretty drafty," Takver said, huddled in blankets. She leaned against him, and he put his arm around her shoulders. "I expect it will," he said.

Long after Takver had fallen asleep that night Shevek lay awake, his hands under his head, looking into darkness, hearing silence. He thought of his long trip out of the Dust, remembering the levels and mirages of the desert, the train driver with the bald, brown head and candid eyes, who had said that one must work with time and not against it.

Shevek had learned something about his own will these last four years. In its frustration he had learned its strength. No social or ethical imperative equaled it. Not even hunger could repress it. The less he had, the more absolute became his need to be.

He recognized that need, in Odonian terms, as his "cellular function," the analogic term for the individual's individuality, the work he can do best, therefore his best contribution to his society. A healthy society would let him exercise that optimum function freely, in the coordination of all such functions finding its adaptability and strength. That was a central idea of Odo's *Analogy*. That the Odonian society on Anarres had fallen short of the ideal did not, in his eyes, lessen his responsibility to it; just the contrary. With the myth of the State out of the way, the real mutuality and reciprocity of society and individual became clear. Sacrifice might be demanded of the individual, but never compromise: for though only the society could give security and stability, only the individual, the person, had the power of moral choice—the power of change, the essential function of life. The Odonian society was conceived as a permanent revolution, and revolution begins in the thinking mind.

All this Shevek had thought out, in these terms, for his conscience was a completely Odonian one.

He was therefore certain, by now, that his radical and unqualified will to create was, in Odonian terms, its own justification. His sense of primary responsibility towards his work did not cut him off from his fellows, from his society, as he had thought. It engaged him with them absolutely.

He also felt that a man who had this sense of responsibility about one thing was obliged to carry it through in all things. It was a mistake to see himself as its vehicle and nothing else, to sacrifice any other obligation to it.

That sacrificiality was what Takver had spoken of recognizing in herself when she was pregnant, and she had spoken with a degree of horror, of self-disgust, because she too was an Odonian, and the separation of means and ends was, to her too, false. For her as for him, there was no end. There was process: process was all. You could go in a promising direction or you could go wrong, but you did not set out with the expectation of ever stopping anywhere. All responsibilities, all commitments thus understood took on substance and duration.

So his mutual commitment with Takver, their relationship, had remained thoroughly alive during their four years' separation. They had both suffered from it, and suffered a good deal, but it had not occurred to either of them to escape the suffering by denying the commitment.

For after all, he thought now, lying in the warmth of Takver's sleep, it was joy they were both after—the completeness of being. If you evade suffering you also evade the chance of joy. Pleasure you may get, or pleasures, but you will not be fulfilled. You will not know what it is to come home.

Takver sighed softly in her sleep, as if agreeing with him, and turned over, pursuing some quiet dream.

Fulfillment, Shevek thought, is a function of time. The search for pleasure is circular, repetitive, atemporal. The variety seeking of the spectator, the thrill hunter, the sexually promiscuous, always ends in the same place. It has an end. It comes to the end and has to start over. It is not a journey and return, but a closed cycle, a locked room, a cell.

Outside the locked room is the landscape of time, in which the spirit may, with luck and courage, construct the fragile, makeshift, improbable roads and cities of fidelity: a landscape inhabitable by human beings.

It is not until an act occurs within the landscape of the past and the future that it is a human act. Loyalty, which asserts the continuity of past and future, binding time into a whole, is the root of human strength; there is no good to be done without it.

So, looking back on the last four years, Shevek saw them not as wasted, but as part of the edifice that he and Takver were building with their lives. The thing about working with time, instead of against it, he thought, is that it is not wasted. Even pain counts.

思考与讨论

(1) 为什么谢维克认为蒂里(Tir)是一个真正的奥多主义者?

(2) 在塔科维亚(Takver)看来,以前女人被统治阶级看作是一种财产的原因是什么?

(3) 奥多主义的词汇"细胞功能"指的是什么?

(4)《类推》这本书的作者认为一个健康的社会应该是什么样的?

(5) 谢维克这个奥多主义者是如何看待社会责任感的?

(6) 如何理解文中"存在的只有过程,过程即全部"这句话?

拓展阅读

[1] Widmer, Kingsley. "The Dialectics of Utopianism: Le Guin's *The Dispossessed*." *Liberal and Fine Arts Review*. vol.3, no.2, 1983, pp.1 - 11.

[2] Easterbrook, Neil. "State, Heterotopia: The Political Imagination in Heinlein, Le Guin, and Delany." *Political Science Fiction*. Columbia, SC: University of South Carolina Press, 1997, pp.43 - 75.

[3] Klarer, Mario. "Gender and the 'Simultaneity Principle': Ursula Le Guin's 'The Dispossessed'." *A Journal for the Interdisciplinary Study of Literature*, vol.25, no.2, 1992, pp.107 - 121.

二、威廉·福特·吉布森

(一) 威廉·福特·吉布森简介

威廉·福特·吉布森(William Ford Gibson, 1948—　)是美国当代科幻小说家和推想小说家。吉布森出生于美国南卡罗来纳州临海城市康威,是公认的赛博朋克科幻分支的创始者,被称作赛博朋克运动之父。他 12 岁时沉迷于科幻小说,渴望成为一名科幻作家。1977 年,在英属哥伦比亚大学选修的科幻文学课结束时,他用小说替代课程论文,完成了处女作《全息玫瑰碎片》(*Fragments of a Hologram Rose*),开启了写作生涯。这是一部短篇小说集,和他后期作品存在较多共同的设定,比如赛博空间、编码记忆、虚拟体验、亡命之人、梦境等。可以说，这部短篇小说集为之后的赛博朋克风格小说奠定了坚实的基础。但是真正让吉布森在科幻界大放光彩的是其在1984年出版的《神经漫游者》，它成为了当时历史上唯一一部获得“三冠王”头衔的作品——同时获得了当年雨果奖、星云奖和菲利普·K.迪克纪念奖。之后他沿用了《神经漫游者》的设定，于1986年写下续篇《零伯爵》(*Count Zero*)，于1987年写下《重启蒙娜丽莎》(*Mona Lisa Overdrive*)，组成了“蔓生三部曲”(Sprawl trilogy)，奠定了他在科幻领域的地位。这两部作品也都获得了星云奖、雨果奖和轨迹奖的提名。“蔓生三部曲”都将背景设定在一个被公司集团和无处不在的先进科技所统治的近未来世界。吉布森用独特的眼光打造了一个反乌托邦和高科技共存的世界，在那里人们享受着先进的科技，但是物质生活却非常落后。这几部小说的主题在于探索科技带来的“意想不到”的后果。当实验室的科技外溢到街头，它也被赋予了新的意义。

在吉布森的小说中，大脑思想直连机器和人工智能，人和人之间能够直接进行思想沟通，并且能够在一个网络虚构的世界中进行互动。然而在获得如此巨大的成功后，吉布森并没有一直沉浸在赛博朋克的领域内，而是在1990年与布鲁斯·斯特林(Bruce Sterling)合作写下了或然性历史小说《差分机》(*The Difference Engine*)。这部作品将背景设定于维多利亚时代科技发达的英国，在第二年获得了星云奖最佳长篇小说奖提名，成为蒸汽朋克小说的开端之作。1993年他再一次另辟蹊径，写出了他个人的第二个系列小说“桥梁三部曲”(Bridge Trilogy)——1993年的《虚拟之光》(*Virtual Light*)、1996年的《虚拟偶像爱朵露》(*Idoru*)和1999年的《明日之星》(*All Tomorrow's Parties*)。在这个系列中，吉布森把社会的邪恶从原来的跨国巨头和人工智能换成了大众媒体，这使得吉布森从一位科幻大神转变成为一名蹩脚的社会学家。之后他还尝试了更加现实主义的写作风格，比如长篇小说《模式识别》(*Pattern Recognition*, 2003)、《幽灵山村》(*Spook Country*, 2007)、《零历史》(*Zero History*, 2010)。虽然这些作品没有像“蔓生三部曲”那么成功，但他在探索的道路上不断前行，为后人留下了一笔宝贵的文化财富。他的作品影响力巨大，受到诸多学者的关注，1999年《卫报》记者史蒂芬·普尔(Stephen Poole)称吉布森为“近二十年最重要的小说家”。

(二)《神经漫游者》简介

这部作品主要讲述的是主角凯斯(Case)在失去网络连接能力后，在一位名叫阿米蒂奇(Armitage)的美国神秘前军官的引导下，去完成一个看似不可能的任务——将控制阿米蒂奇的超级人工智能冬寂(Wintermute)与它的另一半神经漫游者(Neuromancer)合并，变成超级意识。完成任务后，凯斯就能恢复之前失去的黑客能力。

这部小说的成功之处在于它开创了全新的社会背景，构建了一个由全球计算机网络主导的、肮脏的、异化的和反乌托邦的社会。高科技并没有像人们想象的那样带来幸福与快乐，而是被寡头科技企业利用来控制人们。这就是作者想要表达的技术控制论。公司开发超级人工智能，能够主导人的思想，指示雇佣兵去杀人，可以建立自己的信仰，让人把人工智能奉为神明，甚至还能创造出一个虚拟的赛博空间，让人们能够在其中尽情放纵、享乐，甚至是犯罪。就像主角凯斯，通过黑客能力去盗取别人的资料来牟利让他欲罢不能，但这都不是通过他的肉体实现的，而是通过各种能够植入人体的装置和义体实现。因此，强大的科技使人们开始唾弃自己的肉体，转向让自己机械化，严重依赖科技。一旦脱离科技，人类就将一无是处。通过这样的描写，作者展现出对高科技以及对人类未来的忧虑。

除此之外，身份和人格问题也是《神经漫游者》的重要主题。小说对人格的定义非常超前：人格不仅仅存在于活人之中，还存在于虚拟空间、克隆体和人工智能中，它能够被储存，还能被复制，通过更换肉体，意识就能永存。所以小说对人格进行广泛地定义——它赋予任何有意识的人生命和权利，无论是人工的还是其他的。同时，决定人格的方式还有改造。同样的一个人，在被改造之前叫科尔托（Corto），性格不稳定、脾气暴躁，但通过人工智能改造之后就成为阿米蒂奇，拥有超高的服从性。两者都有独立的思想和感觉，但是人格完全不同。人格还能被储存在虚拟空间内，比如迪克西（Dixie Flatline）早在几年前就去世了，但被重建为"ROM 人格矩阵"。凯斯在矩阵中遇到了迪克西的构造，迪克西在那里帮助凯斯完成了阿米蒂奇的任务。迪克西明白自己只是一个构造体，但仍然有思想和感情——他不想永远留在矩阵中，于是恳求凯斯在他们的工作完成后删除他，让他真正死去。

《神经漫游者》的空间叙述也非常独特，尤其是对都市内部的描写，为赛博朋克文化奠定了坚实的基础。小说将高耸密集的摩天大厦和低矮破旧的贫民窟糅合在一起，构建出一幅新旧并置、族裔混杂、底层挣扎的社会景象，如林奇（Kevin Lynch）对波士顿的描述，"比如'新'干线穿过'老'集市区，阿奇大街古老建筑中新建的天主教礼拜堂，古老、阴暗、低矮的'三一'教堂在崭新、明亮、刻板、高耸的约翰·汉考克大厦幕墙上的倒影"[①]。正是这种强烈的反差，让小说后续对犯罪、贫困、失业的描写更加生动，同时也是对未来城市的一种预言。小说通过对城市内部犯罪人群、少数族裔、边缘人群等亚文化的呈现，对未来都市的社会结构和关系进行了想象性构建和批判。

（三）作品选读：《神经漫游者》[②]

The sky above the port was the color of television, tuned to a dead channel.

"It's not like I'm using," Case heard someone say, as he shouldered his way through the crowd around the door of the Chat. "It's like my body's developed this massive drug deficiency." It was a Sprawl voice and a Sprawl joke. The Chatsubo was a bar for professional expatriates; you could drink there for a week and never hear two words in Japanese. Ratz was tending bar, his prosthetic arm jerking monotonously as he filled a tray of glasses with draft Kirin. He saw Case and smiled, his teeth a web work of East European steel and brown decay. Case found a place at the bar, between the unlikely tan on one of Lonny Zone's whores and the crisp naval uniform of a tall African whose cheekbones were ridged with precise rows of tribal scars. "Wage was in here early, with two Joe boys," Ratz said, shoving a draft across the bar with his good hand. "Maybe some business with you, Case?" Case shrugged. The girl to his right giggled and nudged him. The bartender's smile widened. His ugliness was the stuff of legend. In an age of affordable beauty, there was something heraldic about his lack of it. The antique arm whined as he reached for another mug. It was a Russian military prosthesis, a seven-function force-feedback manipulator, cased in grubby pink plastic. "You are too much the artiste, Herr Case." Ratz grunted; the sound served him as laughter. He scratched his overhang of white-shirted belly with the pink claw. "You are the artiste

① 凯文·林奇：《城市意象》，方益萍、何晓军译，北京：华夏出版社，2001 年，第 34 页。

② Gibson, William. *Neuromancer*. London: Gollancz, 2016, pp. 8 - 12.

of the slightly funny deal."

"Sure," Case said, and sipped his beer. "Somebody's gotta be funny around here. Sure the fuck isn't you." The whore's giggle went up an octave.

"Isn't you either, sister. So you vanish, okay? Zone, he's a close personal friend of mine."

She looked Case in the eye and made the softest possible spitting sound, her lips barely moving. But she left. "Jesus," Case said, "what kind a creep joint you running here? Man can't have a drink."

"Ha," Ratz said, swabbing the scarred wood with a rag, "Zone shows a percentage. You I let work here for entertainment value."

As Case was picking up his beer, one of those strange instants of silence descended, as though a hundred unrelated conversations had simultaneously arrived at the same pause. Then the whore's giggle rang out, tinged with a certain hysteria.

Ratz grunted. "An angel passed."

"The Chinese," bellowed a drunken Australian, "Chinese bloody invented nerve-splicing. Give me the mainland for a nerve job any day. Fix you right, mate..."

"Now that," Case said to his glass, all his bitterness suddenly rising in him like bile, "that is so much bullshit."

The Japanese had already forgotten more neurosurgery than the Chinese had ever known. The black clinics of Chiba were the cutting edge, whole bodies of technique supplanted monthly, and still they couldn't repair the damage he'd suffered in that Memphis hotel.

A year here and he still dreamed of cyberspace, hope fading nightly. All the speed he took, all the turns he'd taken and the corners he'd cut in Night City, and still he'd see the matrix in his sleep, bright lattices of logic unfolding across that colorless void... The Sprawl was a long strange way home over the Pacific now, and he was no console man, no cyberspace cowboy. Just another hustler, trying to make it through. But the dreams came on in the Japanese night like live wire voodoo and he'd cry for it, cry in his sleep, and wake alone in the dark, curled in his capsule in some coffin hotel, his hands clawed into the bedslab, temper foam bunched between his fingers, trying to reach the console that wasn't there.

"I saw your girl last night," Ratz said, passing Case his second Kirin.

"I don't have one," he said, and drank.

"Miss Linda Lee."

Case shook his head.

"No girl? Nothing? Only biz, friend artiste? Dedication to commerce?" The bartender's small brown eyes were nested deep in wrinkled flesh. "I think I liked you better, with her. You laughed more. Now, some night, you get maybe too artistic; you wind up in the clinic tanks, spare parts."

"You're breaking my heart, Ratz." He finished his beer, paid and left, high narrow shoulders hunched beneath the rain-stained khaki nylon of his windbreaker. Threading his way through the Ninsei crowds, he could smell his own stale sweat.

Case was twenty-four. At twenty-two, he'd been a cowboy, a rustler, one of the best in the Sprawl. He'd been trained by the best, by McCoy Pauley and Bobby Quine, legends in the biz. He'd operated on an almost permanent adrenaline high, a byproduct of youth and proficiency, jacked into a custom cyberspace deck that projected his disembodied consciousness into the con sensual hallucination that was the matrix. A thief, he'd worked for other, wealthier thieves, employers who provided the exotic software required to penetrate the bright walls of corporate systems, opening windows into rich fields of data. He'd made the classic mistake, the one he'd sworn he'd never make. He stole from his employers. He kept something for himself and tried to move it through a fence in Amsterdam. He still wasn't sure how he'd been discovered, not that it mattered now. He'd expected to die, then, but they only smiled. Of course he was welcome, they told him, welcome to the money. And he was going to need it. Because—still smiling—they were going to make sure he never worked again. They damaged his nervous system with a wartime Russian mycotoxin.

Strapped to a bed in a Memphis hotel, his talent burning out micron by micron, he hallucinated for thirty hours. The damage was minute, subtle, and utterly effective. For Case, who'd lived for the bodiless exultation of cyberspace, it was the Fall. In the bars he'd frequented as a cowboy hotshot, the elite stance involved a certain relaxed contempt for the flesh. The body was meat. Case fell into the prison of his own flesh.

His total assets were quickly converted to New Yen, a fat sheaf of the old paper currency that circulated endlessly through the closed circuit of the world's black markets like the seashells of the Trobriand islanders. It was difficult to transact legitimate business with cash in the Sprawl; in Japan, it was already illegal.

In Japan, he'd known with a clenched and absolute certainty, he'd find his cure. In Chiba. Either in a registered clinic or in the shadow land of black medicine. Synonymous with implants, nerve-splicing, and micro bionics, Chiba was a magnet for the Sprawl's techno-criminal subcultures.

In Chiba, he'd watched his New Yen vanish in a two-month round of examinations and consultations. The men in the black clinics, his last hope, had admired the expertise with which he'd been maimed, and then slowly shaken their heads. Now he slept in the cheapest coffins, the ones nearest the port, beneath the quartz-halogen floods that lit the docks all night like vast stages; where you couldn't see the lights of Tokyo for the glare of the television sky, not even the towering hologram logo of the Fuji Electric Company, and Tokyo Bay was a black expanse where gulls wheeled above drifting shoals of white styrofoam. Behind the port lay the city, factory domes dominated by the vast cubes of corporate arcologies. Port and city were divided by a narrow borderland of older streets, an area with no official name. Night City, with Ninsei its heart. By day, the bars down Ninsei were shuttered and featureless, the neon dead, the holograms inert, waiting, under the poisoned silver sky.

Two blocks west of the Chat, in a teashop called the Jarre de Thé, Case washed down the night's first pill with a double espresso. It was a flat pink octagon, a potent species of Brazilian dex he bought from one of Zone's girls. The Jarre was walled with mirrors, each panel framed in red neon.

At first, finding himself alone in Chiba, with little money and less hope of finding a cure, he'd gone into a kind of terminal overdrive, hustling fresh capital with a cold intensity that had seemed to belong to someone else. In the first month, he'd killed two men and a woman over sums that a year before would have seemed ludicrous. Ninsei wore him down until the street itself came to seem the externalization of some death wish, some secret poison he hadn't known he carried. Night City was like a deranged experiment in social Darwinism, designed by a bored researcher who kept one thumb permanently on the fast-forward button. Stop hustling and you sank without a trace, but move a little too swiftly and you'd break the fragile surface tension of the black market; either way, you were gone, with nothing left of you but some vague memory in the mind of a fixture like Ratz, though heart or lungs or kidneys might survive in the service of some stranger with New Yen for the clinic tanks.

Biz here was a constant subliminal hum, and death the accepted punishment for laziness, carelessness, lack of grace, the failure to heed the demands of an intricate protocol. Alone at a table in the Jarre de Thé, with the octagon coming on, pinheads of sweat starting from his palms, suddenly aware of each tingling hair on his arms and chest, Case knew that at some point he'd started to play a game with himself, a very ancient one that has no name, a final solitaire. He no longer carried a weapon, no longer took the basic precautions. He ran the fastest, loosest deals on the street, and he had a reputation for being able to get whatever you wanted. A part of him knew that the arc of his self-destruction was glaringly obvious to his customers, who grew steadily fewer, but that same part of him basked in the knowledge that it was only a matter of time. And that was the part of him, smug in its expectation of death, that most hated the thought of Linda Lee.

思考与讨论

(1) 港口天空的颜色有什么特殊含义?

(2) 当谈到神经外科技术的时候,凯斯为什么会心中充满了苦涩?

(3) 为什么凯斯会厌恶自己的肉体?

(4) 在孟菲斯饭店,凯斯经历了什么?

(5) 凯斯为什么要来到千叶城?

拓展阅读

[1] Bredehoft, Thomas A. "The Gibson Continuum: Cyberspace and Gibson's Mervyn Kihn Stories." *Science Fiction Studies*, vol.22, no.2, 2003, pp.52-63.

[2] Gibson, William. "Introduction." *Burning Chrome*. New York: Harper Collins, 1986.

[3] McCaffery, Larry. "An Interview with William Gibson." *Storming the Reality Studio: a casebook of cyberpunk and postmodern science fiction*. Durham: Duke University Press, 1991, pp. 263-285.

[4] Myers, Tony. "The Postmodern Imaginary in William Gibson's Neuromancer." *MFS Modern Fiction Studies*, vol.47, no.4, 2001, pp.887-909.

三、奥森·斯科特·卡德

(一) 奥森·斯科特·卡德简介

奥森·斯科特·卡德(Orson Scott Card)于1951年8月24日出生在华盛顿州里奇兰市,是一位以科幻作品而闻名的美国作家。他目前是唯一一个连续几年同时获得雨果奖和星云奖的作家。他凭借小说《安德的游戏》(*Ender's Game*, 1985)和续集《死亡代言人》(*Speaker for the Dead*, 1986)连续获得这两个奖项。

卡德热衷于创造天才少年。在他的作品中,主人公基本都是救世主一般的存在。1977年他发表了处女作短篇小说《安德的游戏》,获得了雨果奖提名和坎贝尔最佳新作家奖。随着这部作品的成功,卡德于1985年把它扩展成中篇小说,并在1986年发表续作《死亡代言人》。随后他快马加鞭,发表了安德系列的《外星异屠》(*Xenocide*, 1991)、《精神之子》(*Children of the Mind*, 1996)、《安德的影子》(*Ender's Shadow*, 1999)、《霸主的影子》(*Shadow of the Hegemon*, 2001)、《影子傀儡》(*Shadow Puppets*, 2002)、《巨人的影子》(*Shadow of the Giant*, 2004)和《安德的放逐》(*Ender in Exile*, 2008),与此前两部小说构成九部曲。

除了安德系列小说之外,卡德的"回家"五部曲——《地球的回忆》(*The Memory of Earth*, 1992)、《地球的呼唤》(*The Call of Earth*, 1993)、《地球飞船》(*The Ships of Earth*, 1994)、《失控的地球》(*Earthfall*, 1995)和《地球的新生》(*Earthborn*, 1995)也深受读者欢迎。和安德系列类似,这个系列的主人公也是一名天才少年,讲述的是在4000万年后,地球因人类战争而变得无法居住,人类前往名叫和谐(Harmony)的星球居住。在这个星球上,殖民者创造了一个超级人工智能"超灵"(Oversoul),它能够监视地球人类,阻止他们进行破坏,但是只能持续一段时间。在这段时间过后,人工智能开始瓦解,于是"超灵"派出一个天才少年小组去地球寻求帮助。

这些作品奠定了卡德在科幻界的重要地位。他的作品风格灵活多变,将宗教色彩融于科幻小说,为科幻小说创造了新面貌。卡德的重要性在于他的观念,在于他的写作技巧。他那明快而开放的文字成功地开拓了科幻读者的思维。

(二)《安德的游戏》简介

《安德的游戏》是一部军事科幻小说,讲述了一名叫作安德·威金(Ender Wiggins)的孩子的故事。那时人类遭到来自外星的"虫族"的袭击,人员伤亡惨重。因此,为了对抗虫族,人类必须要挑选一名才华横溢的指挥官。安德就是这样一名被选中拯救世界的天才儿童。他被格拉夫(Graff)送到战斗学校进行模拟训练,很快就掌握了学校所教的战术并且能够非常熟练地运用策略来对抗敌人。随着他的成长与进步,安德被提升到指挥学校进行进一步训练,在曾经的英雄马泽·雷汉(Maezr Rackham)的带领下进行了无数次战斗模拟测试。在最后一次测试中,安德不惜牺牲整个舰队,向虫族居住的星球发射了一个分子干扰装置,成功地歼灭了外星种族。但是等安德知道这次测试其实是真实的战斗时,他变得非常沮丧,因为自己犯下了种族灭绝罪。

小说比较新颖的一点在于刻画了一位天才儿童主角安德。虽然年纪很小,但是安德在学习能力和适应能力上都非常强,而且思想和行为有时候表现得就像成年人一样,他时而冷酷,时而富有同情心。被送到战斗学校训练后,经历了各种苦难和折磨,安德逐渐从一名乳臭未干的孩子蜕变成一位冷血的战斗指挥官。在作者看来,要成为军官,无论是大人还是孩子,本质上是没有区别的。通过把整个地球的命运交付在一名孩子身上的设定,小说呼吁人们在现实生活中要同等对待孩子,因为他们和成人一样拥有复杂的情感和强大的学习能力。

除此之外,小说中善与恶的界限很模糊,打破了军事类科幻小说的善恶二元论。表面上,人类代表着善良,虫族代表着邪恶,最后善战胜恶,虫族被安德指挥的舰队完全消灭,然后世界归于和平。然而在小说最后一章安德找到母虫虫茧的时候,大家才知道虫族对人类的入侵是一场误会,之后虫族都没有打算再次入侵,甚至在人类消灭虫族后,母虫还让人类去它们的星球耕种和居住。从虫族角度看来,人类反而是恶。这样的善恶变换还体现在安德身上。安德生性善良,但是在战斗学校的训练之下,他失手杀死了自己的战友斯蒂尔森(Stilson)和邦佐(Bonzo),最后还消灭了整个虫族。这时候,安德的角色就从一名天真善良的孩子变成一位冷酷无情的杀手。

(三)作品选读:《安德的游戏》[①]

"Took your time, didn't you, Graff? The voyage isn't short, but the three-month vacation seems excessive."

"I prefer not to deliver damaged merchandise."

"Some men simply have no sense of hurry. Oh well, it's only the fate of the world. Never mind me, you must understand our anxiety. We're here with the ansible, receiving constant reports of the progress of our starships. We have to face the coming war every day. If you can call them days. He's such a very little boy."

"There's greatness in him. A magnitude of spirit."

① Card, Orson Scott. *Ender's Game*. New York: Tom Doherty Associates, 1994, pp. 248 - 252.

"A killer instinct, too, I hope."

"Yes."

"We've planned out an impromptu course of study for him. All subject to your approval, of course."

"I'll look at it. I don't pretend to know the subject matter, Admiral Chamrajnagar. I'm only here because I know Ender. So don't be afraid that I'll try to second guess the order of your presentation. Only the pace."

"How much can we tell him?"

"Don't waste his time on the physics of interstellar travel."

"What about the ansible?"

"I already told him about that, and the fleets. I said they would arrive at their destination within five years."

"It seems there's very little left for us to tell him."

"You can tell him about the weapons systems. He has to know enough to make intelligent decisions."

"Ah. We can be useful after all, how very kind. We've devoted one of the five simulators to his exclusive use."

"What about the others?"

"The other simulators?"

"The other children."

"You were brought here to take care of Ender Wiggin."

"Just curious. Remember, they were all my students at one time or another."

"And now they are all mine. They are entering into the mysteries of the fleet, Colonel Graff, to which you, as a soldier, have never been introduced."

"You make it sound like a priesthood."

"And a god. And a religion. Even those of us who command by ansible know the majesty of flight among the stars. I can see you find my mysticism distasteful. I assure you that your distaste only reveals your ignorance. Soon enough Ender Wiggin will also know what I know; he will dance the graceful ghost dance through the stars, and whatever greatness there is within him will be unlocked, revealed, set forth before the universe for all to see. You have the soul of a stone, Colonel Graff, but I sing to a stone as easily as to another singer. You may go to your quarters and establish yourself."

"I have nothing to establish except the clothing I'm wearing."

"You own nothing?"

"They keep my salary in an account somewhere on Earth. I've never needed it. Except to buy civilian clothes on my vacation."

"A non-materialist. And yet you are unpleasantly fat. A gluttonous ascetic? Such a contradiction."

"When I'm tense, I eat. Whereas when you're tense, you spout solid waste."

"I like you, Colonel Graff. I think we shall get along."

"I don't much care, Admiral Chamrajnagar. I came here for Ender. And neither of us came here for you."

Ender hated Eros from the moment he shuttled down from the tug. He had been uncomfortable enough on Earth, where floors were flat; Eros was hopeless. It was a roughly spindle-shaped rock only six and a half kilometers thick at its narrowest point. Since the surface of the planet was entirely devoted to absorbing sunlight and converting it to energy, everyone lived in the smooth-walled rooms linked by tunnels that laced the interior of the asteroid. The closed-in space was no problem for Ender—what bothered him was that all the tunnel floors noticeably sloped downward. From the start, Ender was plagued by vertigo as he walked through the tunnels, especially the ones that girdled Eros's narrow circumference. It did not help that gravity was only half of Earth-normal—the illusion of being on the verge of falling was almost complete. There was also something disturbing about the proportions of the rooms—the ceilings were too low for the width, the tunnels too narrow. It was not a comfortable place.

Worst of all, though, was the number of people. Ender had no important memories of cities of Earth. His idea of a comfortable number of people was the Battle School, where he had known by sight every person who dwelt there. Here, though, ten thousand people lived within the rock. There was no crowding, despite the amount of space devoted to life support and other machinery. What bothered Ender was that he was constantly surrounded by strangers.

They never let him come to know anyone. He saw the other Command School students often, but since he never attended any class regularly, they remained only faces. He would attend a lecture here or there, but usually he was tutored by one teacher after another, or occasionally helped to learn a process by another student, whom he met once and never saw again. He ate alone or with Colonel Graff. His recreation was in a gym, but he rarely saw the same people in it twice.

He recognized that they were isolating him again, this time not by setting the other students to hating him, but rather by giving them no opportunity to become friends. He could hardly have been close to most of them anyway—except for Ender, the other students were all well into adolescence.

So Ender withdrew into his studies and learned quickly and well. Astrogation and military history he absorbed like water; abstract mathematics was more difficult, but whenever he was given a problem that involved patterns in space and time, he found that his intuition was more reliable than his calculation—he often saw at once a solution that he could only prove after minutes or hours of manipulating numbers.

And for pleasure, there was the simulator, the most perfect videogame he had ever played.

Teachers and students trained him, step by step, in its use. At first, not knowing the awesome power of the game, he had played only at the tactical level, controlling a single fighter in continuous maneuvers to find and destroy an enemy. The computer-controlled enemy was devious and powerful, and whenever Ender tried a tactic he found the computer using it against him within minutes. The game was a holographic display, and his fighter was represented only by a tiny light. The enemy was another light of a different color, and they danced and spun and maneuvered through a cube of space that must have been ten meters to a side. The controls were powerful. He could rotate the display in any direction, so he could watch from any angle, and he could move the center so that the duel took place nearer or farther from him.

Gradually, as he became more adept at controlling the fighter's speed, direction of movement, orientation, and weapons, the game was made more complex. He might have two enemy ships at once; there might be obstacles, the debris of space; he began to have to worry about fuel and limited weapons; the computer began to assign him things to destroy or accomplish, so that he had to avoid distractions and achieve an objective in order to win. When he had mastered the one-fighter game, they allowed him to step back into the four-fighter squadron. He spoke commands to simulated pilots of four fighters, and instead of merely carrying out the computer's instructions, he was allowed to determine tactics himself, deciding which of several objectives was the most valuable and directing his squadron accordingly. At any time, he could take personal command of one of the fighters for a short time, and at first he did this often; when he did, however, the other three fighters in his squadron were soon destroyed, and as the games became harder and harder he had to spend more and more of his time commanding the squadron. When he did, he won more and more often.

By the time he had been at Command School for a year, he was adept at running the simulator at any of fifteen levels, from controlling an individual fighter to commanding a fleet. He had long since realized that as the battleroom was to Battle School, so the simulator was to Command School. The classes were valuable, but the real education was the game. People dropped in from time to time to watch him play. They never spoke—hardly anyone ever did, unless they had something specific to teach him. The watchers would stay, silently, watching him run through a difficult simulation, and then leave just as he finished. What are you doing, he wanted to ask. Judging me? Determining whether you want to trust the fleet to me? Just remember that I didn't ask for it. He found that a great deal of what he had learned at Battle School transferred to the simulator. He would routinely reorient the simulator every few minutes, rotating it so that he didn't get trapped into an up-down orientation, constantly reviewing his position from the enemy point of view. It was exhilarating at last to have such control over the battle, to be able to see every point of it.

It was also frustrating to have so little control, too, for the computer-controlled fighters were only as good as the computer allowed. They took no initiative. They had no intelligence. He began to wish for his toon leaders, so that he could count on some of the squadrons doing well without having his constant supervision. At the end of his first year he was winning every battle on the simulator, and played the game as if the machine were a natural part of his body. One day, eating a meal with Graff, he asked,

"Is that all the simulator does?"

"Is what all?"

"The way it plays now. It's easy, and it hasn't got any harder for a while."

"Oh."

Graff seemed unconcerned. But then, Graff always seemed unconcerned. The next day everything changed. Graff went away, and in his place they gave Ender a companion.

思考与讨论

(1) 隐藏在安德体内的力量是什么?

(2) 为什么军官们不让安德去认识他的同龄人?

(3) 模拟器的意义在哪里?

(4) 为什么学员在围观安德操作模拟器的时候不发出声音?

(5) 选文中最后的对话体现了安德怎样的心态?

拓展阅读

[1] Collings, Michael. *Storyteller: Orson Scott Card*. New York: Overlook Connection Press, 2001.

[2] Reid, Suzanne Elizabeth. *Presenting Young Adult Science Fiction*. New York: Twayne Publishers, 1998.

[3] Lupoff, Richard A. "Card, Orson Scott." Watson, Noelle & Schellinger, Paul E. eds., *Twentieth-Century Science-Fiction Writers* (3rd ed.). Chicago and London: St. James Press, 1991.

[4] Willett, Edward. *Orson Scott Card: Architect of Alternate Worlds*. Berkeley Heights: Enslow Publishers, 2006.

第二章
当代美国气候小说

1962 年，蕾切尔·卡森（Rachel Carson）的经典著作《寂静的春天》（*Silent Spring*）出版，在美国引起强烈反响，成为当代美国环境文学的典范之作，也成为现代环保运动的重要推手。20 世纪 70 年代，美国环保运动日益频繁，人们对工业化、城市化和消费主义模式下的环境恶化问题越来越关注。这种环境意识的觉醒反过来又促进人们对环境文学的进一步关注和探索。在这一时期，环境文学作品的主题开始多样化，涵盖了对自然环境的保护、对工业化进程的质疑和对生态平衡的思考等方面。作家们通过各种文学形式，如小说、诗歌、散文、戏剧等，反思环境恶化的严重后果。这些作品承继 19 世纪中期超验主义作家梭罗（Henry David Thoreau）在《瓦尔登湖》（*Walden; or, Life in the Woods*, 1854）中的自然写作脉络，发扬 19 世纪末缪尔（John Muir）在《加州群山》（*The Mountains of California*，1894）中的自然保护意识，秉承 20 世纪中期利奥波德（Aldo Leopold）在《沙乡年鉴》（*A Sand County Almanac*：*And Sketches Here and There*，1949）中对自然规律的重视，进一步强调人类与自然的互动、依存和共生关系。特别是 20 世纪八九十年代，美国新浪潮科幻小说开始关注全球变暖、环境污染和生物多样性问题，在读者中也产生了较大的影响力。在这样的背景下，越来越多的小说作品开始将气候灾难作为重要的叙事动因，凸显环境批判意识，伸张环境正义，在 20 世纪末、21 世纪初逐渐引发了一股气候变化书写热潮，形成气候小说这一新兴文学样式。

第一节　当代美国气候小说发展史

20 世纪七八十年代，人为引起的全球变暖问题已受到美国作家的关注，并渐渐成为他们书写的对象，但此时，全球升温与森林砍伐、水土流失、毒物垃圾、臭氧层破坏等其他环境问题糅合在一起。1988 年联合国政府间气候变化专门委员会（Intergovernmental Panel on Climate Change, IPCC）成立，1992 年联合国环境与发展会议在巴西里约热内卢举行，155 个国家共同签署了《联合国气候变化框架公约》（The United Nations Framework Convention on Climate Change, UNFCCC），此后便出现了一个相对稳定增长的作家群，以气候变化为书写中心，从文学艺术视角思考推进气候保护政策的方法[①]。20世纪90年代以来，想象气候变化带来的各种灾难场景的文学文化产品（包括小说、电影等）在美国得到蓬勃发展。2007年，美国记者丹·布鲁姆（Dan Bloom）首次提出用"cli-fi"作为气候小说（climate fiction）的简称，这一简称逐渐受到评论界和大众认可。如今，气候小说已发展成一个不容忽视的文类。它旨在想象气候变化带来的各种灾难场景，批判气候变化否定论及美国政府各种不作为现象，关注气候危机中的环境弱势群体和"牺牲区"[②]，以此介入环境政治，从而提升民众的气候危机意识与星球家园意识。

作为一个新兴的文类，气候小说在北美经历了自身的发生发展过程。如上所述，2007年，丹·布鲁姆首次提出"cli-fi"简称；2012年加拿大作家玛格丽特·阿特伍德（Margret Atwood）在推特上使用了这一术语，并促使其得到普及；2014年《纽约时报》撰文讨论气候小说这一新兴文类，扩大了其在普通读者群中的知名度，并促使多部气候小说成为畅销书；2018年亚马逊推出"更暖系列"（Warmer Collection），共包含7部中短篇原创小说，同时推出Kindle版和有声书，供在校学生免费下载；2019年9月8日普利策小说奖获得者乔纳森·弗兰岑（Jonathan Franzen）在《纽约客》撰文，题为《如果我们停止假装》[③]，对缓解气候变化的长远目标和动物保护的现实意义之间的矛盾进行反思，引发了公众的热议，体现出当代美国作家、媒体及公众对气候变化问题的关注，同时也进一步推动了气候小说这一文类在美国的普及与发展。

评论界一般认为第一部气候小说可追溯至英国作家J. G.巴拉德（J. G. Ballad）的《沉没的世界》（*The Drowned World*, 1962），描写全球变暖、冰盖融化后被洪水淹没的伦敦城。20世纪90年代美国相继出现了不少优秀的气候小说作品：大卫·布林（David Brin）的《地球》（*Earth*, 1990）、奥克塔维娅·E.巴特勒的《播种者的寓言》（*Parable of the Sower*, 1993）及续集《天赋寓言》（*Parable of the Talents*, 1998）、布鲁斯·斯特林（Bruce Sterling）的《沉重的天气》（*Heavy Weather*, 1994）、约翰·巴恩斯（John Barnes）的《风暴之母》（*Mother of Storms*, 1994）等。21世纪以来，气候小说发展迅速，尤其是在最近10年，美国作家出版了多部相关作品，包括T. C.博伊尔（T. C. Boyle）的《地球的朋友》（*A Friend of the Earth*, 2000），芭芭拉·金索沃（Barbara Kingsolver）的《逃逸行为》（*Flight Behavior*, 2012），金·斯坦利·罗宾森（Kim Stanley Robinson）的"首都中的科学三部曲"（Science in the Capital Trilogy, 2004, 2005, 2007）、《纽约2140》（*New York 2140*, 2017）、《未来部门》（*The Ministry for the Future*, 2020），吉姆·劳特（Jim Laughter）的《极地红城》（*Polar City Red*, 2012），保罗·巴奇加卢皮（Paolo Bacigalupi）的《水刀子》（*The Water Knife*, 2015），克莱尔·韦恩·沃特金斯（Claire Vaye Watkins）的《金牌柑橘》（*Gold Fame Citrus*, 2015），理查德·鲍尔斯（Richard Powers）的《树语》（*The Overstory*, 2018）等，其中大部分斩获各种文学奖项，包括普利策小说奖、雨果奖、星云奖等。这说明气候小说这一文类不但受到文学评论家的高度关注，也受到普通读者的欢迎。

---

① 详见Trexler, Adam. *Anthropocene Fictions: The Novel in a Time of Climate Change*. Charlottesville and London: University of Virginia Press, 2015, p.9.

② "牺牲区"指由于环境恶化或经济投资失败而遭到永久性破坏的地理区域，其中大部分牺牲区位于少数族裔或低收入社区。英国《卫报》援引联合国专家的报告，指出：在美国路易斯安那州，上百家石油冶炼和化工厂已在美国国内造成多个牺牲区。这种以利益为主导的经济模式对减缓气候变化、保护生物多样性、阻止污染扩散等构成严重的威胁。参见＜https://www.theguardian.com/environment/2022/mar/10/millions-suffering-in-deadly-pollution-sacrifice-zones-warns-un-expert＞。

③ 详见Franzen, Jonathan. "What If We Stopped Pretending? The climate apocalypse is coming. To prepare for it, we need to admit that we can't prevent it." *The New Yorker*. 8 Sept. 2019.4 May.2022. 参见＜https://www.newyorker.com/culture/cultural-comment/what-if-we-stopped-pretending＞。

正如气候小说(cli-fi)的构型源自科幻小说(sci-fi)一样,最早进行气候小说创作的大多为科幻作家。之所以用科幻小说或奇幻小说(fantasy)来书写气候变化,有以下几个原因。第一,气候变化是一个极其缓慢的过程,现实主义线性叙事无法全面描述这样的过程,而科幻或者奇幻小说可以帮助想象这样一个漫长且具有星球尺度的历史进程。第二,气候变化一般无法用肉眼观察,我们日常生活中所见到的山火、洪灾、飓风等气候灾难只是气候变化的结果,或者是变化过程中的一个横断面,因此,小说家需要通过一种具有高度想象性的叙事形式来完成“记录”“见证”甚至是“预警”气候灾难的使命,帮助读者“感受”气候变化的真实影响。第三,气候变化往往会衍生很多社会问题,例如气候难民的出现、“牺牲区”的抗议、资源争夺所引发的战争等,小说家可以将这一系列连锁反应写进作品,对气候变化的社会文化影响进行批判性反思。第四,科幻或者奇幻小说可以最大限度地展现气候变化所衍生的各种情感危机和伦理困境,这与科学家的模型预警不同,是在“冷冰冰的数据”之外的一种人文关怀,也是人文学者参与思考和应对气候变化的重要方略。

当然,也并非只有科幻小说或者奇幻小说才能书写气候变化,当代美国现实主义小说也介入了对这个主题的思考。金索沃的《逃逸行为》就是一部从现实主义视角书写全球变暖对生物多样性影响的作品。鲍尔斯的《树语》则从非人类视角叙述和树木相关的故事,各种不同的树变成了小说中的主角,人类则被弱化为蒂姆西·莫顿(Timothy Morton)所说的“亚主体”(hyposubjects)①,促使读者反思植物在人类历史及全球地质史中所起的作用。《树语》入围2018年布克奖短名单,并获得2019年普利策小说奖。

总而言之,美国气候小说在叙事形式方面进行了多种创新,其主题也呈现出逐渐深化及日益多样化的态势。早期气候小说主要涉及以下三个主题:一是对气候变化的否定、怀疑和接受,二是对于人类世的寓言性警示,三是生态政治。随着这一文类的进一步发展,气候小说可能在未来呈现出新的叙事焦点,即新能源书写和对气候非正义的批判②。下文将从气候小说的情节建构、人物塑造及与末日主题作品的区分等角度详细讨论气候小说的叙事特征,并介绍研究美国气候小说的主要方法和路径。

第二节 为什么是隐性进程:气候小说中的情节建构

在气候小说作为一种文类得到广泛认可之前,气候变化往往会作为小说中的背景加以呈现,在20世纪90年代的大部分美国气候小说作品中即是如此。即使在大众对这一文类有所了解之后,作家在布局小说情节时也一般不会只写气候危机,而不关注人类的情感体验。一方面,西方自文艺复兴以来对“人”的重视使得“文学就是人学”这一理念深入人心;另一方面,如前文所述,气候变化如此缓慢且无法用肉眼观察到的过程很难被作家当作叙事主线,因此,气候变化在大多数气候小说中会以隐性进程的方式呈现。它是小说人物互动的时空背景中的重要组成部分,也成为一股叙事暗流推动着情节的发展。比如小说《无人幸免》(*American War*, 2017)虚构了一场发生在21世纪70年代的美国新南北内战。此

① 参见 Morton, Timothy & Boyer, Domonic. *Hyposubjects: On Becoming Human*. London: Open Humanities Press, 2021.

② 详见 Schneider-Mayerson, Matthew. “Climate Change Fiction.” Rachel Greenwald Smith, ed., *American Literature in Transition, 2000–2010*. Cambridge: Cambridge University Press, pp. 309–310.

时的美国环境污染严重，全球变暖、海平面上升后，整个路易斯安那州和佛罗里达州几乎全部被淹没，南北之间出现了新的裂痕。如果说历史中的南北内战源于自由工业和种植园经济这两种生产方式的冲突，那么《无人幸免》中新的南北内战则源于能源利用方式的矛盾：北方为了减少温室气体排放，要求完全脱离对化石能源的依赖而改用清洁能源，但相对保守的南方则拒绝接受这个规定，仍然大肆使用石油、天然气等化石燃料。小说中的叙事主线是女主人公萨拉特一家在这场新的内战中辗转流离，寄居于佩兴斯难民营的经历。萨拉特的家人或死于战争，或因此失踪，萨拉特则在饱受战争创伤之后反被战争利用，最终通过向北方传播瘟疫进行报复式袭击，导致一亿多人丧生。小说中的气候变化和能源利用问题虽然多次出现，但作者并没有花大量笔墨进行描述，而是将其作为隐性叙事线索跟随主人公复仇故事的展开而缓慢地推进。

气候小说《水刀子》中也有这样一股叙事暗流。由于长期干旱，美国西南部各州对水资源进行明争暗夺。在作者巴奇加卢皮所想象的近未来，全球升温之后，该地区的干旱已发展到一种极端状态，因此，亚利桑那州、德克萨斯州、新墨西哥州以及内华达州的无数居民不得不背井离乡，逐水而居，涌向拥有水权的加利福尼亚州，在自己的国家内沦为气候难民[①]。小说的叙事主线是各方势力关于印第安水权文件的争夺。美国西南部的干旱既是这些气候难民迁徙的背景，也是重要的情节动因，驱使着包括墨西哥非法移民在内的各种人群为获得水资源铤而走险[②]。犹如 20 世纪 30 年代约翰·斯坦贝克（John Steinbeck）在小说《愤怒的葡萄》（*The Grapes of Wrath*, 1939）中所写，沙尘碗事件（Dust Bowl）是造成美国中西部农民西迁加州的重要出发点，但整部小说以俄克拉荷马州的一家人西迁的经历为叙事主线，干旱问题只作为一股叙事暗流隐藏在这条主线之后。

如申丹教授所言，隐性进程是“与情节发展并列前行的一股叙事暗流”[③]，它不同于塞德瑞克·沃茨（Cedric Watts）提出的“隐性情节”（covert plot）。在迄今已有的气候小说作品中，叙事主线大多仍然聚焦于人物之间的矛盾冲突，气候的恶化伴随着人物冲突进程而发展，人物之间的矛盾升级也可能加剧气候恶化。比如《水刀子》中因水权文件的争夺，加州和其他州之间的冲突日趋激烈，西南部各州在州界设防，阻止其他州的人进入。然而州与州之间互相设防并不能从根本上解决水资源短缺的问题，反而导致更多利用非法手段攫取水资源的现象出现，造成更加严重的干旱。可以说，这两个叙述进程互为补充，深刻揭示了在极度干旱中人际及州际的交往困境，展现出危机生存状态下的各种伦理问题和人性弱点。

第三节　为什么是科学家：气候小说中的人物塑造

气候小说涉及气候变化或气候灾难的科学知识，因此在较多气候小说中，会出现一个具有共性身份的人物形象，即科学家。气候小说研究者阿德琳·约翰斯-普特拉（Adeline Johns-Putra）曾在接受采访

① Yazell, Bryan. “A Sociology of Failure: Migration and Narrative Method in US Climate Fiction.” *Configurations*, vol. 28, no. 2, Spring 2020, pp. 155 - 180, p. 166.

② 袁源：《论〈水刀〉中气候难民的流动性》，载《当代外国文学》2023 年第 3 期，第 51 页。

③ 申丹：《“隐性进程”与双重叙事动力》，载《外国文学》2022 年第 1 期，第 63 - 64 页。

时提到:"科学家之所以成为小说人物,其目的主要是使小说中的气候科学知识更容易理解"[①]。因此,这成为气候小说的一种文类特征,也成为读者的一种阅读期待。

气候变化对文学叙事提出了很多挑战。如何更好地讲述全球变暖的故事,并在审美和思想层面对读者形成一定的冲击,是众多气候小说家面临的共同难题。阿米塔夫·高希(Amitav Ghosh)在《大错乱》(*The Great Derangement: Climate Change and the Unthinkable*, 2016)一书第一部分中指出:小说对于气候变化的表征远远不够。迄今书写气候变化最多的是科幻小说,然而科幻小说长期以来却被归类在"严肃小说"的范畴之外。传统讲故事的技艺在面对气候变化的宏大主题时,往往略显乏力。比如现代主义小说过分注重对人物内心世界的描摹,其叙事聚焦具有一定的内敛性,而气候小说本身需要关注各个物种所处的地球气候环境,这是一种外扩性聚焦,所以从类型上而言,现代主义小说缺乏关注气候危机的先决条件。那么,如果想更好地讲述气候变化的故事,科学家的人物设定便为小说叙事提供了独特视角。在气候小说中,科学家不但是气候知识的传播者,同时也在叙事过程中对气候问题构成聚焦。此外,他们处于人类社会的关系网络中,因此也是人物矛盾冲突链条中的重要环节。从这一角度讲,科学家身份使其能够在关于人物冲突的显性叙事进程和关于气候变化的隐性叙事进程中来回穿梭,并将这两种进程有机连接,推动小说情节发展。因此,对于科学家的形象塑造变得格外重要。

气候小说中的科学家大多以正面形象出现,反映出气候小说家对气候科学的尊重。比如,在《逃逸行为》中,科学家奥维德是一个毕业于哈佛大学的生物学教授,带领着他的学生到田纳西农村采集帝王蝴蝶的数据,并试图帮助它们度过严冬。小说第五章则通过奥维德和主人公达拉罗比亚一家的对话,揭示出帝王蝴蝶在阿巴拉契亚山脉停留的原因:全球温度升高,原本冬天栖居于墨西哥的帝王蝴蝶在自加拿大南迁过程中误以为美国田纳西州已经足够温暖,因而停止南飞。在科学家和普通人的谈话中,因气候变化而导致的物候突变知识得以真实、自然地传递给读者,体现出作者金索沃在小说叙事方面的精心布局。此外,奥维德也成为女主人公达拉罗比亚成长过程中的"引路人",引导她通过科学的方法保护帝王蝴蝶,从而保护像帝王蝴蝶一样濒临灭绝的物种,同时也更加深刻地认识自我价值,实现思想和心灵的成长。可以说,对科学家奥维德的人物塑造贯穿小说的整个叙事进程,在揭示气候危机的严重性、传递气候科学知识、推进小说人物心理成长方面起到重要作用。

第四节　如何看待气候小说与末日小说的区别

气候小说的目的在于追寻气候正义,而非渲染末日情结。虽然有不少气候小说采用启示录或者后启示录小说的形式,但作者的最终目的是通过小说写作,提高读者的气候危机意识,从而思考如何改变过于依赖化石燃料的生产和生活方式,采取行动共同应对气候变化。如安东尼娅·梅赫纳特(Antonia Mehnert)所言,气候小说关注的不是简单的气候问题,而是"人为因素引起的气候变化",即排放过多温

① 袁源、阿德琳·约翰斯-普特拉:《21世纪气候小说和人类世批评的语境化:约翰斯-普特拉访谈录(英文)》,载《外国文学研究》2022年第3期,第4页。

室气体导致全球变暖加剧的问题，并通过文学书写透视这一环境危机所映射的各种情感、伦理及政治内涵。气候小说探索的是“气候风险如何具象化地影响社会”，从而帮助大众更好地认识气候变化。因此，气候小说写作是作家“用创造性的方式沟通关于气候变化问题的文化政治努力”[①]。

气候小说与末日小说存在以下三个方面的差异：首先，全球变暖会引发多重气候灾难，因此气候小说不会像传统末日小说那样只聚焦于某个灾难性事件；其次，气候小说更注重“现代风险社会中施害者和受害者的复杂关系”[②]，而不是传统末日小说中那种道德层面的敌我二分；最后，气候小说通过反讽寻求环境正义，从而介入环境政治[③]，其文化政治内涵比大多数末日小说更加丰富深刻。

其实，气候变化“不仅仅是温室气体排放导致全球气温升高的问题，它是一个系统性问题，涉及生物多样性、种群发展、资源利用、城市空间布局、能源经济发展、人际关系变革、心理创伤治疗等方方面面”[④]，这些既是气候小说描摹的对象，也是我们观察这些文本的重要视角。

第五节　关于美国气候小说的研究方法

在美国国内，气候小说研究已经成为一门显学。中国学者近年来也开始关注美国气候小说。在21世纪初，全球气候危机频发的背景下，生态批评界形成一股气候小说研究热潮，基本上从哲学、历史、情感、政治这四大面向形成六种理论进路：解构主义气候批评、历史主义气候批评、整体主义气候批评、气候认知与情感批评、气候正义批评和实证主义气候批评[⑤]。芝加哥大学印度裔历史学家迪佩什·查卡拉巴提（Dipesh Chakrabarty）于2009年发表在《批评探索》（*Critical Inquiry*）上的论文《历史的气候：四个主题》[⑥]在西方批评界具有深刻的影响力，成为气候小说研究的重要参考文献。在过去10年中，查卡拉巴提相继发表了一系列论著，探讨气候变化批评与历史研究的交叉性。他指出，在广大的发展中国家，“全球化”问题已经得到大量的讨论，“全球变暖”问题却还没有引起足够重视[⑦]。所以，气候小说创作与研究也相应有些滞后。实际上，这两个词中的“全球”具有不同的涵义。“全球化”中的“全球”着重讨论全球商品与媒介市场建立的过程，从本质上而言，将人类置于中心地位，描述的是人类“改造—分配—生产”的过程；而“全球变暖”中的“全球”指处于地质及气候变化过程中的整个地球，本质上将人类视作地球上的诸多物种之一。因此，查卡拉巴提认为：气候变化不是某一个历史事件的问题（one-event problem），也不可能用某一种方法便可以应对。“在未来相当长一段时间内，由于全球化和全球变暖的

---

① Mehnert, Antonia. *Climate Change Fictions: Representations of Global Warming in American Literature*. Switzerland: Palgrave Macmillan, 2016, p.4.

② Ibid., p.33.

③ Ibid., p.225.

④ 袁源：《人类纪的气候危机书写——兼评〈气候变化小说：美国文学中的全球变暖表征〉》，载《外国文学》2020年第3期，第171页。

⑤ 详见袁源：《气候变化批评：一种建构世界文学史的理论视角》，载《文艺理论研究》2022年第3期，第69页。

⑥ 参见Chakrabarty, Dipesh. “The Climate of History: Four Theses.” *Critical Inquiry*, vol.35, no.2, 2009, pp.197－222.

⑦ Chakrabarty, Dipesh. “Planetary Crisis and the Difficulty of Being Modern.” *Millennium: Journal of International Studies*, vol.46, no.3, 2018, pp.259－282.

双重影响，由乌尔里希·贝克（Ulrich Beck）提出的‘风险社会’（risk society）概念将得到进一步强化。”[①]由此可见，虽然关注的重点有异，但“全球化”和“全球变暖”都是 21 世纪气候小说研究中需要重点关注的两个理论议题。

气候变化给已有的文学研究范式带来各种冲击。比如，气候变化给后殖民批评带来四大挑战：一是气候变化研究需要把人类行为作为改变地质纪元的一个因素来考量，这就需要把人类当作一个整体，即一个物种来看待，那么人类内部的权力争斗机制很可能被淡化；二是后殖民批评学者往往更关注“有记录的历史”或称“人类历史”，史前史则一般不在其研究的范畴之内，而气候变化的事实要求将这两种历史合为一体，探寻地球作为一个整体何去何从的问题；三是由于气候变化是一个时间跨度很长的概念，人类无法通过有限的生活经验来进行判断，这与后殖民批评所依赖的批评方法相背离；四是气候变化批评将非人的动物、植物、矿物、微生物等物种均纳入讨论范围，而后殖民批评主要讨论的是人类社会的问题，因此，在研究对象方面也需要进行大量拓展。除此之外，美国气候小说研究汲取了性别研究、伦理批评、心理分析、新历史主义、后人类主义等各种理论方法，也关注科技与气候的互动关系等。总而言之，这个新兴的研究领域所考察的文本具有较大的创新性，且在研究方法上也融合了各种理论路径，具有重要的现实意义，值得进一步拓展和探究。

第六节　主要作家介绍与代表作品选读

一、芭芭拉·金索沃

（一）芭芭拉·金索沃简介

芭芭拉·金索沃（Barbara Kingsolver）于 1955 年出生在美国马里兰州，是当代著名的女性小说家、散文家和诗人。在金索沃出生后不久，她们举家搬迁到肯塔基州。金索沃的父亲是当地尼古拉斯县唯一的医生。该县位于贫困的煤矿区和富足的马场之间，是一个比较贫穷的地方，没有游泳池，也没有网球场。大多数人以种植烟草为生。金索沃非常关心自己生活的环境以及周围的人，并希望以小说来改变世界。她的作品多关注环境、女性、人权、正义等主题。她所塑造的女性人物往往会面临艰难的伦理选择，但都具有较强的韧性，小说中也不乏幽默感和诗意的浪漫[②]。她的作品几乎每一部都成为畅销书，曾获得多个文学奖项，被译为 20 多种语言，在中国也有较高的知名度。

在孩童时期，金索沃曾随父母到当时的非洲刚果共和国生活过一段时间。她在非洲的生活经历为小说《毒木圣经》（*The Poisonwood Bible*, 1998）奠定了重要基础。她就读于亚利桑那州立大学，并获得生物学专业的学位。她的科学背景为她在作品中更好地展现动物、植物等方面的科学知识提供了重要

① Chakrabarty, Dipesh. “Postcolonial Studies and the Challenges of Climate Change.” *New Literary History*, vol. 43, no. 1, 2012, pp. 1 - 18, pp. 13 - 14.

② 详见 Pavlos, Suzanne. *Cliff's Notes on Kingsolver's The Bean Trees*. Loncoln: Cliff's Notes, 1999, p. 5.

支撑，在小说《逃逸行为》中，她也塑造了一个颇富魅力的黑人生物学教授形象。

金索沃对写作有一种天生的爱好，在出版小说前，她就是一位自由职业作家。迄今，她已创作8部长篇小说，包括脍炙人口的《豆树青青》(*The Bean Trees*, 1988)、《纵情夏日》(*Prodigal Summer*, 2000)、《毒木圣经》和《逃逸行为》等。另外，金索沃还出版了多部短篇小说集、散文集、诗集等。她的非虚构作品《种花种菜种春风》(*Animal, Vegetable, Miracle: A Year of Food Life*, 2007)记录了她们一家人在弗吉尼亚农村耕种、饲养、与周围邻居交换食物的生活经历。最新小说《无房可住》(*Unsheltered*, 2018)通过19世纪和21世纪两个家庭在新泽西同一个地方居住的两条叙事线索交织推进，指出21世纪人们对全球变暖的态度与19世纪70年代人们对待达尔文进化论的态度有很大的相似性，反映了作者对科学精神、文明进程及未来社会的深度思考。

(二)《逃逸行为》简介

小说《逃逸行为》以阿巴拉契亚山脉中从未走出家乡的年轻母亲达拉罗比亚(Dellarobia)的经历为主线讲述整个故事。达拉罗比亚因看到栖息在山间的成群帝王蝴蝶所构成的橙色景观而获得顿悟，放弃了与年轻的情人幽会的念头，回到丈夫和一双儿女身边。这些帝王蝴蝶一般会从加拿大飞往墨西哥，像候鸟一样在那里度过冬天之后再飞回北方。然而，一方面它们在冬天栖息的墨西哥山间发生了严重的山体滑坡，导致栖息地本身已不复存在；另一方面全球温度升高后，这些蝴蝶在从加拿大往南飞的过程中，误将美国的阿巴拉契亚山脉附近当作墨西哥，于是不再继续南飞。结果可想而知，当冬天来临，这些帝王蝴蝶中的大多数都没法逃离被冻死的命运，因而严重削减了帝王蝴蝶的种群数量。

对于山间突然出现的帝王蝴蝶，小说中的人物采取了不同的处理方法。达拉罗比亚的公公想用违法储存的毒药(DDT)[①]直接进行喷洒以消灭这些蝴蝶，然后继续伐木以支付家庭债务；她的婆婆则据此做起了生意，向来参观蝴蝶景观的人收费；生物学家和气候科学家们则在此建起实验室，通过各种方法将蝴蝶转移至暖房，防止它们被冻死。达拉罗比亚虽未上过大学，但她本能地选择站在科学家一边，不仅把房子租给科研人员使用，还邀请他们共进晚餐，最终她充当了教授的助手，和他的学生们一起拯救这些蝴蝶。在遇见帝王蝴蝶前，达拉罗比亚是一个没有接受过太多教育的农妇。因为厌倦了繁杂的家务和平淡的生活，她试图通过和一个临时电工幽会来满足自己的虚荣心。满山的帝王蝴蝶所构成的橙色景观使她获得一种启示，也彻底改变了她的人生。最终，她勇敢地走出了原来的家庭，一边照顾孩子，一边攻读生物学本科学位，将保护更多像帝王蝴蝶一样濒危的物种作为新的人生目标。

金索沃在这个故事中将女性成长与拯救气候危机中的濒危物种有机融合。女主人公达拉罗比亚逐渐意识到自己与丈夫、孩子、公婆、情人、朋友间关系的本质，这一过程伴随着她对于帝王蝴蝶的怜悯和共情，也伴随着科学知识对这位大山中的年轻女性的影响。从这一角度讲，小说题目"Flight Behavior"既指帝王蝴蝶的飞行行为，又指女主人公达拉罗比亚逃离丈夫所在的保守家庭而重新寻找生活意义的行为。因此，《西雅图时报》(*Seattle Times*)称金索沃在这个故事中不仅描写了基于个人生活经历的微观现象，更建构了"与全球生态系统和社群相关"的宏观世界。《出版人周刊》(*Publishers Weekly*)认为

① DDT(Dichloro diphenyltrichloroe thane)，学名为双对氯苯基三氯乙烷，是一种毒性极高的杀虫剂，不易降解，因此对鱼类和鸟类的繁殖不利。美国著名环保作家蕾切尔·卡森(Rachel Carson)在著作《寂静的春天》(*Silent Spring*, 1962)中重点阐述了因为过度使用DDT而使得鸟类种群数量剧减的问题。这部著作在美国乃至世界环保史上均具有重要的推动作用，在一定程度上也增进了大众对于DDT的认识。

金索沃在这部小说中向社会"传递了一则紧急讯息"，是关于气候变化的一种"感人的号召"，它"如此清晰明了，以至于气候怀疑论者也不能忽视"。这部小说将帝王蝴蝶的命运与女主人公达拉罗比亚的生活糅合在一起，从具体物种层面揭示气候变化对种群可持续发展的影响，激发读者思考在气候变化的时代，人类与非人类物种将以何种形态和谐共生于这个星球。

（三）作品选读：《逃逸行为》①

Dellarobia stood momentarily dumbfounded, which Crystal took as her cue to exit via the kitchen door. Preston went to the front hall to stand with Roy, but she knew he wouldn't open the door, drilled as all kids were in stranger-danger. She peered out the windows in the upper part of the door, but saw nothing. She had to stand on tiptoe and look down before she could see them on the porch, the man and woman both about her own height, possibly even shorter. They looked Mexican, or very dark-skinned at any rate, especially the man. Jehovah's Witnesses? Did they travel the world for their cause?

She opened the door immediately. "May I help you?"

It was the little girl between the adults who spoke: "Preston!"

"Hi, Josefina," he said heartily, sounding like the man of the house.

Dellarobia looked from her son to this child and her parents. "Preston, is this a friend of yours?"

"She's in Miss Rose's room too," he said. The two of them hugged in an obedient, ritualistic way, like children at a family reunion, leaving Dellarobia to meet the parents' gaze feeling thoroughly adrift. The man had a large mustache and wore work clothes, a zippered jacket and billed cap. The wife was a bit more dressed up in a summery flowered shift under her blue cardigan. This family hadn't gotten around to the winter coats either, from the looks of it. They both pumped her hand firmly and said their names, Lupe and Reynaldo and a last name she instantly forgot.

"Well, come in," she said. The child said something to the parents, and they cautiously followed, wiping their shoes on the mat and entering the house so tentatively, Dellarobia had some difficulty getting the door closed behind them. She'd halfway unbuttoned her coat before realizing, startled again, she was half naked underneath. The wet clothes she'd stripped off earlier still lay in a puddle in the hallway. These people must think they'd come calling at a pig house.

"I am so sorry to keep you standing out there. We were out. If you all would please sit down in the living room, I'll join you in just one minute. Preston, would you be a real big boy and go to the kitchen and get everybody a glass of water?"

Again the girl spoke to her parents in Spanish, exchanging several sentences this time. Whatever she told them did the trick, as they walked directly to the sofa and sat down. Dellarobia

---

① Kingsolver, Barbara. *Flight Behavior*. New York: Harper Collins, 2012, pp.96－103.

quickly checked on Cordie, who was sleeping, and then scurried to the bedroom to run a brush through her hair and put on something decent. When she returned to the living room, she saw Preston had delivered water in the plastic cups he was allowed to use: Lupe had Shrek, and Reynaldo had SpongeBob SquarePants. They held their drinks formally. Dellarobia noted the wife's plastic summer sandals worn with pantyhose, and felt for her, knowing exactly what it was like to be a season behind on every kind of payment. The man had removed his cap and placed it on the arm of the sofa. His mustache made two curved lines around the sides of his mouth like parentheses, as if everything he might say would be very quiet, and incidental. Josefina was their princess, in flowered bell-bottom stretch pants and a plaid top. She sat between her parents smiling shyly at Roy while her father held out the back of his hand for the dog to sniff, encouraging her to do the same. Roy let himself be rubbed under the chin, then went and lay down in the entrance hall, satisfied that he had secured the perimeter.

"So," Dellarobia said, wondering whether she should offer cookies. She moved a pile of clothes out of the armchair to sit down, and Preston sidled close, sitting on the carpet at her feet. "It's nice to meet one of Preston's friends. He's my oldest, so it's been kind of strange for me, sending him off to kindergarten, where he's got this whole other world I don't know about."

She instantly regretted the "whole other world," which they might take the wrong way, but it was too late, the little girl was already passing it on. They smiled and nodded, seemingly uninsulted. Dellarobia was coming to understand that these parents did not speak a word of English. They must be living in Feathertown if they had a child enrolled in school. But whatever their situation, they were evidently doing it with a kindergartner as their ambassador. Did she go with them to do their shopping and banking? She couldn't imagine. And could not have been more floored by what the child said next.

"My mother and father wants to see the butterflies."

"You're kidding me!"

The girl began to translate, but Dellarobia stopped her. "No, don't say that. Tell me how they know about the butterflies."

"We know about them a lot," Josefina said, this time without consulting her parents. "They are mariposas monarcas. They come from Mexico." She pronounced it Meheecu, a small, quick slide back to the mother tongue.

"Okay," Dellarobia said, astonished.

"The monarcas are from Michoacán, and we are from Michoacán." Josefina flashed a mouthful of white teeth, gaining poise by the minute. She was a little taller than Preston, and seemed much older. They might have had to enroll an older child in kindergarten, to learn the language, Dellarobia supposed. Or maybe she'd just seen twice as much of life as the kids around here. It seemed probable. "Monarchs," Dellarobia said. "Now see, I've heard that name before." She racked her memory. Animal Planet, maybe.

"Monarch-es," the girl repeated, shifting the emphasis around so it was English, or the next thing to it.

"Are you saying they used to be down there, and now they're all coming up here to live?" Dellarobia recognized a familiar ring to those words, which people often said about immigrants themselves, and again she worried about causing accidental offense. But the girl was focused on the butterfly issue.

"No," she said. "They like to live in Michoacán. On the trees. They live in big, big..." She drew a wide shape with her hands, struggling for a word, then said, "Racimos. Like uvas. Sorry, like grapes."

Dellarobia could have dropped her teeth. "Yes, exactly. Like big bunches of grapes hanging from the trees. You've seen that?"

The girl nodded. She said something rapidly to her parents that made them nod vigorously as well.

"My mother, somebody tells her they are coming here like that. Her friend read in the newspaper. We went to another house to ask for seeing the monarcas. And that lady sayed us to pay money to see them, so we don't go."

"My mother-in-law, Hester, you mean. A lady with a long gray ponytail?" Dellarobia signaled a line from the back of her head.

Josefina nodded. "Yes."

"She was going to charge you money to see the butterflies? When was this?"

"A long time."

"Around Thanksgiving?"

The girl asked her mother a question, who answered with a word that sounded like November. "It was November," Josefina replied.

That witch, thought Dellarobia. Free of charge for churchy locals only. Leave it to Hester to hoard the miracle. "How did you know to come here?"

"Today Preston comes on the bus, and I know you are a nice lady here."

"Well, thank you. You all can go up there and look at the butterflies any day you want to. No charge. That lady you talked to doesn't own them."

The girl translated, and they all smiled. Dellarobia wondered if they meant now.

"The only thing is, I've got a baby here napping, so it's not a good time right this minute. We can go later this week, if you want. Could I get a phone number, to call you?" She tore a page from Preston's drawing pad and handed it to the little girl, who handed it to her father with instructions. He removed a pencil from his pocket, wrote a phone number, and handed it back: ten digits, local area code, but the tidy numbers were foreign-looking. He crossed his sevens, like t's.

"So," she said, folding the paper in quarters. "You've already seen this, back where you come from? Where the butterflies all gang up together?"

"In Michoacán my father is a guía for the mariposas monarcas." The girl was warming up, bouncing just perceptibly on the sofa and speaking a little breathlessly. "He takes the peoples on horses in the forest to see the monarcas, he is explaining the peoples, and counting the mariposas and other things for the, for the científicos. And my mother makes tamales for the lot of peoples."

Dellarobia cupped Preston's head gently in her hand, turning his face upward. "Did you all talk about this at school? The butterflies?"

"Miss Rose said something to Miss Hunt, but not to us," he said. "Josefina asked me if I ever saw the butterflies before, because she did. She said they make the big things all over the trees." He glanced from Josefina to Dellarobia, looking as usual as if he feared he had done something wrong. "That's why I wanted to see them too."

"Shoot! I can't believe this," Dellarobia said, hardly knowing where to start with her questions. "Do you have these butterflies all the time in Mexico? Or do they just show up sometimes?"

"Winter times," the girl said. "In summer days the monarca flies around everywhere drinking the flowers, she flies to here to your country. And in winter she all comes home to Angangueo. My town. Every year the same time coming."

"And that's how your parents make their living? From working with the butterflies, and the people coming to see them?"

"They come, they did came..." Josefina paused a moment, her eyes fixed on the middle distance while she worked out words in her mind. "The peoples came from every places. Every countries."

"You mean tourists from all over the world? Like how many were there, a hundred?" She wondered whether a child so young could possibly know the difference between dozens and hundreds.

"Thousands of peoples. One hundred millions butterflies." That answered that.

"How do you know how many butterflies there are?"

The girl looked a little annoyed. "My father is a guía. I help him riding the horses."

"You can ride a horse?" Preston asked in a reverent whisper. He must think she was the second coming of the Powerpuff Girls.

"If you don't mind my asking, why didn't you stay there?" Dellarobia asked.

"No more. It's gone."

Dellarobia leaned forward, hands pressed between her knees, strangely dreading what might come next. Miracle or not, this thing on the mountain was a gift. To herself in particular, she'd dared to imagine. Not once had she considered it might have been stolen from someone else. "Do you mean the butterflies stopped coming?" she asked. "Or just the tourists stopped coming?"

"Everything is gone!" the girl cried, in obvious distress. "The water was coming and the mud was coming on everything... Un diluvio." She looked at her parents, asking several questions, which they answered, but she did not say more.

"A flood?" Dellarobia asked gently. She thought of the landslide in Great Lick that had taken out a section of Highway 60 in September. On the news they'd called it a maelstrom, the whole valley filled with boulders and mud and splintered trees. She made a downward tumbling motion with her hands. "A landslide?"

Josefina nodded soberly, her body shrinking into the sofa. "Corrimiento de tierras." The mother lifted the girl onto her lap, folding both arms around her protectively. The whole family now looked close to tears.

"I'm sorry," Dellarobia said.

The father spoke quietly in Spanish, and then Josefina said simply, "Everything was gone."

"What was gone?"

"The houses. The school. The peoples."

"You lost your own house?"

"Yes," the girl said. "Everything. The mountain. And the monarcas also."

"That must have been so terrible."

"Terrible, yes. Some childrens did die."

Dear God, she thought. Terrible was a word with many meanings. The landslide at Great Lick had taken a stretch of highway and nothing else. No school, no lives.

"When was this?" she thought to ask. "What year?"

The girl asked a question, and the mother replied with a word that sounded nearly like February. Josefina repeated, "February."

"Of this past winter? So you remember all this? It just happened, what, ten months ago? So you all came here to Feathertown after that, in the spring?"

She nodded. "My cousins and my uncle is working here already a long time."

"Oh, I see. Working the tobacco," Dellarobia said.

"Tabaco," both parents repeated. The man pointed to himself and said, "Tabaco," and something else. He must have been following the conversation to some extent. Her sense of the family kept shifting. They'd had a home they preferred to this, and jobs, scientific things of some type to assist. Now he was evidently hustling for day labor. She felt abashed for the huge things she didn't know. Mountains collapsing on people. Tonight she and Preston would go over to Hester's and get on the computer together.

She handed back the folded piece of paper and asked, "Would you mind writing down the name of your town for me, where you came from? So I can..." What was she going to tell them, that she'd Google it? It sounded ghoulish, like voyeurism. Which, to be honest, was what the daily news amounted to. You could feel more decent watching it when the victims weren't sitting on your sofa.

"So I can learn about your home," she finally said.

The man returned the paper with several words written under the telephone number: Reynaldo Delgado. Angangueo, Michoacán. The last name she'd forgotten, the town that was no more.

They all sat quietly for a long time. Dellarobia had ridden out prayer meetings aplenty, but had no idea what to say to a family that had lost their world, including the mountain under their feet and the butterflies of the air.

思考与讨论

(1) 在选文中,小女孩何塞菲娜(Josefina)的语言中存在很多不合英语语法的现象。这暗示了什么?

(2) 何塞菲娜的父母和帝王蝴蝶之间存在着哪些关联?

(3) 你认为小说中对何塞菲娜一家经历的描写在揭示气候灾难影响方面具有怎样的叙事效果?请用自己的语言进行简要评析。

拓展阅读

[1] Alaimo, Stacy. *Bodily Natures: Science, Environment, and the Material Self*. Bloomington and Indianapolis: Indiana University Press, 2010.

[2] Clark, Timothy. *Ecocriticism on the Edge: The Anthropocene as a Threshold Concept*. London and New York: Bloomsbury Academic, 2015.

[3] Johns-Putra, Adeline. *Climate Change and the Contemporary Novel*. Cambridge: Cambridge University Press, 2019.

二、保罗・巴奇加卢皮

(一) 保罗・巴奇加卢皮简介

保罗・巴奇加卢皮(Paolo Bacigalupi)于1972年出生在美国科罗拉多州,是当代美国科幻作家、气候小说家。他的作品曾获雨果奖、星云奖和坎贝尔奖等科幻大奖。部分作品发表于《阿西莫夫的科幻小说》《奇幻与科幻小说杂志》和《高乡新闻》等期刊。短篇小说集《第六泵和其它故事》(*Pump Six and Other Stories*, 2010)被评为轨迹奖最佳小说集。

巴奇加卢皮大学毕业于东亚研究专业,曾经学过中文。毕业后,他在中国、泰国等亚洲国家生活过,这些经历为他在小说中书写亚洲和亚洲人物提供了素材。第一部长篇小说《发条女孩》(*The Windup*

Girl, 2009)以泰国曼谷为背景，涉及生物科技、环境危机、性别意识及后人类主义等主题。该小说获得2009年星云最佳长篇小说奖、雨果最佳长篇小说奖及2010年坎贝尔奖和轨迹奖，被《时代》杂志评为2009年度十佳小说之一。

巴奇加卢皮的青年文学小说(young adult fiction, YA)《拆船工》(*Ship Breaker*, 2010)以末日后的未来为背景。由于生态恶化，人类文明正在衰落。海平面上升后，新奥尔良已被淹没。人们靠从被冲上岸的油轮中拾荒谋生。15岁的主人公内勒(Nailer)从小就失去了母亲，和嗜赌成性的酒鬼父亲理查德(Richard)生活在一起。一次风暴中，内勒救了富商的女儿尼特(Nita)，却惹怒了尼特的叔叔派斯(Pyce)。内勒本想带尼特逃到新奥尔良，后来却发现理查德和派斯联手劫持了尼特。内勒通过各种努力，学习了各种船舶技术，最终他所在的船追上了劫持尼特的船，再次救了尼特，最后他们两人在最初相遇的海滩重逢。该小说获2010年美国国家图书奖青年文学奖提名，并获得轨迹奖最佳青年图书奖。

短篇小说《柽柳猎人》(*The Tamarisk Hunter*)最早于2006年发表在《高乡新闻》(*High County News*)，后收录于短篇小说集《第六泵和其它故事》。小说假想2030年大干旱背景下，主人公鲁鲁以为加州官方铲除科罗拉多河沿岸吸水过多的柽柳为生，同时获得供水配额。为了能够有源源不断的工资和水配额，鲁鲁一边铲除柽柳，一边种植柽柳。突然有一天，官方通知他不需要再继续这样的工作了，因为加州已经取消了这个项目。鲁鲁面临像大多数人一样不得不北迁逐水而居的命运。这部小说是长篇小说《水刀子》的雏形，也是巴奇加卢皮对美国西南部干旱书写的重要文本。

(二)《水刀子》简介

《水刀子》以21世纪30年代为背景，聚焦美国西南部科罗拉多河流域的干旱问题，塑造了从墨西哥移民到美国的安裘(Angel Velasquez)这样的“水刀子”形象，以及在干旱中挣扎，试图跨越州界到达有水的加州的西南部各州众生相。气候变化背景下，原本干旱的西南部更加缺水，民不聊生。普利策获奖记者露西(Lucy Monroe)到亚利桑那州凤凰城追踪各州间的水权争夺问题。年轻的德州难民玛丽亚(Maria Villarosa)试图在凤凰城艰难度日，存够钱便要逃离到有水的地方。不同身份的人群因为“水”而命运相系。小说中充满各种讽刺，例如，白人殖民者在建立凤凰城时，寓意其将浴火重生，像凤凰一样腾飞。然而，现实中的凤凰城过度依赖科罗拉多河的水源，干旱使凤凰城的居民像蝼蚁一般生活在黑暗之中。他们不得不依靠回收系统，即回收自己的尿液作为珍贵的饮用水。所以，凤凰腾飞只是一个虚幻的梦想，实际上是凤凰降落，干旱将使凤凰城如古代当地的霍霍坎文化一样被历史的沙尘所湮没[①]。

《水刀子》中虚构了一个由中国高科技支持的泰阳生态工程。正如小说中所写：“中国人一点东西都不浪费。他们会烘出甲烷、滤出水分，然后将残余物变成肥料，撒在特区里的奇花异草上，让它们长成大树。”[②]小说中泰阳生态工程成为干旱的凤凰城里的绿洲，是各类人群趋之若鹜的地方。这样的书写反衬出巴奇加卢皮对美国西南部未来生态的担忧，对当今美国浪费能源资源、随意开采蓄水层而不顾未来的短视行为的批判。

---

① 袁源：《论〈水刀〉中气候难民的流动性》，载《当代外国文学》2023年第3期，第51－57页。

② 保罗·巴奇加卢皮：《水刀子》，穆卓芸译，上海：文汇出版社，2019年，第111页。

（三）作品选读：《水刀子》[①]

Michael Ratan—senior hydrology specialist, Ibis Ltd.—lived high up in the Taiyang Arcology and understood what was happening with the world. He spoke a language of acre-feet of water, spring runoff in CFS, and snowpack depths. He spoke of rivers and groundwater. And because he saw the world true and accepted it, instead of living in denial, he was never blindsided.

He told Maria how the Earth held hundreds of millions of gallons of water deep underground. Ancient water that had seeped down into it when glaciers melted. He'd described this world to Maria, hands darting, outlining geological strata, sandstone formations, talking about Halliburton drill soundings, telling her about aquifers.

Aquifers.

Whole huge underground lakes. Of course they were almost pumped dry now, but long ago there had been vast amounts of water down there.

"It's not like the old days," the hydrologist had said, "but if you drill deep enough and frack right, you can open things up. Water will perc okay." He shrugged. "At least in most places there's still an aquifer or two you can crack open and get a little water flowing. Down here, though, it's tougher. Mostly you just got the empty aquifers that Arizona fills up with CAP water."

"CAP water?"

"The Central Arizona Project?" He'd smirked at her ignorance. "Seriously?"

Sarah kicked Maria under the table, but Ratan pushed aside wineglasses and laid his tablet on the table.

"Okay. Here. Look."

He opened a map of Arizona, then zoomed in on Phoenix. He pointed at a thin blue line that wrapped around the northern edge of the city and traced it west across the desert.

In contrast to the lumps of ranged hills and mountains around Phoenix, the blue line was as straight as a ruler. It bent a few times, but it lay on the land as if someone had sliced the desert with an X-Acto blade.

When he zoomed in, Maria could see the pale yellow of the desert and black rocky hills. A few lonely saguaros, casting shadows, and then they were down on top of an emerald river of water, flowing along a concrete-lined canal.

Ratan scrolled the map farther west, following the straight-ruled artificial river until it reached a wide pool of blue, glittering with desert sunlight.

Lake Havasu, it said.

And feeding it, a squiggly blue line: *Colorado River*.

---

① Bacigalupi, Paolo. *The Water Knife*. New York: Alfred A. Knopf, 2015, pp. 44–49.

"The CAP is Arizona's IV drip," Ratan explained. "It pumps water up out of the Colorado River and brings it three hundred miles across the desert to Phoenix. Almost everything else that Phoenix depends on for water is done for. Roosevelt Reservoir is about dried up. The Verde and Salt Rivers are practically seasonal. The aquifers around here are all pumped to hell. But Phoenix still has a pulse because of the CAP."

He drew back the map, showing the distance of the canal again, the slender line crossing all that desert. His finger lingered over it.

"You see how tiny that line is, right? How far it's got to go? And it's coming out of a river that a lot of other people want to use, too. California pumps out of Lake Havasu, too. And Catherine Case up in Nevada doesn't like letting water down into Havasu at all because she needs it up in Lake Mead.

"And then you've got all the lunatics farther upriver in Colorado and Wyoming and Utah who keep saying they aren't going to send any water down to the Lower Basin States at all. They like to say it's theirs. Their mountains. Their snowmelt." He tapped the CAP's slender blue line again. "That's a lot of people fighting over too little water. And that's a mighty vulnerable line. Someone bombed the CAP once, almost knocked Phoenix off."

He leaned back and grinned. "And that's why they're hiring people like me. Phoenix needs backups. If someone comes after them again? Pfft." He made a dismissing gesture. "They're done for. But if I find a decent aquifer? Phoenix is golden. They can even grow again."

"Will you find something?" Maria asked.

Ratan laughed. "Probably not. But people will grab after whatever mirage they think will save them if they're thirsty enough. So I go out with my maps and my drilling crews, and I look busy, and I tell people where to punch holes in the desert, and Phoenix keeps hoping we'll come back with some mother lode of aquifers so they can stop worrying about how they stand on the Colorado River, and they can stop looking over their shoulders at Vegas and California. If I find some new magical water source, they'll be saved. I guess it could happen. I've heard of miracles. Merry Perrys sure believe. Jesus walked on water, so maybe he makes aquifers, too."

The man had laughed at that, but afterward Maria had dreamed about aquifers.

In her dreams they were always vast lakes, deep underground, cooler and more inviting than any abandoned basement, huge caverns filled with water. Sometimes she dreamed that she rowed a boat across those wet cathedral spaces with stalactites phosphorescing overhead like the body paint Sarah wore when she hunted her customers in the dance clubs of the Golden Mile. The roof of the cavern had glowed, and Maria had drifted across those dark reflecting waters, listening to water dripping, trailing her fingers in the soft cool liquid.

Sometimes she dreamed that her family was in the boat with her, and sometimes her father even rowed, carrying them across to China.

And now Maria sat in the darkness beside the oasis of the Red Cross/China Friendship pump and waited to find out if she could see the world as clearly as Sarah's hydrologist. And if Sarah didn't understand, well, Maria would try to help her see clear, too.

"It's market price, girl. The price on the pump right here is all about how much water is down underground. When it gets low, the price goes up so people will slow down and not take so much. When the aquifer gets full, the price goes down because they're not so worried about running out. And sometimes the big vertical farms that the Chinese made stop pumping water so they can dry out for harvest. And they do it all at once, so it fools the water-level monitors. Makes them think there's enough water for everyone, so then sometimes the price—"

The pump's blue glow flickered and dropped to $6.66. Went back up to $6.95.

It flickered again. $6.20. And then back up to $6.95.

"You see that?" Maria asked.

Sarah sucked a breath in surprise. "Whoa."

"You stay with the wagon." Maria sidled closer to the pump. It was late. No one else was watching. No one else had noticed yet. She didn't want them to notice. Didn't want anyone to see what she was about to do.

The price dropped to six dollars, then kicked up a nickel as someone's automated pumps put orders in on the water that was deep down below her feet. But each time the price seemed to dip lower before it went back up.

Maria reached into her bra and pulled out the wadded sweaty bills she kept safe against her skin.

On the pump, the digital readout flickered, prices changing.

$6.95... $6.90... $6.50.

It was dropping—Maria was sure of it. Farmers were still shunting water into drip fields, getting their subsidized price. But the big vertical farms had suddenly stopped pumping, just as the hydrologist had said they would, preparing for a harvest that happened only a few times a year.

And here she was, standing beside the pump, watching the numbers.

$5.95. $6.05.

The price was definitely falling.

Maria waited, her heart beating faster. Around her a crowd began to take notice and press close. $6.15. People started running, seeing finally what was happening. Word spread into the Merry Perry tents and pulled people away from lighting candles at the Santa Muerte shrine to look, but Maria was already there in the sweet spot.

She had her bottles ready. She'd guessed right. Market price, falling like an angel coming down from Heaven to kiss her black hair and whisper hope.

Free fall.

$ 5.85.

$ 4.70.

$ 3.60.

It was lower than she'd ever seen. Maria began shoving bills into the slot, locking in prices as they kept falling. It didn't matter. In a couple more seconds the big boys would sit up. Automated systems would catch the fall and start pumping. She kept jamming in bills. It was almost like buying futures.

She used up all her cash, and still the price was dropping.

"You got any money?" she shouted over to Sarah, not caring now who knew what she was doing. Not caring. She just wanted more of this chance.

"You serious?"

"I'll pay you back!"

Others were swarming over to gawp at the price, then running to tell others about the miraculous plunge. People began crowding the other spigots.

"Hurry up!" Maria was almost shouting with frustration. It was a huge score. And she was here at the perfect moment.

"What if the price doesn't go back up?"

"It'll go up! It'll go up!"

Reluctantly, Sarah handed her a twenty. "This is my rent."

"I need small bills! Nothing big! They won't let you buy big!"

Sarah pulled out more cash, digging fuck money out of her bra.

In the old days, the hydrologist had said, you could do stuff like stick a cool hundred dollars into the machine and walk away with all those gallons. But at the top end of the system some bureaucrat with a sharp pencil had figured out what was going on, and now you could only buy five-dollar increments. So Maria fed fives, watching the price, locking in gallons. Each increment a locked amount. $ 2.44. She'd never seen it go so low. Maria shoved bills in as fast as she could.

The machine jammed. She tried to put more bills in, but it fought her. More people were crowding around now, plugging their own money into spigots, but hers was jammed. Maria swore and slammed her palm against the pump. She'd bought fifty dollars' worth of water, and with Sarah's cash she had more than eighty. And now what? All the other spigots were in use.

Maria gave up and started filling. Already the price was rising. Kicking up as rich people's automated household systems caught the price break and started pumping gallons into cisterns. Or maybe it was the Taiyang Arcology getting in on the action, accelerating the buy as it realized the surplus was worth gorging on. The numbers flickered: $ 2.90... $ 3.10... $ 4.50... $ 4.45...

$ 5.50.

$ 6.50.

$7.05.

$7.10.

Order restored.

Maria lugged her sloshing bottles over to the red wagon and dumped them in. Fifty dollars' worth of water had just become $120, and as soon as she hauled it away from the oasis...

"How much did we make?"

Maria was afraid to say, it felt so good. Once she got the water into the center of town and sidled up beside the Taiyang construction work—people wanted a cool cup of water there. And they had money. She knew the place from when her father had worked the high beams—all those crews coming off shift. And she would be there waiting for them. Offering them relief from the heat. The workers weren't allowed to tap the factory, so if they wanted water out of work, they could either go line up at a Friendship pump and pay the humanitarian pump price, or they could pay Maria and get water conveniently.

"Two hundred," Maria said. "By the time we get all this water away from here, at least two hundred."

"How much for me?"

"Ninety."

Maria could tell Sarah was impressed. The girl chattered the whole way home, thinking about her cut, excited that she'd made a three-day score just from tagging along in the dark with Maria.

"You're just like my fiver," Sarah said. "You get this water thing."

"I'm not a player like that."

But inside, a part of Maria thrilled at the compliment.

Sarah's fiver saw the world clear.

And now Maria did, too.

思考与讨论

(1) 根据文中资深水利学家拉坦(Ratan)的介绍,凤凰城如何依赖中央亚利桑那工程(Central Arizona Project)获得淡水资源?

(2) 科罗拉多河沿岸各州对水资源的态度如何?

(3) 选文中水的价格波动说明了什么?你对水变成一种商品有什么看法?

拓展阅读

[1] Cohen, Tom & Colebrook, Claire. "Vortices: On 'Critical Climate Change' as a Project." *The South Atlantic Quarterly*, vol. 116, no. 1, 2017, pp. 129 - 143.

［2］ Kaplan, E. Ann. *Climate Trauma: Foreseeing the Future in Dystopian Film and Fiction*. New Brunswick and London: Rutgers University Press, 2015.

［3］ Mehnert, Antonia. *Climate Change Fictions: Representations of Global Warming in American Literature*. Switzerland: Palgrave Macmillan, 2016.

三、金·斯坦利·罗宾森

(一) 金·斯坦利·罗宾简介

金·斯坦利·罗宾森(Kim Stanley Robinson)出生于1952年,是迄今创作气候小说最多的美国作家。他师从著名文学批评家弗雷德里克·詹明信(Fredric Jameson),并在詹明信的鼓励和指导下,撰写了研究菲利普·迪克(Phillip K. Dick)的科幻小说的博士论文。罗宾森早在博士毕业前,便开始创作与发表科幻小说。迄今,他已获得雨果奖、星云奖、轨迹奖等多项科幻大奖,是当代美国文坛重要的科幻作家。他的作品关注环境危机,探讨环境、资本与技术的互动关系。近年来,对全球变暖问题的反思是其科幻小说的写作重心,因此他也被称为气候小说家。

罗宾森已出版6部长篇气候小说。其中最早的是"首都中的科学三部曲":《四十种下雨的迹象》(*Forty Signs of Rain*, 2004)、《五十度以下》(*Fifty Degrees Below*, 2005)和《六十天计数》(*Sixty Days And Counting*, 2007)。该三部曲在2015年以《绿色地球》(*Green Earth*)为题出版了修订版合集。此外,罗宾森的气候小说还包括:《2312》(*2312*,2012)、《纽约2140》(*New York 2140*,2017)和《未来部》(*The Ministry for the Future*, 2020)。

在"首都中的科学三部曲"中,第一部《四十种下雨的迹象》以科学家为主要人物,聚焦21世纪早期全球变暖的影响。第二部《五十度以下》承接上一部,继续书写风暴和美国首都华盛顿特区的洪灾,科学家们旨在通过国际合作以重启失控的墨西哥湾暖流,从而寻找应对人为引起的气候变化的策略。第三部《六十天计数》也紧扣前一部的叙事脉络,特别是华盛顿特区的环境问题,通过佛教启示探索使美国及整个世界走出气候危机的可能性。罗宾森的"首都中的科学三部曲"以科学或宗教的方式"从共同体出发",营造了一个"科学乌托邦",并认为这种乌托邦共同体可以减缓甚至是反拨全球变暖的趋势①。

小说《2312》被评为2012年星云最佳长篇小说奖,这是继《红火星》1993年获星云奖之后再次获此殊荣的小说。小说将时间设定在2312年,地球人口已增长到110亿,气温升高,疾病肆虐,水土流失严重,多处海岸线被淹没,整个地球陷入一种失序状态。如小说译者余凌所写:"生活在地球上的人,认为自由呼吸、绿树成荫、碧海蓝天不过是理所当然的事;而发展科技、探索外空,似是解决地上问题的灵丹妙药。本书对此提供了另一个视角。"②值得一提的是,该书中有较多中国元素,比如塑造了一个"举止文明"的中国科学家王伟。小说的最后,移民水星的主人公斯旺决定将暂居于太空中的数千物种送回被气候变化损毁的地球,从而重建这个星球家园。

---

① Johns-Putra, Adeline. *Climate Change and the Contemporary Novel*. Cambridge: Cambridge University Press, 2019, p.139.

② 余凌:译者序,《2312》,金·斯坦利·鲁宾逊著,重庆:重庆出版社,2016年。

《纽约 2140》是罗宾森继“首都中的科学三部曲”之后，再次将视角投向处于气候危机中的城市的小说。在该小说中，海平面上升导致纽约大部分没入海水之中，人们生活在这座“超级威尼斯城”，只能住在高楼的上面几层。罗宾森在一次采访中提到：“之所以选择曼哈顿的大都会人寿保险大楼作为小说中主要人物生活的场所，是因为该楼以威尼斯的圣马可钟楼为模型而建”，建成后便成为当时世界第一高楼。而在小说中，这便成了对被海水淹没的纽约城的一种调侃①。在经历 2100 年的大洪灾之后，纽约的社会阶层进一步分化，低洼的地方恶臭泛滥，乘船甚或游泳成为主要交通方式，这使这部气候小说既带有后启示录特征，也具有一定的喜剧色彩。

(二)《未来部》简介

继《纽约 2140》后，金・斯坦利・罗宾森在 2020 年出版了又一部气候小说力作：《未来部》。以近未来的 2025 年作为时间背景，小说主要通过经历过印度超级热浪的美国志愿者弗兰克・梅(Frank May)的视角，讲述被气候变化改变的未来地球的故事。该书近 600 页，共有 106 个章节。弗兰克并非小说中唯一的叙述者。书中包括大量第一人称复数叙述者(“we”)：印度热浪营救人员、非洲难民、印度生态恐怖组织人员、瑞士石油公司高管的朋友们，等等。此外，还有第三人称全知全觉叙述者。自始至终，小说的叙述视角处于第一人称单复数和第三人称单复数的动态转换过程中，使整部小说犹如交响乐一般，成为关于气候变化未来的多声部叙事。

小说中，由于各国都没能执行《巴黎协定》(Paris Agreement)②中节能减排的目标，联合国成立了“未来部”，和政府间气候变化专门委员会(IPCC)合作，为子孙后代的权益发声。而在该机构成立后不久，印度便发生了超级热浪，即小说第一章描述的情景。此次发生在印度最贫困地区的热浪致使 2000 万人丧生。然而，热浪过后，世界各国，包括印度本国政府却对此没有任何作为，并未减少温室气体排放，而是把这次热浪归结为“地区问题”(regional problem)。弗兰克是此次气候灾难的见证者和幸存者，但也因此患上了创伤后应激障碍(post-traumatic stress disorder，简称 PTSD)，惧怕温暖，只能在冰冷的环境中工作。他还加入了印度的生态恐怖组织，拟暗杀未来部的负责人玛丽・墨菲(Mary Murphy)和石油公司的高管。E.安・凯普兰(E. Ann Kaplan)认为，气候创伤(climate trauma)不只包括弗兰克患上的这种创伤后应激障碍，即使没有经历气候灾难的人，也会对潜在的气候危机存在一种焦虑和恐惧，担心未来地球环境不再宜居，这便是一种和气候相关的创伤前应激障碍(pre-traumatic stress syndrome，简称 PreTSS)③。在 21 世纪，面对不断恶化的气候环境，人们普遍存在这些心理问题。如果不对气候现实加以改变，这些问题会进一步凸显。

正如小说第六章所写：“这次超级热浪就像美国的枪击事件——大家都为此哀痛惋惜，然而很快它

---

① Swearingen, Jake. “Kim Stanley Robinson's *New York 2140*: To Save the City, We Had to Drown It.” *New York*. 27 Mar. 2017. 3 May 2022. See<https://nymag.com/intelligencer/2017/03/kim-stanley-robinsons-new-york-2140-review-a-drowned-nyc.html>.

② 2015 年 12 月 12 日，在联合国气候峰会上通过了新的气候协议《巴黎协定》(Paris Agreement)，取代之前的《京都议定书》。《巴黎协定》的目标是进一步减少温室气体排放，并将全球升温控制在比工业化之前高 2 摄氏度(最好是 1.5 摄氏度)以内。2016 年世界地球日(4 月 22 日)当天，171 个国家或地区签署了《巴黎协定》。关于该协定的具体信息，可参考网站<https://unfccc.int/process-and-meetings/the-paris-agreement/the-paris-agreement>。

③ 详见 Kaplan, E. Ann. “Is Climate-Related Pre-Traumatic Stress Syndrome a Real Condition?” *American Imago*, vol. 77, no. 1, 2020, pp. 81 - 104.

就被忘记，或者代之以另一次类似的事件，直到这样的事件几乎每天都发生，成为了一种新常态。"[①]小说中，发展中国家和西方发达国家一样，承受着全球变暖的各种后果。迄今为止，全球变暖的主要贡献者——西方发达国家仍然继续依赖化石能源，发展传统化石工业，并未如期实现《巴黎协定》中节能减排目标，而作为发展中国家代表的印度亦是如此。因此，气候灾难的发生只是造成一时轰动而已，并没有激发关于减缓气候变化的政策和制度上的改变。小说借此对当今世界的气候变化治理问题进行了批判性反思。在美国国内，2022 年 6 月，最高法院裁决美国国家环境保护局（Environmental Protection Agency）不能通过《空气清洁法》（Clean Air Act）限定现有燃煤和燃气发电厂的温室气体排放量，使拜登政府的气候变化政策严重受挫。由此可见，环境危机与美国政治缠绕交织，使解决气候问题的路径充满荆棘。

小说中还包含大量有关气候变化的科学知识和政策文件，因此，该小说也被归入"硬科幻"类别。罗宾森对于气候现实的描写以及关于气候变化国际治理难题的思考，使这部关于气候未来的小说具有重要的现实意义。比尔·盖茨（Bill Gates）将该书列为 2022 年暑期阅读书目，并认为这是一部"关于气候变化的既令人害怕又带有希望的作品"[②]，书中提到的未来部为子孙后代的权益代言，敦促世界各国各地区减少温室气体排放，为减缓气候变化带来一定的希望。当然，罗宾森并未在该作品中给出解决气候问题的最终方案，这也给读者留下较大的思考空间。

（三）作品选读：《未来部》[③]

Twice a week he visited his therapist. A nice middle-aged woman, intelligent and experienced, calm and attentive. Sympathetic. She was interested in him, he could see that. Probably she was interested in all her clients. But for sure she was interested in him.

She asked him what he was doing, how he was feeling. He didn't tell her about his dreams of vengeance, but what he did tell her was honest enough. Earlier that week, he told her, a hot waft of steam from a giant espresso machine in a coffee emporium had caused him to freak out. Panic attack; he had had to sit down and try to calm his beating heart.

She nodded. "Did you try the eye movements we talked about?"

"No." He was pretty sure this was a bullshit therapy, but the truth was that in the heat of the moment, so to speak, he had forgotten about it. "I forgot. I'll try it next time."

"It might help," she said. "It might not. But nothing lost in trying it."

He nodded.

"Do you want to try it now?"

"Just move my eyes?"

"Well, no. You need to do it when you're dealing with what happened. I don't want you to re-

---

① Robinson, Kim Stanley. *The Ministry for the Future*. New York: Orbit, 2020, p.25.

② Gates, Bill. "A scary but hopeful novel about climate change: Kim Stanley Robinson's *The Ministry for the Future*." *Gatesnotes: The Blog of Bill Gates*. 6 June 2022. 5 July 2022. See <https://www.gatesnotes.com/Books/The-Ministry-for-the-Future>.

③ Robinson, Kim Stanley. *The Ministry for the Future*. New York: Orbit, 2020, pp.66 - 70.

experience anything in a way that feels too bad, but you know we've tried having you tell me what happened from various perspectives, and maybe, if you're up for it, we could try that again, and while you tell me about it you could try the eye movements. It would help build the association."

He shrugged. "If you think it will help."

"I don't know what will help, but it can't hurt to try this. If it's too upsetting just stop. Anytime you want to stop, be sure to stop."

"All right."

So he began to tell the story of how he had first come to his town, and how the heat wave had at first seemed like all the other hot weather they had had. As he spoke he moved his eyes, in tandem of course, as that was the only way he could do it, back and forth, looking as far to the left as he could, vague view of her bookshelves, then in a quick sweep to as far right as he could, catching a vague view of flowers in a vase in front of a window looking out onto a courtyard. This was a voluntary effort that stopped the moment he stopped thinking to do it, so he had to devote some of his attention to it, while at the same time continuing with his story, which as a result was halting and disjointed, unrehearsed and different from what he would have said if he was just telling her the same thing again as before. This he presumed was one benefit of the exercise.

"I got there in the winter so it wasn't that hot to begin with... but it wasn't cold, no. In the Himalayas it was cold, you could even see the snow peaks to the north on clear days, but most days... most days weren't clear. The air was dirty almost all the time. Not that different from anywhere else. So I got settled in and was taking classes in Hindi and working... working at the clinic. Then the heat wave came. It got way hotter than it had been up till then, but everyone... everyone said it was normal, that the time right before the monsoon was the hottest of all. But then it got hotter still. Then it all happened fast, one day it was so hot even the people were scared... and that night some of the older people and the littlest kids died. That sent everyone into shock, but I think they were thinking it was as bad as it could get. Then it got worse, and the power went out, and after that there was no air conditioning... and not much water. People freaked out, and rightfully so. The heat was beyond what the human body can stand. Hyperthermia, that's just a word. The reality is different. You can't breathe. Sweating doesn't work. You're being roasted, like meat in an oven, and you can feel that. Eventually a lot of them went down to the local lake, but its water was like bath temperature, and not... safe to drink. So that's where a lot of them died."

He stopped talking and let his eyes rest. He could feel muscles behind his eyes, pulsing at the unaccustomed efforts. Like any other muscles, they welcomed a rest. That felt odd.

The therapist said, "I noticed that this time you didn't really put yourself in the story."

"No? I thought I did."

"You always talked about them. They did things, things happened to them."

"Well, I was one of them."

"At the time, did you think of yourself as one of them?"

"...No. I mean, they were them, I was me. I watched them, I talked with some of them. The usual stuff."

"Of course. So, could you tell me your part of the story, moving your eyes like that?"

"I don't know."

"Do you want to try?"

"No."

"All right. Maybe some other time. And maybe next time we can try to create the bilateral action by having you hold those little buzzers in your hands. Remember I showed you those? They'll pulse left-right-left-right as you talk it through. It's easier than moving your eyes."

"I don't want to do that now."

"Next time, maybe."

"I don't know when."

"You don't want to?"

"No. Why should I?"

"Well, the theory is that if you tell the story, you're shaping the memory of it to some extent, by putting it into words. And if you do that while making the eye movements, or feeling the hand buzzers, that seems to create a kind of internal distance in you between your memory of the story as you told it, and the, what you might call the reliving of it, the spontaneous reliving of it by way of some trigger setting you off. So that if that were to happen and you wanted some relief from it, you could move your eyes and start maybe thinking of your spoken version of what happened, and it would relieve you from reliving it. If you see what I mean."

"Yes," Frank said. "I understand. I'm not sure I believe it, but I understand."

"That makes sense. But maybe worth a try?"

"Maybe."

One fall he took a Scottish friend's offer to work on a project in Antarctica. She was principal investigator of a small scientific team going to the Dry Valleys, to study the stream that ran there briefly every summer, the Onyx River. And she had room on the team for a field assistant, and wanted to help him out. Since he was having trouble handling the heat, she said, Antarctica ought to be a great place for him.

Sounds good, he said. He was running out of money from a small inheritance left to him by his grandmother, and he still didn't want to contact his parents or his organization, so it would help with that too. And so that fall he flew to Denver and went through the interviews, and altered his résumé to omit his time in India, and then he was hired and off to Auckland, then Christchurch, and from Christchurch south to McMurdo Station on Ross Island, just across McMurdo Sound from the Dry Valleys, which lay between the Royal Society Range and the frozen sea. Even the plane flight to McMurdo was cold, its interior a long open room like a warehouse floor. Same with all the old junky buildings of McMurdo, and the newer buildings too—like warehouses, institutional buildings, and never heated to much more than 60 degrees. Even the line that ran through the buffet in the kitchen was a cool experience. All very congenial.

Then, out in the Dry Valleys, the hut they ate their meals in was kept warm, but not exceptionally so; really it was only warm relative to the outside. The dorm huts were a little hot and stuffy, but it was possible to sleep out in a tent of his own. That was really cold, so cold that the sleeping bag he slept in weighed about ten pounds; it took that much goose down to hold in enough of his own heat to keep him warm. He stuck his nose out of this bag to breathe, and that repeating injection of frigid air reminded him that it was really cold out, even though it was sunny all the time. The continuous light was strange but he soon got used to it.

The problem was that extreme cold somehow led to thoughts of temperature itself, and to warm up their freezing hands after a session of field work, they would heat the dining hut to quite a high temperature, which would make for a stuffy steamy room, and Frank found himself slipping down the slippery slope. Out at this remove from any possibility of relief, freak-outs would be at best inconvenient, at worst a disaster. Medevacs by helo were rare and expensive, he had heard them say. So he had to stay cool. But sometimes he could only hide a freak-out and hope it would go away soon and not come back. Sometimes he torqued his eyes like he was watching a Ping-Pong match.

And they had a sauna hut there. He stayed away from it, of course, but one night, going out to his tent in the bright daylight, he passed it just as a group of scientists burst out of it half naked in bathing suits, shrieking in delighted agony at the instantaneous extreme shift of temperature, evaporative steam bursting off their bodies like they were big pink firecrackers. That sight, which ought to have been beautiful, and their shrieking, which sounded like pain though it was ecstasy, set him off instantly. His heart pounded so fast and hard that he went light-headed, then suddenly fell to his knees and pitched face first onto the snow. No warning, just the sight of the pink firecracker people, a racing heart, then he found himself laid out on the hard cold snow. He had fainted right in front of them. The sauna-goers naturally helped him up, and someone took his pulse as they lifted him and cried out in a panic, Hey feel this tachycardia, my God! Feel it! They said it was 240 beats a minute. Within two hours a helo was thwacking down to medevac him out of there. And once medevacked to McMurdo, and his condition and past experiences made fully known to the NSF brass on site, he was accused of lying on his application form and shipped back home.

思考与讨论

(1) 作为印度热浪的幸存者，弗兰克为什么要去看心理医生？

(2) 印度热浪在这篇选文中起到什么作用?

(3) 根据选文内容并联系生活实际,你认为气候灾难会给普通人带来哪些影响?

拓展阅读

［1］ Morton, Timothy. *Hyperobjects: Philosophy and Ecology after the End of the World*. Minneapolis and London: University of Minnesota Press, 2013.

［2］ Nixon, Rob. *Slow Violence and the Environmentalism of the Poor*. Cambridge and London: Harvard University Press, 2011.

［3］ Weik Von Mossner, Alexa. *Affective Ecologies: Empathy, Emotion, and Environmental Narrative*. Columbus: Ohio State University Press, 2017.

第三章
当代美国(后)“9·11”小说

2001年9月11日,两架被劫持的客机撞向了纽约市的世贸中心,第三架撞向了五角大楼,第四架被劫持的客机在宾夕法尼亚州的开阔地带坠毁,这是自1941年日本轰炸夏威夷珍珠港海军基地以来,美国本土首次遭到外国袭击。现在,“9·11”事件已然成为美国乃至全世界的一个转折点,并依此分为“9·11”之前(pre-9/11或before 9/11)和“9·11”之后(post-9/11或after 9/11)的美国或世界。法国作家、哲学家和社会学家让·鲍德里亚(Jean Baudrillard)认为“9·11”袭击“不仅摧毁了最负盛名的建筑之一,还摧毁了整个(西方)价值体系和世界秩序”[①],双子塔的倒塌是现代城市历史上的一个特殊事件,具有象征意义的建筑被摧毁预示着一种戏剧性的结局,即建筑形式和它所代表的象征意义和世界体系都将消失。

“9·11”事件发生后,美国提出理解“9·11”灾难的两个模式。第一个模式认为,“9·11”事件是一场战争,是可与珍珠港事件相提并论的“偷袭”;第二个模式则认为,“9·11”事件是一种富有生产力、自由、宽容和世俗化(或基督教)的文明与另一种倒退、偏狭和复仇心强的文明之间的互相对抗和斗争。美国的知识分子,如苏珊·桑塔格(Susan Sontag)认为,无论是“战争模式”还是“文明优越模式”都不正确,它们都是“那次罪恶的袭击者和伊斯兰瓦哈比宗教激进主义者的观点”[②]。桑塔格认为,由布什政府宣布的反恐战争永不会终结,所以它并不是一场真正的战争,而是美国用来扩大其强权的信号,不过是美国领导人的借口,是对“假战争的假宣言”[③]。因此,她呼吁美国政府和人民应该自我反省。同时,在桑塔格看来,恐怖分子们披着“貌似委屈的外衣”,以纠正美国的错误为借口,是对“现代性(唯一使妇女解放成为可能的文化)的袭击,以及……对资本主义的袭击”[④]。因此,把恐怖主义视为通过非法手段追求合法要求的这种看法也是错误的。艾弗拉姆·诺姆·乔姆斯基(Avram Noam Chomsky)指出,美国民众的第一反应是震惊、愤怒、恐惧和想要复仇。美国的民意调查结果直观地反映了政府宣传对大众认知判断的影响。“9·11”事件之后,认为伊拉克参与袭击的美国人口比例是3%,而到2003年,大约有一半以上的美国人认为伊拉克应该为“9·11”事件负责。自2002年9月以来,大约60%的美国人认为伊拉克对美国的安全构成威胁。乔姆斯基认为这些态度与美国民众支持对伊拉克发动战争密切相关,

---

① Baudrillard, Jean. *The Spirit of Terrorism* (New Revised Edition). Chris Turner, trans., London: Verso, 2003, p.37.

② Sontag, Susan. *At the Same Time: Essays and Speeches*. Peolo Donerido & Anne hump, eds., New York: Picador, 2007, p. 115.

③ Ibid., p.127.

④ Ibid., p.116.

因为一旦民众认为伊拉克对"9・11"事件负有责任,而且还在策划新的暴行,对他们的安全构成迫在眉睫的威胁,那么美国发动战争进行阻止就是有道理的,而这种宣扬无疑是为布什政府服务。在"团结必胜"的口号下,呼吁反省就等于持有异议,异议就等于不爱国。乔姆斯基提醒大众,美国政府想把他们变成"无知的消费者"[①],这样他们就不会干扰美国政府重组世界。美国民众对该事件的反应矛盾且复杂:他们虽然谴责美国的罪行,对美国给贫困、受压迫的伊拉克人民造成如此巨大的痛苦感到气愤,但是又对美国应该对此次恐怖事件负责、美国咎由自取等言论难以认同,认为无论是想通过归咎于美国,或想以某种方式或程度原谅或宽恕那次暴行都是不道德的行为。2011年,奥萨马・本・拉登(Osama bin Laden)被公开抓获并击毙标志着"9・11"事件10年的自然结束,也标志着恐怖主义叛乱和战争的迅速扩张,"9・11"事件"不再是美国文化史上的里程碑,而成为全球暴力大地图上的一块小拼图"[②]。

第一节　"9・11"文学中的创伤与记忆

创伤和记忆是美国小说家解读"9・11"事件常用的角度。根据西格蒙德・弗洛伊德(Sigmund Freud)的解释,创伤是由战争、焦虑、羞耻或身体疼痛之类的经验引起的痛苦、挫折、伤害或是耻辱,它不仅包括真实的客观存在,也包括长时间内人们的内心体验。卡伊・埃里克森(Kai Erikson)在意识到创伤群体与创伤个体之间的差异后,从全新的角度解释了二者之间的不同。埃里克森认为,个体创伤是一种破坏人的防御体系的心理打击,由于其突发性和暴力性使个体无法有效地回应;集体创伤则是对社会生活基础组织的破坏,它损坏了人们连接的纽带,从而让社会群体产生危机感。埃里克森认为,与个体创伤不同的是,集体创伤对创伤群体的影响是缓慢而危险的,创伤群体慢慢才能意识到社会群体作为一个有效支持体已不再存在,自我中重要的一部分已不复存在[③]。无论"9・11"事件最终是否能被证明是国家和全球变化的一个恶果,但几乎可以肯定的是,"9・11"事件已然成为美国集体记忆中无法抹去的创伤事件。杰弗瑞・亚历山大(Jeffery Alexander)认为集体创伤并非整个群体同时经历痛苦,而是这种严重的不安驻扎在集体感中,对集体意识产生影响。他认为,"当集体的成员感到他们遭受了一个可怕的事件,在他们的集体意识上留下不可磨灭的印记,永远地烙印在他们的记忆中,并以根本和不可逆转的方式改变他们未来的身份时,文化创伤就发生了"[④],这种具有攻击性或不可抗拒的事件会破坏或压制一种文化或文化作为整体存在的一种或多种元素,会威胁到他们的身份感。"9・11"事件给美国人民,甚至全世界带来的这些恐惧和创伤形成了相当常见并且经常被重新想象的历史主题,美国作家试图借用这些历史主题直面"9・11"恐怖事件及其后果。

值得注意的是,在那些直击"9.11"恐怖事件及其后果的文本中,大多数文本侧重于强调创伤的初期

---

① Chomsky, Noam. *Imperial Ambitions: Conversations with Noam Chomsky on the Post 9/11 World*, Interviews with David Barsamian, London: Penguin Books Ltd, 2006, p.32.

② Banita, Georgiana. "Literature after 9/11," *American Literature in Transition, 2000 - 2010*, edited by Rachel Greenwald Smith, Cambridge: Cambridge University Press, 2017, p.154.

③ Erikson, Kai. "Notes on Trauma and Community," *American Imago*, vol.48, no.4, 1991, pp.455 - 472.

④ Alexander, Jeffery C., et al. *Cultural Trauma and Collective Identity*. California: University of California Press, 2004.

症状。美国政府宣称“9·11”事件太恐怖、太具毁灭性、太痛苦、太悲惨，以至于文字无法形容，也不可能表达人们的哀伤和愤慨。在桑塔格看来，怀疑思想和文字，无疑是美国反智主义屡见不鲜的一贯行径。毋庸置疑的是，“9·11”事件重塑了美国人的意识，成为当代美国情感结构的决定性因素，它们必然会对美国写作产生深远的影响，进而重新塑造包括小说、回忆录、诗歌、漫画等文学形式在内的美国文学对“9·11”事件的叙事，也同样转移了美国乃至世界文学的关注焦点。在“9·11”事件发生后，诗人们首当其冲，纷纷为“9·11”事件的受害者致哀，如马丁·埃斯帕达(Martin Espada)的《赞美》(“Alabanza”)、罗伯特·平斯基的(Robert Pinksy)的《9.11》(“9/11”)和比利·柯林斯(Billy Collins)的《名字》(“The Names”)，这些诗既是为了纪念那些逝去的人，也是为了促进个人和国家的创伤愈合。理查德·霍华德(Richard Howard)在《奇迹的谬论》(“Fallacies of Wonder”)一诗中指出双子塔及逝去的生命是用他们的缺席代替他们的存在。2002 年出版的《2001 年 9 月 11 日：美国作家的回应》(*September 11, 2001: American Writers Respond*)诗集收录了苔丝·加拉格尔(Tess Gallagher)、乔伊·哈乔(Joy Harjo)和露西尔·克利夫顿(Lucille Clifton)等诗人的作品。同年出版的诗选《以眼还眼会使全世界盲目：诗人眼中的“9·11”》(*An Eye for An Eye Makes the Whole World Blind: Poets on 9/11*)汇集了 100 位不同诗人的诗，通过诗歌这一独特的文学形式来解读“9·11”事件后人类的处境。丹尼斯·洛伊·约翰逊(Dennis Loy Johnson)和瓦莱丽·梅里安(Valerie Merians)在“9·11”一周年时出版了诗集《“9·11”之后：纽约诗人选集》(*Poetry After 9/11: An anthology of New York Poets*)，其中的诗歌不仅关注“9·11”事件本身，还关注它所带来的恐惧和失落。

威廉·福特·吉布森(William Ford Gibson)的《图像识别》(*Pattern Recognition*, 2003)是第一部直接描写恐怖袭击的小说。小说的主人公是一位营销顾问，在“9·11”事件发生时他的父亲在曼哈顿离奇失踪。法国作家弗雷德里克·贝格贝德(Frédéric Beigbeder)的作品《世界的窗户》(*Windows on the World*, 2003)讲述了一个家庭逃出北塔的故事。此外，阿特·斯皮格曼(Art Spiegelman)影响深远的漫画小说《无塔之影》(*The Shadow of No Towers*, 2004)、乔纳森·萨弗兰·福尔(Jonathan Safran Foer)的《特别响，非常近》(*Extremely Loud and Incredibly Close*, 2005)、朱莉亚·格拉丝(Julia Glass)的《世界覆灭》(*The Whole World Over*, 2006)、杰伊·麦金纳尼(Jay McInerney)的《美好生活》(*The Good Life*, 2006)、唐·德里罗(Don DeLillo)的《坠落者》(*Falling Man*, 2007)、约翰·厄普代克(John Updike)的《恐怖分子》(*Terrorist*, 2007)、保罗·奥斯特(Paul Auster)的《黑暗中的人》(*Man in the Dark*, 2008)、艾米·沃德曼(Amy Waldman)的《屈服》(*The Submission*, 2011)、托马斯·品钦(Thomas Pynchon)的《致命尖端》(*Bleeding Edge*, 2013)等作品都明确地叙述了袭击事件，从多元的视角捕捉美国人在“9·11”当天和之后所经历的困惑、恐惧、愤怒和悲伤。“9·11”小说的特点在于表达袭击发生后，人们陷入了难以理解的沉默。

第二节 “9·11”事件与文学的自省

倘若在“9·11”事件之前，文学经常质疑自身存在的必要性以及它与时间、地点、因果之间的联系，那么“9·11”恐怖袭击则加剧了文学的自省,即文学以何种程度忠实于现实这一问题。早期的“9·11”小说并非一种讲究风格、主题和形式一致的文学类型,因为它关注的是历史事件的影响,因此,“9·11”小说侧重于对事件及大众反应的描写,涉及多文化、多种族问题,甚至国家安全、监管和政策对社会生活的影响。阿特·斯皮格曼的漫画小说《无塔之影》运用文字和图片描述了自己在“9·11”当天和之后的身体和情感反应,凸显了文字和图像之间的张力。与此同时,斯皮格曼质疑了“9·11”事件中的“事实”(facts)和“现实”(reality),通过文本中独特的视觉和语言反复强调了文学作品对生活经验的想象与再现。杰伊·麦金纳尼在其《美好生活》中围绕两对曼哈顿夫妇在“9·11”事件后发生的变化,呈现面对灾难性的事件人们内心最深处的恐惧、兴奋和困惑的矛盾心情。类似的作品还有肯·卡尔弗斯(Ken Kalfus)于2006年出版的《这个国家特有的混乱》(*A Disorder Peculiar to the Country*),其中描写了乔伊斯(Joyce)在双子塔被摧毁期间和之后所做出的古怪的反应,“乔伊斯却感到内心有什么东西在爆发,一种温暖的东西,很像,没错,是一种快感,强烈得几乎像饥饿得到了满足。这是一种眩晕,一种得意。塔楼倒塌的轰鸣声终于传到了她的耳朵里,似乎持续了好几分钟,接着是一阵不自然的暖风,把她的头发往后吹,弄皱了她的衬衫。这座建筑变成了一个蘑菇状的柱状上升的烟,灰尘,和消失的生命,令她感到一种巨大的喜悦”①。不得不承认,“9·11”文学在真实与想象之间、意象与转义之间、私人记忆与公共历史领域之间还存在着很大的间隙。

随着时间的推移,“9·11”小说不再囿于描述事件本身,叙事偏重于描写事件带来的后果。朱奈德·拉纳(Junaid Rana)认为,“9·11”小说无法承担拯救种族主义的大任,反而表现出令人生厌的刻板印象,而诸如阿拉伯裔美国人、亚裔美国人,甚至穆斯林人的复杂经历已经不足以描述超越民族和国家的种族叙述,“种族主义不仅仅是附生现象;相反,它是欧洲启蒙、现代化、殖民主义、资本主义和白人至上主义的历史中固有的一种支配、管理和治理体系”②。知名作家如乔纳森·弗兰岑、保罗·奥斯特以及戴夫·埃格斯(Dave Eggers)把“9·11”事件当作叙事背景,用一种弱化悲剧的方式来处理恐怖事件的后果。后来的“9·11”小说变得更加正式、保守,试图通过对“9·11”事件的简单叙述来应对其复杂的表征和影响带来的挑战。

第三节　“9·11”文学批评

文学评论家理查德·格雷(Richard J. Gray)对2009年以前的“9·11”小说,尤其是美国本土作品,进行了全面的综合评价。他认为大多数“9·11”小说都未能超越创伤的初步阶段,只是简单地记录了一些已发生的创伤性事件。正如格雷所言,尽管美国小说家和权威人士在“9·11”事件后宣布了一个新时代的到来,但他们的作品形式并未见根本的变化。格雷反复强调“9·11”小说关注的问题在文学史上都能找到先例,对“9·11”的虚构反而证明了想象力的失败。格雷发现,在美国作家处理“9·11”事件的小

① Kalfus, Ken. *A Disorder Peculiar to the Country*. London: Harper Collins Publishers, 2006, p.8.

② Rana, Junaid. “The 9/11 of Our Imaginations: Islam, the Figure of the Muslim, and the Failed Liberalism of the Racial Present,” Rajini Srikanth & Min Hyoung Song, eds., *The Cambridge History of Asian American Literature*. Cambridge: Cambridge University Press, 2015, p.504.

说中,“无论从什么意义上讲,这场危机都已被驯化”[①]。“9·11”小说经常挑战公共和集体的历史记忆,黛博拉·艾森伯格(Deborah Eisenberg)在其短篇小说《超级英雄的黄昏》(*Twilight of the Superheroes*, 2006)中就表达了这一观点:“私人生活萎缩到一无所有……一个人日常的乐趣就像架子上积满灰尘的古玩”[②]。唐·德里罗在《坠落的人》中写道,“从9月的那一天起,三年过去了,所有的生活都变得公开了”[③]。

格雷认为许多试图见证当代事件的文本要么夸大创伤,要么关注家庭细节,似乎要将一个国家和国际历史的转折点缩小为情感教育。林恩·莎朗·施瓦茨(Lynne Sharon Schwartz)的《墙上的文字》(*The Writing on the Wall*, 2005)更能说明这一趋势。这部小说讲述了雷娜塔痛苦的过去和不确定的现在,这位在纽约公共图书馆工作的才华横溢的语言学家为这场政治危机提供了一个看似完美、虚构的解决方案。小说的标题指的是在家中张贴的寻找“9·11”失踪人员信息的海报,这也是“9·11”文学作品中经常出现的回忆。此外,移民和差异性问题是“9·11”后美国的核心问题(当然,也是“9·11”前民族国家的核心问题)。自2001年的袭击以来,美国公民身份被激进地重新种族化,边境被封锁,公民自由受到限制。这段不光彩的历史,格雷认为是不同文化在美国相遇、碰撞,甚至在某些情况下相互勾结的结果。格雷以约翰·厄普代克的《恐怖分子》为例,提出美国文学出现了一种富有想象力的转向,即转向从拉丁美洲和东南亚移民的角度重写南方小说,这些小说见证了“9·11”之后的文化变异及文化创伤。格雷在这些作品中看重的是对美国文化融合特征的反应性,以及对混合的、多元的美国进行的非领土化的重新描绘。

然而,也有评论家指出,这种多元化美国的前景是否会耗尽“9·11”文学的视野,因为它不可避免地提出了另一个更具挑战性的议题,即如何应对当代战争和恐怖主义。如果美国在国土遭受袭击后,只强调公民和公民权利的国内空间的重构,就会忽视恐怖袭击最初产生的背景。一旦作家们承认了“9·11”的冲击和创伤,在思想和政治上成熟的文学作品就必须把国内空间留给风险更大的“异族”遭遇。值得注意的是,我们在阅读“9·11”文学的时候,还应该看到美国之外的作家是如何描绘美国的域外扩张,如何探索美国的认识论、现象学、全球影响及其霸权暴露的痕迹。在新时代,小说仍然是表达政治和美学的必要形式,我们需要从“9·11”小说中看到的是认知地图,想象美国在民族国家边界之外的形象和感知。

第四节　主要作家介绍与代表作品选读

一、黛博拉·艾森伯格

(一) 黛博拉·艾森伯格简介

黛博拉·艾森伯格(Deborah Eisenberg, 1945—　)是美国短篇小说作家、演员和哥伦比亚大学艺

① Gray, Richard. *After the Fall: American Literature Since 9/11*. Malden: Wiley Blackwell, 2011, p.134.
② Eisenberg, Deborah. *Twilight of the Superheroes*. New York: Farrar, Straus and Giroux, 2006, p.30.
③ DeLillo, Don. *Falling Man*. New York: Scribner, 2007, p.182.

术学院写作专业的名誉教授。艾森伯格共有五部短篇小说集:《外汇交易》(*Transactions in a Foreign Currency*, 1986)、《第 82 空降兵》(*Under the 82nd Airborne*, 1992)、《环绕亚特兰蒂斯》(*All Around Atlantis*, 1997)、《超级英雄的黄昏》(*Twilight of the Superheroes*, 2006)和《你的鸭子是我的鸭子》(*Your Duck Is My Duck*, 2018)。本·马库斯(Ben Marcus)在《纽约时报》书评上称艾森伯格是“当今最重要的小说作家之一”,其《超级英雄的黄昏》则是部伟大的作品。艾森伯格于 1987 年获得怀丁作家奖(Whiting Award)和古根海姆学者奖(Guggenheim Fellowship),于 2000 年获得了雷亚短篇小说奖(Rea Award for the Short Story),还分别在 1986 年、1995 年、1997 年、2002 年、2006 年和 2013 年 6 次获得欧·亨利奖(O. Henry Awards)。2011 年,艾森伯格因其《黛博拉·艾森伯格故事集》(*The Collected Stories of Deborah Eisenberg*)获得国际笔会/福克纳小说奖(PEN/Faulkner Award for Fiction),又于 2015 年荣获马拉默德短篇小说奖(Malamud Award for Excellence in the Short Story in May),成为第四位同时获得马拉默德奖和福克纳小说奖的作家。她还写过剧本《田园》(*Pastorale*, 1982)、关于艺术家詹妮弗·巴特利特的专著(*Jennifer Bartlett*, 1994)以及文学评论。

艾森伯格专注于短篇小说,不断在越来越复杂、流畅和具有道德深度的故事中对人类心理进行探索。艾森伯格的作品展现了当代美国人与众不同的生活写照。她的故事精雕细琢,描述了男人和女人如何面对他们的个人关系,以及如何应对这些关系发生时不断变化的社会环境。她娴熟地运用对话和不同的视角捕捉人物意识的微妙变化以及描写被命运折磨得伤痕累累的人们的生活,并为读者提供了既真实又具有独创性的观察。艾森伯格的短篇小说体现了她对情感细微差别的敏锐感知和诙谐的机智。艾森伯格会在人物的私生活中注入公众或政治因素,认为作家们应该教会读者如何处理生活中个人隐私和思想与大型公共事件之间错综复杂的关系问题。

(二) 代表作《超级英雄的黄昏》简介

《超级英雄的黄昏》由非线性的、支离破碎的故事片段构成,以第三人称叙事。纳撒尼尔(Nathaniel)是犹太移民罗斯(Rose)和以撒(Isaac)的儿子,吕西安(Lucien)是他的姨父,他的阿姨查莉(Charlie)已经去世。大学毕业后,纳撒尼尔留在了家乡,而他最亲密的朋友艾米蒂(Amity)、麦迪逊(Madison)等搬到了城市,并在公共关系、经纪和艺术领域找到了工作。纳撒尼尔在艾米蒂的鼓励下也搬到了城市。吕西安给纳撒尼尔找了一份建筑行业的工作,并把朋友在曼哈顿的豪华公寓转租给了他。在市场崩溃后,纳撒尼尔的朋友们或失去了工作,或无力支付房租,他们搬去和纳撒尼尔住在一起。一群人一起坐在露台上目睹了“9·11”恐怖袭击和双子塔倒塌。三年后,吕西安和纳撒尼尔以“9·11”事件为背景回忆他们的过去,并意识到现实并非都已恢复正常。为了加深读者对她笔下人物的理解,艾森伯格将灾难对个人的持久影响与平凡的日常生活并置在一起。在这个故事中,她敏感地捕捉了人类经验中常见但又常常被忽视的方面,唤醒了紧张而丰富的人类生活,在这种生活中,“发生的一切都在等待着你的到来”①。

① Eisenberg, Deborah. *Twilight of the Superheroes*, New York: Farrar, Straus and Giroux, 2006, p.133.

（三）作品选读：《超级英雄的黄昏》[①]

THE AGE OF DIGITAL REASONING

One/two. On/off. The plane crashes/doesn't crash.

The plane he took from L. A. didn't crash. It wasn't used as a missile to blow anything up, and not even one passenger was shot or stabbed. Nothing happened. So, what's the problem? What's the difference between having been on that flight and having been on any other flight in his life?

Oh, what's the point of thinking about death all the time! Think about it or not, you die. Besides—and here's something that sure hasn't changed—you don't have to do it more than once. And as you don't have to do it less than once, either, you might as well do it on the plane. Maybe there's no special problem these days. Maybe the problem is just that he's old.

Or maybe his nephew's is the last generation that will remember what it had once felt like to blithely assume there would be a future—at least a future like the one that had been implied by the past they'd all been familiar with.

But the future actually ahead of them, it's now obvious, had itself been implied by a past; and the terrible day that pointed them toward that future had been prepared for a long, long time, though it had been prepared behind a curtain.

It was as if there had been a curtain, a curtain painted with the map of the earth, its oceans and continents, with Lucien's delightful city. The planes struck, tearing through the curtain of that blue September morning, exposing the dark world that lay right behind it, of populations ruthlessly exploited, inflamed with hatred, and tired of waiting for change to happen by.

The stump of the ruined tower continued to smolder far into the fall, and an unseasonable heat persisted. When the smoke lifted, all kinds of other events, which had been prepared behind a curtain, too, were revealed. Flags waved in the brisk air of fear, files were demanded from libraries and hospitals, droning helicopters hung over the city, and heavily armed policemen patrolled the parks. Meanwhile, one read that executives had pocketed the savings of their investors and the pensions of their employees.

The wars in the East were hidden behind a thicket of language: *patriotism, democracy, loyalty, freedom*—the words bounced around, changing purpose, as if they were made out of some funny plastic. What did they actually refer to? It seemed that they all might refer to money.

Were the sudden power outages and spiking level of unemployment related? And what was

① Eisenberg, Deborah. *Twilight of the Superheroes*, New York: Farrar, Straus and Giroux, 2006, pp. 32 - 42.

causing them? The newspapers seemed for the most part to agree that the cause of both was terrorism. But lots of people said they were both the consequence of corporate theft. It was certainly all beyond Lucien! Things that had formerly appeared to be distinct, or even at odds, now seemed to have been smoothly blended, to mutual advantage. Provocation and retribution, arms manufacture and statehood, oil and war, commerce and dogma, and the spinning planet seemed to be boiling them all together at the center of the earth into a poison syrup. Enemies had soared toward each other from out of the past to unite in a joyous fireball; planes had sheared through the heavy, painted curtain and from the severed towers an inexhaustible geyser had erupted.

Styles of pets revolved rapidly, as if the city's residents were searching for a type of animal that would express a stance appropriate to the horrifying assault, which for all anyone knew was only the first of many.

For a couple of months everyone was walking cute, perky things. Then Lucien saw snarling hounds everywhere and the occasional boa constrictor draped around its owner's shoulders. After that, it was tiny, trembling dogs that traveled in purses and pockets.

New York had once been the threshold of an impregnable haven, then the city had become in an instant the country's open wound, and now it was the occasion—the pretext! —for killing and theft and legislative horrors all over the world. The air stank from particulate matter—chemicals and asbestos and blood and scorched bone. People developed coughs and strange rashes.

What should be done, and to whom? Almost any word, even between friends, could ignite a sheet of flame. What were the bombings for? First one imperative was cited and then another; the rationales shifted hastily to cover successive gaps in credibility. Bills were passed containing buried provisions, and loopholes were triumphantly discovered—alarming elasticities or rigidities in this law or that. One was sick of trying to get a solid handle on the stream of pronouncements—it was like endlessly trying to sort little bits of paper into stacks when a powerful fan was on.

Friends in Europe and Asia sent him clippings about his own country. *What's all this*, they asked—secret arrests and detentions, his president capering about in military uniform, crazy talk of preemptive nuclear strikes? Why were they releasing a big science fiction horror movie over there, about the emperor of everything everywhere, for which the whole world was required to buy tickets? What on earth was going on with them all, why were they all so silent? Why did they all seem so confused?

How was he to know, Lucien thought. If his foreign friends had such great newspapers, why didn't *they tell him*!

No more smiles from strangers on the street! Well, it was reasonable to be frightened; everyone had seen what those few men were able do with the odds and ends in their pockets. The heat lifted, and then there was unremitting cold. No one lingered to joke and converse in the course of their errands, but instead hurried irritably along, like people with bad consciences.

And always in front of you now was the sight that had been hidden by the curtain, of all those irrepressibly, murderously angry people.

Private life shrank to nothing. All one's feelings had been absorbed by an arid wasteland—policy, strategy, goals. One's past, one's future, one's ordinary daily pleasures were like dusty little curios on a shelf.

Lucien continued defiantly throwing his parties, but as the murky wars dragged on, he stopped. It was impossible to have fun or to want to have fun. It was one thing to have fun if the sun was shining generally, quite another thing to have fun if it was raining blood everywhere but on your party. What did he and his friends really have in common, anyway? Maybe nothing more than their level of privilege.

In restaurants and cafes all over the city, people seemed to have changed. The good-hearted, casually wasteful festival was over. In some places the diners were sullen and dogged, as if they felt accused of getting away with something.

In other places, the gaiety was cranked up to the level of completely unconvincing hysteria. For a long miserable while, in fact, the city looked like a school play about war profiteering. The bars were overflowing with very young people from heaven only knew where, in hideous, ludicrously showy clothing, spending massive amounts of money on green, pink, and orange cocktails, and laughing at the top of their lungs, as if at filthy jokes.

No, not like a school play—like a movie, though the performances and the direction were crude. The loud, ostensibly carefree young people appeared to be extras recruited from the suburbs, and yet sometime in the distant future, people seeing such a movie might think oh, yes, that was a New York that existed once, say, at the end of the millennium.

It was Lucien's city, Lucien's times, and yet what he appeared to be living in wasn't the actual present—it was an inaccurate representation of the past. True, it looked something like the New York that existed before all this began, but Lucien remembered, and he could see: the costumes were not quite right, the hairstyles were not quite right, the gestures and the dialogue were not quite right.

Oh. Yes. Of course none of it was quite right—the movie was a propaganda movie. And now it seems that the propaganda movie has done its job; things, in a grotesque sense, are back to normal.

Money is flowing a bit again, most of the flags have folded up, those nerve-wracking terror alerts have all but stopped, the kids in the restaurants have calmed down, no more rolling blackouts, and the dogs on the street encode no particular messages. Once again, people are concerned with getting on with their lives. Once again, the curtain has dropped.

Except that people seem a little bit nervous, a little uncomfortable, a little wary. Because you can't help sort of knowing that what you're seeing is only the curtain. And you can't help guessing what might be going on behind it.

THE FURTHE IN THE PAST THINGS ARE, THE BIGGER THEY BECOME

Nathaniel remembers more and more rather than less and less vividly the visit of his uncle and aunt to the Midwest during his childhood.

He'd thought his aunt Charlie was the most beautiful woman he'd ever seen. And for all he knows, she really was. He never saw her after that one visit; by the time he came to New York and reconnected with Uncle Lucien she had been dead for a long time. She would still have been under fifty when she died—crushed, his mother had once, in a mood, implied, by the weight of her own pretensions.

His poor mother! She had cooked, cleaned, and fretted for... months, it had seemed, in preparation for that visit of Uncle Lucien and Aunt Charlie. And observing in his memory the four grown-ups, Nathaniel can see an awful lot of white knuckles.

He remembers his mother picking up a book Aunt Charlie had left lying on the kitchen table, glancing at it and putting it back down with a tiny shrug and a lifted eyebrow. "You don't approve?" Aunt Charlie said, and Nathaniel is shocked to see, in his memory, that she is tense.

His mother, having gained the advantage, makes another bitter little shrug. "I'm sure it's over my head," she says.

When the term of the visit came to an end, they dropped Uncle Lucien and Aunt Charlie at the airport. His brother was driving, too fast. Nathaniel can hear himself announcing in his child's piercing voice, "*I want to live in New York like Uncle Lucien and Aunt Charlie*!" His exile's heart was brimming, but it was clear from his mother's profile that she was braced for an execution.

"Slow *down*, Bernie!" his mother said, but Bernie hadn't. "Big shot," she muttered, though it was unclear at whom this was directed—whether at his brother or himself or his father, or his Uncle Lucien, or at Aunt Charlie herself.

BACK TO NORMAL

Do dogs have to fight sadness as tirelessly as humans do? They seem less involved with retrospect, less involved in dread and anticipation. Animals other than humans appear to be having a more profound experience of the present. But who's to say? Clearly their feelings are intense, and maybe grief and anxiety darken all their days. Maybe that's why they've acquired their stripes and polka dots and fluffiness—to cheer themselves up.

Poor old Earth, an old sponge, a honeycomb of empty mine shafts and dried wells. While he and his friends were wittering on, the planet underfoot had been looted. The waterways glint with weapons-grade plutonium, sneaked on barges between one wrathful nation and another, the polar ice caps melt, Venice sinks.

In the horrible old days in Europe when Rose and Isaac were hunted children, it must have been pretty clear to them how to behave, minute by minute. Men in jackboots? Up to the attic!

But even during that time when it was so dangerous to speak out, to act courageously, heroes emerged. Most of them died fruitlessly, of course, and unheralded. But now there are even monuments to some of them, and information about such people is always coming to light.

Maybe there really is no problem, maybe everything really is back to normal and maybe the whole period will sink peacefully away, to be remembered only by scholars. But if it should end, instead, in dire catastrophe, whom will the monuments of the future commemorate?

Today, all day long, Lucien has seen the president's vacant, stricken expression staring from the ubiquitous television screens. He seemed to be talking about positioning weapons in space, colonizing the moon.

Open your books to page 167, class, Miss Mueller shrieks. *What do you see*?

Lucien sighs.

The pages are thin and sort of shiny. The illustrations are mostly black and white.

This one's a photograph of a statue, an emperor, apparently, wearing his stone toga and his stone wreath. The real people, the living people, mill about just beyond the picture's confines, but Lucien knows more or less what they look like—he's seen illustrations of them, too. He knows what a viaduct is and that the ancient Romans went to plays and banquets and that they had a code of law from which his country's own is derived. Are the people hidden by the picture frightened? Do they hear the stones working themselves loose, the temples and houses and courts beginning to crumble?

Out the window, the sun is just a tiny, tiny bit higher today than it was at this exact instant yesterday. After school, he and Robbie Stern will go play soccer in the park. In another month it will be bright and warm.

PARADISE

So, Mr. Matsumoto will be coming back, and things seem pretty much as they did when he left. The apartment is clean, the cats are healthy, the art is undamaged, and the view from the terrace is exactly the same, except there's that weird, blank spot where the towers used to stand.

"Open the next?" Madison says, holding up a bottle of champagne.

"Strongly agree, agree, undecided, disagree, strongly disagree." "Strongly agree," Lyle says.

"Thanks," Amity says.

"Okay," Russell says. "I'm in." Nathaniel shrugs and holds out his glass.

Madison pours. "Polls indicate that 100 percent of the American public approves heavy drinking," he says.

"Oh, god, Madison," Amity says. "Can't we ever just *drop* it? Can't we ever just have a nice time?" Madison looks at her for a long moment.

"Drop what?" he says, evenly.

But no one wants to get into *that*.

When Nathaniel was in his last year at college, his father began to suffer from heart trouble. It was easy enough for Nathaniel to come home on the weekends, and he'd sit with his father, gazing out the window as the autumnal light gilded the dry grass and the fallen leaves glowed.

His father talked about his own time at school, working night and day, the pride his parents had taken in him, the first college student in their family.

Over the years Nathaniel's mother and father had grown gentler with one another and with him. Sometimes after dinner and the dishes, they'd all go out for a treat. Nathaniel would wait, an acid pity weakening his bones, while his parents debated worriedly over their choices, as if nobody ever had before or would ever have again the opportunity to eat ice cream.

Just last night, he dreamed about Delphine, a delicious champagne-style dream, full of love and beauty—a weird, high-quality love, a feeling he doesn't remember ever having had in his waking life—a pure, wholehearted, shining love.

It hangs around him still, floating through the air out on the terrace—fragrant, shimmering, fading.

WAITING

The bell is about to ring. Closing his book Lucien hears the thrilling crash as the bloated empire tumbles down.

Gold star, Lucien! Miss Mueller cackles deafeningly, and then she's gone.

Charlie's leaving, too. Lucien lifts his glass; she glances back across the thin, inflexible divide.

From farther than the moon she sees the children of some distant planet study pictures in their text: there's Rose and Isaac at their kitchen table, Nathaniel out on Mr. Matsumoto's terrace, Lucien alone in the dim gallery—and then the children turn the page.

思考与讨论

(1) 小说中的每个人物如何看待"9·11"事件?"9·11"事件带给他们什么样的影响?

(2) 如何理解这部短篇小说的题目以及选文中的小标题?

(3) 黛博拉·艾森伯格是如何用短篇小说的形式来呈现"9·11"事件的创伤性的?

拓展阅读

[1] Araújo, Susana. *Transatlantic Fictions of 9/11 and the War on Terror: Images of Insecurity, Narratives of Captivity*. London: Bloomsbury, 2015.

[2] Cristofaro, Diletta De. *The Contemporary Post-Apocalyptic Novel: Critical Temporalities and the End Times.* New York: Bloomsbury Academic, 2020.

[3] Gauthier, Tim. *9/11 Fiction, Empathy, and Otherness*. London: Lexington Books, 2015.

[4] Keeble, Arin. *The 9/11 Novel: Trauma, Politics and Identity*. North Carolina: McFarland & Company, Inc., 2014.

[5] Parr, Adrian. *Deleuze and Memorial Culture: Desire, Singular Memory and the Politics of Trauma*. Edinburgh: Edinburgh University Press, 2008.

二、约翰·厄普代克

(一) 约翰·厄普代克简介

约翰·厄普代克(John Updike, 1932—2009)是一位备受赞誉的美国小说家、诗人、散文家和评论家,其创作生涯非常丰富多彩,著作多达 50 多部。厄普代克的诗集有《美国风物及其他》(*Americana and Other Poems*, 2001)、《1953—1993 诗集》(*Collected Poems 1953—1993*, 1993)、《面对自然》(*Facing Nature*, 1985)、《辗转反侧》(*Tossing and Turning*, 1977)、《七十首诗》(*Seventy Poems*, 1972)、《中点及其他诗歌》(*Midpoint and Other Poems*, 1969)和《做木工的母鸡和其他温顺的生物》(*The Carpentered Hen and Other Tame Creatures*, 1958)。厄普代克的小说和短篇小说集包括《时间的尽头》(*Toward the End of Time*, 1997)、《来世和其他故事》(The *Afterlife and Other Stories*, 1994)、《问题和其他故事》(*Problems and Other Stories*, 1981)、《嫁给我》(*Marry Me*, 1976)、《兔子归来》(*Rabbit Redux*, 1971)、《夫妇》(*Couples*, 1968)。他还著有关于音乐(*Concerts at Castle Hill*, 1982)、艺术(*Just Looking: Essays on Art*, 1989)和高尔夫球(*Golf Dreams: Writing on Golf*, 2011)的评论。厄普代克获得了几乎所有的美国文学奖项和荣誉,包括美国国家图书奖、国家书评界奖和国家艺术俱乐部荣誉勋章。凭借《兔子富了》(*Rabbit Is Rich*)和《兔子歇了》(*Rabbit at Rest*),厄普代克分别于 1982 年和 1990 年获得普利策奖。

厄普代克关注美国新教小镇的中产阶级,善于在日常生活中寻找戏剧性的张力,如婚姻、性和对没有前途的工作的不满。厄普代克想要揭开性的神秘面纱,不断在描写两性关系、肉体及欲望的道路上探索,在他的作品中,极端冲突的中间地带和模棱两可的观点占据了主导地位,而这种模糊性常常在他对待性的方式上显现出来。厄普代克聚焦于自己的民族,竭力把握时代的脉搏,他的作品中也突出了宗教,尤其是传统的新教信仰,关注生活的非理性本质和人类自我反省的需求。

(二)《恐怖分子》简介

约翰·厄普代克笔下的恐怖分子是指18岁的艾哈迈德·马洛伊·阿什莫伊(Ahmad Mulloy Ashmawy)。艾哈迈德的父亲是一名埃及交换生,与美国爱尔兰裔工人特蕾莎·马洛伊(Teresa Mulloy)结婚后,在艾哈迈德三岁时失踪。艾哈迈德虔诚地信奉真主,深受阿訇谢赫·拉希德(Shaikh Rashid)犹太复国主义思想的影响。然而,艾哈迈德时常为自己的宗教信仰与充满物质主义和享乐主义的社会之间的矛盾困惑不已。在他从中央中学(Central High School)毕业之际,63岁的杰克·列维(Jack Levy)成了他的指导教师。列维的犹太身份让他一生受尽折磨,因为他是犹太教的坚定反对者。在毕业之际,艾哈迈德正处在人生的交叉路口,对未来充满了疑惑。他要么如列维所建议的那样上大学,要么遵循阿訇谢赫·拉希德的建议,当一名卡车司机。艾哈迈德喜欢美国非裔女孩泰诺·琼斯(Tylenol Jones),并随她去了基督教堂且深受震撼。虽然艾哈迈德开始怀疑自己的信仰,但他还是决定申请参加商业驾照C级考试并获得驾照。艾哈迈德毕业后成了一名卡车司机,替查理·谢哈卜(Charlie Chehab)工作。查理开始给艾哈迈德灌输圣战思想并安排他去炸隧道。在危急时刻,列维找到艾哈迈德并成功地劝说他放弃了恐怖活动。

在《恐怖分子》中,厄普代克围绕"9·11"事件后恐怖主义威胁的散乱言论,深入分析恐怖主义产生的复杂原因,淋漓尽致地呈现了种族和阶级耻辱感,突出了美国的物质主义和消费文化带来的困惑,认为它既源于美国主流社会信仰丧失对族裔青年造成的冲击,又来自边缘群体深切的异化感和孤独感产生的身份危机,从而在伊斯兰教等宗教组织中寻求归属感。

(三)作品选读:《恐怖分子》[①]

This fragile, misbegotten nation had a history scarcely expressed in the grandiose New Prospect City Hall and the lake of developers' rubble on whose opposite shores stand, with their caged windows, the high school and the sooty black church. Each town bears in its center relics of the nineteenth century, civic buildings of lumpy brown stones or soft red brick with jutting cornices and round arched entryways, ornate proud buildings outlasting the flimsier twentieth-century constructions. These older, ruddier buildings express a bygone industrial prosperity, a wealth of manufacture, machinery and railroads harnessed to the lives of a laboring nation, an era of internal consolidation and welcome to the world's immigrants. Then there is an underlying earlier century, which made the succeeding ones possible. The orange truck rumbles past small iron signs and overlookable monuments commemorating an insurgency that became a revolution; from Fort Lee to Red Bank, its battles had been fought, leaving thousands of boys asleep beneath the grass.

Charlie Chehab, a man of many disparate parts, knows a surprising amount about that ancient conflict: "New Jersey's where the Revolution got turned around. Long Island had been a disaster;

① Updike, John. *Terrorist*. Oxford: ISIS Publishing Ltd., 2007, pp. 202-212.

New York City was more of the same. Retreat, retreat. Disease and desertions. Just before the winter of 'seventy-six-'seventy-seven, the British moved down from Fort Lee to Newark, then to Brunswick and Princeton and Trenton, easy as a knife through butter. Washington straggled across the Delaware with an army in rags. A lot of them, believe it or not, were barefoot. Barefoot, and winter coming on. We were toast. In Philadelphia, everybody was trying to leave except the Tories, who sat around waiting for their buddies the redcoats to arrive. Up in New England, a British fleet took Newport and Rhode Island without a fight. It was *over*."

"Yes, and why wasn't it?" Ahmad asks, wondering why Charlie is telling this patriotic tale with such enthusiasm.

"Well," he says, "several things. Some good things were happening. The Continental Congress woke up and stopped trying to run the war; they said, 'O.K., let George do it.'"

"Is that where the phrase comes from?"

"Good question. I don't think so. The other American general in charge, a silly prick called Charles Lee—Fort Lee is named after him, thanks a bunch—let himself be captured in a tavern in Basking Ridge, leaving Washington in total charge. At this point Washington was lucky to have an army at all. After Long Island, see, the British had gone easy on us. They let die Continental Army retreat and get across the Delaware. That proved to be a mistake, for, as they must have taught you at school—what the fuck do they teach you at school, Madman?—Washington and a plucky band of threadbare freedom fighters crossed the Delaware on Christmas Day and routed the Hessian troops garrisoned in Trenton, and took a whole bunch of prisoners. On top of that, when Cornwallis brought down a big force from New York and thought he had the Americans trapped south of Trenton, Washington snuck off through the woods, around the Barrens and the Great Bear Swamp, and marched north to Princeton! All this with soldiers in rags who hadn't slept for days! People were tougher then. They weren't afraid to die. When Washington ran into a British force south of Princeton, an American general named Mercer was captured, and they called him a damn rebel and told him to beg for quarter, and he said he wasn't a rebel and refused to beg, so they bayoneted him to death. They weren't such nice guys, the British, as Masterpiece Theatre lets on. When things looked their worst at Princeton, Washington on a white horse—this is honest truth, on a truly white horse—led his men into the heart of the British fire and turned the tide, and ran after the retreating redcoats shouting, 'It's a fine fox chase, my boys!'"

"He sounds cruel," Ahmad said.

Charlie made that negative American noise in his nose, *aahnn*, signifying dismissal, and said, "Not really. War is cruel, but not the men who wage it necessarily. Washington was a gentleman. When the battle at Princeton was over, he stopped and complimented a wounded British soldier on what a gallant fight they had put up. In Philadelphia, he protected the Hessian prisoners from the pissed-off crowds, who would have killed them. See, the Hessians, like most professional European soldiers, were trained to give quarter only in certain circumstances, and to take no prisoners otherwise—that's what they did on Long Island, they butchered us—and they were so amazed at the humane treatment they got instead that a quarter of them stayed here when the war was over. They intermarried with the Pennsylvania Dutch. They became Americans."

"You seem very enamored of George Washington."

"Well, why not?" Charlie considers, as if Ahmad has sprung a trap. "You have to be, if you care about New Jersey. Here's where he earned his spurs. The great thing about him, he was a learner. He learned, for one thing, to get along with the New Englanders. From the standpoint of a Virginia planter, the New Englanders were a bunch of unkempt anarchists; they had blacks and red Indians in their ranks as if these guys were white men, just like they had them on their whaling ships. Washington himself, actually, for that matter, had a big black buck for a sidekick, also called Lee, no relation to Robert E. When the war was over, Washington freed him for his services to the Revolution. He had learned to think of slavery as a bad thing. He wound up encouraging black enlistment, after resisting the idea initially. You've heard the word 'pragmatic'?"

"Of course."

"That was Georgie. He learned to take what came, to fight guerrilla-style: hit and hide, hit and hide. He retreated but he never gave up. He was the Ho Chi Minh of his day. We were like Hamas. We were Al-Qaida. The thing about New Jersey was," Charlie hurries to add, when Ahmad takes a breath as if he might interrupt, "the British wanted it to be a model of pacification—winning hearts and minds, you've heard of that. They saw what they did on Long Island was counterproductive, recruiting more resistance, and were trying to play nice here, to woo the colonists back to the mother country. At Trenton, what Washington was saying to the British was, 'This is real. This is beyond nice.'"

"Beyond nice," Ahmad repeats. "That could be the title of a TV series for you to direct."

Charlie doesn't acknowledge the playful idea. He is selling something. He goes on, "He showed the world what can be done against the odds, against a superpower. He showed—and this is where Vietnam and Iraq come in—that in a war between an imperialist occupier and the people who actually live there, the people will eventually prevail. They know the terrain. They have more at stake. They have nowhere else to go. It wasn't just the Continental Army in New Jersey; it was the local militias, little sneaky bands of locals all across New Jersey, acting on their own, picking off British soldiers one by one and disappearing, back into the countryside—not playing fair, in other words, by the other guy's rules. The attack on the Hessians was sneaky, too—in the middle of a blizzard, and on a holiday when not even soldiers ought to have to work. Washington was saying, 'Hey, this is *our* war.' About Valley Forge: Valley Forge gets all the publicity, but the winters after that he camped out in New Jersey—in Middlebrook in the Watchung Mountains, and then in Morristown. In Morristown, the first winter was the coldest in a century. They chopped down six hundred acres of oak and chestnut trees to make huts and have firewood. There was so much snow that winter the provisions couldn't get through and they nearly starved."

"For the state of the world now," Ahmad offers, to get in step with Charlie, "it might have been better if they had. The United States might have become a kind of Canada, a peaceable and sensible country, though infidel."

Charlie's surprised laugh becomes a snort in his nose. "Dream on, Madman. There's too much energy here for peace and sensible. Contending energies—that's what the Constitution allows for. That's what we get." He shifts in his seat and shakes out a Marlboro. Smoke envelops his face as he squints through the windshield and appears to reflect upon what he has told his young driver. "The next time we're south on Route Nine we ought to swing over to Monmouth Battlefield. The Americans fell back, but stood up to the British well enough to show the French they were worth supporting. And the Spanish and Dutch. All of Europe was out to cut England down to size. Like the U.S. now. It was ironical: Louis Seize spent so much supporting us he taxed the French to the point where they revolted and cut off his head. One revolution led to another. That happens." Charlie exhales heavily and in a graver, surreptitious voice pronounces, as if not sure Ahmad should hear the words, "History isn't something over and done, you know. It's now, too. Revolution never stops. You cut off its head, it grows two."

"The Hydra," Ahmad says, to show he is not completely ignorant. The image recurs in Shaikh Rashid's sermons, in illustration of the futility of America's crusade against Islam, and was first encountered by Ahmad in watching children's television, the cartoons on Saturday mornings, while his mother slept late. Just he and the television in the living room—the electronic box so frantic and bumptious with the hiccups and pops and crashes and excited high-pitched voices of cartoon adventure, and its audience, the watching child, utterly quiet and still, the sound turned down to let his mother sleep off her date last night. The Hydra was a comic creature, all its heads chattering with each other on their undulating necks.

"These old revolutions," Charlie continues confidentially, "have much to teach our jihad." Ahmad's lack of a response leads tfie other to ask in a quick, testing voice, "You are with the jihad?"

"How could I not be? The Prophet urges it in the Book." Ahmad quotes: "*Mohammed is Allah's apostle. Those who follow him are ruthless to the unbelievers but merciful to one another*."

Still, the jihad seems very distant. Delivering modern furniture and collecting furniture that had been modern to its dead owners, he and Charlie ride Excellency through a sweltering morass of pizzerias and nail salons, thrift outlets and gas stations, White Castles and Blimpies. *Krispy Kreme* and *Lovely Laundry*, *Rims and Tires* and *877 - TEETH - 14*, *Star-lite Motel* and *Prime Office Suites*, *Bank of America* and *Metro Information Shredding*, *Testigos de Jehovah* and *New Christian Tabernacle*: signs in a dizzying multitude shout out their potential enhancements of all the lives crammed where once there had been pastures and water-powered factories. The thick-walled, eternity-minded structures of municipal purpose still stood, preserved as museums or apartments or quarters for civic organizations. American flags flew everywhere, some so tattered and faded they had evidently been forgotten on their flagstaffs. The world's hopes had centered here for a time, but the time was past. Ahmad sees through Excellency's high windshield clots of males and females his age gathering in gabbling idleness, idleness with an edge of menace, the brown skins of the females bared by skimpy shorts and tight elastic halters, and the males arrayed in tank tops and grotesquely droopy shorts, earrings and wool skullcaps, clownish jokes they play on themselves.

A kind of terror at the burden of having a life to live hits Ahmad through the dusty windshield glare. These doomed animals gathered in the odor of mating and mischief yet have the comfort of their herded kindred, and each harbors some hope or plan of a future, a job, a destination, an aspiration if only to rise in the ranks of dope dealers or pimps. Whereas he, Ahmad, with abilities that Mr. Levy had told him were ample, has no plan: the God attached to him like an invisible twin, his other self, is a God not of enterprise but of submission. Though he endeavors to pray five times a day, if only in the truck body's rectangular cave with its stacked blankets and packing pads, or in a patch of gravel behind a roadside eating place where he can spread his mat for a cleansing five minutes, the Merciful and Compassionate has illuminated no straight path into a vocation. It is as if in the delicious sleep of his devotion to Allah his future has been amputated.

When, in the long lulls of devouring the miles, he confesses his disquiet to Charlie, the usually talkative and well-informed man seems evasive and discomfited.

"Well, in less than three years you'll be getting the Class A CDL and can drive any load—hazmat, trailer rigs—out of state. You'll be making great money."

"But to what end? As you say, to consume consumer goods? To feed and clothe my body that will eventually become decrepit and worthless?"

"That's a way to look at it. 'Life sucks, and then you die.' But doesn't that leave out a lot?"

"What? 'Wife and kids,' as people say?"

"Well, with wife and kids on board, it's true, a lot of these big, meaning-of-it-all existential questions take a back seat."

"You have the wife and kids, and yet you rarely speak of them to me."

"What's to say? I love'em. And what about love, Madman? Don't you feel it? Like I say, we got to get you laid."

"That is a kind wish on your part, but without marriage it would go against my beliefs."

"Oh, come on. The Prophet himself was no monk. He said a man could have four wives. The girl we'd get you wouldn't be a good Muslim; she'd be a hooker. It wouldn't matter to her and shouldn't matter to you. She'd be a filthy infidel with or without whatever you did to her."

"I do not desire uncleanness."

"Well, what the hell do you desire, Ahmad? Forget fucking, I'm sorry I brought it up. What about just being alive? Breathing the air, seeing the clouds? Doesn't that beat being dead?"

A spatter of sudden summer rain from the sky—cloudless, an overall pewter gray shot through with smothered sunlight—speckles the windshield; at the touch of Ahmad's hand the wipers begin their cumbersome flapping. The one on the driver's side leaves a rainbow arc of unswept moisture, a gap in its rubber blade: he makes a mental note to replace that faulty blade. "It depends," he tells Charlie. "Only the unbelievers fear death absolutely."

"What about daily pleasures? You love life, Madman, don't deny it. Just die way you come to work early every morning, eager to see what's on our schedule. We've had other kids on the truck who didn't see a thing, didn't give a damn, they were dead behind the eyes. All they cared about was stopping at the junk-food chains to eat a ton and take a piss and, when the day was over, going out and getting high with their buddies. You, you got potential."

"I have been told that. But if I love life, as you say, it is as a gift from God that He chose to give, and can choose to take away."

"O.K., then. As God wills. In die meantime, enjoy the ride."

"I am."

"Good boy."

思考与讨论

(1) 艾哈迈德的宗教观念是什么?

(2) 是什么促使艾哈迈德变成了恐怖分子?

(3) 厄普代克对恐怖分子是什么态度?

拓展阅读

[1] Banita, Georgiana. *Plotting Justice: Narrative Ethics and Literary culture after 9/11. Lincoln: University of Nebraska Press,* 2012.

[2] O'Gorman, Daniel. *Fictions of the War on Terror: Difference and the Transnational 9/11 Novel*. New York: Palgrave Macmillan, 2015.

[3] Rana, Junaid. "The 9/11 of Our Imaginations: Islam, the Figure of the Muslim, and the Failed Liberalism of the Racial Present." Rajini Srikanth & Min Hyoung Song, eds., *The Cambridge History of Asian American Literature*. Cambridge: Cambridge University Press, 2015, pp. 503-518.

[4] Langah, Nukhbah Taj, ed. *Literary and Non-literary Responses Towards 9/11: South Asia and Beyond*. London: Routledge, 2018.

[5] Muller, Christine. *September 11, 2001 as a Cultural Trauma: A Case Study through Popular*

Culture. New York: Palgrave Macmillan, 2017.

三、托马斯·品钦

(一) 托马斯·品钦简介

托马斯·品钦(Thomas Pynchon, 1937—　)被哈罗德·布鲁姆(Harold Bloom)称作美国当代作家四杰之一,并屡次入围诺贝尔文学奖。作为麦克阿瑟奖获得者,他以其晦涩复杂的小说而闻名。品钦的作品包含着丰富的意旨、风格和主题,通过迷宫式的叙事和对自然科学、前沿科技、高等数学、现代物理等领域的概念借用,描绘了美国光怪陆离的社会全景,道出了现代社会中人类的艰难处境,展现了作家独特的视角以及对黑色幽默、犯罪悬疑、侦探等元素的娴熟运用。品钦的代表作有《万有引力之虹》(*Gravity's Rainbow*, 1973)、《葡萄园》(*Vineland*, 1990)、《性本恶》(*Inherent Vice*, 2009)和《致命尖端》(*Bleeding Edge*, 2013)。

品钦的风格通常被归类为后现代主义。除了强调种族主义和帝国主义等社会政治主题,品钦的作品灵活运用传统高雅文化(high culture)和文学形式的多种元素,以古怪的方式对哲学、神学和社会学思想进行了详尽的探索,但是他的作品又对低俗文化(low culture)及其产品,如漫画书和卡通、低俗小说、流行电影、电视节目、烹饪、城市神话、偏执和阴谋论以及民间艺术表现出很强的亲和力。品钦对流行文化的借鉴模糊了"高雅"和"低俗"文化的传统界限,而其变幻无常的想象力以及作品中复杂的社会背景和人物都被视为其作品的独特特征。

(二) 代表作《致命尖端》简介

《致命尖端》与其他"9·11"小说最不同的是其将21世纪初互联网产业的灾难和世贸中心的灾难放在晚期资本主义的宏大语境下的叙事视角。故事发生在2001年的春天,犹太人玛克欣·塔诺(Maxine Tarnow)是一名被解除职务的调查员,经营着一家名叫"缉凶事务所"的小型欺诈案调查代理公司。她与投资银行家前夫霍斯特·莱夫勒(Horst Loeffler)有两个非常可爱的孩子:齐格(Ziggy)和欧蒂斯(Otis)。玛克欣就像普通的上班族妈妈一样正常生活,直到她开始调查一家计算机安全公司的财务状况以及公司的首席执行官加布里埃尔·艾斯(Gabriel Ice)和他建立的邪恶帝国。玛克欣发现犹太人艾斯把数百万美元非法转移到由恐怖分子控制的账户,甚至发现异常的本福特曲线、幽灵销售商、涌向海湾的资金流以及许多美国政府的合同都与之有关。在"9·11"事件前,玛克欣得到了有人计划击落一架飞机的彩排视频,这使她陷入更深的危机之中。最终,玛克欣凭借自己的经验和智慧脱离危险并回归家庭,但她承认自己无法正确地拼凑出这个世界运行的混乱过程,艾斯团伙也仍逍遥法外。事实上,《致命尖端》的成功并不仅仅是因为"阴谋论"的再次流行,品钦从流行文化、科学和艺术的碎片开始,借玛克欣探求真相的过程,通过民族宗教冲突、各路政治组织的博弈、人类稀奇古怪的癖好、庞大的网络、地下组织、奇异的武器、时间重置等现实和虚拟世界的构建,探讨晚期资本主义的现实处境和未来走向。

(三) 作品选读:《致命尖端》[①]

Chapter 29

...

ON HER WEBLOG, March Kelleher has wasted no time shifting into what she calls her old-lefty tirade mode. Just to say evil Islamics did it, that's so lame, and we know it. We see those official close-ups on the screen. The shifty liar's look, the twelve-stepper's gleam in the eye. One look at these faces and we know they're guilty of the worst crimes we can imagine. But who's in any hurry to imagine? To make the awful connection? Any more than Germans were back in 1933, when Nazis forced the Reichstag within a month of Hitler becoming chancellor. Which of course is not at all to suggest that Bush and his people have actually gone out and staged the events of 11 September. It would take a mind hopelessly diseased with paranoia, indeed a screamingly anti-American nutcase, even to allow to cross her mind the possibility that that terrible day could have deliberately been engineered as a pretext to impose some endless Orwellian 'war' and the emergency decrees we will soon be living under. Nah, nah, perish that thought.

"But there's still always the other thing. Our yearning. Our deep need for it to be true. Somewhere, down at some shameful dark recess of the national soul, we need to feel betrayed, even guilty. As if it was us who created Bush and his gang, Cheney and Rove and Rumsfeld and Feith and the rest of them—we who called down the sacred lightning of 'democracy,' and then the fascist majority on the Supreme Court threw the switches, and Bush rose from the slab and began his rampage. And whatever happened then is on our ticket."

A week or so later, Maxine and March do breakfast at the Piraeus Diner. There is now a huge American flag in the window and a UNITED WE STAND poster. Mike is being extra solicitous to the cops who come in looking for free meals.

"Check this out." March hands over a dollar bill, around the margins of whose obverse somebody has written in ballpoint, "World Trade Center was destroyed by CIA—Bush Senior's CIA is making Bush Jr. Prez for life & a hero." "I got this in change at the corner grocery this morning. That's well within a week of the attack. Call it what you like, but a historical document whatever." Maxine recalls that Heidi has a collection of decorated dollar bills, which she regards as the public toilet wall of the U.S. monetary system, carrying jokes, insults, slogans, phone numbers, George Washington in blackface, strange hats, Afros and dreadlocks and Marge Simpson hair, lit joints in his mouth, and speech-balloon remarks ranging from witty to stupid.

"No matter how the official narrative of this turns out," it seemed to Heidi, "these are the places we should be looking, not in newspapers or television but at the margins, graffiti,

---

① Pynchon, Thomas. *Bleeding Edge*. New York: Penguin Press, 2013, pp. 321－343.

uncontrolled utterances, bad dreamers who sleep in public and scream in their sleep."

"This message on this bill doesn't surprise me so much as how promptly it showed up," March sez now. "How fast the analysis has been."

Like it or not, Maxine has become March's official doubter, and happy to help, usually, though these days like everybody else she's feeling discombobulated. "March, since it happened, I don't know what to believe."

But March, relentlessly on the case, brings up Reg's DVD. "Suppose there was a Stinger crew deployed and waiting for orders to shoot down the first 767, the one that went on to hit the North Tower. Maybe there was another team stationed over in Jersey to pick up the second one, which would've been circling around and coming up from the southwest."

"Why?"

"Anti-compassion insurance. Somebody doesn't trust the hijackers to go through with it. These are Western minds, uncomfortable with any idea of suicide in the service of a faith. So they threaten to shoot the hijackers down in case they chicken out at the last minute."

"And if the hijackers do change their minds, what if the Stinger team do the same and *don't* shoot the plane down?"

"Then that would explain the backup sniper on the other roof, who the Stinger people know is there, keeping them in his sights till their part of the mission is over. Which is as soon as the guy with the phone gets word the plane's committed—then everybody cleans up and clears out. It's full daylight by then, but not that much risk of being seen'cause all the attention is focused downtown."

"Help, too byzantine, make it stop!"

Trying, but is Bush answering my calls?

HORST MEANTIME IS PUZZLED ABOUT something else. "Remember the week before this happened, all those put options on United and American Airlines? Which turned out to be exactly the two airlines that got hijacked? Well, it seems on that Thursday and Friday there were also lopsided put-to call ratios for Morgan Stanley, Merrill Lynch, couple others like them, all tenants of the Trade Center. As a fraud investigator, what does that suggest to you?"

"Foreknowledge of a decline in their stock prices. Who was doing all this trading?" "Nobody so far has stepped forward." "Mystery players who knew it was going to happen. Overseas maybe? Like the Emirates?"

"I try to keep hold of my common sense, but..."

Maxine goes over to her parents' for lunch, and Avi and Brooke are there as expected. The sisters embrace, though you could not say warmly. There's no way not to talk about the Trade Center.

"Nobody that morning had anything to say," Maxine, noticing at some point that there's a NY Jets logo on Avi's yarmulke, "Ain't it awful' is about as profound as it got. Just the one camera angle, the static telephoto shot of those towers smoldering, the same news that's no news, the same morning-show airhead idiocy—"

"They were in shock," Brooke mutters, "like everybody that day, what, you weren't?"

"But why keep showing us that one thing, what were we supposed to be waiting for, what was going to happen? Too high up to run hoses, OK, so the fire will either burn itself out or spread to other floors or—or what else? What were we being set up for, if not what happened? One comes down, then the other, and who was surprised? Wasn't it inevitable by then?"

"You think the networks knew ahead of time?" Brooke, offended, glowering. "Whose side are you on, are you an American or what are you?" Brooke now in full indignation, "this horrible, horrible tragedy, a whole generation traumatized, war with the Arab world any minute, and even this isn't safe from your stupid little hipster irony? What's next, Auschwitz jokes?"

"Same thing happened when JFK was shot," Ernie belatedly trying to defuse things with geezer nostalgia. "Nobody wanted to believe that official story either. So suddenly here were all these strange coincidences."

"You think it was an inside job, Pa?"

"The chief argument against conspiracy theories is always that it would take too many people in on it, and somebody's sure to squeal. But look at the U. S. security apparatus, these guys are WASPs, Mormons, Skull and Bones, secretive by nature. Trained, sometimes since birth, never to run off at the mouth. If discipline exists anywhere, it's among them. So of course it's possible."

"How about you, Avi?" Maxine turning to her brother-in-law. "What's the latest on 4360.0 kilohertz?" Nice as pie. But he gives a violent jump. "Oops, or do I mean megahertz?"

"What The Fuck?"

"Language," Elaine automatically before realizing it's Brooke, who seems to be looking around for a weapon.

"Arab propaganda!" Avi cries. "Anti-Semitic filth. Who told you about this frequency?"

"Saw it on the Internet," Maxine shrugs, "ham operators have known about it forever, they're called E10 stations, operated by Mossad out of Israel, Greece, South America, the voices are women who figure in the erotic daydreams of radio hobbyists everywhere, reciting alphanumerics, encrypted, of course. Widely believed to be messages to agents, salaried and otherwise, out in the Diaspora. Word is that in the run-up to the atrocity, traffic was pretty heavy."

"Every Jew hater in this town," Avi making with the aggrieved tone, "is blaming 9/11 on Mossad. Even a story going around about Jews who worked down at the Trade Center all calling in sick that day, warned away by Mossad through their"—air quotes—secret network.'"

"The Jews dancing on the roof of that van over in Jersey," Brooke fuming, "watching it all collapse, don't forget that one."

Later as Maxine prepares to leave, Ernie catches up with her in the foyer. "Ever call that

FBI guy?"

"I did, and you know what? He thinks Avram really is Mossad, all right? On station, tapping his foot to a klezmer beat only he can hear, waiting to be activated."

"Evil Jewish conspiracy."

"Except you'll notice Avi never talks about what he was doing over in Israel, neither of them do, any more than what he's doing here now for hashslingrz. The one thing I can guarantee you is, is it'll be well compensated, wait and see, he'll give you guys a Mercedes for your anniversary."

"A Nazi car? Good, so I'll sell it..."

Chapter 30

If you read nothing but the Newspaper of Record, you might believe that New York City, like the nation, united in sorrow and shock, has risen to the challenge of global jihadism, joining a righteous crusade Bush's people are now calling the War on Terror. If you go to other sources—the Internet, for example—you might get a different picture. Out in the vast undefined anarchism of cyberspace, among the billions of self-resonant fantasies, dark possibilities are beginning to emerge.

The plume of smoke and finely divided structural and human debris has been blowing southwest, toward Bayonne and Staten Island, but you can smell it all the way uptown. A bitter chemical smell of death and burning that no one in memory has ever in this city smelled before and which lingers for weeks. Though everybody south of 14th Street has been directly touched one way or another, for much of the city the experience has come to them mediated, mostly by television—the farther uptown, the more secondhand the moment, stories from family members commuting to work, friends, friends of friends, phone conversations, hearsay, folklore, as forces in whose interests it compellingly lies to seize control of the narrative as quickly as possible come into play and dependable history shrinks to a dismal perimeter centered on "Ground Zero," a Cold War term taken from the scenarios of nuclear war so popular in the early sixties. This was nowhere near a Soviet nuclear strike on downtown Manhattan, yet those who repeat "Ground Zero" over and over do so without shame or concern for etymology. The purpose is to get people cranked up in a certain way. Cranked up, scared, and helpless.

For a couple of days, the West Side Highway falls silent. People between Riverside and West End miss the ambient racket and don't get to sleep so easily. On Broadway meanwhile it's different. Flatbeds carrying hydraulic cranes and track loaders and other heavy equipment go thundering downtown in convoys day and night. Fighter planes roar overhead, helicopters hang battering the air for hours close above the rooftops, sirens are constant 24/7. Every firehouse in the city lost somebody on 11 September, and every day people in the neighborhoods leave flowers and home-cooked meals out in front of each one. Corporate ex-tenants of the Trade Center hold elaborate memorial services for those who didn't make it out in time, featuring bagpipers and Marine honor guards. Child choirs from churches and schools around town are booked weeks in advance for solemn performances at "Ground Zero," with "America the Beautiful" and "Amazing Grace" being musical boilerplate at these events.

The atrocity site, which one would have expected to become sacred or at least inspire a little respect, swiftly becomes occasion instead for open-ended sagas of wheeling and dealing, bickering and badmouthing over its future as real estate, all dutifully celebrated as "news" in the Newspaper of Record. Some notice a strange underground rumbling from the direction of Woodlawn Cemetery in the Bronx, which is eventually identified as Robert Moses spinning in his grave.

After maybe a day and a half of stunned suspension, the usual ethnic toxicities, fierce as ever, have resumed. Hey, it's New York. American flags appear everywhere. In apartment-building lobbies and up in apartment windows, on rooftops, in storefronts and corner groceries, in eateries, on delivery trucks and hot-dog stands, on motorcycles and bikes, on cabs driven by members of the Muslim faith, who between shifts are taking courses in Spanish as a Second Language with a view to posing as a slightly less disrespected minority, though whenever Latino people try putting out some variation like the Puerto Rican flag, they are reflexively cursed and denounced as enemies of America.

That terrible morning, so it was later alleged, for a radius of many blocks surrounding the towers, every pushcart disappeared, as if the population of pushcart owners, at that time believed to be most of them Muslim, had been warned to keep away. Through some network. Some evil secret rugrider network possibly in place for years. The pushcarts stayed away, and so the morning began that much less comfortably, obliging folks to go in to work without their customary coffees, danishes, donuts, bottles of water, so many bleak appoggiaturas for what was about to happen.

Beliefs like this take hold of the civic imagination. Corner newsagents are raided and Islamic-looking suspects hauled away by the busload. Sizable Mobile Police Command Centers appear at various flashpoints, especially over on the East Side, wherever, for example, a high-income synagogue and some Arab embassy happen to occupy the same block, and eventually these installations grow not so mobile, becoming with time a permanent part of the cityscape, all but welded to the pavement. Likewise, ships with no visible flags, pretending to be cargo vessels, though with more antennas on them than booms, appear out in the Hudson, drop the hook, and become, effectively, private islands belonging to unnamed security agencies and surrounded by stay-away zones. Roadblocks keep appearing and disappearing along the avenues leading to and away from the major bridges and tunnels. Young Guardsfolk in clean new camo fatigues and carrying weapons and ammunition clips are patrolling Penn Station and Grand Central and the Port of Authority. Public holidays and anniversaries become occasions for anxiety.

思考与讨论

(1) "阴谋论"是如何在品钦的《致命尖端》中体现的?

(2) 人们认为是什么导致了“9·11”事件的发生?

(3) 在这部小说中,“9·11”事件的影响是什么?

拓展阅读

[1] Banita, Georgiana. “Literature after 9/11.” Rachel Greenwald Smith, ed., *American Literature in Transition, 2000 -2010*. Cambridge: Cambridge University Press, 2017, pp.152 - 164.

[2] Chomsky, Noam & Barsamian, David. *Imperial Ambitions: Conversations on the Post-911 World*. London: Penguin Books Ltd, 2005.

[3] Gray, Richard. *After the Fall: American Literature Since 9/11*. Malden: Wiley Blackwell, 2011.

[4] Greenberg, Judith, ed. *Trauma at Home: After 9/11*. Lincoln: University of Nebraska Press, 2003.

[5] Langah, Nukhbah Taj, ed. *Literary and Non-literary Responses Towards 9/11: South Asia and Beyond*. London: Routledge, 2018.

[6] Miller, Kristine, ed. *Transatlantic Literature and Culture After 9/11: The Wrong Side of Paradise*. Basingstoke: Palgrave Macmillan, 2014.

[7] Robinson, Alan. *Narrating the Past: Historiography, Memory and the Contemporary Novel*. Basingstoke: Palgrave Macmillan, 2011.

[8] Savvas, Theophilus & Coffman, Christopher K. “American Fiction after Postmodernism.” *Textual Practice*, vol.33, no.4,2019, pp.195 - 212.

第四章
当代美国族裔小说

20 世纪 60 年代，受美国黑人民权运动、奇卡诺运动、印第安人运动、亚裔美国人运动等社会浪潮的深刻影响，以及解构主义、女性主义、后殖民主义、后现代主义、新历史主义等文学思想的大力推动，美国族裔小说的地位发生了根本性的转变，曾一度被边缘化的犹太裔、本土裔、非洲裔、拉美/西语裔、亚洲裔等族裔小说逐步繁荣。

20 世纪 70 年代以来，老一辈族裔作家笔耕不辍，后起之秀又在不断丰富这一传统。他们在传统和革新中摸索前进，努力发掘本族裔历史文化传统，将小说打造成多元文化和意识形态的对话空间，与白人主流文学共同构筑当代美国小说的繁荣景象。他们的共同努力不仅酝酿出“印第安文艺复兴”“奇卡诺文艺复兴”“亚裔美国文艺复兴”等重要的族裔文学文化成果，犹太裔、非洲裔作家更是为美国斩获了包括诺奖在内的各项大奖。在这一时期的文学阵营当中，族裔女性作家不仅是最重要的参与者，她们的文学成就也取得了美国内外的一致认可。

作为体现族裔命运复兴、族裔文化转型和延续的核心，当代美国族裔小说既强调各族裔内部的生命起源、文化传统、语言和历史记忆的多样性内涵，又呼吁对族裔历史文化的批判性继承；围绕异化社会下族裔个体与群体的生存现实，从族裔、阶级、女性等不同立场关注命运、爱情、婚姻和家庭关系等题材，探讨种族主义与多元文化主义之间的矛盾冲突；通过回溯移民经历重构母国历史与民族文化，抵抗由肤色焦虑引起的身份焦虑、生存焦虑与虚无主义情绪，解构白人主流文化的霸权话语压制。就文学性与艺术性而言，族裔作家们普遍将民族文化遗产与后现代写作技巧相融合，同时吸收美洲文学和世界文学之精华，以激发族裔小说的活力和潜质。语言文化的杂糅更是赋予族裔小说高度的异质性与开放性，极大地丰富了小说的文本形式与意义的生成。

美国族裔小说就其族裔历史与文化渊源而言，一般可分为本土裔小说、犹太裔小说、非洲裔小说、拉美/西语裔小说和亚洲裔小说五大类别。从美国小说当代发展的时间线来看，本书重点关注的是 20 世纪 70 年代以后的族裔小说作品。

第一节　当代美国犹太裔小说

20 世纪 70 年代，美国犹太裔小说创作进一步繁荣，见证并参与着同时代美国社会和整个世界的发展。索尔·贝娄(Saul Bellow)、贝纳德·马拉默德(Bernard Malamud)等老一辈作家仍有优秀的作品不断问世。贝娄的《赛姆勒先生的星球》(*Mr. Semler's Planet*, 1970)、《洪堡的礼物》(*Humboldt's Gift*, 1975)描述了犹太裔知识分子的身份困境及其摆脱异化命运的努力。1976年,贝娄以其"对于当代文化富于人性的理解和精妙的分析"[①]荣膺诺贝尔文学奖。与此同时,文坛新人沃特·阿比希(Walter Abish)、菲利普·罗斯(Philip Roth)、保罗·奥斯特(Paul Auster)也开始崭露头角。他们的小说摆脱了犹太裔历史文化传统的视域局限,力求全面深入地展现当代美国社会的方方面面,如罗斯的《我们这一帮》(*Our Gang*, 1971)就以尼克松政府为对象揭示美国政治生活中的尔虞我诈。"美国三部曲"(The American Trilogy)是他最具思想深度的作品,包括《美国牧歌》(*American Pastoral*, 1997)、《背叛》(*I Married a Communist*, 1998)和《人性的污秽》(*The Human Stain*, 2000),塑造了三位现代悲剧意义上的反英雄,透过人物与时代洪流的交锋与碰撞来呈现前者是如何被后者所裹挟及其反抗的无力。

受女权运动的激励,犹太裔女性作家的小说作品也纷纷涌现,如辛西娅·欧芝克(Cynthia Ozick)的《异教徒拉比》(*The Pagan Rabbi*, 1971)和《流血》(*Bloodshed*, 1976)、阿瑟·A.科恩(Arthur A. Cohen)的《西蒙·斯特恩的日子》(*In the Days of Simon Stern*, 1973)、苏珊·弗龙伯格·谢弗(Susan Fromberg Schaeffer)的《安雅》(*Anya*, 1974)和埃斯特·M.布罗纳(Esther M. Broner)的《女人的编织》(*A Weave of Women*, 1975)。这些作品聚焦犹太母女关系,关注其背后新兴的犹太女权运动与传统犹太女性观念之间的激烈碰撞[②],借助犹太神话和神秘主义思想批判僵化的犹太教条,并对犹太大屠杀的历史记忆和创伤经验展开深入的思考。

20世纪80年代,当代美国犹太裔小说出现了一批第二代犹太裔书写的大屠杀文学作品。泰恩·罗森鲍姆(Thane Rosenbaum)在其小说《二手烟》(*Second Hand Smoke*, 1999)中呼吁应充分关注犹太人遭受的灾难,防止种族灭绝这一人类惨剧再次降临。在罗森鲍姆"后大屠杀三部曲"(Post-Holocaust Trilogy)中的另外两部小说《看得见的伊利亚》(*Elijah Visible*, 1996)和《哥谭妖怪》(*The Golems of Gotham*, 2002)以及朱莉·所罗门(Julie Solomon)的《白色谎言》(*White Lies*, 1987)中,这一主题被不断贯彻和深化。此外,宗教在大屠杀的主题和叙事方面也极富活力。在内萨·拉波波特(Nessa Rappoport)的《准备安息日》(*Preparing for Sabbath*, 1989)、阿莱格拉·古德曼(Allegra Goodman)的《完全沉浸》(*Total Immersion*, 1989)、内森·英格兰德(Nathan Englander)的《缓解难以忍受的冲动》(*For the Relief of Unbearable Urges*, 1999)、迈克尔·查本(Michael Chabon)的普利策获奖作品《卡瓦里耶和克莱的奇妙冒险》(*The Amazing Adventures of Kavalier and Clay*, 2000)以及史蒂夫·斯特恩(Steve Stern)和辛西娅·欧艺克的小说中,犹太教神话、象征和语言等内容都被用来探索大屠杀对犹太身份的潜在影响。

21世纪以来,随着美国犹太裔文学复兴的不断深入,犹太裔小说凭借本族裔丰富的文化积淀和对后现代写作手法的娴熟运用,使得任何关于美国犹太裔文学传统已达顶峰转而衰落的观点不攻自破,实现了从边缘文学进入经典文学的华丽转身,正式迈向美国主流文学之列。

---

① 索尔·贝娄:《拉维尔斯坦》,胡苏晓译,北京:人民文学出版社,2015年,第195页。

② Cronin, Gloria & Berger, Alan. *Encyclopedia of Jewish-American Literature*. New York: Facts On File Inc, 2009, p. xxii.

第二节　当代美国本土裔小说

作为“印第安文艺复兴”的中流砥柱，当代美国本土裔小说被视为“致力于抵抗殖民主义和后殖民主义的全球文学的一部分”①。1968年，纳瓦雷·斯科特·莫马迪(N. Scott Momaday)的小说《晨曦之屋》(*House Made of Dawn*)的出版标志着本土裔文学书写的复苏。翌年，该作获得普利策小说奖，激励了不少本土裔作家和读者重新思考“我们是谁以及我们可以成为什么”②等与印第安人的身份和生活密切相关的问题。继莫马迪之后，詹姆斯·韦尔奇(James Welch)、莱斯利·西尔科(Leslie Silko)、杰拉德·维兹诺(Gerald Vizenor)、路易斯·厄德里克(Louise Erdrich)以及谢尔曼·阿莱克西(Sherman Alexie)等优秀作家的作品不断涌现，本土裔小说发展空前繁荣。

印第安部落传统是当代美国本土裔小说重要的文化资源，重新衡量它的价值和意义可以抵抗西方中心思想和文化霸权话语，也是作家们共同的精神追求。为此，莫马迪在《晨曦之屋》中做出了开创性的尝试。小说描绘了印第安士兵阿贝尔从逃离到回归本族文化的精神旅程，挖掘了口述传统和印第安典仪强大的文化力量。无独有偶，西尔科的小说《仪式》(*Ceremony*, 1977)同样围绕印第安老兵塔尤展开，西尔科将他塑造为拉古纳神话人物的当代化身，并让他在面对西方现代文明和印第安文化传统时最终做出回归部落的内心选择。莫马迪的第二部小说《古老的孩子》(*The Ancient Child*, 1989)以基奥瓦神话为蓝本，描写了一位印第安艺术家变身为熊的传奇故事，而这与维兹诺早前的小说《熊心》(*Bearheart: The Heirship Chronicles*, 1978)以及厄德里克的《宾果宫》(*The Bingo Palace*, 1994)有异曲同工之处。在韦尔奇的《血色隆冬》(*Winter in the Blood*, 1974)、《罗尼之死》(*The Death of Jim Loney*, 1979)和《傻瓜乌鸦》(*Fools Crow*, 1986)等作品中，主人公的文化境遇与阿贝尔和塔尤惊人地相似，他们游走在白人和印第安人的世界之间，又与两个世界格格不入。对此，韦尔奇认为只有重新认识印第安人的祖先、历史和文化，意识到“鬼魂的存在”，才能在漂泊和失落的世界里得到精神的安慰。

此外，维兹诺的《忧伤者》(*Griever*, 1987)和《自由的恶作剧者》(*The Trickster of Liberty*, 1988)，迈克尔·多里斯(Michael A. Dorris)的《蓝水河、黄筏子》(*A Yellow Raft in Blue Water*, 1987)，琳达·霍根(Linda Hogan)的《恶灵》(*Mean Spirit*, 1990)、《太阳风暴》(*Solar Storms*, 1995)和《力量》(*Power*, 1998)以及阿莱克西的《保留地布鲁斯》(*Reservation Blues*, 1995)等小说同样致力于维护印第安文化传统，积极构建印第安人的身份形象，并在时代的发展中赋予它新的意义和使命，以谋求本族裔更好的生存和发展空间。

当代美国本土裔小说将民族主义、本土主义和世界主义糅合为互补的视角，用以解读族裔历史、建构族裔身份、抵抗各种形式的殖民与后殖民暴力。“第三空间”和“文化杂糅”为本土裔作家摆脱边缘地位，创造开放包容的身份空间与文化空间提供了有利的思想资源。通过彰显民族差异、模糊文化界限、解构西方固有的时间和历史权威，本土裔小说获得了表达反抗性的叙事能量。“‘属下’不仅开始说话，

---

① Krupat, Arnold & Elliott, Michael A. *A Companion to American Literature and Culture*, Paul Lauter ed., Oxford, U.K.: Blackwell Publisher, 2010, p.622.

② Gray, Richard J. *A History of American Literature* (2nd ed.). Oxford, U.K.: Blackwell Publishers, 2012, p.782.

并开始以强大的力量抵制主流话语，从而撼动了以往高高在上的殖民权威。”①

第三节　当代美国非洲裔小说

20世纪70年代，一大批美国非裔作家开始崭露锋芒，其卓越的小说创作取得了令人瞩目的成就，仅1970年就有25部小说出版。一些评论家将这一年称为非裔女性写作的第二次复兴，也有学者认为美国非裔文学的“后现代时刻”业已来临②。

这一时期，托妮·莫里森（Toni Morrison）、托妮·凯德·班巴拉（Toni Cade Bambara）、艾丽斯·沃克（Alice Walker）、盖尔·琼斯（Gayl Jones）、格洛丽亚·奈勒（Gloria Naylor）等女性作家扛起非裔文学的大旗，其中尤以莫里森的成就最为突出。自发表处女作《最蓝的眼睛》（*The Bluest Eye*, 1970）以来，莫里森在文学创作上涉及小说、诗歌、散文、儿童读物等不同文类，而她的小说紧扣黑人的历史与现实，扎根于非裔文化中的神话、传说和寓言，将口述传统、意识流、多视角、碎片化、魔幻现实主义等叙事手法加以糅合，赋予小说深刻的人文关怀以及超越黑人文学和白人文学的杂糅特质。1993年，莫里森获得诺贝尔文学奖，是首位获此殊荣的美国非裔女性作家。另一位值得一提的作家是沃克。1970年，沃克发表了首部长篇小说《格兰奇·科普兰的第三次生命》（*The Third Life of Grange Copeland*, 1970），之后又继续创作了小说《紫颜色》（*The Color Purple*, 1982）。凭借这部作品，沃克斩获了美国文坛最高荣誉的三大奖项。此外，班巴拉的《大猩猩，我的爱》（*Gorilla, My Love*, 1972）、玛雅·安吉洛（Maya Angelou）的《我知道笼中鸟为何歌唱》（*I Know Why the Caged Bird Sings*, 1970）、琼斯的《科里西多拉》（*Corregidora*, 1975）等作品同样赢得了学术界和大众的一致赞誉。在她们的小说中，祖母、母亲和女儿形成了一个坚固的女性核心，作为叙述者的女儿既吸收祖母宗教福音的影响，亦受母亲“蓝调传统”的熏陶③，非裔文化传统的代际传承为年轻的非裔女性提供了生存的智慧。

自黑人艺术运动结束以来，一种自觉的后现代风格在班巴拉、莫里森、里德等作家的小说中逐渐明晰。他们的小说本质上是反模仿的，质疑线性的叙事结构，通过混淆时间顺序打破现实和虚构的层次，并以拼贴化的语言制造超越文化边界的效果。最早使用语言拼贴的小说之一是弗兰·罗斯（Fran Ross）的《奥利奥》（*Oreo*, 1974）。之后，班巴拉的《食盐者》（*The Salt Eaters*, 1980）、伊什梅尔·里德（Ishmael Reed）的《春季日语教程》（*Japanese by Spring*, 1993）、保罗·比第（Paul Beatty）的《白人男孩洗牌》（*The White Boy Shuffle*, 1996）也以语言跨界等形式呈现后现代美国文化的异质性景观。就主题而言，这些小说既有对种族压迫、种族歧视的揭露，对非裔个性和自我本质失落的抗争，对族裔文化之根和民族文化意识的呼唤，也有对文化冲突与融合和对自我身份的反思。如里德的《芒博琼博》（*Mumbo Jumbo*, 1972）就将黑人文化想象为多元文化的动态融合，通过回归非裔的历史和本源来抵抗文化的单

① 陈靓：《现实维度中的族裔性重构：路易斯·厄德里克作品研究》，上海：复旦大学出版社，2018年，第54页。

② Madhu Dubey, Elizabeth Swanson Goldberg, eds., Maryemma Graham, Jerry W. Ward Jr., *The Cambridge History of African American Literature*. Cambridge: Cambridge University Press, 2011, p.569.

③ Gray, Richard J. *A History of American Literature* (2nd ed.). Oxford, U.K.: Blackwell Publishers, 2012, p.641.

一感。在恩尼斯特·J.盖恩斯(Ernest J. Gaines)的《简·皮特曼小姐自传》(*The Autobiography of Jane Pittman*, 1971)、亚历克斯·哈利(Alex Haley)的《根》(*Roots*, 1976)、约翰·埃德加·维德曼(John Edgar Wideman)的《藏身之所》(*Hiding Place*, 1981)、大卫·布拉德利(David Bradley)的《昌奈斯维尔事件》(*The Chaneysville Incident*, 1981)和查尔斯·R.约翰逊(Charles R. Johnson)的《中间航道》(*Middle Passage*, 1990)等小说作品中,以上主题也有不同程度的体现。

诚如盖恩斯所言,当代非裔小说的"决定性因素不仅仅在于这个主题或那个主题,更在于声音的传达"[①]。凭借对文本与历史高度自觉的反思和修正意识,当代美国非裔小说找到了作为个体、种族和公民的声音,以一种众声喧哗的姿态从边缘走向中心,成功取得与白人主流文学相平等的对话权利。

第四节　当代美国拉美/西语裔小说

当代美国拉美/西语裔小说涵盖墨西哥裔、古巴裔、多米尼加裔、波多黎各裔等众多族裔作家和中南美洲移民作家的小说作品,具有"高度的异质性和典型的地缘文化特征"[②],其中墨裔小说无论在作品数量上还是文学成就上都遥遥领先。

20世纪70年代初,托马斯·里维拉(Tomás Rivera)的《……大地不曾吞噬他》(*. . . And the Earth Did Not Devour Him*, 1971)宣布了"奇卡诺文学运动"的兴起及"奇卡诺/奇卡纳"[③]小说时代的到来。之后优秀的墨裔作家作品层出不穷。鲁道夫·安纳亚(Rudolfo Anaya)的《祝福我,乌蒂玛》(*Bless Me, Ultima*, 1972)、桑德拉·希斯内罗丝(Sandra Cisneros)的《芒果街上的小屋》(*The House on Mango Street*, 1984)、丹尼斯·查韦斯(Denise Chávez)的《最后一个女服务生》(*The Last of the Menu Girls*, 1986)、安娜·卡斯蒂罗(Ana Castillo)的《密西夸华拉书信》(*The Mixquiahuala Letters*, 1986)、亚历杭德罗·莫拉莱斯(Alejandro Morales)的《布娃娃瘟疫》(*The Rag Doll Plague*, 1992)、海伦娜·玛丽亚·维拉蒙特斯(Helena Maria Viramontes)的《在耶稣脚下》(*Under the Feet of Jesus*, 1995)等小说纷纷从不同视角诠释了奇卡诺/奇卡纳的历史与当下、困境与出路。尽管这一时期的小说仍带有强烈的政治色彩,但其主题和范式均显示出多元化的创作趋势,具体表现为:①集中反映墨裔群体的艰难生活、丰富情感和斗争精神;②关注美国、墨西哥及美墨边界中的城市、乡村和荒漠地带的移民群体;③融合本土口述传统、拉美魔幻现实主义与欧美实验主义小说的多种叙事策略;④以诗歌、传记体、回忆录等文本叙事形式消弭小说的文体边界;⑤灵活运用英西双语或西式英语(Spanglish)勾勒杂糅语境下墨裔族群真实的生存体验;⑥奇卡纳小说崛起,对奇卡诺文学权威和父权制提出挑战与解构。

古巴裔小说与多米尼加裔小说常常与西班牙殖民历史和本国当代的政治命运紧密相连,多以国家变革造成的流亡和创伤、移民后的文化冲突与融合为主题。古巴裔作家卡洛斯·艾尔(Carlos Eire)的《在哈瓦那等待风雪》(*Wailing for Snow in Hawana*, 2002)和《在迈阿密学会死亡》(*Learning to Die in*

① Gray, Richard J. *A History of American Literature* (2nd ed.). Oxford, U.K.: Blackwell Publishers, 2012, p.660.

② 李保杰:《当代美国拉美裔文学研究》,济南:山东大学出版社,2014年,第3页。

③ "Chicano/a"为西班牙语"mexicano/a"(墨西哥人)的改写,音译为"奇卡诺/纳",指美国的墨西哥裔。

Miami, 2010),克里斯蒂娜·加西娅(Cristina García)的《梦系古巴》(*Dreaming in Cuban*, 1992)和《阿奎罗姐妹》(*The Agüero Sisters*, 1997)四部小说都以“古巴大革命”为背景,通过人物的命运沉浮透视古巴社会的历史变化。与之相比,奥斯卡·依胡艾罗斯(Oscar Hijuelos)的《曼波歌王奏情歌》(*The Mambo Kings Play Songs of Love*, 1992)则明显褪去了这种政治色彩。多米尼加裔作家茱莉亚·阿尔瓦雷斯(Julia Alvarez)的《蝴蝶时代》(*In the Time of Butterflies*, 1994)、朱诺·迪亚兹(Junot Díaz)的《奥斯卡·瓦奥短暂而奇妙的一生》(*The Brief Wondrous Life of Oscar Wao*, 2007)等小说是对“特鲁希略”[①]独裁统治作出的文学回应,揭露了国家层面的恐怖暴力给本国人民和流亡者带来的毁灭性后果和无法治愈的心灵创伤。尽管同时期波多黎各裔作家的小说成就不及以上族裔,却也不乏优秀的作品出现,如加西亚·拉米斯(García Ramis)的《快乐的日子,塞尔吉奥叔叔》(*Happy Days, Uncle Sergio*, 1986)、朱蒂斯·O.考夫尔(Judith O. Cofer)的《太阳线》(*The Line of the Sun*, 1989)、尼古拉萨·莫尔(Nicholasa Mohr)的《美国梦》(*América's Dream*, 1996)等等。

当代美国拉美/西语裔小说植根于西班牙语美洲悠久灿烂的历史文化遗产,聚焦地理、文化、语言和身份的双重性及其矛盾张力的此消彼长,在边界流动和文化碰撞中汲取经验以再塑身份、重构族裔历史与现实,成为美国文坛极富活力的文学表达。

第五节 当代美国亚裔小说

当代美国亚裔小说枝繁叶茂,包括出自华裔、日裔、韩裔、菲律宾裔、越南裔、印度裔、泰国裔等亚裔作家的小说作品,而其中华裔作家可谓硕果累累、独占鳌头。

1976年,汤亭亭(Maxine Hong Kingston)的《女勇士》(*The Woman Warrior*, 1976)的出版拉开了美国华裔文学重新崛起的序幕。之后,她又陆续发表了《中国佬》(*China Men*, 1980)、《孙行者》(*Tripmaster Monkey*, 1989)、《第五和平书》(*The Fifth Book of Peace*, 2003)等作品,不仅将当代美国华裔文学推向新的高峰,也激励着更多的华裔作家书写自己的声音。继汤亭亭之后,谭恩美(Amy Tan)的《喜福会》(*The Joy Luck Club*, 1989)无疑是过去几十年最引人注目的华裔小说。该作糅合了历史与回忆、真实与虚构,聚焦华裔移民家庭的代际差异和文化错位,以母女关系作为衡量文化和情感变化及延续的尺度,探索种族、性别和身份之间的复杂关系。随着学术界和出版商逐渐发现华裔小说的艺术魅力和市场潜力,以任碧莲(Gish Jen)的《典型的美国人》(*Typical American*, 1991)、赵健秀(Frank Chin)的《唐老亚》(*Donald Duk*, 1991)、李健孙(Gus Lee)的《中国仔》(*China Boy*, 1991)、雷祖威(David Wong Louie)的《爱的痛苦》(*Pangs of Love*, 1991)、伍慧明(Fae Myenne Ng)的《骨》(*Bone*, 1993)为代表的小说作品越来越受欢迎。而曾经一度被忽视的小说,如叶祥添(Laurence Michael Yep)的《龙翼》(*Dragonwings*, 1975)也在美国文坛重放华彩。此外,杨谨伦(Gene Luen Yang)的《美生中国人》(*American Born Chinese*, 2006)是首部获得普林兹奖(Michael L. Printz)的绘本小说,标志着华裔小说的跨界书写与艺术成就得到了充分的认可。就主题而言,

---

① 拉斐尔·莱昂尼达斯·特鲁希略(Rafael Leónidas Trujillo, 1891—1961)曾为多米尼加共和国元首,1930年开始对该国进行了长达31年的独裁统治。

文化身份一直是当代美国华裔小说的核心议题,以上作品在思考华裔文化身份建构与文化传统传承等方面既深刻有力又富有艺术性。比如,在处理文化差异和代际矛盾时,当代美国华裔小说往往通过回忆过去,诉说长期被忽略的族群历史和心声,来达成代际理解与文化融合,纠正主流社会对华裔群体的文化误解,肯定自己的合法地位与多元文化身份,展现中华文化的博大精深与兼容并蓄等内在精神诉求。同时,当代美国华裔小说也会借越南战争、民权运动、女性运动、生态保护等社会现实来表达美国作家所共同关心的问题。

在其他亚裔小说中,日裔作家辛西娅·角畑(Cynthia Kadohata)的《漂浮的世界》(*The Floating World*, 1989)是日裔小说的代表作之一。小说围绕日本移民从日本到夏威夷再到美国内陆的"漂浮"经验展开叙述,隐喻日裔族群如何在不同的文化和身份之间浮浮沉沉,追求美国难以捉摸的承诺,并在不断流动的环境中表演、修改和重塑自己。之后,角畑还接连发表了《在爱之谷的中心》(*In the Heart of the Valley of Love*, 1992)等小说。当代韩裔作家中,苏珊·崔(Susan Choi)曾以小说《美国女人》(*American Woman*, 2003)入围普利策奖。2019 年,她的第五部小说《信任练习》(*Trust Exercise*, 2019)荣获美国国家图书奖。而比恩韦尼多·桑托斯(Bienvenido Santos)的《你为什么把心留在旧金山?》(*What the Hell for You Left Your Heart in San Francisco?*, 1987),杰西卡·哈格多恩(Jessica Hagedorn)的《食狗者》(*Dogeaters*, 1991)和《爱的黑帮》(*The Gangster of Love*, 1996),曹岚(Lan Cao)的《猴桥》(*Monkey Bridge*, 1997)以及芭拉蒂·穆克吉(Bharati Mukherjee)的《中间人和其他故事》(*The Middleman and Other Stories*, 1988)则是菲律宾裔、越南裔和印度裔小说的优秀之作。

正如韩裔学者金惠经(Elaine H. Kim)所言,我们正在见证"美国亚裔文化生产的黄金时代"[①]。当代美国亚裔小说在数量上的爆炸式增长、族裔文化上的异质多元、创作技巧上的混合杂糅使其与本土裔、犹太裔、非洲裔、拉美/西语裔等少数族裔小说并驾齐驱,共同构筑当代美国小说的创作传统与精神内核,丰富并拓展了美国文学的整体面貌。

第六节 主要作家介绍与代表作品选读

一、索尔·贝娄

(一) 索尔·贝娄简介

索尔·贝娄(Saul Bellow, 1915—2005)是美国犹太裔小说家,出生于加拿大蒙特利尔,他的父母是俄国圣彼得堡的犹太移民。1924 年,贝娄随家人赴芝加哥定居,就读于芝加哥大学和西北大学,获得人类学和社会学学士学位。贝娄的职业生涯比较丰富,做过编辑、记者和军人,后执教于明尼苏达大学、普林斯顿大学和芝加哥大学,曾两度获得古根海姆研究基金的资助。

索尔·贝娄的文学成果包括:11 部长篇小说、3 部中篇小说、4 部短篇小说集、1 部戏剧作品和 3 部

① Kim, Elaine H. *Asian American Literature: An Introduction to the Writings and Their Social Context*. *Philadelphia*: Temple University Press, 1982, p. xi.

非虚构性作品。《奥基·马奇历险记》(*The Adventures of Augie March*, 1953)是贝娄的第三部长篇小说,也是他的成名作。小说通过一位犹太青年的人生经历呈现了个体选择、自我位置与归属感等困扰现代人类的普遍难题。1954 年,该小说获得了美国国家图书奖。《雨王汉德森》(*Henderson the Rain King*, 1959)是贝娄的现实主义小说,讲述了一位百万富翁的非洲奇遇及其身体和精神的历练过程。《赫索格》(*Herzog*, 1964)则是贝娄对身为知识分子的苦闷与迷惘和对资产阶级人道主义危机的深描之作。在《赛姆勒先生的星球》(*Mr. Semler's Planet*, 1970)中,贝娄展示了犹太思想的丰富性与深刻性,批判了美国现代社会秩序的错乱与破裂。20 世纪 80 年代起,贝娄陆续发表了长篇小说《院长的十二月》(*The Dean's December*, 1981)、《更多的人死于心碎》(*More Die of Heartbreak*, 1987),中篇小说《只争朝夕》(*Seize the Day*, 1956)、《偷窃》(*A Theft*, 1989)、《贝拉罗萨暗道》(*The Bellarosa Connection*, 1989),短篇小说集《莫斯比的回忆》(*Mosby's Memoirs*, 1968)、《口无遮拦的人》(*Him with His Foot in His Mouth and other stories*, 1984)以及剧本、散文、游记、评论、演讲、回忆录等近 60 篇,写作时间长达半个多世纪,以其敏锐的观察和思考对犹太裔知识分子在当代美国社会的荒谬处境和思想状态进行审视。

索尔·贝娄一生著作等身、获奖无数,包括 1953 年、1964 年、1970 年三次美国国家图书奖,1976 年普利策奖,以及同年的诺贝尔文学奖。在美国文坛,贝娄被认为是继福克纳和海明威之后最重要的少数族裔作家。

(二)《洪堡的礼物》简介

《洪堡的礼物》(*Humboldt's Gift*, 1975)是贝娄最重要的代表作之一。小说主人公之一查理·西特林(Charlie Citrine)是一位青年作家,事业巅峰期过后他的创作开始走下坡路,生活上前妻和情妇都在尽可能地瓜分他的财产。洪堡(Von Humboldt Fleisher)是西特林的导师和挚友,对他有知遇之恩并带领他走进艺术的世界,但在洪堡贫病交加时,西特林却未能伸出援手。对于洪堡事业的潦倒和生命的终结,西特林始终心怀歉疚。小说结尾时,西特林在即将破产之际,凭借洪堡留给他的一个剧本提纲摆脱了物质危机,这时他才真正体会到洪堡当年的精神苦闷。

洪堡和西特林在诸多方面具有相似之处,如族裔身份、职业、婚姻、性格和阅历等。作为出身社会底层的犹太移民后裔,两人终其一生都在追寻身份的认同,而犹太裔身份既是两人身份危机之根源,也是连结两人命运的纽带。洪堡是西特林的前辈,他的诗歌创作才华早已让他在文坛名利双收,可他依然对犹太身份的现实境遇保持相当清醒的态度。从洪堡和西特林两人的职业生涯和命运轨迹来看,我们不难发现功利主义、物质主义和大众文化对高雅艺术的碾压和危害,以及知识分子在面对物质与精神、社会与艺术之间的矛盾冲突时所表现出的挣扎与迷茫。

在被文化工业过滤和重造的整个世界中,洪堡的死和诗歌的衰落是现代主义先锋派文学不敌大众文化的必然结果,折射出贝娄对于人类丧失文学诗性思考能力的担忧,引发人们审视诗人之死的必然性及其背后蕴藏的当代美国文化现实。

(三) 作品选读:《洪堡的礼物》[1]

Humboldt seemed to take this as a compliment, and laughed between his teeth, silently. Then he said, "Here's what you do. Go to Ricketts and say: 'Humboldt is a very distinguished person—poet, scholar, critic, teacher, editor. He has an international reputation and he'll have a place in the literary history of the United States'—all of which is true, by the way. 'And here's your chance, Professor Ricketts, I happen to know that Humboldt's tired of living like a hand-to-mouth bohemian. The literary world is going fast. The avant-garde is a memory. It's time Humboldt led a more dignified settled life. He's married now. I know he admires Princeton, he loves it here, and if you made him an offer he'd certainly consider it. I might talk him into it. I'd hate for you to miss this opportunity, Professor Ricketts. Princeton has got Einstein and Panofsky. But you're weak on the literary creative side. The coming trend is to have artists on the campus. Amherst has Robert Frost. Don't fall behind. Grab Fleisher. Don't let him get away, or you'll end up with some third-rater.'"

"I won't mention Einstein and Panofsky. I'll start right out with Moses and the prophets. What a cast-iron plot! Ike has inspired you. This is what I call high-minded low cunning."

However, he didn't laugh. His eyes were red. He'd been up all night. First he watched the election returns. Then he wandered about the house and yard gripped by despair, thinking what to do. Then he planned out this putsch. Then filled with inspiration he drove in his Buick, the busted muffler blasting in the country lanes and the great long car skedaddling dangerously on the curves. Lucky for the woodchucks they were already hibernating. I know what figures crowded his thoughts—Walpole, Count Mosca, Disraeli, Lenin. While he thought also, with uncontemporary sublimity, about eternal life. Ezekiel and Plato were not absent. The man was noble. But he was all asmolder, and craziness also made him vile and funny. Heavy-handed, thick-faced with fatigue, he took a medicine bottle from his briefcase and fed himself a few little pills out of the palm of his hand. Tranquilizers, perhaps. Or maybe amphetamines for speed. He swallowed them dry. He doctored himself. Like Demmie Vonghel. She locked herself in the bathroom and took many pills.

"So you'll go to Ricketts," Humboldt told me.

"I thought he was only a front man."

"That's right. He's a stooge. But the old guard can't disown him. If we outsmart him, they'll have to back him up."

"But why should Ricketts pay attention to what I say?"

"Because, friend, I passed the word around that your play is going to be produced."

"You did?"

---

[1] Bellow, Saul. *Humboldt's Gift*. New York: Penguin Books, 1984, pp. 126 - 129.

"Next year, on Broadway. They look on you as a successful playwright."

"Now why the hell did you do that? I'm going to look like a phony."

"No, you won't. We'll make it true. You can leave that to me. I gave Ricketts your last essay in the *Kenyon* to read, and he thinks you're a comer. And don't pretend with me. I know you. You love intrigue and mischief. Right now your teeth are on edge with delight. Besides, it's not just intrigue..."

"What? Sorcery! *Fucking sortilegio*!"

"It's not *sortilegio*. It's mutual aid."

"Don't give me that stuff."

"First me, then you," he said.

I distinctly remember that my voice jumped up. I shouted, "What!" Then I laughed and said, "You'll make me a Princeton professor, too? Do you think I could stand a whole lifetime of this drinking, boredom, small talk, and ass-kissing? Now that you've lost Washington by a landslide, you've settled pretty fast for this academic music box. Thank you, I'll find misery in my own way. I give you two years of this goyish privilege."

Humboldt waved his hands at me. "Don't poison my mind. What a tongue you have, Charlie. Don't say those things. I'll expect them to happen. They'll infect my future."

I paused and considered his peculiar proposition. Then I looked at Humboldt himself. His mind was executing some earnest queer labor. It was swelling and pulsating oddly, painfully. He tried to laugh it all off with his nearly silent panting laugh. I could hardly hear the breath of it.

"You wouldn't be lying to Ricketts," he said. "Where would they get somebody like me?"

"Okay, Humboldt. That is a hard question."

"Well, I am one of the leading literary men of this country."

"Sure you are, at your best."

"Something should be done for me. Especially in this Ike moment, as darkness falls on the land."

"But why this?"

"Well, frankly, Charlie, I'm out of kilter, temporarily. I have to get back to a state in which I can write poetry again. But where's my equilibrium? There are too many anxieties. They dry me out. The world keeps interfering. I have to get the enchantment back. I feel as if I've been living in a suburb of reality, and commuting back and forth. That's got to stop. I have to locate myself. I'm here" (here on earth, he meant) "to do something, something good."

"I know, Humboldt. Here isn't Princeton, either, and everyone is waiting for the good thing."

Eyes reddening still more, Humboldt said, "I know you love me, Charlie."

"It's true. But let's only say it once."

"You're right. I'm a brother to you, too, though. Kathleen also knows it. It's obvious how we feel about one another, Demmie Vonghel included. Humor me, Charlie. Never mind how ridiculous this seems. Humor me, it's important. Call up Ricketts and say you have to talk to him."

"Okay. I will."

Humboldt put his hands on Sewell's small yellow desk and thrust himself back in the chair so that the steel casters gave a wicked squeak. The ends of his hair were confused with cigarette smoke. His head was lowered. He was examining me as if he had just surfaced from many fathoms.

"Have you got a checking account, Charlie? Where do you keep your money?"

"What money?"

"Haven't you got a checking account?"

"At Chase Manhattan. I've got about twelve bucks."

"My bank is the Corn Exchange," he said. "Now, Where's your checkbook?"

"In my trench coat."

"Let's see."

I brought out the flapping green blanks, curling at the edges. "I see my balance is only eight," I said.

Then Humboldt reaching into his plaid jacket brought out his own checkbook and unclipped one of his many pens. He was bandoliered with fountain pens and ball-points.

"What are you doing, Humboldt?"

"I'm giving you *carte blanche* power to draw on my account. I'm signing a blank check in your name. And you make one out to me. No date, no amount, just 'Pay to Von Humboldt Fleisher.' Sit down, Charlie, and fill it out."

"But what's it about? I don't like this. I have to understand what's going on."

"With eight bucks in the bank, what do you care?"

"It's not the money..."

He was very moved, and he said, "Exactly. It isn't. That's the whole point. If you're ever up against it, fill in any amount you need and cash it. The same applies to me. We'll take an oath as friends and brothers never to abuse this. To hold it for the worst emergency. When I said mutual aid you didn't take me seriously. Well, now you see." Then he leaned on the desk in all his heaviness and in a tiny script he filled in my name with trembling force.

思考与讨论

(1) 选文中美国犹太裔的身份认同问题体现在哪些方面?

(2) 如何理解洪堡的知识分子形象以及他对文学的观点?

(3) 如何理解洪堡和西特林互换支票的行为?其中体现了何种犹太意识?

(4) 洪堡和西特林的契约关系是否具有稳定性?

拓展阅读

[1] Goldman, L. H. "Saul Bellow and the philosophy of Judaism." *Studies in the Literary Imagination*, vol.17, no.2, 1984, pp.87 - 95.

[2] Kernan, Alvin B. Humboldt's gift. Bloom, Harold (ed.), *Saul Bellow: Modern Critical Views*. New York: Chelsea House, 1986, pp.183 - 187.

[3] Siegel, Ben. "Artists and opportunities in Saul Bellow's *Humboldt's Gift*." Trachtenberg, Stanley, ed., *Critical Essays on Saul Bellow*. Boston: G. K. Hall, 1979, pp.158 - 174.

[4] Zipperstein, Steven J. "Isaac Rosenfeld. Saul Bellow, Friendship and Fate." *New England Review*, vol.30, no.1, 2009, pp.10 - 20.

二、桑德拉·希斯内罗丝

(一) 桑德拉·希斯内罗丝简介

桑德拉·希斯内罗丝(Sandra Cisneros, 1954—　)是美国墨西哥裔作家、诗人,出生于芝加哥波多黎各裔社区,家中有六个兄弟,她是唯一的女孩。希斯内罗丝在1976年毕业于洛约拉大学,获得文学学士学位;两年后她又获得爱荷华大学作家工作坊创意写作硕士学位。正是在爱荷华,希斯内罗丝觉察到墨裔女性的孤独感与异类感,凭借对身份的不懈追求,她发现了自身及其所属群体独特的文学声音。

希斯内罗丝的首部小说《芒果街上的小屋》发表于1984年,翌年获美国国家图书奖,1988年入选《诺顿美国文学选集》(*The Norton Anthology of American Literature*),自此确立了希斯内罗丝在西班牙语裔作家群和在美国文坛的地位。1991年,希斯内罗丝的短篇小说集《喊女溪》(*Woman Hollering Creek and Other Stories*)出版。2002年长篇小说《拉拉的褐色披肩》(*Caramelo*)问世。此外,希斯内罗丝的文学创作还包括诗集《坏男孩》(*Bad Boys*, 1980)、《罗德里戈的诗》(*The Rodrigo Poems*, 1985)、《不择手段》(*My Wicked Wicked Ways*, 1987)、《浪荡女》(*Loose Woman*, 1994),故事集《头发》(*Hairs/Pelitos*, 1994)、《你见过玛丽吗?》(*Have You Seen Marie?*, 2012)和回忆录《芒果街,我自己的小屋》(*A House of My Own: Stories from My Life*, 2015)等作品。

2004年,美国当代极富影响力的文学批评家哈罗德·布鲁姆(Harold Bloom)为《芒果街上的小屋》撰写了十分详尽的导读指南,足见该作品的文学分量。目前希斯内罗丝的作品在世界范围内广泛传播,受到来自美国本土、拉丁美洲和世界各地文学研究者的学术关注。

(二)《芒果街上的小屋》简介

《芒果街上的小屋》由44个短小、独立而又相互关联的故事构成,每个故事在不同的话题上展开,以小女孩埃斯佩朗莎(Esperanza Cordero)的视角讲述其童年经历中的片段与痕迹,以及芒果街上的家人、老屋、玩伴、浮云、瘦树、弃猫和破破烂烂的各种小玩意儿,勾勒出挣扎于美国城市生活中贫苦墨裔少女的成长画卷。

房子是该小说的核心意象，由于生活所迫，埃斯佩朗莎和她的家人不得不四处搬家而成为城市里的游牧者，从一个房子流浪到另一个房子，却没有一座真正属于于自己并且“可以指给别人看的房子”[①]。埃斯佩朗莎的身份意识在对房子的渴求中逐渐觉醒，房子成为她实现理想自我、获得身份归属感的换喻式表达。同时，房子还以物质隐喻的形式道出了墨裔女性的现实遭遇和精神隔绝。比如，住在嬷嬷家地下室来自波多黎各的一家人、凯西走后搬进她家房子的奥提兹一家、躲在阁楼里足不出户的玛玛西塔、住在精美牢笼里的拉菲娜等，生动刻画了墨裔女性被囚禁、被孤立的悲剧命运。此外，小说还展现了主人公埃斯佩朗莎如何通过写作来摆脱“男性注视”，追求女性的自由、独立和成功。

（三）作品选读：《芒果街上的小屋》[②]

Born Bad

Most likely I will go to hell and most likely I deserve to be there. My mother says I was born on an evil day and prays for me. Lucy and Rachel pray too. For ourselves and for each other... because of what we did to Aunt Lupe.

Her name was Guadalupe and she was pretty like my mother. Dark. Good to look at. In her Joan Crawford dress and swimmer's legs. Aunt Lupe of the photographs.

But I knew her sick from the disease that would not go, her legs bunched under the yellow sheets, the bones gone limp as worms. The yellow pillow, the yellow smell, the bottles and spoons. Her head thrown back like a thirsty lady. My aunt, the swimmer.

Hard to imagine her legs once strong, the bones hard and parting water, clean sharp strokes, not bent and wrinkled like a baby, not drowning under the sticky yellow light. Second-floor rear apartment. The naked light bulb. The high ceilings. The light bulb always burning.

I don't know who decides who deserves to go bad. There was no evil in her birth. No wicked curse. One day I believe she was swimming, and the next day she was sick. It might have been the day that gray photograph was taken. It might have been the day she was holding cousin Totchy and baby Frank. It might have been the moment she pointed to the camera for the kids to look and they wouldn't.

Maybe the sky didn't look the day she fell down. Maybe God was busy. It could be true she didn't dive right one day and hurt her spine. Or maybe the story that she fell very hard from a high step stool, like Totchy said, is true.

But I think diseases have no eyes. They pick with a dizzy finger anyone, just anyone. Like my aunt who happened to be walking down the street one day in her Joan Crawford dress, in her funny felt hat with the black feather, cousin Totchy in one hand, baby Frank in the other.

Sometimes you get used to the sick and sometimes the sickness, if it is there too long, gets to

① 桑德拉·希斯内罗丝：《芒果街上的小屋》，潘帕译，南京：译林出版社，2006 年，第 5 页。

② Cisneros, Sandra. *The House on Mango Street*. New York: Vintage Books, 1991, pp.58 – 61.

seem normal. This is how it was with her, and maybe this is why we chose her.

It was a game, that's all. It was the game we played every afternoon ever since that day one of us invented it—I can't remember who—I think it was me.

You had to pick somebody. You had to think of someone everybody knew. Someone you could imitate and everyone else would have to guess who it was. It started out with famous people: Wonder Woman, the Beatles, Marilyn Monroe... But then somebody thought it'd be better if we changed the game a little, if we pretended we were Mr. Benny, or his wife Blanca, or Ruthie, or anybody we knew.

I don't know why we picked her. Maybe we were bored that day. Maybe we got tired. We liked my aunt. She listened to our stories. She always asked us to come back. Lucy, me, Rachel. I hated to go there alone. The six blocks to the dark apartment, second-floor rear building where sunlight never came, and what did it matter? My aunt was blind by then. She never saw the dirty dishes in the sink. She couldn't see the ceilings dusty with flies, the ugly maroon walls, the bottles and sticky spoons. I can't forget the smell. Like sticky capsules filled with jelly. My aunt, a little oyster, a little piece of meat on an open shell for us to look at. Hello, hello. As if she had fallen into a well.

I took my library books to her house. I read her stories. I liked the book *The Waterbabies*. She liked it too. I never knew how sick she was until that day I tried to show her one of the pictures in the book, a beautiful color picture of the water babies swimming in the sea. I held the book up to her face. I can't see it, she said, I'm blind. And then I was ashamed.

She listened to every book, every poem I read her. One day I read her one of my own. I came very close. I whispered it into the pillow:

> I want to be
> like the waves on the sea,
> like the clouds in the wind,
> but I'm me.
> One day I'll jump
> out of my skin.
> I'll shake the sky
> like a hundred violins.

That's nice. That's very good, she said in her tired voice. You just remember to keep writing, Esperanza. You must keep writing. It will keep you free, and I said yes, but at that time I didn't know what she meant.

The day we played the game, we didn't know she was going to die. We pretended with our heads thrown back, our arms limp and useless, dangling like the dead. We laughed the way she did.

We talked the way she talked, the way blind people talk without moving their head. We imitated the way you had to lift her head a little so she could drink water, she sucked it up slow out of a green tin cup. The water was warm and tasted like metal. Lucy laughed. Rachel too. We took turns being her. We screamed in the weak voice of a parrot for Totchy to come and wash those dishes. It was easy.

We didn't know. She had been dying such a long time, we forgot. Maybe she was ashamed. Maybe she was embarrassed it took so many years. The kids who wanted to be kids instead of washing dishes and ironing their papa's shirts, and the husband who wanted a wife again.

And then she died, my aunt who listened to my poems.

And then we began to dream the dreams.

思考与讨论

(1) 选文中美国墨裔女性的遭遇和问题体现在哪些方面？解决方案又是什么？

(2) 如何理解卢佩婶婶和她的房子的内在关系？

(3) 作者在圣母瓜达卢佩的当代改写中传达出何种文化意识？

(4) 选文中文本的音乐性体现在哪些方面？具有何种文体意义？

拓展阅读

[1] Bloom, Harold, ed. *Bloom's Guides: The House on Mango Street*. New York: Infobase Publishing, 2010.

[2] Madsen, Deborah L. *Understanding Contemporary Chicana Literature*. Columbia: University of South Carolina Press, 2001.

[3] Herrera, Cristina. *Contemporary Chicana Literature: (Re) Writing the Maternal Script*. New York: Cambria Press, 2014.

[4] Kevane, Bridget. *Latino Literature in America*. Westport: Greenwood Press, 2003.

三、托妮·莫里森

(一) 托妮·莫里森简介

托妮·莫里森(Toni Morrison, 1931—2019)是美国非洲裔小说家，出生于俄亥俄州洛雷恩市。莫里森在1953年毕业于霍华德大学，两年后获康奈尔大学硕士学位，先后在兰登书屋、南得克萨斯大学、霍华德大学、纽约州立大学、耶鲁大学和普林斯顿大学执教，是一位兼具创作才华与批评精神的作家。

1970年，莫里森的首部小说《最蓝的眼睛》一经发表便深受好评。接着，小说《秀拉》(*Sula*, 1974)和《所罗门之歌》(*Song of Solomon*, 1977)更是为这位年轻的作家赢得广泛认可，并相继获得1975年国家图书奖小说提名奖和1978年美国书评家协会奖。在此之后，莫里森笔耕不辍，陆续创作了《柏油娃娃》(*Tar Baby*, 1981)、《宠儿》(*Beloved*, 1987)、《爵士乐》(*Jazz*, 1992)、《天堂》(*Paradise*, 1998)等长篇小说，其中《宠儿》被评论界普遍视为莫里森的代表作品。小说讲述了非裔母亲如何亲手杀死女儿以避免奴隶制对她的残害以及女儿如何重返人间的故事，该作曾获1988年普利策最佳小说奖。1993年，莫里森"以其富有洞察力和诗情画意的小说把美国现实的一个重要方面写活了"[①]，成为首摘诺贝尔文学奖的美国非裔作家。

2000年以来，莫里森创作了《爱》(*Love*, 2003)、《恩惠》(*A Mercy*, 2008)、《家园》(*Home*, 2012)、《上帝帮助孩子》(*God Help the Child*, 2015)等长篇小说。此外，她还撰写了剧本《做梦的艾美特》(*Dreaming Emmett*, 1986)、文学评论《黑暗里的游戏》(*Playing in the Dark: Whiteness and the Literary Imagination*, 1993)、儿童文学《大盒子》(*The Big Box*, 1999)和《拜托了，路易斯》(*Please, Louise*, 2014)等不同体裁和文类的作品。

莫里森的小说融合了种族与阶级、神话与现实，她以非裔文化传统为内源，以反映本族群人民的生活为动力，以揭示美国黑人的残酷现实以及主流和边缘之间的对峙与冲突为目的，努力克服性别、种族和阶级的多重障碍，展现了对本族群甚至对整个人类命运的深刻思考和人文关怀。

(二)《宠儿》简介

《宠儿》的核心情节是莫里森根据一位名叫玛格丽特·加纳(Margaret Garner)的黑奴的真实经历所写成。美国内战前后，黑人女奴塞丝(Sethe)不堪忍受"甜蜜之家"(Sweet Home)农场残酷的身心虐待，身怀六甲的她冒死带着两个儿子和一个女儿逃到辛辛那提，在即将被猎奴者抓获之时，为了不让孩子们重蹈自己的苦难，塞丝亲手锯断了不满两岁女儿的喉咙。此后18年，塞丝深受杀婴行为的折磨，她的房子因闹鬼变成凶宅，两个儿子被死去婴儿的怨毒逼出家门，女儿丹芙(Denver)沉默寡言、没有朋友，而被塞丝杀死的孩子更是化作少女"宠儿"重返人间，和塞丝一家生活在同一屋檐下，无休止地向她索求母爱，直到最终被人们驱除和遗忘。

"杀婴"是《宠儿》的核心事件，也是小说引发的热点问题。在评价母亲杀死婴儿的场景时，美国学者角谷美智子(Michiko Kakutani)认为这一幕"如此残酷和令人不安以至于扭曲了其前后的时间"[②]。在对"杀婴"的叙事建构上，小说运用多元化的叙述话语和视角，通过非线性的叙事方式拼凑出整个"杀婴"事件的来龙去脉。声音的多样性极大增强了事件本身的神秘色彩，也意味着"杀婴"背后潜藏着大量可待挖掘的文本内涵，比如奴隶制对黑人的摧残，母性神话的颠覆与重构，杀婴行为的伦理危机，以及黑人如何走出阴霾、寻找生存的意义等不同方面的内容，这些叩问与思考对于重新审视美国非裔族群的生命困境与精神重负有着十分重要的启示意义。

凭借丰富的想象力、诗化的语言、意识流和碎片化的叙事，莫里森向我们展示了"母爱"一词的丰富蕴意，而母爱与暴力的矛盾并置不单单揭示出奴隶制背景下母性问题的复杂性，更折射出肉身死亡与精神死亡的伦理困境，以此再现黑人女性在性别与种族双重压迫下的沉重心灵史。

---

① 托妮·莫里森:《宠儿》,潘岳、雷格译,北京:中国文学出版社,1996年。

② Hevesi, Dennis. "Toni Morrison's Novel *'Beloved'* Wins the Pulitzer Prize in Fiction," *The New York Times*, April 1,1988, Section A, p1, Retrieved April 29,2017.

(三) 作品选读:《宠儿》[1]

When the four horsemen came—schoolteacher, one nephew, one slave catcher and a sheriff—the house on Bluestone Road was so quiet they thought they were too late. Three of them dismounted, one stayed in the saddle, his rifle ready, his eyes trained away from the house to the left and to the right, because likely as not the fugitive would make a dash for it. Although sometimes, you could never tell, you'd find them folded up tight somewhere: beneath floorboards, in a pantry—once in a chimney. Even then care was taken, because the quietest ones, the ones you pulled from a press, a hayloft, or, that once, from a chimney, would go along nicely for two or three seconds. Caught red-handed, so to speak, they would seem to recognize the futility of outsmarting a whiteman and the hopelessness of outrunning a rifle. Smile even, like a child caught dead with his hand in the jelly jar, and when you reached for the rope to tie him, well, even then you couldn't tell. The very nigger with his head hanging and a little jelly-jar smile on his face could all of a sudden roar, like a bull or some such, and commence to do disbelievable things. Grab the rifle at its mouth; throw himself at the one holding it—anything. So you had to keep back a pace, leave the tying to another. Otherwise you ended up killing what you were paid to bring back alive. Unlike a snake or a bear, a dead nigger could not be skinned for profit and was not worth his own dead weight in coin.

Six or seven Negroes were walking up the road toward the house: two boys from the slave catcher's left and some women from his right. He motioned them still with his rifle and they stood where they were. The nephew came back from peeping inside the house, and after touching his lips for silence, pointed his thumb to say that what they were looking for was round back. The slave catcher dismounted then and joined the others. Schoolteacher and the nephew moved to the left of the house; himself and the sheriff to the right. A crazy old nigger was standing in the woodpile with an ax. You could tell he was crazy right off because he was grunting—making low, cat noises like. About twelve yards beyond that nigger was another one—a woman with a flower in her hat. Crazy too, probably, because she too was standing stock-still—but fanning her hands as though pushing cobwebs out of her way. Both, however, were staring at the same place—a shed. Nephew walked over to the old nigger boy and took the ax from him. Then all four started toward the shed.

Inside, two boys bled in the sawdust and dirt at the feet of a nigger woman holding a blood-soaked child to her chest with one hand and an infant by the heels in the other. She did not look at them; she simply swung the baby toward the wall planks, missed and tried to connect a second time, when out of nowhere—in the ticking time the men spent staring at what there was to stare at—the old nigger boy, still mewing, ran through the door behind them and snatched the baby from the

---

① Morrison, Toni. *Beloved*. New York: Alfred A. Knopf, 1996, pp. 148 - 150.

arch of its mother's swing.

Right off it was clear, to schoolteacher especially, that there was nothing there to claim. The three (now four—because she'd had the one coming when she cut) pickaninnies they had hoped were alive and well enough to take back to Kentucky, take back and raise properly to do the work Sweet Home desperately needed, were not. Two were lying open-eyed in sawdust; a third pumped blood down the dress of the main one—the woman schoolteacher bragged about, the one he said made fine ink, damn good soup, pressed his collars the way he liked besides having at least ten breeding years left. But now she'd gone wild, due to the mishandling of the nephew who'd overbeat her and made her cut and run. Schoolteacher had chastised that nephew, telling him to think—just think—what would his own horse do if you beat it beyond the point of education. Or Chipper, or Samson. Suppose you beat the hounds past that point thataway. Never again could you trust them in the woods or anywhere else. You'd be feeding them maybe, holding out a piece of rabbit in your hand, and the animal would revert—bite your hand clean off. So he punished that nephew by not letting him come on the hunt. Made him stay there, feed stock, feed himself, feed Lillian, tend crops. See how he liked it; see what happened when you overbear creatures God had given you the responsibility of—the trouble it was, and the loss. The whole lot was lost now. Five. He could claim the baby struggling in the arms of the mewing old man, but who'd tend her? Because the woman—something was wrong with her. She was looking at him now, and if his other nephew could see that look he would learn the lesson for sure: you just can't mishandle creatures and expect success.

The nephew, the one who had nursed her while his brother held her down, didn't know he was shaking. His uncle had warned him against that kind of confusion, but the warning didn't seem to be taking. What she go and do that for? On account of a beating? Hell, he'd been beat a million times and he was white. Once it hurt so bad and made him so mad he'd smashed the well bucket. Another time he took it out on Samson—a few tossed rocks was all. But no beating ever made him... I mean no way he could have... What she go and do that for? And that is what he asked the sheriff, who was standing there amazed like the rest of them, but not shaking. He was swallowing hard, over and over again. "What she want to go and do that for?"

The sheriff turned, then said to the other three, "You all better go on. Look like your business is over. Mine's started now."

Schoolteacher beat his hat against his thigh and spit before leaving the woodshed. Nephew and the catcher backed out with him. They didn't look at the woman in the pepper plants with the flower in her hat. And they didn't look at the seven or so faces that had edged closer in spite of the catcher's rifle warning. Enough nigger eyes for now. Little nigger-boy eyes open in sawdust; little nigger-girl eyes staring between the wet fingers that held her face so her head wouldn't fall off; little nigger-baby eyes crinkling up to cry in the arms of the old nigger whose own eyes were nothing but slivers looking down at his feet. But the worst ones were those of the nigger woman who looked like she didn't have any. Since the whites in them had disappeared and since they were as black as her skin, she looked blind.

思考与讨论

(1) 如何理解塞丝杀婴的举动?

(2) 选文中的其他人物对杀婴事件持何种态度?

(3) 塞丝弑女与奴隶主占有奴隶是否具有本质上的相似性?

(4) 在"学校老师"看到塞丝时,作者使用了何种写作手法?

拓展阅读

[1] Baillie, Justine. *Toni Morrison and Literary Tradition: The Invention of an Aesthetic.* London: Bloomsbury Academic, 2013.

[2] Birch, Eva Lennox. *Black American Women's Writing: A Quilt of Many Colours*. London: Harvester Wheatsheaf, 1994.

[3] David, Ron. *Toni Morison Explained: A Reader's Map to the Novels*. New York: Random House, 2000.

[4] Fultz, Lucille P. *Toni Morrison: Playing with Difference*. Urbana: University of Ilinois Press, 2003.

[5] Winsbro, Bonnie. *Supernatural Forces: Belief, Difference, and Power in Contemporary Works by Ethnic Women*. Amherst: University of Massachusetts Press, 1993.

四、谭恩美

(一) 谭恩美简介

谭恩美(Amy Tan, 1952—)是美国华裔作家,出生于加州的奥克兰市,父母是第一代中国移民。青少年时期的谭恩美曾遭遇哥哥和父亲相继离世的精神打击,后与母亲、弟弟远赴瑞士。重返加州后,谭恩美就读于圣何塞州立大学,获得了文学学士学位和语言学硕士学位。在加州大学伯克利分校攻读博士学位的第二年,谭恩美因故放弃学业,自此踏上文学创作之旅。

1989 年,谭恩美的首部小说《喜福会》发表,并使其成功跻身美国畅销小说家之列。该书被翻译为包括中文在内的 30 多种语言,在世界各地发行,先后赢得美国国家图书奖、1991 年最佳小说奖、1990 年海湾地区小说评论奖以及国家图书评论奖提名等奖项,还被选入《诺顿美国文学选集》,进入美国文学经典作品之林。1993 年《喜福会》被著名导演王颖(Wayne Wang)和制片人奥利弗·斯通(Oliver Stone)搬上银幕,取得了不错的票房成绩。之后,谭恩美接连创作了长篇小说《灶神之妻》(*The Kitchen God's*

Wife, 1991)、《灵感女孩》(*The Hundred Secret Senses*, 1995)、《接骨师之女》(*The Bonesetter's Daughter*, 2001)、《沉没之鱼》(*Saving Fish From Drowning*, 2005)和《奇幻山谷》(*The Valley of Amazement*, 2013),以及散文、儿童读物等不同体裁的文学作品,进一步奠定了她在当代美国华裔文学史上的地位。

凭借东方元素、母女冲突、身份认同及女性自我成长等丰富多样的主题,谭恩美的作品超越了族裔、性别和阶级的局限,神奇地"震动了美国社会精神的意识之弦"[①],为当代美国小说和少数族裔文学开创了新的叙事风格。

(二)《喜福会》简介

《喜福会》围绕四对母女讲述了华裔移民家庭麻将桌上的故事。主人公之一吴宿愿(Suyuan Woo)在抗日战争期间借打麻将来排解战乱之苦,将其组织的麻将俱乐部称作"喜福会"以图吉利。赴美后的她联合许家、顾家和江家开启了第二个"喜福会"麻将俱乐部,小说大部分内容即从这项娱乐活动出发,以四对母女为主线展开叙事。她们边打麻将边拉家常,攀比子女或回忆往事,轮流讲述一个个故事和一段段历史,年复一年不曾中断,"喜福会"就这样成为她们的生活模式和礼仪习俗。

"幸福的家庭是相似的,不幸的家庭各有各的不幸。"[②]"喜福会"里的四位母亲都有不幸的过往,她们在残酷现实的逼迫下离开中国远赴美国,四个女儿也都有各自的艰辛,如两种文化压力下自我的艰难成长、两代华裔女性间的情感隔膜、文化和身份认同障碍等等。在小说的四个部分中,每部分开篇都有一个引子,第一篇和最后一篇由母亲们叙述其人生阅历,中间两篇由女儿们叙述其成长经历、文化碰撞和母女关系,"如同麻将桌上的四方轮流坐庄,各家的故事就在轮流坐庄中娓娓道出"[③]。

小说将华裔女性的自我经历放大,将家庭矛盾和母女冲突提升到文化冲突的层面,并使之象征化、寓言化,传递出中国与美国、东方与西方、主流与族裔、男性与女性、汉语和英语两种文化秩序间的判断和抉择,并巧妙地通过人物命运的多元化走向破解二元对立困境,彰显出小说在文化内涵上的开放性和艺术性。

(三)作品选读:《喜福会》[④]

When I arrive at the Hsus' house, where the Joy Luck Club is meeting tonight, the first person I see is my father. "There she is! Never on time!" he announces. And it's true. Everybody's already here, seven family friends in their sixties and seventies. They look up and laugh at me, always tardy, a child still at thirty-six.

I'm shaking, trying to hold something inside. The last time I saw them, at the funeral, I had broken down and cried big gulping sobs. They must wonder now how someone like me can take my mother's place. A friend once told me that my mother and I were alike, that we had the same wispy hand gestures, the same girlish laugh and sideways look. When I shyly told my mother this, she

---

① 张子清:《善待别人,尊重别人的生存权——李健孙访谈录》,南京:译林出版社,2002年,第86页。

② 列夫·托尔斯泰:《安娜·卡列宁娜》,周扬译,《列夫·托尔斯泰文集第九卷》,北京:人民文学出版社,2015年,第3页。

③ 程爱民等:《20世纪美国华裔小说研究》,南京:南京大学出版社,2010年,第147页。

④ Amy, Tan. *The Joy Luck Club*. New York: Penguin Books, 2006, pp.27-29.

seemed insulted and said, "You don't even know little percent of me! How can you be me?" And she's right. How can I be my mother at Joy Luck?

"Auntie, Uncle," I say repeatedly, nodding to each person there. I have always called these old family friends Auntie and Uncle. And then I walk over and stand next to my father.

He's looking at the Jongs' pictures from their recent. China trip. "Look at that," he says politely, pointing to a photo of the Jongs' tour group standing on wide slab steps. There is nothing in this picture that shows it was taken in China rather than San Francisco, or any other city for that matter. But my father doesn't seem to be looking at the picture anyway. It's as though everything were the same to him, nothing stands out. He has always been politely indifferent. But what's the Chinese word that means indifferent because you can't *see* any differences? That's how troubled I think he is by my mother's death.

"Will you look at that," he says, pointing to another nondescript picture.

The Hsus' house feels heavy with greasy odors. Too many Chinese meals cooked in a too small kitchen, too many once fragrant smells compressed onto a thin layer of invisible grease. I remember how my mother used to go into other people's houses and restaurants and wrinkle her nose, then whisper very loudly: "I can see and feel the stickiness with my nose."

I have not been to the Hsus' house in many years, but the living room is exactly the same as I remember it. When Auntie An-mei and Uncle George moved to the Sunset district from Chinatown twenty-five years ago, they bought new furniture. It's all there, still looking mostly new under yellowed plastic. The same turquoise couch shaped in a semicircle of nubby tweed. The colonial end tables made out of heavy maple. A lamp of fake cracked porcelain. Only the scroll-length calendar, free from the Bank of Canton, changes every year.

I remember this stuff, because when we were children, Auntie An-mei didn't let us touch any of her new furniture except through the clear plastic coverings. On Joy Luck nights, my parents brought me to the Hsus'. Since I was the guest, I had to take care of all the younger children, so many children it seemed as if there were always one baby who was crying from having bumped its head on a table leg.

"You are responsible," said my mother, which meant I was in trouble if anything was spilled, burned, lost, broken, or dirty. I was responsible, no matter who did it. She and Auntie An-mei were dressed up in funny Chinese dresses with stiff stand-up collars and blooming branches of embroidered silk sewn over their breasts. These clothes were too fancy for real Chinese people, I thought, and too strange for American parties. In those days, before my mother told me her Kweilin story, I imagined Joy Luck was a shameful Chinese custom, like the secret gathering of the Ku Klux Klan or the tom-tom dances of TV Indians preparing for war.

But tonight, there's no mystery. The Joy Luck aunties are all wearing slacks, bright print blouses, and different versions of sturdy walking shoes. We are all seated around the dining room table under a lamp that looks like a Spanish candelabra. Uncle George puts on his bifocals and starts the meeting by reading the minutes:

"Our capital account is $24,825, or about $6,206 a couple, $3,103 per person. We sold Subaru for a loss at six and three-quarters. We bought a hundred shares of Smith International at seven. Our thanks to Lindo and Tin Jong for the goodies. The red bean soup was especially delicious. The March meeting had to be canceled until further notice. We were sorry to have to bid a fond farewell to our dear friend Suyuan and extended our sympathy to the Canning Woo family. Respectfully submitted, George Hsu, president and secretary."

That's it. I keep thinking the others will start talking about my mother, the wonderful friendship they shared, and why I am here in her spirit, to be the fourth corner and carry on the idea my mother came up with on a hot day in Kweilin.

But everybody just nods to approve the minutes. Even my father's head bobs up and down routinely. And it seems to me my mother's life has been shelved for new business.

思考与讨论

(1) 为什么母亲要让同为小孩的叙事者"负责任"?

(2) 将喜福会比喻为三K党或印第安战舞具有何种文化寓意?

(3) 如何理解喜福会里人们穿着的改变?

(4) 选文中"我怎么可能在喜福会里取代母亲呢?"这句话透露出怎样的母女关系?

拓展阅读

[1] Bernier, Lucie, ed. *Aspects of Diaspora: Studies on North American Chinese Writers*. Berne: Peter Lang, 2000.

[2] Hamilton, Patricia L. "Feng Shui, Astrology, and the Five Elements: Traditional Chinese Belief in Amy Tan's The Joy Luck Club." *MELUS*, vol.24, no.2, 2000, pp.125-145.

[3] Huntley, E.D. *Amy Tan: A Critical Companion*. New York: Greenwood Press, 1998.

[4] Ma, Sheng-mei. *Immigrant Subjectivities: In Asian American and Asian American Literature*. New York: State University of New York Press, 1988.

五、路易斯·厄德里克

(一) 路易斯·厄德里克简介

路易斯·厄德里克(Louise Erdrich, 1954—)是美国本土裔作家,出生于明尼苏达州。她的父亲是德裔美国人，母亲是奥吉布瓦（Ojibwa）族人。厄德里克先后就读于达特茅斯学院和霍普金斯大学，出版文学作品 20 余部，涉及小说、诗歌、儿童文学等多个领域，是美国当代最富创作力的女作家之一。

1984 年，厄德里克发表了长篇小说《爱药》（*Love Medicine*），该作畅销全美并被授予美国书评家协会奖等多个奖项，从此奠定了她在当代美国文坛的地位。之后，厄德里克陆续出版了《甜菜女王》（*Beet Queen*，1986）、《痕迹》（*Tracks*，1988）、《宾果宫》。这四部小说组成了著名的"北达科他四部曲"（North Dakota Quartet），真实再现了北达科他龟山保留地齐佩瓦印第安人的生存现状。2000 年后，厄德里克的《小无马地奇迹的最后报告》（*The Last Report on the Miracles at Little No Horse*，2001）、《屠夫俱乐部》（*The Master Butchers Singing Club*，2003）、《四灵魂》（*Four Souls*，2004）、《鸽灾》（*The Plague of Doves*，2008）、《踩影游戏》（*Shadow Tag*，2010）、《圆屋》（*The Round House*，2012）、《拉罗斯》（*La Rose*，2016）等一系列作品的相继发表，成功引起了美国国内新一轮的厄德里克阅读热。近年来，厄德里克还发表了《永生上帝的未来家园》（*Future Home of the Living God*，2017）和《守夜人》（*The Night Watchman*，2020）两部小说。前者以反乌托邦小说的形式"展现了一幅并不遥远的未来图景"①；后者则借印第安部落捍卫土地权利的艰辛往事反思族裔群体的生存困境与对策。从体裁上看，厄德里克几乎涉猎了除戏剧外的所有文学形式，包括 17 部长篇小说、2 部短篇小说集、6 部儿童小说、3 部诗集和两部回忆录。

至今，厄德里克以丰富娴熟的文学笔触斩获了六次欧·亨利小说奖、《洛杉矶时报》小说奖、司各特·奥台尔历史小说奖、苏·考夫曼奖和内森·阿尔格伦短篇小说奖等美国各大文学奖项，文学成就可以与莫马迪、韦尔奇等本土裔文学前辈相比肩，无可争议地成为美国印第安文艺复兴第二次大潮的代表人物。

（二）《踩影游戏》简介

小说《踩影游戏》围绕一对夫妻的婚姻与情感展开，将妻子艾琳（Irene）的红色日记和蓝色日记作为两条线索讲述了一个破碎家庭的悲剧故事。艾琳具有多重身份：她是印第安人和白人的混血后代，是印第安知名画家吉尔（Gil）的妻子兼模特，是弗洛里安（Florian）、瑞尔（Riel）和斯托尼（Stoney）的母亲，是正在完成艺术史论文的博士生。日记中的艾琳以第一人称"我"的声音出现，丈夫吉尔则是日记中的"你"。吉尔事业成功，但他脾气暴躁，常对妻儿拳脚相向。在吉尔的肖像画创作中，艾琳是他永恒的主题、凝视的对象。吉尔不断寻找新的方式塑造艾琳，其中很多都带有强烈的侵略性和羞辱意味。在外界眼中，他们的婚姻幸福美满，然而吉尔对艾琳的占有和压迫令艾琳感到窒息。当艾琳发现吉尔一直在偷看她的红色日记时，夫妻间的尊重和信任立刻瓦解。于是，艾琳决定用一本蓝色日记来记录生活和婚姻的真相，将它藏在银行的保险箱里，并在红色日记里杜撰了自己的婚外情，故意把它放在吉尔可以找到的地方。就这样，艾琳和吉尔的关系变成艾琳的一场操纵性游戏，冷战和暴力随即而来，最终导致两人双双殒命这一无法挽回的悲剧性结局。

《踩影游戏》延续了厄德里克一贯的叙事风格，人物、日记、叙述者的声音交织重叠，形成多声部的叙事效果，幽闭的家庭叙事同样渗透着厄德里克作品中一些共同的主题，尤其是探索了爱情的复杂本质、

① 张琼：《身体控制与文化失控——论厄德里克的〈永生上帝的未来家园〉》，载《国外文学》2019 年第 4 期，第 117 页。

身份的流动性以及一个家庭为生存和救赎而进行的激烈斗争。

（三）作品选读:《踩影游戏》[①]

After our mother waded into the lake and then threw herself forward and began to swim, we watched a moment, we hesitated. Then one of us cried out and we all—Florian, Stoney, and me, Riel—we all rushed into the knifelike cold. It sliced out our breath. Stoney could not go far and I struggled from the water with him, so numbed I couldn't think, and bitterly shaking. Florian got farther, but finally he quit, too. Out there, we saw, Mom was still swimming forward, her head out of water like a dog's. She didn't turn or make any sign that she noticed us at all. She just went to him. By the time she reached our father, he had floundered, but we saw her clutch his head and turn, dragging him by the hair. Her arm was straight out and she kicked, sidestroking. He was afloat behind her. We stood on the end of the silver dock. She was coming back to us—she had once showed us how you save someone: we knew what you do—and we had stopped crying. Then she disappeared. At first, we thought that she was swimming underwater. But then the dogs started barking in a different tone. A drawn-out sound almost like the braying of wild animals, and it struck us deeply. Stoney shrieked and I took the phone from the pocket of Mom's shirt where it was lying on her chair, and dialed 911.

When Florian hit the skids in high school, dropped out, and became addicted to everything he tried—booze, grass, cocaine, meth—Mom's sister, our aunt now, Louise, put him through treatment the first time. His high school teachers helped him through the second time. He is now in college. We talk. Last time, he told me that he was back into explaining the universe, and laughingly said he'd fried a few too many neurons and his classes were actually difficult. He's studying dark matter and supersymmetry again. He said that sometimes in human terms a broken supersymmetry—like his brain, our childhood, or the human face—can be the more elegant or at least more useful solution.

Solution to what? I said.

But he just smiled, one incisor crooked and black.

Stoney came out all right. He went to school in Hawaii, but he's on leave and I heard he went to Molokai and maybe wants to live there. I don't know exactly how. He doesn't often talk to me or Florian. He didn't like living with a big family, but I did. We grew up with Louise and Bobbi's family—we had a traditional adoption and I got brothers, sisters, twenty cousins, and it was all of them who mainly raised me. Which turned out to be a good thing, I think. I also found that the old-time Indians are us, still going to sundances, ceremonies, talking in the old language and even using the old skills if we feel like it, not making a big deal.

---

① Erdrich, Louise. *Shadow Tag*. New York: Harper (Luxe). 2010, pp. 259 - 265.

As for the dogs, they would still be alive if this was a movie. I haven't written down their names because if anything is sacred, they are. Do you understand? I'm not sure I do, but there it is. Snowball or one of his versions probably does live on in Stoney's old first-grade classroom yet. Schrodinger got fed a tab of acid and went down a storm drain. Pretty much, Florian always blamed himself.

Two years ago, just after I graduated from the University of Minnesota, and before I entered this graduate writing program, I turned twenty-one. On the day of my birthday, the lawyer who handled my parents' estate appeared at the doorway to the house. Gerald Oberfach is a good-natured, round sort of person with a hoarse, high-pitched voice, not the type at all you would think of as a tough lawyer. But he did a lot to shield us in those years following our parents' death. We just call him Ober.

Ober came into the house and asked if we could sit down and talk, alone. My sisters and brothers or cousins were in their rooms, and my aunts were gone somewhere. Things were quiet. I said sure and we walked into the cluttered, sunny kitchen. He sat down at the white table, which was flecked with gold glitter. I poured Ober a cup of coffee from the Mr. Coffee pot. He put a tiny red cardboard envelope on the table, and told me it was the key to a safe-deposit box. I just stared at it.

My feeling is that I don't want this, I said.

Ober drank the coffee and nodded, and nodded some more. He has the knack of saying nothing. But I could outlast him, and finally he had to speak.

Your mother told me that this should be given to you when you turned twenty-one. So...

I have been through a great deal of therapy, so it doesn't bother me anymore to say that I am angriest at my mother. The reason I am angriest at her is that she should have saved herself for us—not for him, for us. She died because she could not let go of him. But she should have let go, for us.

Yet I also know she thought she could save anyone, which makes it a stupid accident. So then I want to think she saw in our father's heart an unwavering light. Through all the shitstorms, a steady flame.

I can't decide.

I once asked Florian if an absolutely steady flame was possible. In an airless void, he said, an absolutely steady flame is theoretically possible and yet impossible. There would of course be no oxygen and without it a true fire could not exist.

I said to Ober again that I didn't want the key. Ober said I didn't have to take it, but he was leaving it all the same.

He gave me one of his overlong hugs, said good-bye, and walked out. The door closed and the key sat there. And I sat there, too, just looking at the key. Then not looking at the key. I was thinking of something else. For a long time, I just sat there, thinking.

All of a sudden, my sister or aunt or one of my cousins was making noise in the house, and I picked up the key. I put it in my pocket and I walked out the back door. It was early in the afternoon.

The address of the bank was printed on the little red envelope.

I hope there's lots of money in the box, I thought as I went there. But I knew there wouldn't be any money in the box. I think I knew that there would just be writing. And now, as you see, I have put it all together, both of her diaries. The Red Diary. The Blue Notebook. Her notes on Catlin. My memory charts. I have also filled in certain events and connections. Sometimes, it has helped me to talk to Louise. Other times, I imagined that I was my mother. Or my father. I have written about them in many ways. I interviewed their therapist, who decided it was better to serve the living than the dead, and went over her notes with me and laughed with me and cried. So you see, I am the third person in the writing. I am the one with the gift of omniscience, which is something—I don't know if it's generally known—that children develop once they lose their parents. This is also, of course, my master's thesis. I am a writer in a writing program and here is the place where I thank my mentors. Thank you, parents, you left me with your marriage, my material, the stuff of my life.

I am angriest at you, Mom, but there is this: you trusted me with the narrative.

I said that I was thinking after Ober left and as I stood in the warm dog—smelling kitchen. I was looking at the key, not knowing whether I would pick it up, leave it, or pick it up and throw it in the trash. Actually, I wasn't thinking, or deciding; I was remembering. I was caught in a memory I have had many times. It is always so real I lose track of what's around me and it seems to be happening again.

思考与讨论

(1) 瑞尔在选文中有几个角色？分别承担什么功能？各角色之间又有着怎样的内在关系？

(2) 瑞尔的第三人称叙述使小说的叙述重心发生了何种性质的转变？

(3) 如何理解艾琳死后留给瑞尔日记的行为和意义？

拓展阅读

[1] Noori, Margaret. "Shadow Tag (review)." *Studies in American Indian Literatures*, vol. 22, no.2, 2010. p.89-96.

[2] Owens, Louis. *Other Destinies: Understanding the American Indian Novel*. Norman: University of Oklahoma Press, 1992.

[3] Treuer, David. *Native American Fiction: A User's Manual*. Saint Paul: Graywolf Press, 2006.

[4] Vecsey, Christopher. *Traditional Ojibwa Religion and Its Historical Changes*. Philadelphia: The American Philosophical Society, 1983.

第五章
当代美国女性小说

2020 年 1 月 15 日，在第四波女权主义浪潮[①]的影响下，弗吉尼亚州议会投票通过男女平等权利修正案(Equal Rights Amendment, ERA)，成为通过该修正案的第 38 个州[②]，这意味着性别平等有望被写入美国宪法。爱丽丝·保罗(Alice Paul)于 1923 年提出该修正案，呼吁宪法自第十九条修正案赋予女性选票权后，继续赋予女性与男性平等的权利。1972 年 3 月，在第二波女权主义浪潮的推动下，参议院通过男女平等权利修正案，并将其提交至州立法机构以获批准，拟定时效为 7 年，后被延长至 10 年。弗吉尼亚州通过该修正案的时间晚于既定日期 38 年，其间更有个别保守州申请撤回曾经通过修正案的决定。时至今日，女权主义者们仍在为将男女平等编入宪法而奋斗。

虽然男女平等权利修正案尚未正式生效，但是在其推进过程中，女性的社会地位随之提升。在数波女权主义浪潮的影响下，女权主义发展出多种理论批评流派，女性小说也由小众逐步走向文学主流。其中，第二波女权主义浪潮标志着当代美国女性小说兴起的开端。1963 年贝蒂·弗里丹(Betty Friedan)出版《女性的奥秘》(*The Feminine Mystique*)，掀起美国第二波女权主义浪潮。第二波女权主义者借用反殖民抗争的"自我决定理论"(self-determination)以及美国非裔民权运动的政治观念[③]，认为女性文化不平等与政治不平等密不可分。因此，女性不能仅被动地拒绝其备受压迫的身份，而是应该发自内心、积极自主地参与女权主义对"政治、精神性、审美、性别的变革"[④]。彼时女权主义的政治议程之一便是围绕女性主体与女性经历建立女性自己的历史与文学传统，寻找女性在历史与文学史中被埋藏的声音。在当时的女权主义者眼中，这么做不仅可以挑战男性视角在文学正典中的统治地位，而且能够以史为鉴，通过研究历史中女性的社会地位与性别角色，了解并改善女性当下的生存现状。得益于此，1970 年起，多家女性出版社(如 The Feminist Press, des femmes, Virago Press, Attic Press, Spinifex Press 等)纷纷建立，女性小说数量激增。

1993 年，托妮·莫里森获得诺贝尔文学奖，成为第一位获得诺贝尔文学奖的非裔女性作家。在赛

① 第四波女权主义浪潮(Fourth-wave feminism)是 2012 年左右掀起的女权主义运动，其特征是利用互联网带来的全球化对身材羞辱、性虐待、性骚扰、性暴力进行发声(尤其是 MeToo 运动)。

② 美国宪法第五条规定，一条修正案需要在全国四分之三的州议会被通过，才能正式生效。美国共 50 州，故需至少 38 州通过一条修正案，方可使其被纳入宪法。

③ Bhavnani, Kum-Kum & Coulson, Meg. "Race." Mary Eagleton, ed., *A Concise Companion to Feminist Theory*. Oxford, U.K.: Blackwell Publishing, 2003, p.73.

④ Showalter, Elaine. *A Jury of Her Peers, American Women Writers from Anne Bradstreet to Annie Proulx*. New York: Alfred A. Knopf, 2009, p.536.

珍珠(Pearl S. Buck)于1938年获奖后,时隔55年,终有女性作家再次登上诺贝尔文学奖的舞台。除此之外,多位女性作家的作品,如艾丽斯·沃克(Alice Walker)的《紫颜色》(*The Color Purple*)、简·斯迈利(Jane Smiley)的《一千英亩》(*A Thousand Acres: A Novel*, 1991)、安妮·普鲁(Annie Proulx)的《船讯》(*The Shipping News*, 1993)、玛丽莲·罗宾逊(Marilynne Robinson)的《基列家书》(*Gilead*, 2004)、唐娜·塔特(Donna Tartt)的《金翅雀》(*The Goldfinch*, 2013),陆续获得普利策小说奖、美国国家图书奖等代表美国小说最高荣誉的奖项。这些作品的获奖昭示着当代女性小说在文学性上取得的成就,说明女性小说在正典文学中拥有了一席之地,受众也不再局限于女性读者。

当代美国女性小说多受后现代主义与后结构主义影响,打破体裁限制,风格繁杂多元,难以在传统文学类别范畴下进行归类,故笔者根据各作家对其女性身份的理解,将当代美国女性小说大致分为以下三类:①以女性视角改写传统文学的女性成长小说与女权主义元小说;②讲述女性多重身份的种族、族裔、多文化杂糅女性小说;③挣脱女性身份束缚,拥抱创作自由的女性作家作品。这三类小说涵盖的创作主旨如下:一、围绕女性主体,叙述女性经历;二、找寻被历史遗忘的女性,发现女性的文学传统,建立属于女性的文学正典与历史;三、反抗父权社会给女性安排的性别角色;四、摆脱男性凝视与白人至上的审美,根据种族与族裔文化,建立女性个人审美价值;五、将女性身份与种族/族裔身份结合,创造出属于自己种族/族裔的女性小说;六、摆脱性别限制,以平等身份与男性作家公平竞争,拥抱正典文学的多元性。

第一节 以女性视角改写传统文学——女性成长小说与女权主义元小说

盖尔·格林(Gayle Greene)将女权主义元小说视为20世纪70年代最具影响力的女性写作类型:"书中女性主角指望在文学传统中找到现存问题的答案,推测'形式'(the forms)与她生活和写作的关系,寻找不同于传统安排的,即婚姻或死亡,'属于自己的结局',以及免于以往情节的自由"①。女权主义小说中的女性多与经典文学作品中的女性形成互文。她们以离经叛道的女性角色为榜样,却拒绝其榜样的悲惨结局。这些女性角色对既定社会角色的反抗与对自由的追寻大都体现在对传统家园空间的叛逃中。

女权主义小说强调对女性传统空间的反抗。一些西方启蒙运动理论对性别进行二元区分,由此划分两性所属的不同空间:男性是理性的、受教化的,属于公共场合,擅长政治与经济;女性是有依赖性的、柔弱的,需要受监护,适合相夫教子,属于闲适的家庭空间②。这般武断的区分将女性限制在家庭空间里,要求她们扮演"家中天使"(the angel in the house)的角色。二战之后,后现代与后结构主义提出移

① Greene, Gayle. "Ambiguous Benefits: Reading and Writing in Feminist Meta-fiction." Carol J. Singley & Susan Elizabeth Sweeney, eds., *Anxious Power: Reading, Writing, and Ambivalence in Narrative by Women*. Albany: State University of New York Press, 1993, p.315; Showalter, 2009, p.537.

② McDowell, Linda. "Place and Space." Mary Eagleton, ed., *A Concise Companion to Feminist Theory*. Oxford, U.K.: Blackwell Publishing, 2003, p.13.

动性(mobility)、杂糅性(hybridity)、游牧身份(nomadic identity)、边界(borderlands)构建,力求打破空间的单一性。同时,第二波女权主义者借用加斯东·巴什拉(Gaston Bachelard)对家园的定义,主张家园概念并非一成不变,而是流动的、多样的,为女权主义对传统家园空间的反抗打下了基础。

家园承载着其成员的记忆、人文活动、社会关系、家庭关系、两性关系,它会随着主体年龄、经历与想法的改变而改变,对不同的主体具有不同的意义。于女性,家园承载的关系中通常充斥着性别专制与不平等、对免费劳动力的压榨、暴力、恐惧、虐待①。因此,在女权小说中,部分女性通过私奔或离婚的形式挣脱家园的束缚,反抗传统的家庭模式。她们试图建立独属于女性的家园、社区、关系网与精神空间。

埃里卡·琼(Erica Jong)的女性成长小说《怕飞》(*Fear of Flying*, 1973)展示了当代女性成长小说的特性:"一些新的事情正在发生。女性开始书写她们自己的生活,就好像她们的生活与男性的同等重要"②。书名中的"飞"代表性欲、独立、创造性、野心③等鲜少由女性表达的品质。《怕飞》的主角是二十九岁的曼哈顿犹太裔女诗人伊莎多拉·温(Isadora Wing),她试图以私奔的方式逃离自己一成不变的生活。然而,私奔的无疾而终宣告温对新的家园空间与女性身份找寻失败。此外,返程途中遭受的性侵令她精神崩溃,她甚至无法找回其私奔前拥有的家园空间与女性身份。所幸,私奔途中获得的精神解放使温意识到自己遭受的一切痛苦本质上源于男性对女性身体的物化与剥削,并非全为自身之过,因此,她选择了自我接纳。其自我接纳的结局符合女性主义元小说特征,即对文学传统中拥有相似经历的女性结局之反抗。在她能找到的、为数不多的女性榜样中,大部分渴望觉醒的女性角色最终都屈从于命运,不是退缩回丈夫的监管,为其生儿育女,就是难以忍受痛苦,选择自我了结④。

同样,玛丽莲·弗伦奇(Marilyn French)的小说《醒来的女性》(*The Women's Room*, 1977)以空间为名,讲述米拉(Mira)在传统家庭空间中所受的剥削。米拉的丈夫不支持其上学,认为那些知识与经验对她毫无作用,并用大量的家务将她困在了家里。米拉对此选择反抗,丈夫也因此与她离婚。生活的剧变对米拉打击极大,一度使她与大多失去妻子身份和家园空间的女性一样,在绝望中选择自我了结。幸运的是,其女性好友玛莎(Martha)恰好上门拜访,及时将她救下。米拉在玛莎的鼓励下重振旗鼓,决定重返校园。由女性构成的关系网与精神家园使米拉得以避免文学传统中女性的悲剧式结局。

与此同时,弗伦奇在《醒来的女性》中提及她对经典文学结局的幻想。她认为莎剧中的李尔王最后变成了一个成天胡言乱语的老疯子,坐在里根家的炉火边,对着燕麦粥流口水;罗密欧与茱丽叶虽然结婚生子,但是因为茱丽叶想重返校园读研,罗密欧却想住进新墨西哥的某个社区,两人分道扬镳;茶花女在波尔多开了一家小旅馆,生意还不错⑤。弗伦奇认为,婚姻不是一部女性成长小说的结束,而是开始,传统小说的结尾其实诉说着另一个故事的开端。《怕飞》与《醒来的女性》都试图拆解传统文学的剧情设计,拒绝典型角色的固有结局。

此外,格雷斯·佩利(Grace Paley)也表达了对三段式传统剧情,即开头、展开、结局的反抗。其小说集《最后一刻的巨大变化》(*Enormous Changes at the Last Minute*, 1974)的 17 个短故事中,有 11 个

① McDowell, 2003, p.15.

② Templin, Charlotte. *Feminism and the Politics of Literary Reputation: The Example of Erica Jong*. Lawrence: University Press of Kansas, 1995, p.29.

③ Showalter, 2009, p.540.

④ Ibid., pp.540 - 541.

⑤ French, Marilyn. *The Women's Room*. New York: Penguin Books, 2009, p.137.

故事都出现了没有丈夫，或是不提及丈夫的女性角色。短故事之一“与我父亲的一次谈话”（A Conversation with My Father）中，佩利借着费丝（Faith）之口传达自己对一成不变的传统剧情的鄙视：“剧情把所有的希望都拿走了。所有人，真实的、虚构的，都值得拥有不被剧情束缚的命运。”①

1992年，简·斯迈利凭借小说《一千英亩》获得普利策小说奖。《一千英亩》对莎士比亚的经典悲剧《李尔王》（*King Lear*，1606）进行颠覆性改写，将李尔王的故事转移到美国艾奥瓦州的一座农场，并以原型为《李尔王》中恶毒姐姐贡纳莉（Goneril）的吉妮（Ginny）的视角，揭露其父对三位女儿的压榨与侵犯。斯迈利的小说大多传达出对充斥着白人男性偏见的文学传统的不屑与挑战，而《一千英亩》的获奖证明其女权小说在文学性上获得的认可不亚于当时以男性视角为主调的主流文学。以女性视角改写传统文学不仅成为当代美国女性小说的一大特点，还挑战了此前近乎被白人男性视角统治的文学传统，使得文学正典更加多元。

第二节　女性的多重身份——种族、族裔、多文化杂糅女性小说

20世纪40年代至60年代开展的民权运动中，由美籍非裔男性书写的反抗文学时常不自觉地透露出对女性的物化与歧视。因此，在民权运动后，部分非裔女权主义者逐渐脱离男性民权斗士阵营，转而专注于自身经验，将自己描绘为“自治主体”（autonomous subjects）②。她们开始挖掘非裔女性的生活，使用非裔方言写作，以女性视角重温非裔的历史。但同时，非裔女权主义者意识到她们无法抛弃自身的非裔特征，加入以白人女性利益为重的女权主义阵营。部分白人女权主义者也察觉她们在这运动中仅仅考虑了中产阶级白人女性的利益，对非裔及其他族裔女性的权益提及太少。第二波女权主义浪潮对少数族裔女性的忽视使女权主义“为所有女性发声”的概念站不住脚，第三波女权主义浪潮随之顺势而起。第三波女权主义浪潮发起于20世纪80年代，强调差异性（difference）与交错性（intersectionality），将种族看成一个重要分类，也尝试分开对待不同族裔的女性所拥有的不同经历，因为“女性没有共同的过去”③。

托妮·莫里森在《最蓝的眼睛》中揭示了白人审美对非裔女性造成的审美误导，尤其是对正在形成审美观念的非裔少女造成的伤害。白人资本赞助的商业广告使非裔少女们将白人长相定为审美标准，认为蓝眼睛、金头发、白皮肤最美丽。书中的佩科拉（Pecola）由于肤色过深认为自己很丑陋。这样的认知不仅来源于佩科拉身边白人商业的广告宣传，也源于她的家庭环境：佩科拉的母亲对她很冷漠，却对雇主家的白人女孩宠爱有加。因此，佩科拉一直祈祷可以拥有一双蓝眼睛。眼睛在书中具有象征意义，代表凝视与征服。拥有美丽的眼睛可以让佩科拉具备反凝视的力量④。小说呼应了非裔赋权运动

---

① Showalter, 2009, p.565.

② Cudjoe, Selwyn R. “Maya Angelou: The Autobiographical Statement Updated.” Henry Louis Gates, Jr. ed., *Reading Black, Reading Feminist*. New York: Meridian, 1990, pp.282－283.

③ Cowman, Krista & Jackson, Louise A. “Time.” Mary Eagleton, ed., *A Concise Companion to Feminist Theory*. Oxford, U.K.: Blackwell Publishing, 2003, p.39.

④ Scott, Lynn. “Beauty, Virtue and Disciplinary Power: A Foucauldian Reading of Toni Morrison's *The Bluest Eye*.” *Midwestern Miscellany* 24, 1996, pp.9－23.

(Black Empowerment Movement)的主旨,“黑色即美丽”(Black is Beautiful)的口号同样意在扭转白人至上的审美。

《最蓝的眼睛》主要展现了对非裔女性的同情,但是莫里森也对非裔男性示以同情。她同样透露出对佩科拉的父亲乔利(Cholly)的怜悯。即使乔利侵犯了佩科拉,莫里森依然坚持强调乔利对女儿的爱,声称他由于对女儿的痛苦现状无能为力,被迫走向极端。莫里森对非裔男性与女性的同等怜悯说明她对自己非裔身份的强调。虽然莫里森以黑人女性的身份创作,但是她坚持族裔比性别更加重要,认为非裔女性的文学与白人女性的文学不同:非裔女性不像白人女性,白人女性由于受到良好的保护,从未感受过外界的攻击与侵犯。非裔女性由于遭受种族歧视,从小对攻击与侵略习以为常。因此,非裔女性可以将家园与冒险结合在一起,“她们既是港湾也是渔船,既是小酒馆也是道路。我们,非裔女性,两者皆占”[①]。

艾丽斯·沃克的《紫颜色》同样将种族矛盾立于性别矛盾之上。小说前半部分充斥着丈夫与妻子的矛盾,如某某先生(Mr. ________)对西丽(Celie)的行为暴力及言语暴力,某某先生之子哈波(Harpo)以暴力驯服妻子索菲亚(Sophia)的尝试。然而,这样的性别矛盾在索菲亚因为种族矛盾被镇长关押入狱后悄然消解。所有知道消息的同族都因此愤怒,也因这股共同的愤怒放下个人矛盾,团结一心,为营救索菲亚出谋划策。在此之后,某某先生开始反思自己,最终向西丽道歉,两人成为了朋友。哈波及其新女友也与索菲亚开始和平相处,小说前半部分产生的性别矛盾从而得以和解。

沃克在她的作品集《寻找我们母亲的花园》(*In Search of Our Mother's Gardens*, 1983)中提出“妇女主义”(Womanism[②])的概念。“妇女主义”是对以白人女性为中心的女权主义的补充,强调女性的精神力量与精神联系。在沃克的描述中,妇女主义者是“一个非裔女权主义者或有色人种女权主义者……一位爱其他女性的女性,无论是不是与性取向相关。欣赏并偏向女性文化、女性的情绪弹性(将眼泪视为笑声的平衡)、女性的力量。有时候爱个别男人,无论是不是与性取向相关。投身于全部人类的生存与完整性,男性与女性。不是分裂主义者,除非偶尔这样做,作为精神释放。爱音乐。爱舞蹈。爱月亮。爱灵魂。爱爱本身、食物、圆形。爱苦难。爱人类。爱她自己。无论何时”[③]。妇女主义强调对种族、阶级、性向的包容以及无差别的爱。对沃克而言,妇女主义对于白人女权主义,就像“紫色对于薰衣草一样不可或缺”[④]。

妇女主义的理念顺应当时文化战争提出的“多元文化论”(multiculturalism)。文化战争的战场主要在人文学术界。革新派提出扩展大学课程的文化与种族多样性,将女性、少数群体、种族、族裔性、移民文化都纳入研究范围,因为它们都是美国文化历史的一部分。虽然多元文化论没有发展成文学运动,但在其影响下,身份背景为少数群体或跨文化的女性作家数量激增,如墨西哥裔、亚裔、阿拉伯裔女性作家等。这些女性族裔作家通过描绘家庭矛盾,揭示移民人口后代在族裔文化与美国主流文化双重挤压下的身份认知危机。知名女性族裔小说作家有桑德拉·希斯内罗丝、谭恩美、任璧莲、芭拉蒂·穆克吉、路

---

① Tate, Claudia. "Morrison." *Black Women Writers at Work*. England: Oldcastle Books, 1989, p.125; Showalter, 2009, pp. 545 - 546.

② Womanism 有时也被译成非裔女权主义。

③ Walker, Alice. *In Search of Our Mother's Gardens: Womanist Prose*. New York: Harcourt Brace Jovanovich, 1983, pp. xi - xii.

④ Ibid., p. xxi.

易斯·厄德里克、茱帕·拉希丽(Jhumpa Lahiri)等。[①]

第三节　挣脱女性身份的束缚——女性小说的无限可能

女性小说从不局限于女权主义。在当代女权主义浪潮刚掀起之时，一些女性作家就认为女权主义把所有女性作家扔进了同一个刻板印象里，淡化了个人不同的经历、风格、写作目的。辛西娅·欧芝克(Cynthia Ozick)在文章《文学与性政治：异议》(*Literature and the Politics of Sex: A Dissent*, 1983)中反对当代女权主义对自己的标签化与政治化，强调自己的创作自由："我写作的时候是自由的。我是任何一种我想要成为的作家。我可以把自己当成一位男性、一位女性、一块石头、一滴雨水、一块木头、一个西藏人、一根仙人掌的刺"[②]。

玛丽莲·罗宾逊对女权主义浪潮充满欣赏，并认为无论男性还是女性都受惠于此。但同时，她希望写出一本关于女性，却无关女权主义的小说，认为那才是终极女权(ultimate feminism)："当你可以放下女权的范畴书写女性，不是好像在写一些次要的、有污点的人种，而是简简单单的人类"[③]。罗宾逊认为，女性的自身魅力足以让她们成为受欢迎的小说角色。她希望写出一本只有女性角色，但是男性也会爱看的文学作品，这一想法在《管家》(*Housekeeping*, 1980)中实现。

《管家》一书展示了女性可以选择的不同道路。露西尔(Lucille)甘于做一个普通少女，拥有并守护属于自己的女性传统家园。她无法忍受姨妈西尔维(Sylvie)把家中弄得乱七八糟，因此最终选择离开家人，与自己的家政老师一起生活。露丝(Ruth)则在西尔维的带领下，逐渐培养出反叛精神，最后和西尔维一起逃离老房子与家乡，选择流浪。

女权主义小说的故事背景大多围绕美国东北部，非裔女权主义小说大多发生在美国南部，而崇尚创作自由的女性作家不受地域限制，她们笔下的故事可以发生在任何地方。玛丽莲·罗宾逊的《管家》发生在美国西北部爱达荷州的一个虚构小镇——指骨镇。安妮·普鲁的数部小说也以美国西部为背景，并认为人们对西部的英雄幻想言过其实[④]。她的小说《船讯》则主要描绘了加拿大的纽芬兰岛。

普鲁并不认为自己的作品属于传统女性小说(women's writing)范畴，因为她可以轻易地在男性视角与女性视角间切换。对普鲁来说，"作家可以写她/他想写的任何事、任何性别、任何地点"[⑤]。她选择男性作为小说主角主要是因为她的小说情节发生在较早的时期，在尊重历史背景的前提下，男性角色可以合法合理地做到更多女性角色做不到的事。但普鲁笔下的女性绝非做不了事的柔弱角色，在她的短篇小说集《好吧，就这样》(*Fine Just the Way It Is*, 2008)中，普鲁讲述了怀俄明州女性的艰苦生活。在

---

① Showalter, 2009, pp.585 - 586.

② Ozick, Cynthia. "Literature and the Politics of Sex: A Dissent." *Art and Ardor: Essays by Cynthia Ozick*. New York: Knopf, 1983, p.285; Showalter, 2009, p.568.

③ Maguire, James H. "Marilynne Robinson." *Dictionary of Literary Biography 206: Twentieth-Century American Western Writers*, ed. Richard H. Cracroft. Farming-ton, Mich.: The Gale Group, 1999, pp.251 - 260; Showalter, 2009, p.577.

④ Showalter, 2009, p.621.

⑤ Kanner, Ellen. "After the Pulitzer Prize-winning *Shipping News*, a Story of the Immigrant Experience." interview with Annie Proulx, August 31, 1997; Showalter, 2009, p.603.

以男性为主角的《船讯》中，每一个女性角色都意志坚定、个性鲜明，对男主角的人生道路产生不同的影响。

女性作家创作自由的实现代表着文学市场已经完全向女性敞开怀抱。那些曾经独属于女性的内部隐喻与象征如今已成为了美国英语词典的一部分。据纽约时报（*The New York Times*，1997.03.17）报道，小说市场70～80%的买家都是女性。女性读者对阅读市场的占领使无论男性作家还是女性作家都更加注重对女性角色的人物刻画，以满足大多读者希望看到作品中包含强大女性角色的需求。

当然，逐渐女性化的文学市场也带来了一些弊端。文学批评家开始担心文学成为女性，尤其是家庭主妇特有的消遣，阅读行为被打上女性化的烙印①，成为男性不必保持的习惯。随着新媒体、互联网的普及，纸质阅读的生存空间被挤压，传统文学的地位进一步受到挑战。女性文学如何做出调整，在全球化、互联网化、娱乐至上的世界中立足，吸引所有性别读者，是一个值得思考的问题。

第四节 主要作家介绍与代表作品选读

一、玛丽莲·弗伦奇

（一）玛丽莲·弗伦奇简介

玛丽莲·弗伦奇（Marilyn French，1929—2009）是美国小说家，也是激进女权主义者。弗伦奇出生于纽约布鲁克林，来自第三代波兰移民家庭。自幼年起，弗兰奇的母亲就是家中的主导人物，弗兰奇由此学会不屈从于男性权威。弗兰奇于1950年结婚，于1951年取得霍夫斯特拉学院（今霍夫斯特拉大学，Hofstra University）哲学与英语文学学士学位。此后，她生了两个孩子，并一直供其丈夫读法学院。1964年，弗伦奇返回霍夫斯特拉学院学习，取得硕士学位，并留校担任讲师。1967年，弗伦奇与丈夫离婚，前往哈佛大学学习，并于5年后取得博士学位，学位论文主题为乔伊斯（James Joyce）的《尤利西斯》。

从哈佛毕业后，弗伦奇在伍斯特圣十字学院（College of the Holy Cross in Worcester）任教四年，担任英语文学助理教授，并开始研究父权与女性历史。凯特·米利特（Kate Millet）的《性政治》（*Sexual Politics*，1970）成为其女权主义思想启蒙，失败的婚姻以及女儿18岁时遭受的性侵更促使其女权主义思想的成长。同时，她以玛拉·索沃斯卡（Mara Solwoska）的笔名撰写了不少论文。

1977年，弗伦奇出版了她的第一部，也是最负盛名的一部小说——《醒来的女性》。小说影射了她自己的生活：不被丈夫支持学业的太太离婚后重新进入校园，女儿遭受的性侵致使母亲走向极端女权主义。这部备受争议的小说被翻译成20多种语言，并售卖出两千多万份。她之后的小说《流血的心》（*The Bleeding Heart*，1980）、《她母亲的女儿》（*Her Mother's Daughter*，1987）、《我们的父亲》（*Our Father*，1994）、《我与乔治的夏天》（*My Summer with George*，1996）等都着重描写二战后女性在婚姻中

① Showalter，2009，p.605.

受到的压迫，这使她成为了一名社会性别问题的意见领袖。

弗伦奇在其出版的论文集《莎士比亚对经历的分隔》(*Shakespeare's Division of Experience*, 1981)中声称，一直以来，女性的生育能力都将其与自然结盟，而男性总有着战胜并征服自然的冲动，因此，男性总是试图征服女性，而女性容易受到男性的压迫。在《对抗女人的战争》(*The War Against Women*, 1992)中，弗伦奇以全球化的视野研究历史中女性所受的迫害，比如非洲毁坏女性生殖器的仪式、印度焚烧新娘的习俗、男女的贫富差距。她认为女性被父权社会压抑了个性，丧失了本该拥有的社会权益与个人自由。

1995年，弗伦奇出版了荷兰语作品《从夏娃到黎明：一段女性的历史》(*From Eve to Dawn: A History of Women*, 1995)，该书于2002年被翻译成英语。这部小说检阅了思想文化史如何将女性排斥在外，否认了她们的历史、现在、未来。所以，女权主义者应当自己挖掘并书写女性的历史。

2009年5月2日，弗伦奇在曼哈顿因心力衰竭去世，享年79岁。

(二)《醒来的女性》简介

《醒来的女性》以米拉为中心，描绘了20世纪60年代的女性群像。米拉是哈佛大学的学生，骨子里是自由派的作风，毫不避讳地与他人公开讨论传统道德、宗教、两性相关的话题，也因此在校园里名声不佳。在与男友兰尼(Lanny)出现分歧后，兰尼将米拉带去酒吧后丢下了她。被认定为“无主之物”的米拉险些被轮奸，这让她开始畏惧独立女性的身份，屈服于传统，最后与认识不久的诺姆(Norm)结了婚。

婚后，米拉离开学校，找了一份打字员的工作，以供诺姆攻读医学院。她想回学校，却被诺姆以资金不足和精力有限劝退。诺姆甚至在米拉怀孕后痛斥她毁掉了自己按部就班的生活，仿佛怀孕都是她一个人的错。米拉将全部精力奉献给家庭，然而诺姆认为她的辛苦是理所应当的：她住着自己买的房子，理应付出劳动。诺姆的压迫让米拉喘不过气，好在孩子们让她感受到了爱与安慰，可随着男孩子们逐渐长大，米拉与他们的联结也越来越弱。

除了孩子外，米拉所有的慰藉都来自周边的女性邻居。她们没有米拉的学历与教养，但是她们与米拉互相陪伴、聊天，支撑起了米拉的精神世界。对米拉来说，“她们对彼此的重要性远大于她们的丈夫。她不知道，没有彼此，她们能不能生存下去，她爱她们。”因此，即使后来布利斯(Bliss)为了与情夫私奔污蔑米拉，米拉也从未责怪过她，甚至在丈夫评判布利斯时为她辩护。并且，诺姆决定与米拉离婚的诱因之一就是米拉不顾他的反对，执意出钱帮助萨曼莎(Samantha)还房贷，米拉为了她的女性朋友违背了他的权威。

离婚后，米拉在女性朋友的鼓励下，回到哈佛继续自己未完成的学业，在那里结识不少婚姻破裂后回到学校的女性，并与热衷于参加各类社会维权小组的瓦尔(Val)建立了友谊。在与朋友们的相处中，米拉逐渐找回自己的女性意识，摆脱了他人对自己女性身份所施加的枷锁。然而，在瓦尔的女儿被非裔男性性侵，瓦尔却无法在法庭上保护自己的女儿免受歧视与羞辱后，瓦尔觉得性别歧视远大于种族歧视与其他不公正，因此彻底转变为极端女权，与米拉分道扬镳。

“醒来的女性”并无法完全翻译出原标题的深意。原标题(The Women's Room)指向多层空间。首先，它可以指代女洗手间，也就是小说开头米拉所处的空间。女士洗手间是女权主义者们最热衷于张贴宣传海报与口号的地方，其一是因为在此的女性一定有独处的空间与时间去注意到这些标语，其二是因为这是当时少数往墙上贴东西不会被撕掉的地方。同时，女洗手间与女性的月经息息相关。在文中，月经代表性觉醒、私密，伴随着腐败的味道与男性嫌恶的目光，米拉一度因此认为自己是污秽的。

其次，它可以是一间供女性聚集的房间。小说中存在着不少这样的房间，功能不一，氛围不一。例如，家庭主妇们频繁举办的派对中存在一间供女性聊天的房间。在跳舞前，男士和女士由于没有共同话题，会在不同的房间聊天，免得相互打扰。在平日，这些女士也会相聚在一起聊天，打发时光。

此外，第三章中，莉莉（Lily）被其丈夫送进精神病医院，玛莎（Martha）进过精神病医院，特里萨（Theresa）一直被关在那里，罗杰（Roger）与多丽丝（Doris）认为米拉有精神病。弗伦奇笔下的精神病院关押的大多数病人都是丈夫眼中不称职的妻子。精神病院似乎成为了惩治不听话女性的空间。

最后，"room"一词可以指向抽象空间，也就是女性的精神空间。米拉和丈夫搬去了更大的房子，他们拥有了更多间房间，甚至拥有了四间厕所，但米拉反而觉得自己拥有的"空间"变少了，因为她的时间被更多的家务塞满了，也无法再像从前那样随便走到相熟的邻居家坐下聊天。她认为自己开始下沉。她与其他女性建立的精神羁绊也可以称得上是女性共同的精神空间，因此女性朋友的分道扬镳也使米拉的空间更加狭窄。

值得注意的是，米拉所处的大多空间依然主要由白人构成。她是一个自由主义者，但除了朋友家的女佣，并没有接触过其他黑人，也没有接触过什么印第安人、墨西哥裔或是东方人。因此，她保留了白人的一部分偏见。看到瓦尔的非裔朋友巴特（Bart）与白人朋友格兰特（Grant）假意争执时，米拉下意识觉得巴特会抽出一把刀把她们都杀了。并且，她对巴特的触碰感到恐惧，认为如果换成一个白人男性，自己并不会拥有这样的感觉。她意识到了自己的偏见，认为其原因在于她对有色人种的陌生感，也希望自己可以克服这些偏见。米拉的反应影射了当时女权主义的不完善性，也为第三波女权主义浪潮就种族问题、族裔性与多样性对女权主义发起挑战做出了铺垫。

（三）作品选读：《醒来的女性》①

1

...

Mira debated. She would like to have the house, of course: she too had wanted material success. But it frightened her. She felt she was sinking, sinking—into what she wasn't sure. Norm's parents were proud of their son: to be able to own a house like that at only thirty-seven! But they were also a bit anxious: he wasn't getting himself too far in debt now, was he? Paying off the new partnership, buying the house and another car too. They glanced significantly at Mira. She was an ambitious driving woman, she supposed, in their eyes. She no longer cared what they thought, but the injustice nevertheless scratched her. Her own parents were more enthusiastic: Mira had really done well for herself, marrying a man who could afford a house like that.

Mira sank. She was thirty when they moved to Beau Reve.

2

Yes, I know, you think you see it all. Having shown you the nasty underside of life in the

---

① French, Marilyn. *The Women's Room*. New York: Penguin Books, 2009, pp.131 - 141.

young, struggling white middle class, I will now show you the nasty underside of life in the older, affluent, white middle class. You are a bit chagrined. I start you off at Harvard, in the middle of an exciting period full of young exciting people with new ideas, only to drag you through an afternoon of soap opera. I'm sorry. Really. If I knew any exciting adventure tales, I'd write them, I assure you. If I think of any as we go, I'll be glad to insert them. There were important things happening during the years just described: there was the Berlin Wall, John Foster Dulles, Castro, who was the darling of the liberals until he shot all those people (having read his Machiavelli) and became suddenly the devil. And a senator of less than national fame took the Democratic nomination and forced Lyndon Johnson to go along with him.

Sometimes I get as sick of writing this as you may be at reading it. Of course, you have an alternative. I don't. I get sick because, you see, it's all true, it happened, and it was boring and painful and full of despair. I think I would not feel so bad about it if it had ended differently. Of course, I can't talk about ends, since I am still alive. But I would have a different slant on things, perhaps, if I were not living in this inconsolable loneliness. And that is an insoluble problem. I mean, you could go up to a stranger on the street and say. "I am inconsolably lonely," and he might take you home with him and introduce you to his family and ask you to stay for dinner. But that wouldn't help. Because loneliness is not a longing for company, it is a longing for kind. And kind means people who can see you who you are, and that means they have enough intelligence and sensitivity and patience to do that. It also means they can accept you, because we don't see what we can't accept, we blot it out, we jam it hastily in one stereotypic box or another. We don't want to look at something that might shake up the mental order we've so carefully erected. I have respect for this desire to keep one's psyche unviolated. Habit is a good thing for the human race. For instance, have you ever traveled from place to place, spending no more than a day or two in each? You wake up in the morning a bit unnerved, and every day you have to search for where you put your toothbrush last night, and figure out whether you unpacked your comb and brush. Every morning you have to decide where to have your *café* and croissant, or your *cappuccino* or *kawa*. You even have to find the right word. I said *si* for two weeks after I entered France from Italy, and *oui* for two weeks after I entered Spain from France. And that's an easy enough word to get right. You have to spend so much energy just getting through the day when you have no habits that you don't have any left for productive labor. You get that glazed look of tourists staring up at one more church and checking the guidebook to see what city they're in. Each day you arrive in a new place you have to spend two or more hours finding a decent cheap hotel: subsisting becomes the whole of life.

Well, you see what I mean. Every new person you meet and really take in violates your psyche to some degree. You have to juggle your categories to fit the person in. Here where I am, people see me some way—I don't know exactly how. Middle-aged matron, rabid feminist, nice lady, madwoman: I don't know. But they can't see me who I am. So I'm lonely. I guess maybe I wouldn't be able to say who I am myself. One needs some reflection from the outside to get an image of oneself. Sometimes, when I am really low, the words of Pyotr Stephanovich come into my mind: You must love God because He is the only one you can love for Eternity. That sounds very profound to me, and tears come into my eyes whenever I say it. I never heard anyone else say it. But I don't believe in God and if I did I couldn't love Him/Her/It. I couldn't love anyone I thought had created this world.

Oh God. (Metaphorically speaking.) So people handle loneliness by putting themselves into something larger than they are, some framework or purpose. But those big exterior things—I don't know, they just don't seem as important to me as what Norm said to Mira or Bliss to Adele. I mean, do you really care about 1066? Val would scream that it was significant, but my students don't care about 1066. They don't even care about World War II or the Holocaust. They don't even remember Jean Arthur. For them, Elvis Presley is part of the quaint, irrelevant past. No, it's the little things that mater. But when you're dealing with a lot of insignificant lives, how do you put things together? When you look back on your life, are there places where you can put your finger, like crossroads on a map or a scholar's crux in Shakespeare, where you can say, "There! That is the place where everything changed, the word upon which everything hinged!"

I find that difficult. I feel like a madwoman. I walk around my apartment, which is a shithouse, full of landlord's odds and ends of leftover furniture and a few dying plants on the windowsills. I talk to myself, myself, myself. Now I am smart enough to provide a fairly good running dialogue, but the problem is there's no response, no voice but mine. I want to hear another's truth, but I insist it be a truth. I talk to the plants but they shrivel and die.

I wanted my life to be a work of art, but when I try to look at it, it swells and shrinks like the walls you glean in a delirious daze. My life sprawls and sags, like an old pair of baggy slacks that still, somehow, fits you.

Like Mira, Val, and lots of others, I went back to the university late in life. I went with despair and expectations. It was a new life. It was supposed to revitalize you, to send you radiant to new planes of experience where you would get tight with Beatrice Portinari and be led to an earthly paradise. In literature, new lives, second chances, lead to visions of the City of God. But I have been suspecting for a while now that everything I ever read was lies. You can believe the first four acts, but not the fifth. Lear really turned into a babbling old fool drooling over his oatmeal and happy for a place by the fire in Regan's house in Scarsdale. Hamlet took over the corporation by bribing the board and ousting Claudius, and then took to wearing a black leather jacket and German Army boots and sending out proclamations that everyone would refrain from fornication upon pain of death. He wrote letters to his cousin Angelo and together they decided to purify the whole East Coast, so they have joined with the Mafia, the Marines, and the CIA to outlaw sex. Romeo and

Juliet marry and have some kids, then separate when she wants to go back to graduate school and he wants to go live on a commune in New Mexico. She is on welfare now and he has long hair and an Indian headband and says *Oooom* a lot.

Camille lives: she runs a small popular hotel in Bordeaux. I've met her. She has bleached blond hair, thick orange makeup, and a hard mouth, and she knows everything about the price of vermouth, clean sheets, bottled orange drink, and certain available female bodies. She's thicker all around than she used to be, but she still has a shape. She meanders around in a shiny pale blue pantsuit, and sits in her bar laughing with friends and keeping an eye out for Bernard, the married man who is her latest lover. Except for her passion for Bernard, she is tough and fun. Don't ask what it is about Bernard that makes her so adore him. It is not Bernard, but love itself. She believes in love, goes on believing in it against all odds. Therefore, Bernard is a little bored. It is boring to be adored. At thirty-eight, she should be tough and fun, not adoring. When he leaves her, a month or two from now, she will contemplate suicide. Whereas, if she had been able to bring herself to stop believing in love, she would have been tough and fun and he would have adored her forever. Which would have bored her. She then would have had to be the one to tell him to clear out. It is a choice to give one pause.

Tristan and lsolde got married after Issy got a divorce from Mark, who was anyhow turned on to a groupie at that point. And they discovered the joys of comfortable marriage can't hold a candle to the thrill of taboo, so they have placed an ad in the Boston *Phoenix* asking for a third, fourth, or even fifth party of any gender to join them in tasting taboo joys. They will smoke, they will even snort a little coke, just to assure a degree of fear about being intruded upon by the local police. Don't judge: they, at least, are trying to hold their marriage together. And you?

The problem with the great literature of the past is that it doesn't tell you how to live with real endings. In the great literature of the past you either get married and live happily ever after, or you die. But the fact is, neither is what actually happens. Oh, you do die, but never at the right time, never with great language floating all around you, and a whole theater full of witnesses to your agony. What actually happens is that you do get married or you don't, and you don't live happily ever after, but you do live. And that's the problem. I mean, think about it. Suppose Antigone had lived. An Antigone who goes on being an Antigone year after year would be not only ludicrous but a bore. The cave and the rope are essential.

It isn't just the endings. In a real life, how can you tell when you're in Book I or Book Ⅲ, or Act Ⅱ or Act Ⅴ? No stagehands come charging in to haul down the curtain at an appropriate moment. So how do I know whether I'm living in the middle of Act Ⅲ and heading toward a great climax, or at the end of Act Ⅴ and finished? I don't even know who I am. I might be Hester Prynne, or Dorothea Brooke, or I might be the heroine of a TV drama of some seasons back—what was her name?—Mrs. Muir! Yes, she walked on the beach and was in love with a ghost and originally she looked like Gene Tierney. I always wanted to look like Gene Tierney. I sit in the chair and I have no one to knit woolen stockings for so it's irrelevant that I don't know how to knit. (Val could, oddly. Nothing works the way it does in books. Can you imagine Penthesilea knitting?) I'm just sitting here living out even to the edge of doom—what? Valerie's vision? Except she forgot to tell me what comes next.

3

MIRA HAD a new life. It was supposed to be glorious, it was supposed to be what all those hard years in the two- or three-room apartments were for. This was what it was all about. Norm had worked hard for long hours, so had she: for this. Not everyone who worked hard for long hours achieved this; they were lucky. She had her own car—Norm's old one; he bought a new little MG for himself—and a house with four bathrooms. She also had (after some wrestling with her conscience and some tense discussion with Norm, who did not want to say straight out that he did not want to pay for help in the house, so said instead that they could only get a colored woman and she would no doubt rob them blind—as if they had anything to steal) a washer-dryer, a dishwasher, a man to wax the kitchen floor every two weeks, and a laundry to do the sheets and Norm's shirts. Never again, frozen sheets in January.

She told herself this as she paced the large, mostly empty rooms. She stood in the wide foyer, with its impressive chandelier and the winding staircase, and told herself she must be happy, she had to be. She had no other choice: there was a moral imperative on her to be happy. She was not actively unhappy. She was just—nothing.

The rhythms of life were different in Beau Reve. She would get up at seven with Norm, and make coffee while he showered and shaved. He no longer ate breakfast at home. She would sit with him over the coffee for a few minutes while he gave her her chores for the day—suits to be cleaned, shoes to be mended, some business at the bank, a telephone call to the insurance agent about the dent in his car. Then he left and she woke the children, who dressed as she prepared their eggs. She dressed as they ate them, then she drove them the mile to the school bus stop. Everyone but Norm was grouchy in the morning and they spoke little. Then she returned to the house.

That was the worst time. She would come in through the door from the garage to the kitchen and the house would smell of bacon and toast. The greasy frying pan sat on the stove, the spattered coffeepot behind it. Dirty dishes lay on the kitchen table. The four beds were unmade and there was soiled underwear lying about. There was dust in the living and dining rooms, the family room held used soda glasses and potato chip crumbs from the night before.

What bothered her was not that the tasks that had to be done were exerting. It was not even that they were tedious. It was that she felt that the three others lived their lives and she went around after them cleaning up their mess. She was an unpaid servant, expected to do a superlative job. In return, she was permitted to call this house hers. But so did they. Most of the time she did not think about it: only every morning, when she returned from dropping the kids at the bus. She made up little rewards for herself: I will do this and that, then I will sit and read the paper. She charged into it, sticking a batch of wash in the machine, cleaning the kitchen, making up beds and straightening rooms, and then attacked the rest of the house, in which something had to be done every day, it was so big. Down on her hands and knees in one of the endless bathrooms, she would tell herself that in a way she was fortunate, Washing the toilet used by three males, and the floor and walls around it, is, Mira thought, coming face to face with necessity. And that was why women were saner than men, did not come up with the mad, absurd schemes men developed: they were in touch with necessity, they had to wash the toilet bowl and floor. She kept telling herself that.

About eleven thirty, she made a fresh pot of coffee and sat down with *The New York Times*, which (another new luxury) she had delivered. She sat for an hour at least, savoring it. In the afternoon, she did her errands, or on days when there were no errands, she might visit Lily or Samantha or Martha. But she had to be home by three, when the boys got in. They were not yet old enough to be left alone. She didn't mind that too much, although it would have been nice, just once in a while, to feel free to stay out as long as she wanted. She didn't know what she would have done with such freedom—Lily's, Martha's, and Samantha's children came in around then too, and the women were involved with the children. It was just the feeling of freedom she craved. But she enjoyed talking to the boys when they got in. They were smart and funny, and she hugged them a lot. They would talk over a snack, then change their clothes and go out. She had another hour to herself. She would take the laundry out of the dryer and fold it carefully, patiently. She would take something out of the freezer to defrost. Then she would take a book and sit down. The boys ran in and out and she was frequently interrupted, so she read only light things in the afternoons. Then it was time to prepare dinner. Norm usually got in about six thirty, and nowadays they all ate together. But Norm continually picked on the boys at the dinner table: they were using the wrong fork, they had their elbows on the table, they were chewing with their mouths open. So dinnertime was always tense. Afterward, the boys would go off to do homework, Norm would settle in the family room with the paper, and Mira would clean up the kitchen. The boys took their own baths now, and all she had to do was remind them about it, keep track that they did it, and wash the tubs afterward. They would come in to watch TV for a while before bed, but they had to watch what Norm wanted to see. Once she insisted they be allowed to see a children's special, and Norm had sulked the rest of the night. She would sit with them, reading or mending. Then they would go to bed. Norm would sit for a while longer, and by ten he would be asleep in the chair. She would go over and shake him: "Norm, don't fall asleep in the chair." He would awake and stand and stumble groggily to the bedroom.

Then Mira would switch off the TV set. She was too tired now to read seriously, but she did not want to go to bed. She would pour a snifter of brandy and turn out all the lights and sit in the corner of the family room, by the window—sit and drink and smoke until eleven or twelve, then go to bed.

She was living the American Dream, she knew that, and she tried to get her mask on straight. She had her hair done at the right shop and when they saw gray and advised dye, she let them dye it. She bought expensive three-piece knit suits; she had her nails manicured. She had a holder full of charge cards.

There were moments of beauty. Sometimes, before she made the boys' beds, she would think about them, and love would gush into her heart, and she would lie down on their beds and smell the sheets, bury her face in them. Their beds smelled just like the boys. Sometimes, when she was having her coffee and reading her paper, the sun would slant in through the big kitchen window and pour across the wooden table and her heart would be still. And sometimes, dressed to go out, she would walk slowly through the large house and feel its cleanliness and order and would think that the comfort of order might after all be the best one could hope for, might even be enough.

She was not unhappy. She lived much through her friends, all of whom were having troubles. After listening to Lily or Sam or Martha all afternoon, it felt good to come home to her peaceful and orderly house. Given what she knew about others' lives, how could she complain about her own?

思考与讨论

(1) 搬家对米拉有着什么样的意义?

(2) 如何理解米拉与"美国梦"的关联?

(3) 在米拉的第三人称叙事中,弗伦奇偶尔会切换至第一人称讲述一些感受,这么做的效果是什么?

(4) 选文中多次出现的"孤独感"有什么意义?

(5) 选文中,弗伦奇以第一人称提及许多经典名著,并尝试改写它们的结局,如何看待这其中的互文性?

拓展阅读

[1] Elliott, J.K. "Time of Death: the End of the 1960s and the Problem of Feminist Futurity in *The Women's Room* and *Vida*." *Modern Fiction Studies*, vol.52, no.1, 2006, pp.143-168.

[2] French, Marilyn. "Preface." *The Women's Room*. New York: Penguin Books, 2009, pp. xxi-xxviii.

[3] Marshall, L. "The Women's Room." Frank N. Magill, ed., *Cyclopedia of Literary Characters 5*. Ipswich, Massachusetts: Salem Press, 2015, pp.2714-2715.

二、艾丽斯·沃克

(一) 艾丽斯·沃克简介

艾丽斯·沃克(Alice Walker, 1944—)是美国女性小说家、短篇故事作家、诗人、社会活动积极分子。哈罗德·布朗姆称其为当代文学界最具代表性的作家之一。沃克出生在美国佐治亚州的伊腾顿市(Eatonton),是家中的第八个孩子。8岁时,沃克的哥哥失误将她的右眼打伤,因救治不及时导致永久失明,留下的伤疤也让她自卑很久。在家人的鼓励下,沃克走出了心理阴影。她在文章《美丽:当另一位舞者是自我》(*Beauty: When the Other Dancers is the Self*)中记载了自己右眼留下的伤疤。

由于难以忍受吉姆·克劳法(Jim Crow laws),沃克的兄弟姊妹都试着逃离南方。沃克的姐姐梅蜜(Mamie)成为了一名研究殖民主义的学术专家,在欧洲、南美洲和非洲游历。然而,当梅蜜回家时,她无法再适应家里人的生活方式、说话方式、知识水平。受其影响,沃克的小说中饱含离开家园与背弃过去者的心理矛盾,这样的矛盾构成了她小说中的姐妹角色,如《紫颜色》中逃离父亲掌控,被姐夫赶走,后与牧师一家前往非洲传教的耐蒂(Nettie)。

沃克在家人的鼓励下发现了自己的文学才华。作为同级最优秀的学生,沃克拿着乔治亚州全额奖学金入学斯帕尔曼学院(Spelman College),后转学至纽约的莎拉·劳伦斯学院(Sarah Lawrence College)。沃克在莎拉·劳伦斯学院研读托尔斯泰、杜斯妥也夫斯基、加西亚·马尔克斯以及当代非洲小说家的作品,于1965年毕业。

毕业后,沃克前往肯尼亚参加国际生活实验(Experiment in International Living),并拜访了室友在乌干达的家人。返回美国后,她因跨种族恋爱意外怀孕,一度抑郁并产生了轻生的想法。其间,沃克的大学同学、诗人简·库柏(Jane Cooper)与穆里尔.鲁凯泽(Muriel Rukeyser)都为其提供大量支持与帮助。穆里尔·鲁凯泽将沃克介绍给了自己的文稿代理人莫妮卡·麦考尔(Monica McCall)。麦考尔后将沃克介绍给不少有名的作家,包括兰斯顿·休斯(Langston Hughes),并帮助她出版诗集《曾经》(*Once*)。然而,由于沃克除了在自己第一本短篇小说集的致谢中感谢鲁凯泽外,没有再公开感谢身为白人女性的鲁凯泽,引起了鲁凯泽的不满,两人因此决裂。沃克与鲁凯泽的矛盾是当时白人女权主义者与非裔女权主义者矛盾的缩影:一方期待感激与战友情;另一方憎恨无论是来自男性还是女性的恩赐态度(patronage/matronage)。

20世纪60年代末,受马丁·路德·金(Martin Luther King Jr.)影响,沃克搬去密西西比州杰克逊市,在美国全国有色人种协进会(National Association for the Advancement of Colored People/NAACP)工作,后以进驻作家的身份在杰克逊州立学院(Jackson State College)与陶格鲁学院(Tougaloo College)任教,并出版了自己的第一本小说,即《格兰奇·科普兰的第三次生命》(*The Third Life of Grange Copeland*, 1970)。1972年,沃克前往马萨诸塞州,开设了女性研究课程。这是美国最早的一批女性研究课程。

1982年,沃克凭借《紫颜色》成为第一个获得普利策小说奖的非裔女性。《紫颜色》同时得到美国国家图书奖与美国书评家协会奖。沃克在她的职业生涯中共出版了 17 部小说与短篇故事集、12 本非小说类文学作品、论文集以及诗集。沃克的作品大多聚焦于非裔，尤其是非裔女性，描述她们在充满种族歧视、性别歧视、暴力行为的社会中的生活。沃克的其他小说包括《梅丽迪恩》(*Meridian*, 1976)、《我灵物的圣殿》(*The Temple of My Familiar*, 1989)、《寻找那块绿色的石头》(*Finding the Green Stone*, 1991)、《拥有快乐的秘诀》(*Possessing the Secret of Joy*, 1992)、《在我父亲微笑的光芒下》(*By the Light of My Father's Smile*, 1998)、《前进之路伴随破碎之心》(*The Way Forward is With a Broken Heart*, 2000)、《现在是敞开心扉的时间》(*Now is the Time to Open Your Heart*, 2004)等。

(二)《紫颜色》简介

《紫颜色》以书信体的方式讲述了一对黑人姐妹，西丽与耐蒂的生活。故事发生在 20 世纪初期美国南部佐治亚州的乡村。西丽被她一直以来当做父亲的男人性侵后，生下了两个孩子。为此卧病在床、不明真相的母亲被活活气死。她的"父亲"处理掉了两个孩子后，强迫她辍学，把她丢给了本想娶耐蒂，有四个孩子的鳏夫。西丽称其为某某先生。西丽忍受着某某先生对她的嫌恶与打骂，只能向上帝写信，倾诉自己的痛苦。

耐蒂逃离"父亲"后来找西丽，但某某先生恼于她拒绝自己的调情，把她赶了出去，并扣下了耐蒂写来的所有讲述自己生活的信件。耐蒂离开后，在牧师塞缪尔(Samuel)家中干活，后来跟着他们去非洲传教，并发现牧师的两个孩子是西丽丢失的孩子。尽管耐蒂从未收到西丽的回信，但她依然坚持给西丽写信，并像西丽给上帝写信那样，将给姐姐写信视为自己的精神寄托。

某某先生将曾经的情人莎格(Shug)接回家养病，本想借此举动挑衅西丽，却没想到西丽喜欢上了莎格。她悉心照料莎格，使她恢复健康，两人因此成为了挚友。在莎格的帮助下，西丽找到某某先生藏起来的耐蒂的信，并因此决定离婚。离婚后，西丽与莎格去孟非斯打拼，开了一家裁缝铺谋生。她不再给上帝写信，而是给耐蒂写，两人都在作者的身份上又获得了读者的身份。在小说结尾，耐蒂带着西丽的两个孩子回到了美国，与西丽团聚。

《紫颜色》中的女权主义与族裔性密不可分。西丽一直羡慕索菲亚的勇敢与果断：某某先生的大儿子哈波想驯服妻子索菲亚，于是决定向父亲学习，用暴力驯服她，却被强壮的索菲亚揍得鼻青脸肿。索菲亚为哈波生了好几个孩子，在忍受不了哈波后毅然决然地离开他，开始新的生活。索菲亚的果敢彰显女权主义提倡的独立女性意识。同时，她与哈波几乎决裂，和哈波的新恋人玛丽·阿格纽斯(Mary Agnes)也两看相厌。然而，哈波与玛丽很快就放下了与索菲亚的矛盾。索菲亚因断然拒绝去镇长家当女佣，被镇长扇了一个耳光，她选择反击，但被警察关进了监狱。在监狱里，索菲亚被打瞎一只眼睛，肋骨断了，浑身浮肿，也失去了说话能力。西丽和玛丽想尽办法，最后靠着玛丽的关系成功将索菲亚从监狱里救了出来。索菲亚的经历让某某先生与哈波放下了由性别带来的矛盾，也让玛丽放下了个人恩怨，种族歧视让所有非裔克服性别冲突，一致对外。此外，索菲亚在获得自由后，不再像从前一样，拥有那股女权主义不屈服的女性精神，种族迫害剥夺了她大女子的勇敢与果断。由此可以看出，在沃克笔下，非裔女性的身份由族裔与性别同时建构，缺一不可。

(三) 作品选读:《紫颜色》[①]

Dearest Celie,

It was the funniest thing to stop over in Monrovia after my first glimpse of Africa, which was Senegal. The capital of Senegal is Dakar and the people speak their own language, Senegalese I guess they would call it, and French. They are the blackest people I have ever seen, Celie. They are black like the people we are talking about when we say, "So and so is blacker than black, he's *blue*black." They are so black, Celie, they shine. Which is something else folks down home like to say about real black folks. But Celie, try to imagine a city full of these shining, blueblack people wearing brilliant blue robes with designs like fancy quilt patterns. Tall, thin, with long necks and straight backs. Can you picture it at all, Celie? Because I felt like I was seeing black for the first time. And Celie, there is something magical about it. Because the black is so black the eye is simply dazzled, and then there is the shining that seems to come, really, from moonlight, it is so luminous, but their skin glows even in the sun.

But I did not really like the Senegalese I met in the market. They were concerned only with their sale of produce. If we did not buy, they looked through us as quickly as they looked through the white French people who live there. Somehow I had not expected to see any white people in Africa, but they are here in droves. And not all are missionaries.

There are bunches of them in Monrovia, too. And the president, whose last name is Tubman, has some in his cabinet. He also has a lot of white-looking colored men in his cabinet. On our second evening in Monrovia we had tea at the presidential palace. It looks very much like the American white house (where our president lives) Samuel says. The president talked a good bit about his efforts trying to develop the country and about his problems with the natives, who don't want to work to help build the country up. It was the first time I'd heard a black man use that word. I knew that to white people all colored people are natives. But he cleared his throat and said he only meant "native" to Liberia. I did not see any of these "natives" in his cabinet. And none of the cabinet members' wives could pass for natives. Compared to them in their silks and pearls, Corrine and I were barely dressed, let alone dressed for the occasion. But I think the women we saw at the palace spend a lot of their time dressing. Still, they look dissatisfied. Not like the cheery school teachers we saw only by chance, as they herded their classes down to the beach for a swim.

Before we left we visited one of the large cacoa plantations they have. Nothing but cacoa trees as far as the eye can see. And whole villages built right in the middle of the fields. We watched the weary families come home from work, still carrying their cacoa seed buckets in their hands (these double as lunch buckets next day), and sometimes—if they are women—their children on their

---

① Walker, Alice. *The Color Purple*. New York: Washington Square Press, 1983, pp.131 - 133, pp.245 - 248.

backs. As tired as they are, they sing! Celie. Just like we do at home. Why do tired people sing? I asked Corrine. Too tired to do anything else, she said. Besides, they don't own the cacoa fields, Celie, even president Tubman doesn't own them. People in a place called Holland do. The people who make Dutch chocolate. And there are overseers who make sure the people work hard, who live in stone houses in the corners of the fields.

Again I must go. Everyone is in bed and I am writing by lamp-light. But the light is attracting so many bugs I am being eaten alive. I have bites everywhere, including my scalp and the bottoms of my feet.

But—

Did I mention my first sight of the African coast? Something struck in me, in my soul, Celie, like a large bell, and I just vibrated. Corrine and Samuel felt the same. And we kneeled down right on deck and gave thanks to God for letting us see the land for which our mothers and fathers cried—and lived and died—to see again.

Oh, Celie! Will I ever be able to tell you all? I dare not ask, I know. But leave it all to God.

Your everloving sister, Nettie

Dear Nettie,

Mr. ________ talk to Shug a lot lately by telephone. He say as soon as he told her my sister and her family was missing, she and Germaine made a beeline for the State department trying to find out what happen. He say Shug say it just kill her to think I'm down here suffering from not knowing. But nothing happen at the State department. Nothing at the department of defense. It's a big war. So much going on. One ship lost feel like nothing, I guess. Plus, colored don't count to those people.

Well, they just don't know, and never did. Never will. And so what? I know you on your way home and you may not git here till I'm ninety, but one of these days I do expect to see your face.

Meanwhile, I hired Sofia to clerk in our store. Kept the white man Alphonso got to run it, but put Sofia in there to wait on colored cause they never had nobody in a store to wait on'em before and nobody in a store to treat'em nice. Sofia real good at selling stuff too cause she act like she don't care if you buy or not. No skin off her nose. And then if you decide to buy anyhow, well, she might exchange a few pleasant words with you. Plus, she scare that white man. Anybody else colored he try to call'em auntie or something. First time he try that with Sofia she ast him which colored man his mama sister marry.

I ast Harpo do he mind if Sofia work.

What I'm gon mind for? he say. It seem to make her happy. And I can take care of anything come up at home. Anyhow, he say, Sofia got me a little help for when Henrietta need anything special to eat or git sick.

Yeah, say Sofia. Miss Eleanor Jane gon look in on Henrietta and every other day promise to cook her something she'll eat. You know white people have a look of machinery in they kitchen. She whip up stuff with yams you'd never believe. Last week she went and made yam ice cream.

How this happen? I ast. I thought the two of you was through.

Oh, say Sofia. It finally dawn on her to ast her mama why I come to work for them.

I don't expect it to last, though, say Harpo. You know how they is.

Do her peoples know? I ast.

They know, say Sofia. They carrying on just like you know they would. Whoever heard of a white woman working for niggers, they rave. She tell them, Whoever heard of somebody like Sofia working for trash.

She bring Reynolds Stanley with her? I ast. Henrietta say she don't mind him.

Well, say Harpo, I'm satisfied if her menfolks against her helping you, she gon quit.

Let her quit, say Sofia. It not my salvation she working for. And if she don't learn she got to face judgment for herself, she won't even have live.

Well, you got me behind you, anyway, say Harpo. And I loves every judgment you ever made. He move up and kiss her where her nose was stitch.

Sofia toss her head. Everybody learn something in life, she say. And they laugh.

Speaking of learning, Mr. ________ say one day us was sewing out on the porch, I first start to learn all them days ago I use to sit up there on my porch, staring out cross the railing.

Just miserable. That's what I was. And I couldn't understand why us have life at all if all it can do most times is make us feel bad. All I ever wanted in life was Shug Avery, he say. And one while, all she wanted in life was me. Well, us couldn't have each other, he say. I got Annie Julia. Then you. All them rotten children. She got Grady and who know who all. But still, look like she come out better than me. A lot of people love Shug, but nobody but Shug love me.

Hard not to love Shug, I say. She know how to love somebody back.

I tried to do something bout my children after you left me. But by that time it was too late. Bub come with me for two weeks, stole all my money, laid up on the porch drunk. My girls so far off into mens and religion they can't hardly talk. Everytime they open they mouth some kind of plea come out. Near bout to broke my sorry heart.

If you know your heart sorry, I say, that mean it not quite as spoilt as you think.

Anyhow, he say, you know how it is. You ast yourself one question, it lead to fifteen. I start to wonder why us need love. Why us suffer. Why us black. Why us men and women. Where do children really come from. It didn't take long to realize I didn't hardly know nothing. And that if you ast yourself why you black or a man or a woman or a bush it don't mean nothing if you don't ast why you here, period.

So what you think? I ast.

I think us here to wonder, myself. To wonder. To ast. And that in wondering bout the big things and asting bout the big things, you learn about the little ones, almost by accident. But you never know nothing more about the big things than you start out with. The more I wonder, he say, the more I love.

And people start to love you back, I bet, I say.

They do, he say, surprise. Harpo seem to love me. Sofia and the children. I think even ole evil Henrietta love me a little bit, but that's cause she know she just as big a mystery to me as the man in the moon.

Mr. ________ is busy patterning a shirt for folks to wear with my pants.

Got to have pockets, he say. Got to have loose sleeves. And definitely you not spose to wear it with no tie. Folks wearing ties look like they being lynch.

And then, just when I know I can live content without Shug, just when Mr. ________ done ast me to marry him again, this time in the spirit as well as in the flesh, and just after I say Naw, I still don't like frogs, but let's us be friends, Shug write me she coming home.

Now. Is this life or not?

I be so calm.

If she come, I be happy. If she don't, I be content.

And then I figure this the lesson I was suppose to learn.

Oh Celie, she say, stepping out of the car, dress like a moving star, I missed you more than I missed my own mama.

Us hug.

Come on in, I say.

Oh, the house look so nice, she say, when us git to her room. You know I love pink.

Got you some elephants and turtles coming, too, I say.

Where your room? she ast.

Down the hall, I say.

Let's go see it, she say.

Well, here it is, I say, standing in the door. Everything in my room purple and red cept the floor, that painted bright yellow. She go right to the little purple frog perch on my mantlepiece.

What this? she ast.

Oh, I say, a little something Albert carve for me.

She look at me funny for a minute, I look at her. Then us laugh. Where Germaine at? I ast.

In college, she say. Wilberforce. Can't let all that talent go to waste. Us through, though, she say. He feel just like family now. Like a son. Maybe a grandson. What you and Albert been up to?

she ast.

Nothing much, I say.

She say, I know Albert and I bet he been up to something, with you looking as fine as you look.

Us sew, I say. Make idle conversation.

How idle? she ast.

What do you know, I think. Shug jealous. I have a good mind to make up a story just to make her feel bad. But I don't.

Us talk bout you, I say. How much us love you.

She smile, come put her head on my breast. Let out a long breath.

Your sister,

Celie

思考与讨论

(1) 西丽与耐蒂书信中的用语有什么区别？作者这样安排有何用意？沃克为何选用书信体裁？

(2) 小说以颜色为名，选文中描绘了哪些颜色？分别代表了什么？

(3) 西丽与某某先生的关系是如何发生变化的？为何发生改变？

(4) 选文中，非裔如何看待非洲土地？耐蒂对非洲生活的描绘有什么意义？

拓展阅读

[1] Bloom, Harold. *Alice Walker*. New York: Chelsea House Publishers, 1989.

[2] Selzer, Linda. "Race and Domesticity in *The Color Purple*." *African American Review* vol.29, no.1, 1995, pp.67 - 82.

[3] White, Evelyn C. *Alice Walker: A Life*. New York: Norton, 2004.

三、安妮・普鲁

(一) 安妮・普鲁简介

安妮・普鲁(Annie Proulx, 1935—　)是美国作家、编剧，于1935年出生在美国康涅狄格州诺维奇市(Norwich, Connecticut)，全名是艾德娜・安妮・普鲁(Edna Annie Proulx)，以纪念其母亲的姨母。她曾于20世纪50年代前往科尔比学院(Colby College)短暂就读，1966年重返校园，在佛蒙特大学(University of Vermont)取得学士学位，1973年在乔治威廉斯爵士大学(现康考迪亚大学，Concordia University)取得硕士学位。1999年，康考迪亚大学授予她荣誉博士学位。

20世纪60年代早期至70年代，普鲁以E. A. Proulx的笔名在数本杂志上发表短篇小说。她在

1988年出版了第一部作品集《心灵之歌与其他故事》(*Heart Songs, and Other Stories*),随后于1992年出版了第一部小说《明信片》(*Postcards*)。小说视角在逃亡的洛亚尔·布拉德(Loyal Blood)与他远在福蒙特的家人间来回切换。洛亚尔误杀了自己的女友,因此踏上逃亡之路。他不定期给家人邮寄明信片,讲述自己的生活与经历,但从没有留下过回信地址,因此错过了家里发生的所有大事,如他父亲的自杀、母亲的惨死、家庭农场的出售、妹妹与一个虚拟陌生人的婚姻。《明信片》获得了国际笔会/福克纳奖,是《船讯》的前身。

1993年,普鲁凭借《船讯》获得普利策小说奖与美国国家图书奖。她的短篇小说《断背山》(*Brokeback Mountain*, 1997)与《脏泥》(*The Mud Below*, 1999)获得了欧·亨利短篇小说奖。这两篇小说都被收录于她1999年的短篇小说集。2017年,普鲁获得美国国家图书奖终身成就奖。

普鲁的小说具有黑色幽默喜剧的风格,小说中充满了古怪的、令人印象深刻的人物,以及非传统结构的家庭。她擅长运用出人意料的词汇、尖刻的语言以及不寻常的情节转折讲述支离破碎的家庭对脚下土地的依恋。同时,她热衷于研究北美边缘小镇的自然地理与风土人情,因此她经常在小说中使用区域性语言。她的其他长篇小说包括《手风琴罪行录》(*Accordion Crimes*, 1996)、《老谋深算》(*That Old Ace in the Hole*, 2002)、《树民》(*Barkskins*, 2016)等。

(二)《船讯》简介

受克利福德·沃伦·阿什利(Clifford W. Ashley)影响,《船讯》以不同的绳结系法为题,讲述了与绳结(coil)同音的男主角,奎尔(Quoyle)的成长故事。奎尔并不是他的名字,而是家族姓氏——他的名字一直到最后才出现在小说中,却是以缩写的形式。奎尔从小就生活在家人、同学、老师厌恶的目光下。他长得丑陋、身形臃肿、性格愚钝,没有什么特长。因此,他自卑、逆来顺受、沉默寡言。由于奎尔的下巴格外巨大且怪异,他经常用一只手捂住它。大学辍学后,奎尔的非裔朋友帕特里奇(Partridge)给他介绍了一份小报社中薪水微薄的工作。奎尔符合布鲁门贝格(Blumenberg)对缺陷本质(Mängelwesen)的定义:一个不被期待出生的人,必须克服生理与心理的缺陷。

奎尔一直过着浑浑噩噩的生活,他不停地被报社解雇、返聘。帕特里奇与妻子很快踏上了新生活的道路,再次落单的奎尔踏进了一段不幸的婚姻,他的妻子佩塔尔·贝尔(Petal Bear)只对他的性能力感兴趣,但很快由于他的丑陋与无趣移情别恋。奎尔为了两个女儿努力维护这个家,但只换来佩塔尔挑衅般地当着他的面带着其他男人回家寻欢作乐。奎尔的父母因为生病选择自杀,佩塔尔卖了她和奎尔的两个女儿,卷走了家里的钱与情夫私奔,当时的奎尔甚至付不起保姆的工资。在一片混乱中,奎尔接到警方电话,通知他佩塔尔与其情夫在一场车祸中死亡,脖子折断,胸口烧焦。警察找到了他的女儿,她们被卖给了恋童癖人贩子,被找到的时候赤身裸体,但好在不幸的事情还没有发生。

在奎尔浑浑噩噩时,他的姑妈果断地决定带着奎尔和两个孩子离开美国,前往他们祖辈的家园,纽芬兰岛。奎尔在到达之前就通过帕特里奇找到了新工作,在《拉呱鸟》(*The Gammy Bird*)报社当记者。编辑杰克·巴吉特(Jack Buggit)安排他报道汽车残骸的新闻,最好可以拍到大火与烧焦的胸口,这让奎尔不断想起自己的心理创伤。此外,奎尔需要报道船讯,也就是船进出港口的新闻与故事。同时,奎尔的姑妈提出了很多计划,她想修好他们的老房子,还要买一条船,可奎尔因为小时候学不会游泳,多次被父亲按在水里,差点溺死,所以对开船这一想法十分恐惧。在多方面压力的鞭策下,奎尔开始成长。他买了一条船，并克服坠落的恐惧帮姑妈修屋顶。

随着奎尔适应并喜欢上自己的新生活，纽芬兰的风土面貌慢慢展开。奎尔通过报道一条传闻属于希特勒的船，开发出自己的专栏。这条船不但让他第一次得到外界的肯定，让他知晓自己姑妈装修游轮的工作，还让他见证了一场谋杀案——奎尔跟着比利(Billy)去瞭望岛参观奎尔家族墓地时，在被礁石卡住的手提箱里发现了该船主丈夫的头颅。奎尔在新历险中成长，了解了自己家族的背景，逐渐学会与女儿们相处，也终于收获爱情。

《船讯》中，奎尔一直在寻找自己的容身之处。在前往纽芬兰之前，他不被家人喜欢，在学校、报社、社区也一直是边缘化角色，这使他收到的评价一直是负面的："一块巨大的长方形湿面包""猪油脑袋""一条穿了人的衣服去拍滑稽照片的狗"等等。他所在的社区并没有给他展现自己优点的机会，而他的温和、善良、内心敏感都在融入纽芬兰社区后才慢慢展现出来。奎尔家族在纽芬兰臭名昭著，他们是海盗出身，家族历史充斥着血腥与冷漠。奎尔展现出与自己家族男性全然不同的温和品质，因此他逐渐被社区所接受且喜爱。在奎尔成为《拉呱鸟》主编后，他的全名"R·G·奎尔"第一次出现，代表着他找到了真正的自我。

《船讯》与《紫颜色》都没有完全使用标准英语。《紫颜色》中耐蒂的书信语言是较为标准的英语，而西丽在信中使用了具有非裔口语化特征的非正式英语。《船讯》中经常出现一些没有主语及动词的短句，普鲁将阅读单元从单句扩大到了段落，以此呈现更丰富的变化。

(三) 作品选读：《船讯》[①]

11

A Breastpin of Human Hair

In the nineteenth century jewelers made keepsake ornaments from the hair of the dead, knotting long single hairs into arabesqued roses, initials, singing birds, butterflies.

THE AUNT set out for the house on Friday morning. She was driving her new truck, a navy blue pickup with a silver cap, the extra-passenger cab, a CD player and chrome running boards.

"We need it. Got to have a truck here. Got to get back and forth to my shop. You got a boat, I got a truck. They've got the road fixed and the dock in. Upstairs rooms done. There's an outhouse. For now. Water's connected to the kitchen. Some of that new black plastic waterline. Later on we can put in a bathroom. He's working on the roof this week. If the weather holds. But it's good enough. We might as well get out there. Out of this awful motel. I'll pick up groceries and kerosene lamps. You come out with the girls-and your boat-tomorrow morning."

Her gestures and expressions swift, hands clenching suddenly as though on the reins of a fiery horse. Wild to get there.

The aunt was alone in the house. Her footsteps clapping through the rooms, the ring of bowl

---

① Proulx, Annie. *The Shipping News.* New York: Scribner, 1999, pp. 99 - 107.

and spoon on the table. Her house now. Water boiled magnificently in the teakettle. Upstairs. Yet climbing the stairs, entering that room, was as if she ventured into a rough landscape pocked with sinks and karst holes, abysses invisible until she pitched headlong.

The box holding the brother's ashes was on the floor in the corner.

"All right," she said, and seized it. Carried it down and through and out. A bright day. The sea glazed, ornamented with gulls. Her shadow streamed away from her. She went into the new outhouse and tipped the ashes down the hole. Hoisted her skirts and sat down. The urine splattered. The thought that she, that his own son and grandchildren, would daily void their bodily wastes on his remains a thing that only she would know.

On Saturday morning Quoyle and his daughters came along, suitcases humped in the backseat, the speedboat swaying behind on the rented trailer. He steered over the smoothed road. Starting where the road ended in the parking lot of the glove factory, the bulldozer had scraped a lane through the tuckamore to the house. New gravel crunched under the tires. Clouds, tined and serrated, and ocean the color of juice. The sun broke the clouds like a trout on the line.

"A ladder house," said Sunshine, seeing the scaffolding.

"Dad, I thought it was going to be a new house," said Bunny. "That Dennis was making it new. But it's the same one. It's ugly, Dad. I hate green houses." She glared at him. Had he tricked her?

"Dennis fixed up the inside. We can paint the house another color later on. First we have to fix up the holes and weak spots."

"Red, Dad. Let's paint it red."

"Well, the aunt has the say. It's mostly her house, you know. She might not be crazy about red."

"Let's paint her red, too," said Bunny. Laughed like a hyena.

Quoyle pulled in beside the aunt's truck. He'd wrestle with the trailer and the boat on Sunday. Dennis Buggit on the roof, tossing shingles into the wind. The aunt opened the door and cried "Ta-TA!"

Smooth walls and ceilings, the joint compound still showing trowel marks, the fresh window sills, price stickers on the smudgy window glass. A smell of wood. Mattresses leaned against a wall. The girls' room. Bunny piled wood shavings on her head.

"Hey, Dad, look at my curly hair, Daddy, look at my curly hair. Dad! I got curly hair." Shrill and close to tears. Quoyle picked at melted cheese on her shirt.

In the kitchen the aunt ran water into a sink, turned on the gas stove to show.

"I've made a nice pot of stewed cod," she said. "Dennis brought a loaf of Beety's homemade bread. I got bowls and spoons before I came over, butter and some staples. Perishables in that ice cooler. You'll have to bring ice over. I don't know when we can get a gas refrigerator in here.

Nephew, you'll have to manage with the air mattress and sleeping bag in your room for a while. But the girls've got bed frames and box springs."

Quoyle and Bunny put a table together of planks and sawhorses.

"This is heavy," said Bunny, horsing up one end of a plank, panting in mock exhaustion.

"Yes," said Quoyle, "but you are very strong." His stout, homely child with disturbing ways, but a grand helper with boards and stones and boxes. Not interested in the things of the kitchen unless on a platter.

Dennis came down from the roof, grinned at Quoyle. There was nothing in him of Jack Buggit except eyes darting to the horizon, measuring cuts of sky.

"Great bread," said Quoyle, folding a slice into his mouth.

"Yeah, well, Beety makes bread every day, every day but Sunday. So."

"And good fish," said the aunt. "All we need's string beans and salad."

"So," said Dennis. "The caplin run'll be soon. Get a garden in. Caplin's good fertilizer."

In the afternoon Quoyle and Bunny wiped at the lumpy joint compound with wet sponges until the seams were smooth. Bunny intent, the helpful child. But glancing in every corner. On the roof Dennis hammered. The aunt sanded windowsills, laid a primer coat.

In the last quarter-light Quoyle walked with Dennis down to the new dock. On the way they passed the aunt's amusement garden, a boulder topped with silly moss like hair above a face. Scattered through the moss a stone with a bull's-eye, a shell, bits of coral, white stone like the silhouette of an animal's head.

The wood of the new dock was resinous and fragrant. Water slapped beneath. Curdled foam.

"Tie your boat up now, can't you?" said Dennis. "Pick up a couple old tires so she don't rub."

Dennis slipped the mooring lines, jumped into his own boat, and hummed into the dusk on curling wake. The lighthouses on the points began to wink. Quoyle went up the rock to the house, toward windows flooded with orange lamplight. Turned, glanced again across the bay, saw Dennis's wake like a white hair.

In the kitchen the aunt shuffled cards, dealt them around.

"We'd play night after night when I was a girl," she said. "Old games. Nobody knows them now. French Boston, euchre, jambone, scat, All-Fours. I know every one."

Slap, slap, the cards.

"We'll play All-Fours. Now, every jack turned up by the dealer counts a point for him. Here we are, clubs are trumps."

But the children couldn't understand and dropped their cards. Quoyle wanted his book. The aunt's blood boiled up.

"Everlasting whining!" What had she expected? To reconstruct some rare evening from her ancient past? Laughed at herself.

So Quoyle told his daughters stories in the dim bedroom, of explorer cats sighting new lands, of birds who played cards and lost them in the wind, of pirate girls and buried treasure.

Downstairs again, looked at the aunt at the table, home at last. Her glass of whiskey empty.

"It's quiet," said Quoyle, listening.

"There's the sea." Like a door opening and closing. And the cables' vague song.

Quoyle woke in the empty room. Grey light. A sound of hammering. His heart. He lay in his sleeping bag in the middle of the floor. The candle on its side. Could smell the wax, smell the pages of the book that lay open beside him, the dust in the floor cracks. Neutral light illumined the window. The hammering again and a beating shadow in the highest panes. A bird.

He got up and went to it. Would drive it away before it woke the aunt and the girls. It seemed the bird was trying to break from the closed room of sea and rock and sky into the vastness of his bare chamber. The whisper of his feet on the floor. Beyond the glass the sea lay pale as milk, pale the sky, scratched and scribbled with cloud welts. The empty bay, far shore creamed with fog. Quoyle pulled his clothes on and went downstairs.

On the threshold lay three wisps of knotted grass. Some invention of Sunshine's. He went behind the great rock to which the house was moored and into the bushes. His breath in cold cones.

A faint path angled toward the sea, and he thought it might come out onto the shore north of the new dock. Started down. After a hundred feet the trail went steep and wet, and he slid through wild angelica stalks and billows of dogberry. Did not notice knots tied in the tips of the alder branches.

Entered a band of spruce, branches snarled with moss, whiskey jacks fluttering. The path became a streambed full of juicy rocks. A waterfall with the flattened ocean at its foot. He stumbled, grasping at Alexanders, the leaves perfuming his hands.

Fountains of blackflies and mosquitoes around him. Quoyle saw a loop of blue plastic. He picked it up, then a few feet farther along spied a sodden diaper. A flat stick stamped "5 POINTS Popsicle Pete." When he came on a torn plastic bag he filled it with debris. Tin cans, baby-food jars, a supermarket meat tray, torn paper cajoling the jobless reader.

> ... perhaps you are not quite confident that you can successfully complete the full program in Fashion Merchandising. Well, I can make you a special offer that will make it easier for you. Why not try just Section One of the course to begin with. This does not involve you in a long-term commitment and it will give you the opportunity to...

Plastic line, the unfurled cardboard tube from a roll of toilet paper, pink tampon inserters.

Behind him a profound sigh, the sigh of someone beyond hope or exasperation. Quoyle turned. A hundred feet away a fin, a glistening back. The Minke whale rose, glided under the milky surface. He stared at the water. Again it appeared, sighed, slipped under. Roiling fog arms flew fifty feet above the sea.

A texture caught his eye, knots and whorls down in the rock. The object was pinched in a cleft. He worked it back and forth and then jerked at it. Held it on his palm. Intricate knots in wire, patterned spirals and loops. Wires broken where he had torn the thing loose from the rock. He turned it over, saw a corroded fastening pin. And, turning it this way and that, he caught the design, saw a fanciful insect with double wings and plaited thorax. The wire not wire but human hair—straw, rust, streaky grey. The hair of the dead. Something from the green house, from the dead Quoyles. He threw the brooch, with revulsion, into the pulsing sea.

Climbing again toward the house, he reached the spruce trees, heard a rough motor. A boat veered toward the shore and he thought it was Dennis until he saw the scabbed paint, fray and grime. The dory idled. The man in the stern cut the motor, raised the propeller. Drifted in the fog. The man's head was down, white stubble and gapped mouth. His jacket crudely laced with thrummy twine. Old and strong. Jerked up a line of whelk pots. Nothing. He lowered the propeller, pulled again and again on the greasy rope. The engine settled into a ragged beat. In a minute man and boat were eaten by mist. The motor faded south in the direction of the glove factory, the ruins of Capsize Cove.

Quoyle clawed up. Thought that if he got in there with axe and saw, set some pressure-treated steps in the steepest pitches, built a bridge over the wet spots, gravel and moss—it would be a beauty of a walk down to the sea. Some part of this place as his own.

"We thought the gulls had carried you off." The smell of coffee, little kid hubbub, the aunt in her ironed blue jeans, hair done up in a scarf, buttering toast for Sunshine.

"Dennis was here in his truck. He's got to go cut wood with his father-in-law. Said bad weather was coming, you might want to get the rest of the shingles on. Says it ought to take a day, day and a half. Left you his carpenter's belt. Wasn't sure if you had tools. Said there's five or six more squares under that sheet of plastic. He's not sure when he'll be able to get back. Maybe by Wednesday. Look what he brought the girls."

Two small hammers with hand-whittled handles lay on the table. The throats of the handles painted, one with red stripes, the other with blue.

But Quoyle felt a black wing fold him in its reeking pit. He had never been on a roof, never put down a shingle. He poured a cup of coffee, slopping it in the saucer, refused the toast made from Dennis's wife's bread.

Went to the foot of the ladder, looked up. A tall house. How tall, he didn't know. Steep pitch of roof. In all Newfoundland the roofs were flat, but the Quoyles had to have a wild pitch.

He took a breath and began to climb.

The aluminum ladder bounced and sang as he went up. He climbed slowly, gripped the rungs. At the edge of the roof he looked down to see how bad it was. The rock glinted cruelly with mica. He raised his eyes to the roof. Tar paper stapled down. New shingles halfway. There was a wooden brace nailed above the shingles. Crouch on the brace and nail the shingles? The worst part would be getting up to the brace. Slowly he got back down to the ground. He heard Sunshine laughing in the kitchen, the tap of the small hammer. Sweet earth beneath his feet!

But buckled on Dennis's carpenter's belt, the pouch heavy with roofing nails, the hammer knocking his leg as he climbed. Halfway up he thought of the shingles, went back down and got three.

Now climbed with only one hand, the other clenching the asphalt pieces. At the top of the ladder he had a bad moment. The ladder rose up several rungs above the roof and he had to step off to the side onto the roof, to crawl up with the deep air beneath him.

He crouched awkwardly on the brace, saw that Dennis put the shingles on in tiers that he could reach comfortably, then set the brace in a new position. The tops of the spruces were like stains in the fog below. He could hear the slow pound of the sea. He did nothing for a few minutes. It wasn't so bad.

Quoyle put his three shingles up behind him on the slant. Took one, slowly butted it to Dennis's last, taking care to maintain the five-inch reveal. He got a few nails out of the apron, gingerly eased the hammer from under his buttock, got it out of the leather loop. He nailed the shingle. As he pounded the third nail home he heard a sliding sound, saw the two loose shingles he had carried up, slipping down. He stopped them with his hammer. Placed a shingle, nailed it. The third. It was not difficult, only awkward and breathless.

Now Quoyle balanced half a square of shingles on his shoulder, climbed back. It was easier, and he got up the roof without crawling, laid the shingles over the ridge and set to work. He glanced at the sea once or twice, saw the profile of a tanker on the horizon like a water snake floating in ease.

He was on the last row. It was fast now because he could straddle the ridge. The nails sank into the wood.

"Hi, Daddy."

He heard Bunny's voice, glanced toward the ground, but the glance stopped high. She stood on one of the rungs above the roof level, straining to put her foot on the roof. She held the hammer with the red-striped neck. Quoyle saw in a tiny vivid window that Bunny was going to put her foot on the roof, was going to step forward onto the edge of the steep pitch as though on a level path, was going to fall, to pinwheel shrieking to the rock.

"I'm going to help you." Her foot reached for the roof.

"Oh, little child," breathed Quoyle. "Wait there." His voice was low but passionately urgent. "Don't move. Wait there for me. I'm coming to get you. Hold on tight. Don't come on the roof. Let me get you." The mesmerizing voice, the father fixing his child in place with his starting eyes, inching down the evil slope on the wrong side of everything, then grasping the child's arm, her hammer falling away, he saying "Don't move, don't move, don't move," hearing the painted hammer clatter on the rock below. And Quoyle, safe on the rungs, Bunny pinned between his chest and the ladder.

"You're squashing me!"

Quoyle went down with trembling legs, one hand on the rungs, his left arm folded around his daughter's waist. The ladder shook with his shaking. He could not believe she hadn't fallen, for in two or three seconds he had lived her squalling death over and over, reached out time after time to grip empty air.

思考与讨论

(1) 作者往往用名字直呼大多数角色，但主角奎尔从来都只有姓氏没有名字，奎尔的姑妈也一直被叫作"姑妈"(the aunt)，鲜少被提及姓名，二者独特的称呼有什么意义?

(2) 普鲁如何刻画奎尔的父亲角色? 其父亲角色与传统女性小说中的母亲角色有什么区别?

(3) 选文中的短句子对小说内容表达起什么作用?

(4) 小说中的大海与船有什么隐喻意义?

拓展阅读

[1] Moss, Maria. "The Search for Sanctuary: Marilynne Robinson's *Housekeeping* and E. Annie Proulx's *The Shipping News*." *Amerikastudien/American Studies*, vol.49, no.1, 2004, pp.79-90.

[2] Requena-Pelegrí, Teresa. "Fathers Who Care: Alternative Father Figures in Annie E. Proulx's *The Shipping News* and Jonathan Franzen's *The Corrections*." Àngels Carabí & J. M. Armengol, eds., *Alternative Masculinities for a Changing World. Global Masculinities.* New York: Palgrave Macmillan, 2014, pp.115-128.

[3] Stewart, Robert Scott. "Tayloring the Self: Identity, Articulation, and Community in Proulx's *The Shipping News*." *Studies in Canadian Literature*, vol.23, no.2, 1998, pp.49-70.

[4] 王弋璇.记忆、空间与主体建构——安妮·普鲁的小说《船讯》中的"绳结"意象解读[J].河南教育学院学报(哲学社会科学版),2012,31(2):117-121.

第六章 当代美国战争小说

美国作为一个在战争中独立和成长起来的国家，其战争小说毫无疑问成为美国文学的一个重要组成部分。詹姆斯·费尼莫尔·库柏(James Fenimore Cooper)以美国独立战争为背景创作的小说《间谍》(*The Spy*, 1821)，成为美国战争小说的发端。其后，以战争为创作背景、以战争双方参与者的个人生存与命运为观照的基本书写模式，传承了美国战争小说的书写。

第二次世界大战之后，美国为谋求自身的政治利益和经济利益，多次发动规模不等的海外战争，包括朝鲜战争、越南战争、海湾战争、阿富汗战争等。其中朝鲜战争和越南战争都是美国以阻止共产主义为目的且损失严重的军事行动。1950年，朝鲜战争(Korean War)爆发，美国出于政治原因参与其中。然而在这场战争中，美国没有像二战或越战那样全面参战，所以并没有引起国内较大的震荡。此外，作为二战后美国参与的第一次付出高昂代价却未能打赢的战争，朝鲜战争让美国颜面尽失，因此被贴上了“被遗忘的战争”的标签。由于这些原因，以朝鲜战争为主题的小说并未得到较多的关注。1959年，越南战争(Vietnam War)爆发。1961年，美国再次介入其中。这是二战后美国参与的规模最大、时间最长、人数最多、影响最深远的一次战争。因此，至20世纪70年代，以越战为背景的美国战争小说陆续出现并达至繁盛。

进入20世纪90年代，能源短缺成为整个世界关注的焦点与重点。伊拉克为掌控科威特石油，于1990年2月入侵科威特。为恢复科威特的领土完整，在联合国安理会授权下，以美国为首的多国联盟对伊拉克采取了军事行动，揭开了海湾战争(Gulf War)，亦称波斯湾战争或第一次伊拉克战争(The Persian Gulf War/The First Iraq War)的序幕。2001年10月，美国联合多个国家对阿富汗“基地”组织和塔利班发动军事行动。此次军事行动是美国对“9·11”事件的报复性反击，同时也标志着美国反恐战争的开始，史称阿富汗战争(The War in Afghanistan)。这个时期，与伊拉克战争和阿富汗战争相关的小说多以参战士兵的返乡、对战争的回忆和在战争中遭到的创伤为主题。

当代美国战争小说可以分为以下几类：一、以回忆录的方式创作的非虚构小说，主要包括参战人员和非参战人员所经历的战争前线和后方境况的文本再现，参战人员退伍返乡后与社会再次融合的艰涩心路历程，创伤后应激障碍给参战人员及其家人带来的身心伤害；二、客观如实反映战争事件的现实主义小说，包括描写战争场面的恐怖与暴力，返乡人员的真实生活境遇，以及对战争事件的回忆；三、以虚构和事实相结合为内容，以叙事事件和时间相交错为叙事方式，介于现实与想象之间的后现代主义小说，包括对战争事实的描述和逃离战争的想象，对和平生活的向往和渐趋浓重的反战思想。

美国战争小说深受独立战争、内战、两次世界大战、朝鲜战争、越南战争等多次战争的影响，其主题和关注的社会问题也不断扩大丰富。此外，受当时存在主义的影响，当代美国战争小说更多地倾向于体现人的自我价值与社会价值，其主题主要集中在以下七个社会问题：一、个人在战争中的价值、命运与地位；二、战争的荒谬性和对人性的摧毁；三、战争中的移民和难民问题，以及战争对他们及其后代造成的持续性负面影响和历史记忆等话题；四、女性在以男性为主的军队中的性别歧视和地位问题；五、战争中的平民和战争的道德伦理问题；六、种族歧视和性别歧视问题；七、创伤后应激障碍给参战人员带来的伤害及影响。伊拉克战争和阿富汗战争发生后，这一时期的美国战争小说更多地关注到了平民和参战人员，多维度地展现了受到美国军事政策和军事行动影响的参战双方平民和士兵的生活。随着人类继续参与不断升级的破坏性战争，战争小说带给我们的是对战争意义深入的和持续的再思考：我们将继续与暴力及其后果和影响作斗争，并试图通过书写的形式对战争的目的及意义进行阐明、质疑和反对。

第一节 从现实主义到后现代主义的转向

20 世纪 70 年代之后的美国战争小说多以越战为主要创作背景，相关作家大都亲历了第二次世界大战、朝鲜战争和越南战争。这一时期的作家以战场上的亲身经历作为写作主题和第一手素材，通过现实主义的表现方法真实地还原了残酷混乱的战争场面，并结合战争典型环境的描写、客观事实的描述和具体细节的重现来塑造人物形象和刻画人物心理，从而在更大程度上真实地反映了战时和战后参战人员与平民的生存和生活现状，这样的内容更贴近平民阶层，也拉近了读者与小说中人物和情节的心理距离，同时也为读者创造了参与思考的语境和机会。

越南战争的失败无情地打破了美国人引以为傲的美国常胜的神话，这促使他们开始反思自己的文化传统，由此出现了一批发起“反正统文化运动”(counter-culture)的激进青年。他们承继 20 世纪 50 年代时期“垮掉的一代”(The Beat Generation)的反社会和寻求绝对自由的思想，借用奇装异服、吸毒、组织“公社”群居等极端行为表达对现实社会的不满与绝望，借此反对政府、反对越战，罗伯特·斯通(Robert Stone)就是其中之一。

罗伯特·斯通曾在美国海军服兵役，在越战期间做过战地记者。他以亲历的战争事件为素材，于 1974 年出版了现实主义小说《亡命之徒》(*Dog Soldiers*, 1974)，并于 1975 年获得美国国家图书奖。《亡命之徒》以流畅平实的叙事语言和严密清晰的叙事结构，将美国军人把毒品从越南战场转移到美国国内这一犯罪事件娓娓道来。作者把战争、吸毒、嬉皮士等当时美国的社会焦点问题作为小说主题，揭露了越南战争期间缉毒警察与毒贩之间的黑恶交易，以及美国军队和政府内部的官僚主义与腐败现象。

拉里·海涅曼(Larry Heinemann)是美国小说家，他于 1967 年至 1968 年间在越南战场服兵役。他的三部小说和一部回忆录均以越南战争为主题，其中《帕科的故事》(*Paco's Story*, 1986)就是依据自己的参战经历写成的。1987 年，这部小说获得了美国国家图书奖。作者借用士兵幽灵自述这一独特且神秘的人物叙事视角，在文本中重现主人公的参战经历和战后重返社会的遭遇。通过对战场上的尸体、实际环境、人物对话、俚语口语、人物行为等细节的现实主义书写，借用士兵幽灵自述的陌生化叙事视角，该小说给读者描绘了一幅血腥暴力的现实主义画面，同时呈现了战后成为街头流浪者的退伍士兵的真实生活境遇。20 世纪 70 年代至 80 年代，与越战相关的现实主义小说不仅反映了东南亚人民遭受的战争带来的灾难，还呈现了战后返乡士兵的真实境遇，这些残酷的现实让美国国民对越南战争有了更加真实的认识和理解。基于战争的现实和文学作品的推动，美国民众的反战主义思想日趋强烈。

二战结束后，美苏进入“冷战”对峙时期。到 20 世纪 50 年代，美国国内麦卡锡主义对知识分子的迫害加剧了国内民权运动。同时期朝鲜战争、越南战争的失败，国内经济的萧条，妇女解放运动和黑人运动的蓬勃发展，一系列暗杀领袖的暴力事件和日本原子弹爆炸的后续影响，不断出现与激化的国际争端和国内矛盾，致使美国国内的社会冲突继续扩大，进一步加剧了动荡不稳的社会局势和政治局面。这种社会现状引发了黑色幽默(Black Humour)作家们的关注和反思：科技、经济的发展和进步，为什么会造成人类愈发严重的不安与恐惧？1961 年，约瑟夫・海勒(Joesph Heller)发表了黑色幽默长篇小说《第二十二条军规》(*Catch-22*, 1961)，标志着后现代主义正式进入美国文学。

蒂姆・奥布莱恩(Tim O'Brien)，是在美国屡获殊荣且在越南战场服过兵役的著名越战小说家。他的后现代主义小说《追寻卡西艾托》(*Going after Cacciato*, 1978)获得了美国国家图书奖，小说《士兵的重负》(*The Things They Carried*, 1990)获得了法国最佳外国图书奖(Prix du Meilleur Livre Etranger)，小说《在森林之湖》(*In the Lake of the Woods*, 1994)获得了美国历史学家协会(Society of American Historians)颁发的詹姆斯・费尼莫尔・库柏奖，并被《时代》杂志评为年度最佳小说。蒂姆・奥布莱恩借助自己的越战亲身经历，用小说的形式让人们更加全面地理解越南战争的复杂性和战争对人类道德的挑战。小说《追寻卡西艾托》打破了叙事时间的连贯性，模糊了叙事空间的界限性，把过去、现在、未来与回忆、现实、幻想进行了巧妙地交织融合，形成了魔幻的后现代派叙事结构和叙事风格。这种时间与空间的混乱，反映了士兵对这场战争的混乱理解和战争本身的混乱，而作者正是借用这种后现代主义魔幻的混乱叙事和结构，呈现战争对参战士兵造成的不可逆的精神创伤。

从罗伯特・斯通、拉里・海涅曼的现实主义小说，到约瑟夫・海勒、蒂姆・奥布莱恩的后现代主义小说，这个历时性的变化过程，既反映出二战以后美国国内各种社会矛盾的激化和动荡不安的社会现状，也反映出随着工业的迅速发展，西方资本主义把理性和科技物化为纯粹的工具理性和掠夺他人的机器，进而走向人的对立面。因此，作家们认为传统的现实主义叙事模式已经无法呈现这些社会问题，以及这些问题对美国社会、国民心理、家庭和个人造成的负面影响，也不足以引起美国民众对人的存在与理性的再思考。所以他们通过战争小说的书写，对现实主义的传统叙事模式进行反驳和解构，以颓废、暴力、死亡等极端的社会现象为叙事内容，以时间、空间的碎片化与混乱性为叙事结构，以象征、荒诞、虚构为叙事方法，来反思人的存在与人的本质和理性的问题。虽然这些小说呈现的主题是战争，但其目的和意义都是超越战争的，以反战为主要目的，并提出了对战争的目的和意义的再思考。

第二节　以新新闻主义和回忆录为主的非虚构小说

新新闻主义(New Journalism)又被称为“新新闻体小说”“新新闻报道”或“非虚构小说”，出现于 20

世纪60年代的美国。作为两个不同的书写和叙事领域，新闻强调报道事件的客观性和真实准确性，新新闻主义则强调新闻写作技巧的文学化，如人物、场景、情节、心理等细节描写。这种将新闻报道的真实性和文学写作的艺术性相结合的方式，模糊了艺术与非艺术之间的界限，从而关注到了更多的社会真实现状，加强了文本的阅读性和读者的阅读兴趣，并且依靠作家的想象力和认知力的延展，发掘出新闻事件中的潜在意义。同时，新新闻主义也是作家群体对当时现实主义书写表达不满与反驳的另一种方式。

第二次世界大战后，美国虽然处在经济复苏繁荣和科技飞速发展的阶段，但国际争端不断扩大，国内社会矛盾进一步激化，致使一向崇尚“个人主义”的美国民众的精神危机愈加严重，“反叛”“颠覆”“颓废”成为当时的时代精神和社会主题。20世纪50年代，存在主义哲学的相关著作和学说通过翻译被陆续引入美国，如让・保罗・萨特(Jean Paul Sartre)的《存在与虚无》(*Being and Nothingness*, 1956)，马丁・海德格尔(Martin Heidegger)的《存在与时间》(*Being and Time*, 1965)等。存在主义哲学以人为中心、尊重人的个性和自由的精神恰好与美国民众的本土“个人主义”哲学相契合。于是，存在主义哲学就为新新闻主义打破常规的叙事视角、叙事话语、叙事内容和叙事模式提供了哲学上的价值观认同和理论支持。

美国当代战争的新新闻体小说或非虚构小说，最早出现在越南战争的新闻报道里。之后，包括回忆录在内的这种新的艺术创作形式，成为亲历参战人员讲述战争经历的主要叙事策略。

美国作家迈克尔・赫尔(Michael Herr)在越战期间以记者身份进入越南，他在当时的杂志上连续发表了有关越南战争的相关报道，后来这些报道收录为合集《新闻快报》(*Dispatches*, 1977)。这部作品以第一人称的叙事视角呈现了赫尔作为记者在越南战争中的经历。赫尔通过对多名美国士兵的言语、行为和心理的细致描写，以及他本人所见所闻的真实记录，呈现了一幅真实的越南战场图景，揭露了美国官方新闻媒体对战争的虚假宣传。诺曼・梅勒(Norman Mailer)的非虚构小说《夜幕下的大军》(*The Armies of the Night*, 1968)于1969年同时获得普利策非虚构小说类奖和美国国家图书奖。小说叙述了1967年10月，美国10万余名抗议者聚集在华盛顿林肯纪念堂和五角大楼，以抗议美国卷入越南战争的反战事件。梅勒在《夜幕下的大军》中，以第一人称的叙事视角，通过实、虚结合以及叙、议结合的新闻报道方式和小说的艺术创作方法，真实地记录了这一反战、反征兵、反极权主义的游行示威活动。

作为一种对战争“到底是什么”的经历或解读，回忆录成为诸多参战人员更为偏好的一种书写形式。此外，亦有一些作者通过网络分享自己的参战经历和深度思考，把战争以更加直观和真实的方式呈现给读者。从士兵到记者，再到作家的菲力普・卡普托(Philip Caputo)在军队服役三年后，于1977年出版了他在越南参战和生活的回忆录《战争谣言》(*A Rumor of War*, 1977)。作者通过自己和周围人有关战争的回忆与记录，真实刻画了参战士兵在战争中的“所作所为”和战争对他们的深重影响，揭示了战争以及政府虚假宣传战争目的的“谣言”给人类带来的伤害与灾难。科比・巴泽尔(Colby Buzzell)于2005年出版了他的博客小说《我的战争：在伊拉克消磨时光》(*My War: Killing Time in Iraq*, 2005)，杰森・克里斯托弗・哈特利(Jason Christopher Hartley)出版了网络回忆录《另一个战士：在伊拉克的一年》(*Just Another Soldier: A Year on the Ground in Iraq*, 2006)。这些回忆录聚焦于战争期间士兵们对所执行任务目的的不明确而产生的困惑感，在与伊拉克人合作过程中的无效沟通与挫败感，表达了他们只能依靠网络打发兵役时间等多种负面情绪，以及创伤后应激障碍给战后士兵的身体和生活带来的痛苦与影响。所有这些回忆和叙述都呈现了参战人员对战争的厌烦与不信任，与官方媒体的报道形成了鲜明的对比。

无论是在越南战争、伊拉克战争还是阿富汗战争中，女性作为参战人员的一部分，她们面临的在以男性为主的军队中的性别歧视、身份地位等问题也成为美国战争小说中的一个重要主题，相关作品有战地护士琳达·范·德万特（Lynda Van Devanter）的回忆录《天亮前回家：一个越南战地护士的故事》（*Home Before Morning: The Story of an Army Nurse in Vietnam*, 1983），温妮·史密斯（Winnie Smith）的《战场上的美国女儿：与越南战地护士在前线》（*American Daughter Gone to War: On the Front Lines with an Army Nurse in Vietnam*, 1992），以及记者海伦·本尼迪克特（Helen Benedict）取材于真实事件的小说《沙女王》（*Sand Queen*, 2011）。这些作品聚焦于女性在战争中的生存状态，让读者清楚地认识到女性在军队遭到的性别歧视、性伤害等问题，以及美国军事政策对参战双方女性带来的身心影响和伤害。

迈克尔·赫尔认为，战争作为真实发生的事件，这一性质本身就对特定的报告文学产生了特定的需求①。这既是对新新闻主义小说或非虚构小说产生的一种解释，也是对其所具有的客观性描述和主观性议论的跨界陈述。但是小说中事件的客观性并不能保证其历史真实性，这很有可能会对读者造成主观上的误解与误导。也正是这种文体间跨界的模糊性，导致了这种新的体裁在事件的真实性报道和文学性书写间存在不确定性和不平衡性。这种跨界的模糊性、不确定性和不平衡性，使得这类文学体裁在20世纪70年代后一度隐匿。即便如此，美国非虚构作家罗伯特·博因顿（Robert S. Boynton）在他的《新新闻主义：与美国顶级非虚构作家的访谈录》中以比较视域的观点强调了新新闻主义的优势和未来发展的趋向："'新闻学'和'文学'——在'主观'和'客观'报道之间的争议——对这一代影响并不太大，这使他们能随意将两种体裁进行优势组合。没有宣言，没有公开辩论，就是这样做了。新新闻主义已经领衔美国文学了。"②

第三节 主题书写与审美视角的多元并置与融合

美国战争小说多元化的原因在于战争本身就具有政治、经济、历史、文化等多元复杂性，美国在第二次世界大战后参与并发起的战争体现出强烈的极权主义，而且当时美国社会经济、科技、文化迅速发展，国内各种社会矛盾不断激化，这些因素都是促使美国战争小说多元化的根源。国际争端激烈、国内社会矛盾加剧，反映在文学创作上就是创作方法、主题、审美视角等的多变性和多元化。

当代美国战争小说主题的多元化表现在对战争真实目的和意义的书写，用以表达反战、反政府的目的，揭露美国政府和军队的内部腐败、美国发动战争的真实动机等，同时也有为数不多的描写士兵的英勇行为和献身精神的英雄主义、浪漫主义主题，如罗宾·莫尔（Robin Moore）的《绿色贝雷帽》（*The Green Berets*, 1965），但是该小说对战争英雄主义和浪漫主义的宣扬，掩盖了美国政府参与干涉越南内

① Haytock, Jennifer. *Routledge Introductions to American Literature*. London & New York: Routledge, 2018, p.131.
② 罗伯特·博因顿：《新新闻主义：美国顶尖非虚构作家写作技巧访谈录》，刘蒙之译，北京：北京师范大学出版社，2005年，第13页。

政的事实和参战的真实目的。

越战之后，美国战争小说的主题范围逐渐宽泛，更多地涉及与战争相关的文化、经济、性别、种族等社会问题，如创伤后应激障碍给参战人员及其家人带来的精神与身体上的影响与伤痛，以及战后返乡人员重新融入社会的艰辛与无奈。凯文·鲍尔斯（Kevin Powers）是一位在伊拉克服役一年的机枪手，他的小说《黄鸟》（*The Yellow Birds*，2012）以第一人称的叙述视角，讲述了主人公因战争受到的精神创伤，这种创伤使得他在道义和人性之间产生了人格分裂，即便是在战后多年也仍然无法愈合或消除。身体上留下的创伤不是勇敢的标志，而是那段永远不能忘却的伤痛和记忆，这就是战争留给参战人员永久的创伤。

女性无论是在前线参战还是在后方赡养家庭，都被作为一个特殊群体对待而产生相应的性别歧视、性侵害等问题。在伊拉克和阿富汗战争小说中，对女性参战人员的关注成为该战争小说的特点之一。乔治·布兰特（George Brant）的小说《搁浅》（*Grounded*，2012），讲述了一名女战斗机飞行员因为战争新技术的挑战和性别问题而遭到的严重的心理创伤。女记者海伦·本尼迪克特的小说《孤勇者：在伊拉克孤军奋战的女人们》（*The Lonely Soldier: The Private War of Women Fighting in Iraq*，2010），通过对四十名伊拉克战争退伍军人的采访，呈现了战争、阶级、种族、同性恋恐惧症和创伤后应激障碍等诸多复杂问题。小说中的女兵们在战争中所遭受的性别歧视甚至性伤害，带给她们的是一生难以抹去的残酷记忆和不可逆的精神创伤。

迈克尔·皮特雷（Michael Pitre）和艾略特·阿克曼（Elliot Ackerman）是前美国海军陆战队队员，都曾在伊拉克或阿富汗战争期间服役。迈克尔·皮特雷的小说《五人组和二十五人组》（*Fives and Twenty-Fives*，2014），聚焦于战争期间的修路工人，同时也涉及军队内部的士兵、军医、翻译员等人物。艾略特·阿克曼的小说《蓝底绿色》（*Green on Blue*，2015）把关注点投向参战双方的平民，以此来反映美国入侵伊拉克、干涉伊拉克事务给美国人民和伊拉克人民带来的影响与伤害。

美国战争小说创作形式的多元化主要体现在小说叙事策略和叙事风格的多元化上，如小说叙事视角、叙事动机、叙事人称、叙事空间的多变性。同时，黑色幽默和非虚构小说等创作方法的使用，丰富和拓展了美国战争小说的创作形式。这些多样化的创作方法使得战争小说的叙事更加全面，主题更加宽泛突出。其次，审美视角的多元化，如后现代主义、超现实主义、新历史主义的诗学理论和文学审美批评理论，使美国战争小说在其发展过程中不断地趋向于书写、结构、叙事等文学创作方法和文学审美批评的多元化并置与融合。

黑色幽默是后现代主义在文学形式上的一种表现方法。20世纪60年代，在美国国内极端混乱、动荡的社会状态下，作家借用黑色幽默这种极端的方式反叛传统的、循规蹈矩的现实主义，用喜剧的方式表达悲剧的主题，使小说的艺术效果得到最大化的延展，使主题进一步深化。约瑟夫·海勒（Joseph Heller）的《第二十二条军规》（*Catch-22*，1961），成为美国黑色幽默战争小说的开山扛鼎之作。库特·冯内古特（Kurt Vonnegut）的《第五号屠场》（*Slaughterhouse-Five*，1969）、托马斯·品钦（Thomas Pynchon）的《万有引力之虹》（*Gravity's Rainbow*，1973）都是前期美国黑色幽默战争小说中的经典作品。

黑色幽默小说的后期作家加贝·哈德森（Gabe Hudson），是一位参加过海湾战争的前海军陆战队士兵。他的小说《亲爱的总统先生》（*Dear Mr. President*，2002），沿袭了梅勒、冯古内特等人的黑色幽默的创作方法，通过短故事呈现了战争的幻想与荒谬。黑色幽默小说以“反理性”“反小说”的形式，摆脱了传统小说的严谨性和完整性。这些标新立异的创作手法，如打乱叙事顺序、颠倒叙事空间、错置叙事结构，使得读者在一系列错乱中感受到了战争的荒诞与绝望，迷茫与困惑，从而进一步反思战争的目的和意义，反思人性的善良与邪恶。

战争小说不是历史，但它以文本书写和艺术审美的方式见证了历史，参与了历史的建构。美国战争小说既是个人的记忆与创伤，也是整个民族的集体记忆与创伤；既是个人和集体对战争的反思和反省，也是对时代特征和历史事件的见证。美国新历史主义代表路易斯·蒙特罗斯(Louis Montrose)明确指出“文本的历史性”(the historicity of texts)和“历史的文本性”(the textuality of history)，即历史文献与文学文本同样具有叙事性甚至虚构性，因而“客观历史”是不可能存在的。但是历史的文本性和文本的历史性之间的互动，使得战争小说的主题不再囿于简单的二元对立，而是生与死、荣与辱、道义与人性、责任与诱惑等多重主题的并置，也构建了浪漫主义与现实主义、现实主义与现代主义、现代主义与后现代主义、后现代主义与新历史主义等创作方法的多元书写模式和多元交错融合的审美视角。

海伦·本尼迪克特的小说《沙女王》，既关注了美国军队中女性士兵的身份地位和性别歧视问题，又关注了伊拉克平民在美国入侵后的生存状态等多重主题。丹尼斯·约翰逊(Denis Johnson)获得美国国家图书奖的小说《烟树》(*Tree of Smoke*, 2007)，从美国军官、士兵、越南人、加拿大妇女等多个视角对战争进行了大规模的描绘。伊丽莎白·安·斯卡伯勒(Elizabeth Ann Scarborough)的小说《治疗师的战争》(*The Healer's War*, 1988)，将传统小说与奇幻题材混合在一起，对她所经历的战争进行了视角、空间的多元书写。亚裔美籍小说家阮越清(Viet Thanh Nguyen)的小说《同情者》(*The Sympathizer*, 2015)，叙述了越南战争期间一名北越间谍在南越潜伏的故事。这部小说打破了传统小说的叙事结构和叙事方式，构建了叙事者在种族、文化和政治上的多重身份，使小说的叙事具有了叙事者种族、身份间的悖立和文化与意识形态间的冲突与迷茫。

二战后美国经济、科技迅速发展，新闻媒体的传播方式也不断更新，隐藏在传统的文字书写背后的真实的战争通过新的媒介如影像、音频、图片等呈现。因而，美国战争小说的主题、创作方法、审美视角等的发展趋势必然以更加多元化的形式存在。

第四节　主要作家介绍与代表作品选读

一、蒂姆·奥布莱恩

(一) 蒂姆·奥布莱恩简介

蒂姆·奥布莱恩(Tim O'Brien，全名为 William Timothy O'Brien, 1946—　)，是美国作家，越战退伍军人，1946 年 10 月出生于美国明尼苏达州的奥斯汀市。奥布莱恩 12 岁时，全家移居到沃辛顿，这个地方对他的艺术感悟力和想象力的培养起到了重要的作用，他的诸多小说也以沃辛顿的自然环境为背景。1968 年，他取得玛卡莱斯特学院（Macalester College）政治科学学士学位。1969 年至 1970 年，他应征入伍并在越南服兵役。服役期满后，他进入哈佛大学研究生院学习，并在华盛顿邮报担任实习生。1973 年，奥布莱恩根据自己在越南战场的经历写成小说《如果我死在战区》（*If I Die in a Combat Zone, Box Me Up and Ship Me Home*），正式开启了他的写作生涯。

奥布莱恩的小说以鲜明的人物形象和扣人心弦的情节著称，以模糊现实与虚构之间的界限为主要创作方法。虽然他的作品多以越战为主题，但同时关涉了爱与恨、生与死、记忆与想象等社会主题，他的作品也因此获得多项荣誉。他的小说《追寻卡西艾托》于 1979 年获美国国家图书奖。1990 年，小说《士兵的重负》获得芝加哥论坛报小说奖（Chicago Tribune Heartland Award for fiction）、法国最佳外国图书奖。

奥布莱恩的小说《士兵的重负》是美国文学的经典作品，是对战争、记忆、想象力所承载的救赎力量的思考。小说通过第三人称的叙述，详细描述了小说中每个士兵随身携带的物品，包括武器装备、药物、口粮、防护用具等作战物资，以及他们携带的对战争的恐惧和悲伤、对爱的渴望和对生命的尊重。作者通过士兵们携带的物资，让读者感受到了战争所负载的物理、心理和生命的重量。

奥布莱恩的另一部小说《林中之湖》（*In The Lake of the Woods*, 1994），是一部有关失踪、失落和欺骗的作品。小说通过一起失踪案，牵涉出了美国在越南美莱地区的大屠杀事件。作者打破了历史和小说之间的界限，暴露出美国在犯下滔天罪行后却不愿承认，也不愿承担该有的责任的问题，构成了集体暴力与民族遗忘之间的心理和审美的张力。同时，作者将真实与虚幻、残酷与甜蜜混合在一起，表现了创伤后应激障碍对参战士兵的身体、精神以及与其相关的周围人的生活带来的深重影响。1995 年，该小说获得詹姆斯·费尼莫尔·库柏奖最佳历史小说奖。

奥布莱恩著有 7 部小说和 1 部回忆录，还有大量的短篇小说、非虚构小说和评论文章。2013 年，他成为第一位获得普利兹克军事写作终身成就文学奖的小说作家（Pritzker Military Library Literature Award for Lifetime Achievement in Military Writing）。

（二）《追寻卡西艾托》

小说《追寻卡西艾托》是一部关于越南战场上年轻士兵的故事。小说的叙事时间在不同时间段之间来回切换，造成现实与虚构之间的不确定性和魔幻性。小说以三条叙事主线展开：保罗·柏林（Paul Berlin）回忆在越南期间的往事；保罗在观察哨彻夜沉思；保罗和他的部队为追捕逃兵卡西艾托，穿越亚洲进入欧洲，最后到达巴黎。

小说以"那是一段糟糕的时光"开始，紧接着列出了一串阵亡者的名单。"战争就是寒冷的、灰色的、腐烂的。"[①]这样的开端，在阅读的一开始就给读者在感官上形成了对战争这个残酷事实的感受——恐惧。士兵们则试图以各种方式应对他们每天经历的恐怖事件，于是他们中的一些人因无法接受这种现实逃跑了。卡西艾托失踪了，他的朋友保罗·柏林声称他去了巴黎。中尉科森（Corson）决定派出一个小分队去寻找卡西艾托。在小分队追捕到第六天的时候，他们找到了卡西艾托，并试图说服他投降，但是卡西艾托拒绝并继续逃离。

---

① O'Brien, Tim. *Going After Cacciato*. New York: Broadway, 1999, p.1.

从这里开始，小说沿着三条叙事主线展开。第一条叙事线，是保罗对自己来到越南后的回顾，关于他初次到越南接受训练的经历、他对这个地方以及战友们的细致观察，以及他所在的部队在战争中的伤亡情况的陈述。这一部分以叙述战争中发生的真实事件为主，但是没有按事件发生的时间顺序进行叙述。第二条叙事线，是保罗在独自一人站岗时的幻想，这些幻想构成了小说的另一部分——虚构事件的叙事。这一部分的叙述时间是从午夜到黎明，按照时间顺序展开。在这段时间里，有保罗的回顾和反思，还有他对战争的深重的恐惧。这些事件看似真实，但都是在保罗的想象中发生的。第三条叙事线，小分队继续追捕卡西艾托，他们穿越丛林，途经老挝、曼德勒、德黑兰、喀布尔、雅典、卢森堡，一路追到巴黎。这一路上他们既遇到了各种障碍，也感受到了正常生活带给他们的愉悦和美好。这些带有超现实主义色彩的叙事，是他们企望逃脱军队、远离战争，对和平生活的向往和反战思想的呈现。

这部小说叙述的不仅是保罗一个人的逃离，也是其他士兵逃离战争的愿望。可悲的是，这种逃离只是一种幻想，一种心理上的逃避，现实中的他们无法逃离这场残酷的战争，以及战争带给他们的不可逆的身体与精神的创伤。小说表达的不仅是想象的美好与现实的残酷，还有在这种鲜明对比之下战争带给美国国民深远的影响和伤害，更是对战争目的的拷问和反驳，对真理和现实问题的本质探索。

（三）作品选读：《追寻卡西艾托》①

It was a bad time. Billy Boy Watkins was dead, and so was Frenchie Tucker. Billy Boy had died of fright, scared to death on the field of battle, and Frenchie Tucker had been shot through the nose. Bernie Lynn and Lieutenant Sidney Martin had died in tunnels. Pederson was dead and Rudy Chassler was dead. Buff was dead. Ready Mix was dead. They were all among the dead. The rain fed fungus that grew in the men's boots and socks, and their socks rotted, and their feet turned white and soft so that the skin could be scraped off with a fingernail, and Stink Harris woke up screaming one night with a leech on his tongue. When it was not raining, a low mist moved across the paddies, blending the elements into a single gray element, and the war was cold and pasty and rotten.

Lieutenant Corson, who came to replace Lieutenant Sidney Martin, contracted the dysentery. The tripflares were useless. The ammunition corroded and the foxholes filled with mud and water during the nights, and in the mornings there was always the next village, and the war was always the same. The monsoons were part of the war. In early September Vaught caught an infection. He'd been showing Oscar Johnson the sharp edge on his bayonet, drawing it swiftly along his forearm to peel off a layer of mushy skin. "Like a Gillette Blue Blade," Vaught had said proudly. There was no blood, but in two days the bacteria soaked in and the arm turned yellow, so they bundled him up and called in a dustoff, and Vaught left the war. He never came back. Later they had a letter from him that described Japan as smoky and full of slopes, but in the enclosed snapshot Vaught looked happy enough, posing with two sightly nurses, a wine bottle rising from between his

① O'Brien Tim. *Going After Cacciato*. New York: Broadway, 1999, pp.1-10.

thighs. It was a shock to learn he'd lost the arm. Soon afterward Ben Nystrom shot himself through the foot, but he did not die, and he wrote no letters. These were all things to joke about. The rain, too. And the cold. Oscar Johnson said it made him think of Detroit in the month of May. "Lootin' weather," he liked to say. "The dark an' gloom, just right for rape an' lootin'." Then someone would say that Oscar had a swell imagination for a darkie.

That was one of the jokes. There was a joke about Oscar. There were many jokes about Billy Boy Watkins, the way he'd collapsed of fright on the field of battle. Another joke was about the lieutenant's dysentery, and another was about Paul Berlin's purple biles. There were jokes about the postcard pictures of Christ that Jim Pederson used to carry, and Stink's ringworm, and the way Buff's helmet filled with life after death. Some of the jokes were about Cacciato. Dumb as a bullet, Stink said. Dumb as a month-old oyster fart, said Harold Murphy.

In October, near the end of the month, Cacciato left the war.

"He's gone away," said Doc Peret. "Split, departed."

Lieutenant Corson did not seem to hear. He was too old to be a lieutenant. The veins in his nose and cheeks were broken. His back was weak. Once he had been a captain on the way to becoming a major, but whiskey and the fourteen dull years between Korea and Vietnam had ended all that, and now he was just an old lieutenant with the dysentery.

He lay on his back in the pagoda, naked except for green socks and green undershorts.

"Cacciato," Doc repeated. "The kid's left us. Split for parts unknown."

The lieutenant did not sit up. With one hand he cupped his belly, with the other he guarded a red glow. The surfaces of his eyes were moist.

"Gone to Paris," Doc said.

The lieutenant put the glow to his lips. Inhaling, his chest did not move. There were no vital signs in the wrists or thick stomach.

"Paris," Doc Peret repeated. "That's what he tells Paul Berlin, and that's what Berlin tells me, and that's what I'm telling you. The chain of command, a truly splendid instrument. Anyhow, the guy's definitely gone. Packed up and retired."

The lieutenant exhaled.

Blue gunpowder haze produced musical sighs in the gloom, a stirring at the base of Buddha's clay feet. "Lovely," a voice said. Someone else sighed. The lieutenant blinked, coughed, and handed the spent roach to Oscar Johnson, who extinguished it against his toenail.

"Paree?" the lieutenant said softly. "Gay Paree?"

Doc nodded. "That's what he told Paul Berlin and that's what I'm telling you. Ought to cover up, sir."

Sighing, swallowing hard, Lieutenant Corson pushed himself up and sat stiffly before a can of Sterno. He lit the Sterno and placed his hands behind the flame and bent forward to draw in heat.

Outside, the rain was steady. "So," the old man said. "Let's figure this out." He gazed at the flame. "Trick is to think things clear. Step by step. You said Paree?"

"Affirm, sir. That's what he told Paul Berlin, and that's—"

"Berlin?"

"Right here, sir. This one."

The lieutenant looked up. His eyes were bright blue and wet. Paul Berlin pretended to smile.

"Jeez."

"Sir?"

"Jeez," the old man said, shaking his head. "I thought you were Vaught."

"No."

"I thought he was you. How... how do you like that? Mixed up, I guess. How do you like that?"

"Fine, sir."

The lieutenant shook his head sadly. He held a boot to dry over the burning Sterno. Behind him in shadows was the crosslegged Buddha, smiling from its elevated stone perch. The pagoda was cold. Dank from a month of rain, the place smelled of clays and silicates and dope and old incense. It was a single square room built like a pillbox with stone walls and a flat ceiling that forced the men to stoop or kneel. Once it might have been a fine house of worship, neatly tiled and painted, but now it was junk. Sandbags blocked the windows. Bits of broken pottery lay under chipped pedestals. The Buddha's right arm was missing but the smile was intact. Head cocked, the statue seemed interested in the lieutenant's long sigh. "S. Cacciato, he's gone. Is that it?"

"There it is," Doc said. "You've got it." Paul Berlin nodded.

"Gone to gay Paree. Am I right? Cacciato's left us in favor of Paree in France." The lieutenant seemed to consider this gravely. Then he giggled. "Still raining?"

"A bitch, sir."

"I never seen rain like this. You ever? I mean, ever?"

"No," Paul Berlin said. "Not since yesterday."

"And I guess you're Cacciato's buddy. Is that the story?"

"No, sir," Paul Berlin said. "Sometimes he'd tag along. Not really."

"Who's his buddy?"

"Nobody. Maybe Vaught. I guess Vaught was, sometimes."

"Well," the lieutenant murmured. He paused, dropping his nose inside the boot to sniff the sweating leather. "Well, I reckon we better get Mister Vaught in here. Maybe he can straighten this shit out."

"Vaught's gone, sir. He's the one—"

"Mother of Mercy."

Doc draped a poncho over Lieutenant Corson's shoulders. The rain was steady and thunderless and undramatic. It was midmorning, but the feeling was of endless dusk.

The lieutenant picked up the second boot and began drying it. For a time he did not speak. Then, as if amused by something he saw in the flame, he giggled again and blinked. "Paree," he said. "So Cacciato's gone off to gay Paree—bare ass and Frogs everywhere, the Follies Brassiere." He glanced up at Doc Peret. "What's wrong with him?"

"Just dumb. He's just awful dumb, that's all."

"And he's walking. You say he's walking to gay Paree?"

"That's what he claims, sir, but you can't trust—"

"Paree! Jesus Christ, does he know how far it is? I mean, does he know?"

Paul Berlin tried not to smile. "Eight thousand six hundred statute miles, sir. That's what he told me—eight thousand six hundred on the nose. He had it down pretty good. Rations, fresh water, a compass, and maps and stuff."

"Maps," the lieutenant said. "Maps, flaps, schnaps." He coughed and spat, then grinned. "And I guess he'll just float himself across the ocean on his maps, right? Am I right?"

"Well, not exactly," said Paul Berlin. He looked at Doc Peret, who shrugged. "No, sir. He showed me how...See, he says he's going up through Laos, then into Burma, and then some other country, I forget, and then India and Iran and Turkey, and then Greece, and the rest is easy. That's what he said. The rest is easy, he said. He had it all doped out."

"In other words," the lieutenant said, and hesitated. "In other words, fuckin AWOL."

"There it is," said Doc Peret. "There it is."

The lieutenant rubbed his eyes. His face was sweating and he needed a shave. For a time he lay very still, listening to the rain, hands on his belly, then he shook his head and laughed. "What for? Just tell me: What the hell for?"

"Easy," Doc said. "Really, you got to stay covered up, I told you that."

"What for? Answer me one thing. What for?"

"Shhhh. He's dumb, that's all."

The lieutenant's face was yellow. He rolled onto his side and dropped the boot. "I mean, why? What sort of silly crap is this—walking to gay Paree? What's happening? Just tell me, what's wrong with you people? All of you, what's wrong?"

"Relax."

"Tell me."

"Easy does it," Doc said. He picked up the fallen poncho and shook it out and then arranged it around the old man's shoulders.

"Answer me. What for? What's wrong with you shits? Walking to gay Paree, what's wrong?"

"Not a thing, sir. We're all wonderful. Aren't we wonderful?"

From the gloom came half-hearted applause.

"There, you see? We're all wonderful. It's just that ding-dong, Cacciato. That's the whole of it."

The lieutenant laughed. Without rising, he pulled on his pants and boots and a shirt, then rocked miserably before the blue Sterno flame. The pagoda smelled of the earth. The rain was unending. "Shoot," the lieutenant sighed. He kept shaking his head, wearily, grinning, then at last he looked up at Paul Berlin. "What squad you in?"

"Third, sir."

"That's Cacciato's squad?"

"Yes, sir."

"Who else?"

"Me and Doc and Eddie Lazzutti and Stink and Oscar and Harold Murphy. That's it, except for Cacciato."

"What about Pederson?"

"Pederson's no longer with us, sir."

The lieutenant kept rocking. He did not look well. When the flame was gone, he pushed himself to his feet, coughed, spat, and touched his toes. "All right," he sighed. "Third Squad goes after Cacciato."

Leading to the mountains were four klicks of level paddy. The mountains jerked straight out of the rice; beyond those mountains and other mountains was Paris. The tops of the mountains could not be seen for the mist and clouds. Everywhere the war was wet.

They spent the first night in laager at the base of the mountains, a long miserable night, then at dawn they began the ascent.

At midday Paul Berlin spotted Cacciato. He was half a mile up, bent low and moving patiently against the steep grade. A smudged, lonely-looking figure. It was Cacciato, no question. Legs much too short for the broad back, a shiny pink spot at the crown of the skull. Paul Berlin spotted him, but it was Stink Harris who spoke up.

Lieutenant Corson took out the binoculars.

"Him, sir?"

The lieutenant watched Cacciato climb toward the clouds.

"That him?"

"Oh, yes. Yes."

Stink laughed. "Dumb-dumb. Right, sir? Dumb as a dink."

The lieutenant shrugged. He watched until Cacciato was lost in the higher clouds, then he mumbled something and put the glasses away and motioned for them to move out.

"It's folly," Oscar said. "That's all it is. Foolish folly."

Staying in the old order, they climbed slowly: Stink at point, then the lieutenant, then Eddie and Oscar, then Harold Murphy, then Doc Peret. At the rear of the column, Spec Four Paul Berlin walked with his head down. He had nothing against Cacciato. The whole thing was silly, of course, immature and dumb, but even so, he had nothing against the kid. It was just too bad. A waste among infinitely wider wastes.

Climbing, he tried to picture Cacciato's face. He tried hard, but the image came out fuzzy. "It's the Mongol influence," Doc Peret had once said. "I mean, hey, just take a close look at him. See how the eyes slant? Pigeon toes, domed head? My theory is that the guy missed Mongolian idiocy by the breadth of a genetic hair. Could've gone either way."

And maybe Doc was right. There was something curiously unfinished about Cacciato. Open-faced and naive and plump, Cacciato lacked the fine detail, the refinements and final touches, that maturity ordinarily marks on a boy of seventeen years. The result was blurred and uncolored and bland. You could look at him then look away and not remember what you'd seen. All this, Stink said, added up to a case of gross stupidity. The way he whistled on guard, the funny little trick he had of saving mouthwash by spitting it back into the bottle, fishing for walleyes up in Lake Country. It was all part of a strange, boyish simplicity that the men tolerated the way they might tolerate a frisky pup.

Humping to Paris, it was one of those crazy things Cacciato might try. Paul Berlin remembered how the kid had spent hours thumbing through an old world atlas, studying the maps, asking odd questions: How steep were these mountains, how wide was this river, how thick were these jungles? It was just too bad. A real pity. Like winning the Bronze Star for shooting out a dink's front teeth. Whistling in the dark, always whistling, chewing Black Jack, always chewing and whistling and smiling his frozen white smile. It was silly. It had always been silly, even during the good times, but now the silliness was sad. It couldn't be done. It just wasn't possible, and it was silly and sad.

The rain made it a hard climb. They did not reach the top of the first mountain until late afternoon.

After radioing in position coordinates, they moved along the summit to a cluster of granite boulders that overlooked the Quang Ngai plain. Below, clouds hid the paddies and the war. Above, in more clouds, were more mountains.

It was Eddie Lazzutti who found the spot where Cacciato had spent the night, a gently recessed rock formation roofed by a slate ledge. Inside was a pile of matted grass, a can of burnt-out Sterno, two chocolate wrappers, and a partly burned map. Paul Berlin recognized the map from Cacciato's atlas.

"Cozy," Stink said. "A real nest for our pigeon."

The lieutenant bent down to examine the map. Most of it was burned away, crumbling as the old man picked it up, but parts could still be made out. In the left-hand corner a red dotted line ran through paddyland and up through the first small mountains of the Annamese Cordillera. The line ended there, apparently to be continued on a second map.

Lieutenant Corson held the map carefully, as if afraid it might break apart. "Impossible," he said softly.

"True enough."

"Absolutely impossible."

They rested in Cacciato's rock grotto. Tucked away, looking out over the wetly moving mountains to the west, the men were quiet. Eddie and Harold Murphy opened rations and ate slowly, using their fingers. Doc Peret seemed to sleep. Paul Berlin laid out a game of solitaire. For a long while they rested, no one speaking, then at last Oscar Johnson took out his pouch of makings, rolled a joint, inhaled, and passed it along. Things were peaceful. They smoked and watched the rain and clouds and wilderness. Cacciato's den was snug and dry.

No one spoke until the ritual was ended.

Then, very softly, Doc said, "Maybe we should just turn back. Call an end to it."

"Affirmative," Murphy said. He gazed into the rain. "When the kid gets wet enough, cold enough, he'll see how ridiculous it is. He'll come back."

"Sure."

"So why not?" Doc turned to the lieutenant. "Why not pack it up, sir? Head back and call it a bummer."

Stink Harris made a light tittering sound, not quite mocking.

"Seriously," Doc kept on. "Let him go... MIA, strayed in battle. Sooner or later he'll wake up, you know, and he'll see how nutty it is and he'll—"

The lieutenant stared into the rain. His face was yellow except for webs of shattered veins.

"So what say you, sir? Let him go?"

"Dumber than marbles," Stink giggled. "Dumber than Friar Tuck."

"And smarter than Stink Harris."

"You know what, Murph?"

"Pickle it."

"Ha! Who's saying to pickle it?"

"Just stick it in vinegar," said Harold Murphy. "That's what."

Stink giggled again but he shut up. Murphy was a big man.

"So what's the verdict, sir? Turn around?"

The lieutenant was quiet. At last he shivered and crawled out into the rain with a wad of toilet paper. Paul Berlin sat alone, playing solitaire in the style of Las Vegas. Pretending ways to spend his earnings. Travel, expensive hotels, tips for everyone. Wine and song on white terraces, fountains blowing colored water. Pretending was his best trick to forget the war.

When the lieutenant returned he told them to saddle up.

"Turning back?" Murphy said.

The lieutenant shook his head. He looked sick.

"I knew it," Stink crowed. "Can't just waddle away from a war, ain't that right, sir? Dummy's got to be taught you can't hump your way home." Stink grinned and flicked his eyebrows at Harold Murphy. "Damn straight, I knew it."

Cacciato had reached the top of the second mountain. Bareheaded, hands loosely at his sides, he looked down on them through a mix of fog and drizzle. Lieutenant Corson had the binoculars on him.

"Maybe he don't see us," Oscar said. "Maybe he's lost."

The old man made a vague, dismissive gesture. "He sees us. Sees us real fine."

"Pop smoke, sir?"

"Why not? Sure, why not throw out some pretty smoke?" The lieutenant watched through the glasses while Oscar took out the smoke and pulled the pin and tossed it onto a level ledge along the trail. The smoke fizzled for a moment and then puffed up in a heavy cloud of lavender. "Oh, yes, he sees us. Sees us fine."

"Bastard's waving."

"Isn't he? Yes, I can see that, thank you."

"Will you—?"

"Mother of Mercy."

High up on the mountain, partly lost in the drizzle, Cacciato was waving at them with both arms. Not quite waving. The arms were flapping.

"Sick," the lieutenant murmured. He sat down, handed the glasses to Paul Berlin, then began to rock himself as the purple smoke climbed the face of the mountain. "I tell you, I'm a sick, sick man."

"Should I shout up to him?"

"Sick," the lieutenant moaned. He kept rocking.

Oscar cupped his hands and hollered, and Paul Berlin watched through the glasses. Cacciato stopped waving. His head was huge through the binoculars. He was smiling. Very slowly, deliberately, Cacciato was spreading his arms out as if to show them empty, opening them up like wings, palms down. The kid's face was fuzzy, bobbing in and out of mist, but it was a happy face. Then his mouth opened, and in the mountains there was thunder.

"What'd he say?" The lieutenant rocked on his haunches. He was clutching himself and shivering. "Tell me, what'd he say?"

"Can't hear, sir. Oscar—?"

And there was more thunder, long-lasting thunder that came in waves.

"What's he saying?"

"Sir, I—"

"Just tell me."

Paul Berlin watched through the glasses as Cacciato's mouth opened and closed and opened, but there was only more thunder. And the arms kept flapping, faster now and less deliberate, wide-spanning winging motions—flying, Paul Berlin suddenly realized. Awkward, unpracticed, but still flying.

"A chicken!" Stink squealed. He pointed up the mountain. "Look it! See him?"

"Mother of Children."

"Look it!"

"A squawking chicken, you see that? A chicken!"

The thunder came again, and Lieutenant Corson clutched himself and rocked.

"Just tell me," he moaned. "Just tell me, what's he saying?"

Paul Berlin could not hear. But he saw the wide wings, and the big smile, and the movement of the boy's lips.

"Tell me."

So Paul Berlin, watching Cacciato fly, repeated it: "Good-bye."

In the night the rain became fog. They camped near the top of the second mountain, and the fog and thunder lasted through the night. The lieutenant vomited. Then afterward he radioed back that he was in pursuit of the enemy.

From far off, a radio-voice asked if gunships were needed.

"Negative on gunships," said the old lieutenant.

"Negative?" The radio-voice sounded disappointed. "Tell you what, how about some nice arty? We got—"

"Negative," the lieutenant said. "Negative on artillery."

"We got a real bargain going on arty this week—two for the price of one, no strings and a warranty to boot. First-class ordnance, real sweet stuff. See, we got this terrific batch of 155 in, a real shitload of it, so we got to go heavy on volume. Keeps the prices down."

"Negative."

"Well, jeez." The radio-voice paused. "Okay, Papa Two-Niner. Tell you what, I like the sound of your voice. A swell voice, really lovely. So here's what I'm gonna do. I'm gonna give you a dozen nice illum, how's that? Can you beat it? Find a place in town that beats it and we give you a dozen more, no charge. Real boomers with genuine sparkles mixed in. A closeout sale, one time only."

"Negative. Negative, negative, negative."

"You're missing out on some fine shit, Two-Niner."

"Negative, you monster."

"No offense—"

"Negative."

"As you will, then." The radio-voice buzzed. "Happy hunting."

"Mercy," the lieutenant said into a blaze of static.

The night fog was worse than the rain, colder and more saddening. They lay under a sagging lean-to that seemed to catch the fog and hold it like a net. Oscar and Harold Murphy and Stink and Eddie Lazzutti slept anyway, curled around one another like lovers. They could sleep and sleep.

"I hope he keeps moving," Paul Berlin whispered to Doc Peret. "That's all I hope, I just hope he's moving. He does that, we'll never get him."

"Sure thing."

"That's all I hope."

"Then they chase him with choppers. Planes or something."

"Not if he gets himself lost," Paul Berlin said. His eyes were closed. "Not if he hides."

"Yeah." A long silence. "What time is it?"

"Two?"

"What time you got, sir?"

"Very lousy late," said the lieutenant from the bushes. "Come on, what—"

"Four o'clock. Zero-four-hundred. Which is to say a.m."

"Thanks."

"Charmed." There was a soft warm glow where the old man squatted. After a time he grunted and stood up, buttoned his trousers, and crawled back under the lean-to. He lit a cigarette and sighed.

"Feel better, sir?"

"Smashing. Can't you see how wonderful I feel?"

"I just hope Cacciato keeps moving," Paul Berlin whispered. "That's all. I hope he uses his head and keeps moving."

"It won't get him anywhere."

"Get him to Paris, maybe."

"Maybe," Doc sighed, turning onto his side, "and where is he then?"

"In Paris."

"Nope. I dig adventure, too, but you can't get to Paris from here. Just can't."

"No?"

"No way. None of the roads lead to Paris."

The lieutenant finished his cigarette and lay back. His breath came hard, as if the air were too heavy or thick for him, and for a long time he twisted restlessly from side to side.

"Maybe we better light a Sterno," Doc said gently. "I'm pretty cold myself."

"No."

"Just for a few minutes maybe."

"No," the lieutenant said. "It's still a war, isn't it?"

"I guess."

"There you have it. It's still a lousy war."

There was thunder. Then lightning lighted the valley deep below, then more thunder, then the rain resumed.

They lay quietly and listened.

Where was it going, where would it end? Paul Berlin was suddenly struck between the eyes by a vision of murder. Butchery, no less: Cacciato's right temple caving inward, silence, then an enormous explosion of outward-going brains. It scared him. He sat up, searched for his cigarettes. He wondered where the image had come from. Cacciato's skull exploding like a bag of helium: boom. So simple, the logical circuit-stopper. No one gets away with gross stupidity forever. Not in a war. Boom, and that always ended it.

What could you do? It was sad. It was sad, and it was still a war. The old man was right about that.

Pitying Cacciato with wee-hour tenderness, pitying himself, Paul Berlin couldn't help hoping for a miracle. The whole idea was crazy, of course, but that didn't make it impossible. A lot of crazy things were possible. Billy Boy, for example. Dead of fright. Billy and Sidney Martin and Buff and Pederson. He was tired of it. Not scared—not just then—and not awed or overcome or crushed or defeated, just tired. He smiled, thinking of some of the nutty things Cacciato used to do. Dumb things. But brave things, too.

"Yes, he did," he whispered. It was true. Yes... then he realized that Doc was listening. "He did. He did some pretty brave stuff. The time he dragged that dink out of her bunker, remember that?"

"Yeah."

"And the time he shot that kid. All those teeth."

"I remember."

"You can't call him a coward. You can't say he ran out because he was scared."

"You can say a lot of other shit, though."

"True. But you can't say he wasn't brave. You can't say that."

Doc yawned. He sat up, unlaced his boots, threw them off, and lay back on his belly. Beside him the lieutenant slept heavily.

Paul Berlin felt himself grinning. "I wonder... You think maybe he talks French? The language, I mean. You think he knows it?"

"You're kidding."

"Yeah. But, jeez, it's something to think about, isn't it? Old Cacciato marching off to Paris. It's something."

"Go to sleep," Doc said. "Don't forget, cowboy, you got your own health to think about. You're not exactly a well man."

思考与讨论

(1) 这部小说的叙事背景是什么？作者想要通过小说向读者传递什么信息？

(2) "Cacciato"这个名字来自哪种语言？在源语中，这个名字有什么寓意？

(3) 为什么用"神秘"来形容观察哨？有什么隐喻意义？

(4) 当卡西艾托被士兵们包围时，为什么保罗要冲着他大喊"快走！"？

(5) 小说中巴黎的象征意义是什么？

拓展阅读

[1] Boyle, Brenda M., ed. *The Vietnam War: Topics in Contemporary North American Literature*. New York: Bloomsbury, 2015.

[2] Couser, G. Thomas. Going after Cacciato: The Romance and the Real War. *The Journal of Narrative Technique*, vol.13, no.1, 1983, pp.1 - 10.

[3] Silbergleid, Robin. Making Things Present: Tim O'Brien's Autobiographical Metafiction. *Contemporary Literature*, vol.50, no.1, 2009, pp.129 - 155.

[4] 胡亚敏.叙述的惶惑？战争的惶惑！——论蒂姆·奥布莱恩的《追寻卡西艾托》[J].解放军外国语学院学报，2008(06):81 - 84.

二、海伦·本尼迪克特

(一) 海伦·本尼迪克特简介

海伦·本尼迪克特(Helen Benedict, 1952—　)是英裔美国作家、记者，出生于英国伦敦，父母都是美国人类学家。她的作品以关注种族、社会非正义和伊拉克战争而著名，现任哥伦比亚大学新闻专业教授。

本尼迪克特的小说《沙女王》被美国《出版商周刊》誉为"最佳当代小说"。她的非虚构小说《孤勇者：

在伊拉克孤军奋战的女人们》讲述了在伊拉克的美国女性军人和伊拉克平民女性在这场战争中遭受的苦难。这两部小说的内容均来自真实事件，都对美国军队里发生的性侵犯事件做了深入的报道和严厉的批判，由此也引发了美国民众对五角大楼的集体控诉。本尼迪克特本人也因这两部小说获得艾达·威尔斯新闻勇敢奖（the Ida B. Wells Award for Bravery in Journalism）和詹姆斯·阿伦森社会正义新闻奖（the James Aronson Award for Social Justice Journalism）。

她的新作《希望与悲伤的地图》（*Map of Hope and Sorrow: Stories of Refugees Trapped in Greece*, 2022）深度讲述了5位难民艰辛残酷的生活，讲述了他们的坚韧、痛苦和希望。2021年，本尼迪克特因为对难民所做的杰出贡献而获得美国笔会吉恩·斯坦因口述历史奖（The PEN/Jean Stein Grant for Literary Oral History）。

（二）《沙女王》简介

《沙女王》是本尼迪克特根据对四十多位美国女兵和伊拉克人的采访写成的真实故事，讲述了女性对生存的希望、勇气和坚持不懈的斗争。作者围绕两个主要角色构建了沙女王：凯特（Kate Brady）和娜依玛（Naema Jassim）。她们年龄相同，都想保护自己所爱的人，都面临着艰难境遇中的生存挑战。

19岁的凯特·布雷迪参军是为了给她的家庭带来荣誉，为了给中东带来民主。然而事与愿违，她被遗忘在伊拉克沙漠的一个角落里，守卫着一个临时的美国监狱。在这里，凯特遇到了伊拉克医学生娜依玛·贾西姆。娜依玛和父亲、弟弟因为巴格达被入侵而逃难至此，她的父亲和弟弟又遭受不公正待遇而被拘禁在这座监狱里。凯特冒险帮助娜依玛获取亲人在监狱里的信息，她们允诺在今后的日子里要互相帮助，但战争很快就使她们之间的友谊破裂。

和每个士兵一样，凯特必须面对日常战斗任务所带来的生命威胁。同时，凯特又是33名军人中仅有的三名女性之一。因此，她最大的敌人不是伊拉克人，而是可能随时骚扰她的战友科米克（Kormick）和博纳（Boner）。终于有一天，当凯特独自在哨塔执勤时，他们对她进行了性侵犯。在一系列的反抗无果之后，凯特变成了一个充满愤怒情绪和极具伤害性的女兵。她将自己的愤怒迁移到了其他无辜的伊拉克囚犯身上，并对这些人进行殴打虐待，其中一个人就是娜依玛的父亲。而凯特对囚犯的施暴，又招致了囚犯们对她进行性骚扰，这样凯特就处于一个恶性的循环内无法摆脱。

娜依玛是一个医学生，但是家园的沦落导致她无法继续求学，只能四处逃难以求生存。她和家人遭受了炸弹袭击、饥饿、失去家园和家人的痛苦。而朋友凯特在无法自控下对娜依玛父亲的虐待殴打，加剧了两人之间的紧张关系。当两个女人挣扎于既想生存又想保护她们所爱之人的这个冲突时，每个人都对对方的生活和未来产生了巨大而不可预见的影响。

尽管这两位女性有着相似的特点，但是作者还是对她们予以了区分，一个受过教育，一个没有；一个有着严格的宗教观念，一个现实理性。因此，在艰苦危险的战争环境下，她们一个能够设法应对，一个却不知所措最终走向崩溃。

这部小说探讨了伊拉克战争对参战双方女性的生活和未来带来的深重的负面影响和不可逆的精神伤害，揭露了美国女兵在以男性为主的军队里的真实生存境遇和地位，以及遭受战争之苦的伊拉克女性为生存而做出的巨大努力和牺牲。这是一部震撼人心的小说，但因女性在社会中所受到的不公正待遇而让人感到无比凄凉和沮丧，这也是作者本尼迪克特多年对战争、难民的关注而倾注的心血。

(三) 作品选读:《沙女王》[①]

[NAEMA]

IT WAS THE looting that finally drove my family from Baghdad. During the bombing in March, we stayed, enduring the explosions that shattered windows and cracked open the earth, that left corpses rotting in the streets and poisoned the air with the stench of burning flesh. After each attack, Papa and Mama, Zaki and I would climb to the roof, handkerchiefs pressed to our mouths, to survey the damage. The house across the street, where we used to watch five little sisters play, was now nothing but dust and bricks, every one of those children dead. The café where I would buy my tea on the way to classes had been turned into a mound of smashed stone and twisted wire. Baghdad's ancient buildings, mosques and markets, her elegant avenues of bright palm trees—all this we saw reduced to rubble and blood. Yet we were no more able to leave our beloved Baghdad than if she were our dying mother.

At the end of May, though, when the streets were swarming with thieves and thugs and the desperate and angry poor from Sadr City, released by war like wasps from a broken nest—this we could not endure.

In the beginning we thought the Americans would stop it. After all, they had their tanks and guns, their soldiers, and we had nothing since they had dismantled our army and police. But no. They lounged on their trucks in the sun, smoking and taking photographs while looters stripped our shops, our homes, our museums. Zaki could not go back to school for fear of being kidnapped or killed by criminals who would snatch anybody for ransom. (Our poor neighbor's son, a little boy of twelve, was shot dead in the street for nothing but his CD player.) And I could not go to my classes at Baghdad Medical College for fear of the same, or of being raped. Many girls and women were being raped.

"We can't stay here any longer," Papa told us one morning after we'd eaten what breakfast we could find, his thin face sad and gray. "Your mother and I have decided to go to your grandmother's house. Umm Qasr has been badly bombed, but the Americans have moved on from there now and it's more peaceful than this place. Pack up one bag each, only. We leave tomorrow at dawn."

"Tomorrow?" Zaki jumped up from the kitchen table, panic in his eyes. "But I haven't said good-bye to Malik yet, or any of the others! Can't we wait a few days?"

"No, little one, it's too risky." Papa stood and took Zaki in his arms, patting his back and stooping to kiss the top of his head. "I spent all day yesterday waiting for petrol so we could leave," he added in his quiet way. "We have no time to delay. Now go pack, children, and please, don't fuss."

---

① Benedict, Helen. *Sand Queen*. New York: Soho Press, 2011, pp. 29 - 32, 79 - 87.

But I could hear the shame in Papa's voice. I knew he thought it cowardly to run from Baghdad, even then; that he felt he was abandoning his city in her time of need.

Some speak of how hard it is to choose among their possessions when they must flee their homes like this; it is an old refugee story. But for me, it was not hard. All I needed were a few clothes and my medical books so I could continue my studies. Photographs, ornaments, childhood souvenirs—what did these matter anymore? If I wanted memories, I had them in my head. I could have jumped in the car with nothing at all, so eager was I to escape the sight of my city being smashed and pillaged.

No, the hardship for me was having to leave my friends, and most of all, my fiancé, Khalil. I telephoned him as soon as Papa finished telling us to pack and he ran right over to see me. We clung to each other in shock. "I'll count every minute until we can be together again," he said urgently, holding me tightly to his chest. "And as soon as the war ends and we're reunited, *inshallah*, we will celebrate our new freedoms, our new Iraq, right, my love?"

"Yes, God willing, yes," I replied, weeping. But when Papa gently told Khalil that he must go, I could not watch him walk out the door. I had to turn and run into another room, for I was afraid. Already I sensed that even the deepest of loves and most earnest of promises can be crushed by war.

For Mama, it was leaving our house itself that hurt the most. She had been raised in a simple village of farmers, steeped in the old peasant ways, so to her our Baghdad home and belongings were proof of how far she had come and she could not bear to let any of it go. All night long, she agonized over which tea set to bring, which scarves, which dishes and dresses and photographs and letters, until I was mad with impatience.

Zaki was also distraught. He had spent years obsessively collecting souvenirs of his favorite musicians, and more years accumulating bootleg tapes and CDs and lovingly arranging them in categories on his shelves, as if building a nest to keep himself safe from the world. He wept frantically when Papa told him he must abandon these things, just as he wept at being separated from his friends. His only comfort was that when he appeared at his door, hugging his guitar to his chest as desperately as he had once hugged his baby blanket, not even Papa had the heart to make him leave it behind.

At dawn the next morning, we climbed into our old red car to set off, Mama openly crying, Papa grim, his glasses already grimy with dust and sweat. Zaki huddled in the rear seat with me, clutching his guitar. "Don't look back, Zaynab," Papa said to our mother. "It will only hurt more. And when this is over, Allah willing, we will come home."

We knew not to count on this, but it was necessary to hope.

The drive was long and hot and excruciatingly slow. Every corner brought a tangle of traffic and soldiers shouting and waving their incomprehensible signals, their faces livid and sunburned. Checkpoints, barricades or tanks blocked every road we needed to go down, or so it seemed. People were running this way and that, their mouths contorted in panic. Along the roads, trails of looters filed like ants, carrying or dragging their stolen trophies: plush red seats torn from theaters, restaurant tables, office cabinets, vases and televisions and statues. What use do they have for all this rubbish? I wondered. Why are we tearing apart our own city?

The many roadblocks forced us in the wrong direction over and over, and once a soldier made us drive right into a market. Just as we got there, a military truck came roaring in, the gunner on top pointing his killing machine at the women selling their eggplants and melons. The soldiers were shouting and waving but we could not tell what they wanted. Stop? Turn around? Go to the left, to the right? Why did they not make themselves clear? The driver in front of us tried to turn and get out of the way, but he must have panicked and hit the accelerator instead of the brake because his car catapulted into a market stand, crushing two children and their mother. Then the soldiers began to shoot—why? People screaming, running, guns exploding, blood drenching the vegetables. Five people dead, among them a mother and her baby, the child's pink dress matted with blood, her arm a ragged stump.

Zaki put his head out of the window and vomited.

Papa set his jaw—I could see it in the mirror. Slowly, he backed up, turned and wove the car like a needle around the market stalls and out the other side. He knocked nobody down, showing it was possible to do.

It took us four hours to get out of Baghdad. Mama found her strength at last and stopped weeping. She sat forward, her slim back straining as she peered through the dust-covered windshield, on the lookout for the slightest sign of danger. Papa drove without a word, his jaw clenched, his hands gripped tightly on the steering wheel, his frail shoulders hunched with tension. Zaki huddled in my arms, trembling, the little man he so wished to be swept away by fear.

I sat up straight and fierce. It would have to be my strength that would carry us through, I knew that then. Zaki was too young, my father too fragile and my mother too stunned by loss. It was up to me now, and me alone, to make sure that my family survived.

[KATE]

THE FIRST MORNING of my new job, Jimmy comes right to the entrance of my tent to pick me up. He pretends he's just here to take back his blouse, but I know he's really trying to protect me and I don't like it any better than I did last night. I don't want him escorting me to the Humvee like a prisoner, and I don't want him causing a lot of gossip, either. I want to walk around free, prove that no shitbag on earth, not Kormick, not Boner—not the whole frickin' Army—can stop me from being a soldier.

It isn't even dawn by the time I clamber into the Humvee with my new team, so other than saying hi, nobody's awake enough to feel like talking, thank God. But I lean my head back and pretend to sleep in case they try. My scarf's still around my neck to cover the bruises, the sweat gathering underneath it. My right boob throbs, and my throat feels so crushed and raw it hurts even to turn my head. As for the rest of me—my soul or whatever you want to call it—that's still flapping away in the sky.

My new team consists of three guys and me: Jimmy, who's been promoted to E5 sergeant and team leader. Our driver, a big muscled blond called Ned Creeley, with a button-nosed face that makes him look fourteen. And Tony Mosca, a.k.a. Mosquito, a hairy little Italian from New Jersey with twinkly brown eyes and a mouth as filthy as Yvette's. I know they must have heard about last night—me covered in puke and Jimmy in blood—but nobody says anything. It might be tact, embarrassment or just laziness, I don't know, but it's fine with me. Far as I'm concerned, it never fucking happened at all.

Our assignment is to guard a prison compound near the rear of the camp. A compound is what we call a block of forty or so rectangular tents, lined up in rows to make a square. Each tent is twelve feet long and holds about twenty-two prisoners. And each compound is surrounded by a corral of sand and a fence made of three giant coils of razor wire stacked in a pyramid, two on the bottom and one on top. Typically, one soldier guards each side of the block, either on the ground or in a guard tower, while a few extra, like Jimmy, are stationed at the entrance.

My post turns out to be a tower on the west side, so after button-nose Creeley drops me off, I climb up its ladder to look around. The tower's about as high as a streetlight, just a platform on a wobbly scaffold made of plywood and two-by-fours, with a flat roof no bigger than a beach umbrella. I'm only ten feet away from the rolls of wire, so the prisoners can come up pretty close if they want. But not another soldier's in sight.

This is what I have with me for the job: My rifle. Two MREs. Three one-liter bottles of water. A pack of cigarettes. A walkie-talkie that crackles but doesn't work. A radio that doesn't work either. A chair. And a headache.

I play with the walkie-talkie a while to see if I can get it to do something, but it really is a piece of crap. It looks exactly like the toy one Tyler gave April for her seventh birthday, except that one worked better than this. We let her bring it once when she came camping with us, and we had a lot of fun hiding in the woods where we couldn't see each other and being able to talk anyhow. When she lost hers and cried, because in our family that would have got her spanked, Tyler crouched down beside her and said, "Hey there, everybody loses things sometimes. I'll get you another. So no April showers, okay?"

"I hate that joke," April said between sobs, but she was smiling a little, too.

Tyler's often kind like that. His whole family is. His mom and dad take things easy, like he did with the lost walkie-talkie, even though they've got five kids and not much money. They could hardly be more different from my parents. Dad runs us like we're part of his sheriff's department. Rules here, rules there—not just about saying grace before we talk and locking the gun in the sideboard, but all day long. He even puts lists of our daily schedules up on the fridge. I think he'd make April and me call him "sir" if Mom let him. He likes posting mottos around the house, too. Take responsibility for your actions. Don't blame others for your mistakes. If you dig your own grave, you must lie in it.

Guess that's what I've done. Dug my own grave.

It only takes the prisoners about ten minutes to realize that their new guard is a female. At first they ignore me and wander around in their man-dresses, some of them in head rags, most not, smoking the cheap cigarettes we give them for free and kicking the bits of dried shrub that grow out of the sand. But when one of them comes up close enough to see my face, all hell breaks loose. He laughs and beckons some others over. They point. They jeer. They gesture at me over and over to take off my helmet and show them my hair. And then one guy swaggers up, pulls out his dick and jerks off right in front of me.

And this is just my first hour.

I'm shocked and disgusted, but I'm not about to show it. I look away, glad my eyes are hidden behind my shades, chew my gum and try to act like he and the other men are no more important to me than ants. All right, I tell myself, this must be a test from God, having to endure one piece of crap after another like this. I'll handle it, pray when I need to, suck it up like the soldier I am. Anyhow, I don't really blame the prisoners for being angry. I mean, look at the poor fuckers, stuck in overcrowded, stinking hot tents for reasons they probably don't understand. I know most of them are innocent because we've been told as much. Some are criminals who escaped in the war—you can tell which ones are thieves because they have a hand cut off. A lot are Saddam's soldiers who deserted soon as the war began and turned themselves in to us, skinny and ragged and desperate for food and protection. Some are real bad guys, of course, Saddam loyalists or insurgents. But most are just ordinary people who got caught by mistake. Like Naema's little brother—perhaps.

So I try to be Jesus-like and forgiving about it, the way Mom and Father Slattery would want. Remember those who are in prison, as though in prison with them—isn't that how the verse in Hebrews goes? It isn't me they hate, I tell myself, it's what I represent. The power behind those bombs, the foreigners who arrested them and put those hoods on their heads. And from what I've heard, all Arab men think Western women are whores anyhow.

These are the things I think about during my first few hours as a prison guard, sitting up here on my tower in a fold-up metal chair, cooking in the heat like an egg on a skillet. These, and how much I long for Tyler, for his soft singing, his eyes so full of love—for the days when I could trust people. The one thing I don't let myself think about is what happened with Kormick.

"Kate?" A voice floats up from the ground.

I peer over the edge of my platform. Jimmy's looking up at me from behind a new pair of prescription shades. They suit him a lot better than his basic combat glasses—a. k. a. BCGs. Those make you so ugly we call them Birth Control Glasses, 'cause no one will sleep with you when you're wearing them. "What're you doing here?" I call down to him.

"I got a break. There's a bunch of HHC guys working the entrance with me and we're spelling each other." He holds out a paper cup. "Ice. Can I come up?"

Ice is like gold around here, so I tell him he's more than welcome. Slinging his rifle strap over his shoulder, he climbs the ladder and offers me the cup.

"All for me?" I'm still croaking, throat raw and sore.

"No way, we're sharing." He looks at me with concern. "You sound terrible—sure you're okay?"

"Yup. Don't worry about it." We dig out an ice chip each and stand there sucking it in bliss, staring out at the sand. Ice chips in the desert: the best ice cream in the world. It helps my throat feel a little better, too.

"Can I ask you something?" Jimmy says then. He has this soothing voice, low and calm. Perhaps that's why I'm letting him talk to me.

"Depends."

"Well, no pressure, but I was wondering—now you've had time to sleep on it, are you going to report Kormick?"

I keep my gaze on the sand. "Why would I want to do that? To win myself more friends?"

"Well, in case, you know, he tries to hurt somebody else." Jimmy sounds embarrassed, but he forges ahead anyhow. "I meant it when I said I'll back you up if you do. So will DJ. We talked about it. That shitbag should be thrown in the brig, have his big-ass career ended. Boner, too."

"What did DJ have to do with it?"

"He took care of Boner while I was busy with Kormick."

I shake my head. If Jimmy or DJ stick their necks out for me like this, their careers will be fucked. I can't ask them to do that. And if I report Kormick, he'll only make my life even more fun-and-games than it already is. Anyhow, it isn't like he actually raped me, only tried to, so what's there to report? That he attacked me and I failed to be a soldier and fight him off? No, anything I say will only make me sound like one of those whiny pussies all the guys think we females are anyway.

"I'll think about it," I tell Jimmy finally.

"You're pretty tough, aren't you? Were you always like this?" "Who, me?" I look at him in surprise. He's smiling at me teasingly.

"No way. I was little Miss Innocent at home. Served the pie at church picnics. You know the type."

"You weren't so innocent. You had that boyfriend you told me about."

"I have that boyfriend. Fiancé, in fact." We fish out another ice chip each.

"What about you?" I say then, happy to keep off the topic of Kormick. "You got anyone waiting for you at home?"

The age-old question. The stuff soldiers have been talking about since war was invented.

"Nope," Jimmy says, looking away from me. "I had this girlfriend, but when she found out I was coming here... well, you know."

"You mean she dumped you? What happened to standing by your man while he serves his country and all that shit?"

He shrugs.

"Well, that sucks. Sounds like she didn't deserve you. You'll find someone better. You've got plenty of time."

He glances at me, then gazes over the concertina wire at the prisoners.

"We're in a war, Kate. What fucking time?"

On my second morning of guard duty I get up even earlier than usual, determined to fit in a run. My throat's still bruised and aching but at least my boob feels a little better. If I put on my tightest sports bra, I think I can run without it hurting too much. But the idea of being trapped up in my tower, facing another long day of masturbating perverts without even having had my precious morning exercise is more than I can stand.

Third Eye won't come, which surprises me. She just rolls over, growls, "Leave me the fuck alone," and goes back to sleep. But Yvette's ready. I'm still pissed at both of them for not speaking to me the night after Kormick, but since I can't go running by myself—too dangerous and against the rules—I appreciate her company, at least.

The air feels thicker than usual, even though the sun hasn't risen yet, and a light wind's already stirring up the moondust, making it hard to breathe. "Looks like we're in for another frickin' sandstorm," I say while we jog down the road.

"Shit. It'll suck to have to drive in this." Yvette's been going out on convoys for weeks now, often at night, which is way more dangerous than anything I have to do. Her MOS is convoy security, which means she rides in the passenger seat of a convoy truck with her weapon out the window, scanning the desert for danger. I'm still a fob-goblin, a soldier who's never left base.

We run in silence for a time, sinking into the rhythm of it. The sand road's a pretty good running track as long as you keep your eye out for stones, but one step off it into the soft stuff on either side can twist your ankle in a flash. Ahead of us the road stretches straight as a plank till it disappears in a haze. I swear the Iraq desert must be the flattest damn place on the planet.

"You okay?" Yvette says after a while, her voice strained. "I heard some shit went down the other day."

"What did you hear?"

"Oh, the usual BS. Fuck, this moondust's hard to breathe." We run for a while without saying anything.

"Well?" she says eventually. "You ain't answered me yet." "Oh. Yeah, I'm okay thanks."

"You sure? Your voice sounds funny." "It's nothing. Just a sore throat."

"Is that why you're wearing a scarf in one hundred and fortydegree weather?"

"Yep."

She eyes me skeptically. "If you say so. But talk to me anytime you need to, all right, babe? I mean it."

I glance over at her bony little face and for a moment I feel a flash of love for her. Or maybe it's just abject gratitude. She knows something happened to me and she's acknowledged it, which is more than anyone else in my frigging unit has done, aside from Jimmy. We never confide how we really feel—we're much too busy keeping up a front. Specially Third Eye, with that tough-guy act of hers. Some days it seems like all we do is brag, tease or lie to each other. Whatever happened to the band of brothers and sisters we're supposed to be at war, I don't know. In my company we're more like a band of snakes.

By the time we get back to the tent, the horizon's turned a dark streaky orange and the air's clogged with dust. I rinse off with a bottle shower the best I can, although it only makes the dust stick to me worse than ever, then go inside to change into my uniform. Third Eye's sitting on her rack giving me the strangest look. "What's the matter with you?" I say, squeezing my hair carefully with a towel. I have to be careful since so much of it's been falling out lately. "You're looking at me like I turned green or something."

"You been to the crapper yet?" "What kind of a question is that?"

"You better go look. Come on, I'll go with you." She has this heavily serious expression on her face, so I guess she isn't kidding, although you can never be sure with Third Eye.

"Okay. Whatever."

I slip into my fart sack to change (no need to give the guys any more eye candy than they take already), pick up my gear and trudge out after her, the men following our asses with their eyes, like always. She doesn't say anything more.

When we get to the Porta-Johns, panting from trying to breathe through the whirling sand and pizza-oven air, she points at one. Through the dust I can just make out some writing on it in big black letters. I walk up to see.

TITS BRADY IS A COCK-SUCKIN SAND QUEEN.

SIGN IF YOU'VE FUCKED HER.

Under it are fourteen names: Boner. Rickman. Mack. And close to half the guys in my tent. At least DJ's name isn't there. Nor is Kormick's—doesn't want to draw attention to himself, I guess. But Jimmy's is.

Third Eye comes up beside me and stares at the list. "All I can say, kiddo, is I warned you."

Without looking at her, I turn and walk back alone.

"Mom?" I'm behind the tent, my cell phone crackling in my ear. "I know it's late for you, did I wake you up?" My words echo back at me.

"Katie, is that you?" Her voice is delayed by the distance, so it's overlapping the echo of mine, tangling up our sentences.

"Yeah, it's me. Did I wake—"

"It's so good to hear your voice, sweetie! You know you can call any hour you want. You okay? Not hurt or anything?"

"No, no, I'm fine. But Mom?" My voice is trembling. I can hear it echoing in a pathetic whine. Mom, Mom... "It isn't going so good out here—"

"Thank the Lord."

"No... did you hear me? I don't know if I can hack it—"

"What? Oh yes, I can hear you now. I'm sorry you feel that way, honey, but don't give up. You're just adjusting, I'm sure. It'll get easier. And if you just pray to the Lord Jesus, He will help you. He'll help you be strong."

"I am being strong. That's not what I—"

"Katie?" Dad's on the other extension but I can hardly hear his voice between the echoes of mine and Mom's. "Don't worry, little girl. Just hang in there. Everyone has a rough time in the Army sometimes. It was hard for me, too, when I first entered the Force. But I know you can do it. We have faith in you, sweetheart."

"But—"

"Be brave, my girl. Remember, we love you. God loves you. Make us proud."

A few minutes later, I'm in my team's Humvee again, on our way to the compound. Jimmy's in the front, as usual, next to baby-faced Creeley, and hairy little Mosquito is squashed into the back with me, cracking obscene jokes with the guys. I stare blindly through the yellow plastic side window, my arms crossed tightly over my chest. I can feel their eyes raking over me—I know they've all seen the latrine. They were probably snickering about it on their way to pick me up—the Sand Queen, the list of names, everything. Sand Queen is one of the worst things a female can get called in the Army. It means an ugly-ass chick who's being treated like a queen by the hundreds of horny guys around her because there's such a shortage of females. But she grows so swellheaded over their attention that she lets herself be passed around like a whore at a frat party, never realizing that back home those same guys wouldn't look at her twice.

In other words, she's a pathetic slut too desperate and dumb to know she's nothing but a mattress.

I'm trying to hang in there, like Dad said. I'm trying hard. But in a way, that graffiti is worse than Kormick.

When the Humvee stops on my side of the compound, I climb out without looking at anybody and set off for my tower. The sandstorm's blowing stronger by the minute, so I pull my scarf over my mouth to keep out the grit. Right now, I wouldn't care if the sand just buried me forever.

"Wait!" Jimmy calls. Normally he drives on with the others, but this time he jumps out, sends Creeley off without him and runs after me. The whole frickin' base is going to hear about that in a flash.

I ignore him and keep walking.

"Listen, can I explain something?" he says. I speed up.

"It wasn't me put my name there. You've got to believe me. Some other fucker did it. You know I wouldn't do that!"

I keep going. "Kate!"

He reaches out for my arm. I shake him off. "Listen to me!"

"Go fuck yourself." I walk even faster. "Kate, come on! Don't be like this."

I climb the ladder to my tower, refusing to answer. He stands there in the wind for a long time looking up at me. But I won't look back at him.

Only after he gives up and leaves do I drop my head onto my arms. Whatever made me think Jimmy would be any better than the other guys in this craphole? It's a boy's club and it's never going to be anything else. Bros before hos, as they like to say.

I'm such a fucking fool.

思考与讨论

(1) 在这场战争中，凯特和娜依玛各自的处境如何？

(2) 凯特与其他士兵之间存在什么样的关系？

(3) 如何理解凯特和娜依玛所面对的战争冲突、文化冲突和反抗男权统治的冲突？

(4) 试以女性主义角度思考，你认为作者使用第一人称的叙事目的是什么？

(5) 凯特为什么被称为“沙女王”，这个名称的隐喻意义是什么？

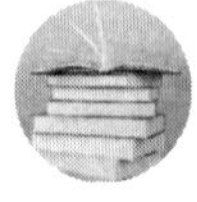

拓展阅读

[1] Johnson, Leola. "Review of Virgin or Vamp: How the Press Covers Sex Crime." *Gender and Society*, vol. 8, no. 3, 1994, pp. 467 – 469.

[2] Mathers, Jennifer G. "I Am Not the Wonderful Person I Was." *The Women's Review of Books*, vol. 27, no. 1, 2010, pp. 8 – 9.

[3] Ghandeharion, Azra. "Gendered Narrative in Female War Literature: Helen Benedict's Sand Queen." *Hawwa*, vol. 19, no. 2, 2021, pp. 202 – 222.

三、阮越清

(一) 阮越清简介

阮越清(Viet Thanh Nguyen，1971—　)是越南裔美籍作家，1971年出生于越南。他4岁时跟随父母从南越逃至美国，经历了一段时间的难民营生活后，与家人定居在加州圣何塞市。1997年，阮越清毕业于加州大学伯克利分校，取得英语博士学位，后任教于南加州大学至今，现为英美研究和民族学、比较文学教授。2018年，阮越清入选美国人文与科学院院士。同为该院院士的还有石黑一雄(Kazuo Ishiguro)、玛格丽特·阿特伍德(Margaret Atwood)、米兰·昆德拉(Milan Kundera)等。

他的长篇小说《同情者》被《纽约时报》评选为畅销书，并获2016普利策小说奖、戴顿文学和平奖(Dayton Literary Peace Prize)、埃德加奖最佳小说奖(the Edgar Award for Best First Novel)、安德鲁·卡内基最佳文学奖(the Andrew Carnegie Medal for Literary Excellence)、加利福尼亚图书奖(California Book Award)等多项大奖和荣誉。他的非虚构族裔研究作品《不朽：越南和战争的记忆》(*Nothing Ever Dies: Vietnam and the Memory of War*, 2016)入围2016年美国国家图书奖、2017年全美书评人协会奖(National Book Critics Circle Award in General Nonfiction)、美国比较文学协会的勒内·韦勒克比较文学最佳图书奖(Réné Wellek Prize for the Best Book in Comparative Literature)。他的有关文化与种族、政治关系的著作《种族与抵抗：亚裔美国人的文学与政治》(*Race and Resistance: Literature and Politics in Asian America*, 2002)，以及新作短篇小说集《难民》(*The Refugees*, 2017)和《同情者》的续集《承诺者》(*The Committed*, 2020)已出版面世。

他的族裔研究作品《不朽：越南和战争的记忆》是关于历史批判和伦理的理论著作，探讨了从美国到越南、老挝、柬埔寨和韩国等许多国家和人民的意识中，什么是越南战争、如何记忆越南战争等问题。在著作《种族与抵抗：亚裔美国人的文学与政治》中，阮越清认为，亚裔美国知识分子将亚裔美国人理想化，这种理想化意味着亚裔美国知识分子无法应对其文化的意识形态、种族身份的多样性，这样就无法应对亚裔美国人文化的复杂性、冲突和潜在的未来选择。

短篇小说集《难民》探索了移民、种族身份、文化身份、爱情和家庭问题，思考了战争与和平，国家、家庭与个人的命运问题。小说《同情者》的续集《承诺者》是一部悬疑犯罪小说，也是一部把美国极权主义、法国殖民主义、女权主义、共产主义与反共产主义等哲学理论与文学融合为一体的哲学小说，探讨了命运与自由意志、权力与无能为力之间存在的紧张关系。

(二)《同情者》简介

小说《同情者》集历史、政治、种族身份、文化身份、间谍、惊悚等元素于一体，讲述了一个潜伏于南越的北越双面间谍的故事。故事发生在1975年，越共占领西贡，美军因此大撤退。真实身份是越南共产党的主人公也随其南越"长官"逃难至美国，并在美国继续进行间谍工作。在此期间，他作为难民和间谍，身心经历了政治信仰与忠诚、道义与人性、爱与恨、生与死的挣扎和磨难。

小说主人公是一个法越混血儿，是南越军队情报组织高级将军的副官，也是小说中"将军"核心圈子中最受信任的成员之一。但实际上,他是一名北越共产党间谍,在他的"生死兄弟"——曼(Man)的指示下进行间谍活动。小说从主人公回忆1975年4月30日西贡沦陷开始,他和将军一家以及另一位"生死兄弟"邦(Bon)一起逃离西贡,前往美国并定居洛杉矶,曼则继续留在西贡进行间谍指挥活动。

在洛杉矶期间,主人公通过秘密信件与曼继续交流情报获取工作,以便曼了解将军在美国筹划的反共产主义计划。同时,他认识了一位美籍日裔女人莫莉(Mori),他们彼此因为美籍亚裔的共性而建立了浪漫的爱情关系。这期间,他还与他的大学同学桑尼相逢,桑尼也是越南人,是一家报纸的记者。

将军在洛杉矶开始谋划返回越南并重新获取政权,但是他发现在洛杉矶有共产党的间谍。为了洗脱将军对自己的嫌疑,主人公把一位无辜的少校作为替罪羊,并在将军的授意下,让邦开枪杀了这名少校。然而,主人公却因为杀害无辜者而产生了强烈的负罪感。在主人公前往菲律宾期间,同学桑尼与莫莉在一起的事实激怒了他。这时,桑尼撰写了那位无辜少校死亡事件的报道,将军便命令主人公杀了桑尼。其实,这一切都是主人公为报背叛之仇而筹划的阴谋。

为了夺取越南的政权,将军派兵前往越南,主人公为了保护邦一同前往,但是这一行为违背了曼让他留在美国继续监视将军的指令。在越南,他和邦被俘并被关在监狱遭受严刑逼供。最终,他见到了自己的上司——曼。但是他在监狱遭受的所有酷刑都是在曼的指令下进行的。最终,在主人公承认了一些所谓的罪行后,曼释放了他们并强迫他们离开了越南。

小说主人公对自己在政治信仰和所处真实环境中的立场感到矛盾,他努力在两个世界中生存,最终导致他被最信任的人抓获并折磨。"同情者",表达的是对越南的同胞、北越的同志、南越的士兵、美国白人社会中处于弱势的越南难民和其他少数族群的深切的同情。主人公背负多重身份,在感受和跨越不同的文化、种族、政治信仰的张力中,在对自我和身份的追问中艰难前行。

(三) 作品选读:《同情者》[1]

CHAPTER 8

We own the day, but CHARLIE owns the night. Never forget that. These are the words that blond twenty-one-year-old Sergeant JAY BELLAMY hears on his first day in the torrid tropics of Nam from his new commanding officer, Captain WILL SHAMUS. Shamus was baptized in the blood of his own comrades on the beaches of Normandy, survived another near-death experience under a Chinese human-wave attack in Korea, then hauled himself up the ranks on a pulley oiled with Jack Daniel's. He knows he will not ascend any higher, not with his Bronx manners and his big, knobby knuckles over which no velvet gloves fit. This is a political war, he informs his acolyte, the words emanating from behind the smoke screen produced by a Cuban cigar. But all I know is a killing war. His task: save the prelapsarian Montagnards of a bucolic hamlet perched on the border of wild Laos. What's threatening them is the Viet Cong, and not just any Viet Cong. This is the baddest of the bad—King Cong. King Cong will die for his country, which is more than can be said for most Americans. More important, King Cong will kill for his country, and nothing makes King

[1] Nguyen, Viet Thanh. *The Sympathizer*. New York: Grove Press, 2015, pp. 65 - 73.

Cong lick his lips like the ferric scent of the white man's blood. King Cong has stocked the dense jungle around the hamlet with veteran guerrillas, battle-wizened men (and women) who have slaughtered Frenchmen from the Highlands to the Street Without Joy. What's more, King Cong has infiltrated the hamlet with subversives and sympathizers, friendly faces only masks for calculating wills. Standing against them are the hamlet's Popular Forces, a ragtag bunch of farmers and teenagers, Vietnam's own minutemen trained by the dozen Green Berets of the US Army Special Forces A-Team. This is enough, Sergeant Bellamy thinks, alone in his watchtower at midnight. He's dropped out of Harvard and run far from his St. Louis home, his millionaire daddy, and his fur-cloaked mother. This is enough, this stunningly beautiful jungle and these humble, simple people. This is where I, Jay Bellamy, make my first and maybe my last stand—at THE HAMLET.

This, at any rate, was my interpretation of the screenplay mailed to me by the director's personal assistant, the thickish manila envelope arriving with my name misspelled in a beautifully cursive hand. That was the first whiff of trouble, the second being how the personal assistant, Violet, did not even bother to say hello or good-bye when she called for my mailing information and to arrange a meeting with the director in his Hollywood Hills home. When Violet opened the door, she continued with her bewildering manner of discourse in person. Glad to see you could make it, heard a lot about you, loved your notes on The Hamlet. And that's precisely how she spoke, trimming pronouns and periods, as if punctuation and grammar were wasted on me. Then, without deigning to make eye contact, she inclined her head in a gesture of condescension and disdain, signaling me to enter.

Perhaps her abruptness was merely part of her personality, for she had the appearance of the worst kind of bureaucrat, the aspiring one, from blunt, square haircut to blunt, clean fingernails to blunt, efficient pumps. But perhaps it was me, still morally disoriented from the crapulent major's death, as well as the apparition of his severed head at the wedding banquet. The emotional residue of that night was like a drop of arsenic falling into the still waters of my soul, nothing having changed from the taste of it but everything now tainted. So perhaps that was why when I crossed over the threshold into the marble foyer, I instantly suspected that the cause of her behavior was my race. What she saw when she looked at me must have been my yellowness, my slightly smaller eyes, and the shadow cast by the ill fame of the Oriental's genitals, those supposedly minuscule privates disparaged on many a public restroom wall by semiliterates. I might have been just half an Asian, but in America it was all or nothing when it came to race. You were either white or you weren't. Funnily enough, I had never felt inferior because of my race during my foreign student days. I was foreign by definition and therefore was treated as a guest. But now, even though I was a card-carrying American with a driver's license, Social Security card, and resident alien permit, Violet still considered me as foreign, and this misrecognition punctured the smooth skin of my self-confidence. Was I just being paranoid, that all American characteristic? Maybe Violet was stricken with colorblindness, the willful inability to distinguish between white and any other color, the only infirmity Americans wished for themselves. But as she advanced along the polished bamboo floors, steering clear of the dusky maid vacuuming a Turkish rug, I just knew it could not be so. The flawlessness of my English did not matter. Even if she could hear me, she still saw right through me, or perhaps saw someone else instead of me, her retinas burned with the images of all the castrati dreamed up by Hollywood to steal the place of real Asian men. Here I speak of those cartoons named Fu Manchu, Charlie Chan, Number One Son, Hop Sing—Hop Sing!—and the bucktoothed, bespectacled Jap not so much played as mocked by Mickey Rooney in Breakfast at Tiffany's. The performance was so insulting it even deflated my fetish for Audrey Hepburn, understanding as I did her implicit endorsement of such loathsomeness.

By the time I sat down opposite the director in his office, I was seething from the memory of all these previous wounds, although I did not show it. On the one hand, I was sitting for a meeting with the famed Auteur, when once I was just another lovelorn movie fan passing Saturday afternoons in the cinematic bliss of matinee screenings from which I emerged, blinking and slightly shocked, into sunlight as bright as the fluorescent bulbs of a hospital birthing room. On the other hand, I was flummoxed by having read a screenplay whose greatest special effect was neither the blowing up of various things nor the evisceration of various bodies, but the achievement of narrating a movie about our country where not a single one of our countrymen had an intelligible word to say. Violet had scraped my already chafed ethnic sensitivity even further, but since it would not do to make my irritation evident, I forced myself to smile and do what I did best, remaining as unreadable as a paper package wrapped up with string.

The Auteur studied me, this extra who had crept into the middle of his perfect mise-en-scène. A golden Oscar statuette exhibited itself to the side of his telephone, serving as either a kingly scepter or a mace for braining impertinent screenwriters. A hirsute show of manliness ruffled along his forearms and from the collar of his shirt, reminding me of my own relative hairlessness, my chest (and stomach and buttocks) as streamlined and glabrous as a Ken doll. He was the hottest writer-director in town after the triumph of his last two films, beginning with *Hard Knock*, a critically lauded movie about the travails of Greek American youth in the inflamed streets of Detroit. It was loosely autobiographical, the Auteur having been born with an olive-tinged Greek surname he had bleached in typical Hollywood fashion. His most recent film declared that he had had enough with off-white ethnicity, exploring cocaine-white ethnicity instead. *Venice Beach* was about the failure of the American Dream, featuring a dipsomaniac reporter and his depressive wife writing competing versions of the Great American Novel. As the foolscap mounted endlessly, their money and their lives slowly drained away, leaving the audience with a last image of the couple's dilapidated cottage strangled by bougainvillea while beautifully lit by the sun setting beyond the Pacific. It was Didion crossed with Chandler as prophesied by Faulkner and shot by Welles. It was very good. He had talent, no matter how much it might have pained me to say so.

Great to meet you, the Auteur began. Loved your notes. How about something to drink. Coffee, tea, water, soda, scotch. Never too early for scotch. Violet, some scotch. Ice. I said ice. No ice, then. Me too. Always neat for me. Look at my view. No, not at the gardener. José! José! Got to pound on the glass to get his attention. He's half deaf. José! Move! You're blocking the view. Good. See the view. I'm talking about the Hollywood sign right there. Never get tired of it. Like the Word of God just dropped down, plunked on the hills, and the Word was Hollywood. Didn't God say let there be light first. What's a movie but light. Can't have a movie without light. And then words. Seeing that sign reminds me to write every morning. What. All right, so it doesn't say Hollywood. You got me. Good eye. Thing's falling to pieces. One O's half fallen and the other O's fallen altogether. The word's gone to shit. So what. You still get the meaning. Thanks, Violet. Cheers. How do they say it in your country. I said how do they say it. Yo, yo, yo, is it. I like that. Easy to remember. Yo, yo, yo, then. And here's to the Congressman for sending you my way. You're the first Vietnamese I've ever met. Not too many of you in Hollywood. Hell, none of you in Hollywood. And authenticity's important. Not that authenticity beats imagination. The story still comes first. The universality of the story has to be there. But it doesn't hurt to get the details right. I had a Green Beret who actually fought with the Montagnards vet the script. He found me. He had a screenplay. Everyone has a screenplay. Can't write but he's a real American hero. Two tours of duty, killed VC with his bare hands. A Silver Star and a Purple Heart with oak leaf clusters. You should have seen the Polaroids he showed me. Made my stomach turn. Gave me some ideas, though, for how to shoot the movie. Hardly had any corrections to make. What do you think of that.

It took me a moment to realize he was asking me a question. I was disoriented, as if I were an English as a second language speaker listening to an equally foreign speaker from another country. That's great, I said.

You bet it's great. You, on the other hand. You wrote me another screenplay in the margins. You ever even read a screenplay before.

It took me another moment to realize there was another question. Like Violet, he had a problem with conventional punctuation. No—

I didn't think so. So why do you think—

But you didn't get the details right.

I didn't get the details right. Violet, hear that. I researched your country, my friend. I read Joseph Buttinger and Frances FitzGerald. Have you read Joseph Buttinger and Frances FitzGerald. He's the foremost historian on your little part of the world. And she won the Pulitzer Prize. She dissected your psychology. I think I know something about you people.

His aggressiveness flustered me, and my flustering, which I was not accustomed to, only flustered me further, which was my only explanation for my forthcoming behavior. You didn't even get the screams right, I said.

Excuse me.

I waited for an interjection until I realized he was just interrupting me with a question. All right, I said, my string starting to unravel. If I remember correctly, pages 26, 42, 58, 77, 91, 103, and 118, basically all the places in the script where one of my people has a speaking part, he or she screams. No words, just screams. So you should at least get the screams right.

Screams are universal. Am I right, Violet.

You're right, she said from where she sat next to me. Screams are not universal, I said. If I took this telephone cord and wrapped it around your neck and pulled it tight until your eyes bugged out and your tongue turned black, Violet's scream would sound very different from the scream you would be trying to make. Those are two very different kinds of terror coming from a man and a woman. The man knows he is dying. The woman fears she is likely to die soon. Their situations and their bodies produce a qualitatively different timbre to their voices. One must listen to them carefully to understand that while pain is universal, it is also utterly private. We cannot know whether our pain is like anybody else's pain until we talk about it. Once we do that, we speak and think in ways cultural and individual. In this country, for example, someone fleeing for his life will think he should call for the police. This is a reasonable way to cope with the threat of pain. But in my country, no one calls for the police, since it is often the police who inflict the pain. Am I right, Violet?

Violet mutely nodded her head.

So let me just point out that in your script, you have my people scream the following way: *AIIEEEEE!!!* For example, when VILLAGER #3 is impaled by a Viet Cong punji trap, this is how he screams. Or when the LITTLE GIRL sacrifices her life to alert the Green Berets to the Viet Cong sneaking into the village, this is how she screams before her throat is cut. But having heard many of my countrymen screaming in pain, I can assure you this is not how they scream. Would you like to hear how they scream?

His Adam's apple bobbed as he swallowed. Okay.

I stood up and leaned on the desk to look right into his eyes. But I didn't see him. What I saw was the face of the wiry Montagnard, an elder of the Bru minority who lived in an actual hamlet not far from the setting of this fiction. Rumor had it he served as a liaison agent for the Viet Cong. I was on my first assignment as a lieutenant and could not figure out a way to save the man from my captain wrapping a strand of rusted barbed wire around his throat, the necklace tight enough so that each time he swallowed, the wire tickled his Adam's apple. That was not what made the old man scream, however. It was just the appetizer. In my mind, though, as I watched the scene, I screamed for him.

Here's what it sounds like, I said, reaching across the desk to pick up the Auteur's Montblanc fountain pen. I wrote onomatopoeically across the cover page of the screenplay in big black letters:

AIEYAAHHH!!! Then I capped his pen, put it back on his leather writing pad, and said, That's how we scream in my country.

After I descended from the Auteur's home to the General's, thirty blocks distant and down the hills to the Hollywood flatlands, I reported my first experience with the motion picture industry to the General and Madame, both of whom were infuriated on my behalf. My meeting with the Auteur and Violet had gone on for a while longer, mostly in a more subdued fashion, with me pointing out that the lack of speaking parts for Vietnamese people in a movie set in Vietnam might be interpreted as cultural insensitivity. True, Violet interjected, but what it boils down to is who pays for the tickets and goes to the movies. Frankly, Vietnamese audiences aren't going to watch this movie, are they? I contained my outrage. Even so, I said, do you not think it would be a little more believable, a little more realistic, a little more authentic, for a movie set in a certain country for the people in that country to have something to say, instead of having your screenplay direct, as it does now, cut to villagers speaking in their own language? Do you think it might not be decent to let them actually say something instead of simply acknowledging that there is some kind of sound coming from their mouths? Could you not even just have them speak a heavily accented English—you know what I mean, ching-chong English—just to pretend they are speaking in an Asian language that somehow American audiences can strangely understand? And don't you think it would be more compelling if your Green Beret had a love interest? Do these men only love and die for each other? That is the implication without a woman in the midst.

The Auteur grimaced and said, very interesting. Great stuff. Loved it, but I had a question. What was it. Oh, yes. How many movies have you made. None. Isn't that right. None, zero, zilch, nada, nothing, and however you say it in your language. So thank you for telling me how to do my job. Now get the hell out of my house and come back after you've made a movie or two. Maybe then I'll listen to one or two of your cheap ideas.

Why was he so rude? Madame said. Didn't he ask you to give him some comments? He was looking for a yes man. He thought I'd give him a rubber stamp of approval. He thought you were going to fawn over him.

When I didn't do it, he was hurt. He's an artist, he's got thin skin.

So much for your career in Hollywood, the General said.

I don't want a career in Hollywood, I said, which was true only to the extent that Hollywood did not want me. I confess to being angry with the Auteur, but was I wrong in being angry? This was especially the case when he acknowledged he did not even know that Montagnard was simply a French catchall term for the dozens of Highland minorities. What if, I said to him, I wrote a screenplay about the American West and simply called all the natives Indians? You'd want to know whether the cavalry was fighting the Navajo or Apache or Comanche, right? Likewise, I would want to know, when you say these people are Montagnards, whether we speak of the Bru or the Nung or the Tay.

Let me tell you a secret, the Auteur said. You ready. Here it is. No one gives a shit.

He was amused by my wordlessness. To see me without words is like seeing one of those Egyptian felines without hair, a rare and not necessarily desirable occasion. Only later, driving away from his house, could I laugh bitterly about how he had bludgeoned me into silence with my own weapon of choice. How could I be so dense? How could I be so deluded? Ever the industrious student, I had read the screenplay in a few hours and then reread and written notes for several more hours, all under the misguided idea my work mattered. I naively believed that I could divert the Hollywood organism from its goal, the simultaneous lobotomization and pickpocketing of the world's audiences. The ancillary benefit was strip-mining history, leaving the real history in the tunnels along with the dead, doling out tiny sparkling diamonds for audiences to gasp over. Hollywood did not just make horror movie monsters, it was its own horror movie monster, smashing me under its foot. I had failed and the Auteur would make The Hamlet as he intended, with my countrymen serving merely as raw material for an epic about white men saving good yellow people from bad yellow people. I pitied the French for their naïveté in believing they had to visit a country in order to exploit it. Hollywood was much more efficient, imagining the countries it wanted to exploit. I was maddened by my helplessness before the Auteur's imagination and machinations. His arrogance marked something new in the world, for this was the first war where the losers would write history instead of the victors, courtesy of the most efficient propaganda machine ever created (with all due respect to Joseph Goebbels and the Nazis, who never achieved global domination). Hollywood's high priests understood innately the observation of Milton's Satan, that it was better to rule in Hell than serve in Heaven, better to be a villain, loser, or antihero than virtuous extra, so long as one commanded the bright lights of center stage. In this forthcoming Hollywood trompe l'oeil, all the Vietnamese of any side would come out poorly, herded into the roles of the poor, the innocent, the evil, or the corrupt. Our fate was not to be merely mute; we were to be struck dumb.

Have some pho, Madame said. It will make you feel better.

She had been cooking and the house smelled of sentiment, a rich aroma of beef broth and star anise I can only describe as the bouquet of love and tenderness, all the more striking because Madame had never cooked before coming to this country. For women of Madame's rarefied class, cooking was one of those functions contracted out to other women, along with cleaning, nursing, teaching, sewing, and so on, everything except for the bare biological necessities, which I could not imagine Madame performing, except, perhaps, for breathing. But the exigencies of exile had made it necessary for Madame to cook, as no one else in the household was capable of anything more than boiling water. In the General's case, even that was beyond him. He could fieldstrip and reassemble an M16 blindfolded, but a gas stove was as perplexing as a calculus equation, or at least he pretended so. Like most of us Vietnamese men, he simply did not want to be even brushed with domesticity. The only domestic things he did were sleep and eat, both of which he was better at than me. He finished his pho a good five minutes before I did, although my slow speed of consumption was not due to lack of will but because Madame's pho had dissolved me and transported me back in time to my mother's household, where she concocted the broth from the gray beef bones given by my father from his leftovers. Usually, we ate the pho without the thin slices of beef that were its protein, we being too poor to afford the meat itself, except for those rare occasions when my suffering mother scraped together enough wherewithal. But poor as she was, my mother brewed the most wonderfully aromatic soup, and I helped her by charring the ginger and onion that would be plunked into the iron pot for flavor. It was also my task to skim the scum that boiled to the top of the broth as the bones simmered, leaving the broth clear and rich. As the bones continued to simmer for hours, I tortured myself by doing my homework by the pot, the aroma taunting and tantalizing. Madame's pho harkened back to the warmth of my mother's kitchen, which was probably not as warm as it was in my memories, but never mind—I had to stop periodically to savor not only my soup but the marrow of my memories.

Delicious, I said. I haven't had this in years.

Isn't it amazing? I never suspected she had this talent. You should open a restaurant, I said.

The way you talk! She was clearly pleased.

Have you seen this? The General pulled a newspaper from the stack on the kitchen countertop, the latest edition of Sonny's biweekly paper. I had not seen it yet. What disturbed the General was Sonny's article on the major's funeral, now a few weeks past, and the coverage of the wedding. On the major's demise, Sonny wrote that "the police call this a robbery-homicide, but are we sure an officer of the secret police was without enemies who might want him dead?" And in regards to the wedding, Sonny summarized the speeches and concluded by observing that "perhaps it is time for the talk of war to cease. Isn't the war over?"

He's doing what he's supposed to be doing, I said, even though I knew that he had gone too far. But I agree he may be a little naive.

Is it naïveté? That's a generous reading. He's supposed to be a reporter. That means to report the facts, not to make things up or interpret them or put ideas in people's heads.

He isn't wrong about the major, is he?

Whose side are you on? Madame said, completely shedding the role of cook. Reporters need editors and editors need beatings. That's the best newspaper policy. The problem with Son is that he is his own editor and he goes unchecked.

You're absolutely right, Madame. The Auteur's punch had unnerved me, knocked me out of character. Too much freedom of the press is unhealthy for a democracy, I declared. While I did not believe this, my character, the good captain, did, and as the actor playing this role I had to sympathize with this man. But most actors spent more time with their masks off than on, whereas in my case it was the reverse. No surprise, then, that sometimes I dreamed of trying to pull a mask off my face, only to realize that the mask was my face. Now, with the face of the captain readjusted for a proper fit, I said, the citizenry can't sift out what is useful and good if there's too much opinion circulating.

No more than two opinions or ideas on any one issue should be out there, the General said. Look at the voting system. Same concept. We had multiple parties and candidates and look at the mess we had. Here you choose the left hand or the right and that's more than enough. Two choices and look at all the drama with every presidential election. Even two choices may be one too many. One choice is enough, and no choice may be even better. Less is more, isn't it? You know the man, Captain. He'll listen to you. Remind him of how we did things back home. Even though we're here, we still need to remember the ways we did things.

In the good old days, Sonny would already be sweating in a holding cell. Out loud, I said, speaking of the old days, sir, are we making any progress on winning them back again?

Progress is being made, the General said, leaning back in his chair. We have friends and allies in Claude and the Congressman, and they tell me they are not alone. But it's a difficult time for getting support publicly, since the American people don't want to fight another war. So, we have to assemble ourselves slowly.

We need a network here and there, I suggested.

I have a list of the officers for our first meeting. I've talked to all of them in person and they are dying for the chance to fight. There's nothing for them here. The only chance for them to regain their honor and be men again is to reclaim our country.

We'll need more than a vanguard.

Vanguard? Madame said. That's communist talk.

Maybe so. But the communists won, Madame. They weren't just lucky. Perhaps we should learn from some of their strategies. A vanguard can lead the rest of the people toward where it is they don't even know they want to go but should go.

He's right, the General said.

The vanguard works clandestinely but sometimes shows the public a different face. Voluntary organizations and the like become the fronts for the vanguard.

Exactly, the General said. Look at Son. We need to make his newspaper one of those front organizations. And we need a youth group, a women's group, even an intellectuals' group.

We also need cells. Parts of the organization need to be secluded from one another so that if one cell is lost, others can survive. This is one cell right here. Then there are the cells Claude and the Congressman are involved in, which I know nothing about.

In due time, Captain. One step at a time. The Congressman is working on certain contacts to clear the way for us to send men to Thailand.

That will be the staging area.

Exactly. A return by sea is too difficult. We have to go overland back into the country. Meanwhile, Claude is finding us money. Money can get us the rest of what we need. We can get the men, but they will need weapons, training, a place to train. They'll need transport to Thailand. We must think like communists, as you say. We must plan far ahead for decades. We must live and work underground, as they did.

At least we're already acquainted with darkness.

We are, aren't we? We had no choice. We have never had a choice, not really, not when it matters. Communism forced us to do everything we have done to oppose it. History has moved us. We have no choice but to fight, to resist evil and to resist being forgotten. This is why—and here the General picked up Sonny's newspaper—even talking about the war being over is dangerous. We must not allow our people to grow complacent.

And neither must we let them forget their resentment, I added. That's where newspapers can play a role, on the culture front.

But only if the journalists do their work as they should. The General tossed the newspaper back on the table. "Resentment." That's a good word. Always resent, never relent. Perhaps that should be our motto.

There's a ring to it, I said.

思考与讨论

(1) 小说中"剧本"的隐喻意义是什么?

(2) 小说主人公多重身份的困境以及这种身份所具有的优势是什么?

(3) 小说主人公作为亚裔在美国的生存处境如何?

(4) "同情者"表达的是对何人、何事的同情?

(5) 如何理解作者在小说主人公多重身份上建构的多元文化冲突与融合?

拓展阅读

[1] Hoy, Pat C. "Spying with Sympathy and love." *The Sewanee Review*, Vol. 123, No. 4, 2015, pp. 685 - 690.

[2] Williams, Michael. "Kafka in Saigon." *The World Today*, Vol. 71, No. 4, 2015, pp. 47 - 47.

[3] 孙璐. 同情的困境:《同情者》中的世界主义伦理与反讽主义实践[J]. 外国文学研究, 2017(3): 112 - 121.

第七章
当代美国喜剧小说

20 世纪 60 年代以来，美国喜剧小说在秉承马克·吐温（Mark Twain）美国乡土幽默（American humor）讽刺文风的同时，更加凸显政治性、族裔性和女性主义等显著特征。圆滑可笑的新英格兰北方佬小商贩形象，慢吞吞的南方农民典型，充满喜剧风情的西部边疆汉子形象等，各移民种族的幽默特质都是当代美国喜剧小说幽默的表征。

当代美国喜剧小说往往与宗教、族裔和地域有关。黑人、天主教徒和犹太教徒各具独特的喜剧特征，西部小说在幽默讽刺中对比乡土与都市、自然与工业等社会变化，本土裔小说塑造鬼怪精灵的恶作剧者（the trickster）反抗形象，犹太裔作家极力刷新犹太刻板印象，将犹太人的幽默机智特征注入美国文化，非裔喜剧小说借用反讽缓解来自社会和生活的压力，女性作家笔下的家常幽默（domestic humor）常常带有幽怨情绪。当代美国喜剧小说在表现幽默风趣文风的同时也饱含嘲笑奚落等苦涩的深意，用幽默的方式表征身份与生活的迷茫困境。幽默在当代美国小说中不仅仅是一种修辞，更是一种赋予政治含义的抵抗策略。

黑色幽默是现代美国小说的典型特征。1965 年，一本名为《黑色幽默》（*Black Humor*）的专著在美国畅销。1973 年，舒尔茨（Max F. Schulz）在《60 年代的黑色幽默小说》（*Black Humor Fiction of the Sixties*）一书中集中研究现代美国黑色幽默作家，将黑色幽默作家归属为后存在主义者，以应对没有目标、没有终点的现代社会终局。

进入 90 年代，华莱士（David Foster Wallace）的小说以近似讽刺（proximal irony）风格著称，运用人物嵌入式视角讽刺世界的滑稽可笑。自后“9·11”（post - 9/11）小说产生以来，美国喜剧小说幽默的伦理内涵和政治寓意又增加了一个新的种族审视的语境。

第一节　美国喜剧小说传统及其当代特征

喜剧风格是美国小说的典型特征。美国小说从写作素材、叙事技巧到创作形式都具有美国式幽默。美国式幽默主要源于民间，民间口头传统为美国文学注入了地方特色。幽默也是美国小说区别于欧洲大陆小说的显著特征。美国小说的幽默主要指美国乡土幽默，以幽默讽刺著称的美国乡土作家马克·

吐温代表了美国式幽默的语言风格。

20世纪60年代和70年代是美国社会受到强烈冲击的年代。长达十年之余的越南战争引起了美国国内外的反战情绪，同时，青年学生发起对正统文化反叛的反文化运动，美国国内掀起解放妇女权力的女权运动，马丁·路德·金为黑人争取与白人平等的权利，以乘坐公共交通工具为开端的民权运动等在60年代风起云涌。这些政治文化运动给美国政治、社会、文学、艺术、文化提出了极大的挑战，也提供了诸多解读视角来看待美国60年代至70年代混乱的社会局面、复杂的文化背景和由此滋生的新的文学动向。

20世纪60年代黑人文艺复兴运动促使黑人文学空前繁盛，黑人文学与生俱来的幽默传统也得以绽放，美国非裔作家在文学作品中很自然地表现出黑人民族文化中的幽默、神话等创作手法，这一时期最有代表性的非裔作家是托妮·莫里森。60年代美国印第安文艺复兴意味着美国本土裔文学走向现代性，本土裔作家以莫马迪为首在美国主流文学史上崭露头角，"恶作剧者"等独特的幽默形象在本土裔作家的创作中深入人心。20世纪犹太喜剧演员和犹太幽默为美国幽默注入新的元素，第二次世界大战以后，索尔·贝娄(Saul Bellow)、伯纳德·马拉默德(Bernard Malamud)等第二代在美国生长的犹太移民作家面对美国的同化开始思考个人生活和传统价值观念。黑色幽默自20世纪60年代起也应运而生，主要用来描述美国60年代出现的那些常常令读者感到既好笑又苦涩，既诙谐又悲哀的小说[①]。

总体而言，60年代以来，美国白人主流文学依然强势，就小说的喜剧特性而言，白人主流文学的幽默继承了马克·吐温的辛辣讽刺，南方文学也秉承了传统的口语幽默等表现方式。同时，美国白人主流文学的边界被打破，族裔文学、女性文学等进入主流文学领域，不同种族、不同阶层、不同性别的幽默特征在美国文学中得以呈现，共同促成美国喜剧小说的多维特征。

第二节　美国文学的幽默多样性成因及特征

美国文学的幽默主要体现在人物塑造和话语模式等方面，美国不同种族的幽默表现特征往往有所不同。可以说，正是美国处处可见的种族差异和偏见使得美国文学呈现出幽默的多样性：从以"美国佬"著称的白人男性幽默形象到西部边疆粗糙汉子的幽默风趣，再到南方文学中注重民间口语的幽默表现；从以自嘲为特征的犹太幽默到具有嘻哈之风的黑人幽默，再到以笑声作为抵抗策略的本土裔印第安幽默，美国幽默往往与政治有关联，幽默为美国文学增添了民族独特性和审美特征。

一、白人男性喜剧形象

美国作为一个多民族多种族国家，其族群特征是不可忽视的文学文化因素。美国文学在以白人男

① 李维屏、戴鸿斌：《什么是现代主义文学》，上海：上海外语教育出版社，2011年，第61页。

性为中心人物的宏大叙事之隙，族裔群体、女性群体也成为主要的喜剧人物形象。美国小说的喜剧传统正是在以白人男性为中心的人物与非白人男性喜剧人物穿插中得以形成。

美语俚语中常用“美国佬”（Yankee）指白人男性。康斯坦斯·洛克（Constance Rourke）认为，美国的喜剧传统自美国独立战争时期开始流传，“美国佬”常常是一帮旅行者，他们爱讲故事爱讲笑话，天真又狡猾，几乎没受过教育。“美国佬”是美国最初的喜剧人物形象，以新英格兰的恶作剧者或是以典型的美国傻乐滑稽可笑的形象著称[①]。“美国佬”指新英格兰的品行正直、头脑简单、思想天真的白人男性，区别于欧洲大陆圆滑世故的人物形象。

除了“美国佬”，来自欧洲大陆的美国人还创造了一个西部边疆喜剧形象——“吹牛大王”[②]。“吹牛大王”将想象的故事与现实混在一起讲述。二战后的美国文学中，小说家不乏借用棒球意象丰富并延伸“吹牛大王”的形象。

二、犹太幽默

美国犹太幽默有“贫民窟幽默”之称，犹太幽默突显受难的主题和郁郁不得志的精神状态。犹太民族的排他性和民族内部的不团结“使他们永久地处于软弱无力的地位，当他们陷入不幸时，往往行动上屈从，观念上却抗争，这恰恰导致了犹太民族幽默感的产生”[③]。美国犹太作家将幽默渗透在严肃主题的写作中，作品往往带有自嘲的语气，犹太幽默是犹太作家为缓解历史迫害的创伤记忆和压力而采取的一种策略。

犹太幽默是犹太人在流散漂泊环境中的生存之道和逃避危险、缓解压力的途径。犹太人深信自己是上帝的选民，可是历史上犹太人遭受了深深的磨难和歧视，信仰与现实的巨大反差造就了犹太幽默，犹太幽默不乏用自嘲的口吻来审视磨难。马拉默德往往选取犹太小人物为写作对象，在嘲讽小人物可笑行为的同时表现对人性和人的心理的理解，而菲利普·罗斯善于在严肃中达到嘲讽的效果。

自 20 世纪 50 年代以来，美国犹太作家不再囿于体现犹太性，而是去反映美国社会普通人的生活。犹太作家用英语写作屡屡获奖，犹太小说从边缘走向美国主流文学。战后最杰出的犹太作家索尔·贝娄自第一部小说《荡来荡去的人》（*Dangling Man*，1944）开始大放异彩，60 年代发表《赫索格》（*Herzog*，1964）讲述犹太知识分子的婚姻生活；70 年代发表《洪堡的礼物》（*Humboldt's Gift*，1975）探讨美国知识分子的地位，获得 1975 年普利策文学奖；1982 年发表《院长的十二月》（*The Dean's December*），1987 年发表《更多的人死于心碎》（*More Die of Heartbreak*）讲述犹太知识分子的生活；1997 年发表中篇小说《真情》（*The Actual*）。

伯纳德·马拉默德是战后另一个重要的美国犹太作家。马拉默德出生在美国布鲁克林区的一个俄国犹太移民家庭，其代表作《店员》（*The Assistant*，1957）叙述主人公弗兰克在磨难中获得新生，阐明犹太教的道德观念。1966 年写犹太人困难的小说《基辅怨》（*The Fixer*）发表，次年获得普利策小说奖。

---

① Rourke, Constance. "*American Humor: A Study of the National Character*." *New York Review of Books*, 2004, pp. 6 - 12.

② Bendixen, Alfred. *A Companion to the American novel*. West Chichester: Blackwell Publishing Ltd. 2012, p 224.

③ 苏晖：《黑色幽默与美国小说的幽默传统》，北京：中国社会科学出版社，2013 年，第 148 页。

1979年《杜宾的生活》(*Dubin's Lives*)发表。马拉默德在小说中处处表现犹太幽默的特征。

艾萨克·巴什维斯·辛格(Issac Bashevis Singer)是另一个犹太文学创作大师。辛格出生在波兰,早期用意第绪语写作,于1935年移居美国。《傻瓜吉姆佩尔》(*Gimpel the Fool*, 1957)是辛格最著名的短篇故事集,辛格借着吉姆佩尔面对妻子侮辱的逆来顺受,表现了犹太人面对纳粹迫害无力反抗的现实。《卢布林的魔术师》(*The Magician of Lublin*, 1959)是辛格的代表作,60年代辛格出版多部小说,如《市场街的斯宾诺莎》(*The Spinnnoza of Market Street*, 1961)、《奴隶》(*The Slave*, 1962)、《庄园》(*The Manor*, 1967)、《地产》(*The Estate*, 1969)等。1978年,辛格获诺贝尔文学奖。

20世纪80年代之后,以索尔·贝娄、辛格、菲利普·罗斯等为代表的一大批犹太作家更加关注当下美国犹太人的生活状态,他们的文学成就确立了美国犹太文学在世界文学中的地位。犹太性是探讨犹太作家的关键词,而幽默也是阅读犹太作家在作品中叙说犹太人现实生活与精神生活不可小觑的元素。

三、黑人喜剧模式

非裔美国喜剧人物和创作技巧表现出黑人传统的幽默元素。美国黑人文学中的笑声和俚语根植于黑人民族固有的幽默传统,笑声是掩饰生活苦难的策略。幽默是美国黑人生存的方式和长久以来生成的心理机制,也是美国黑人文学的主要特征。黑人幽默在美国文学与文化中的地位不容忽视。黑人的幽默似乎与生俱来,幽默是美国黑人对生活经验和生活现实的反映,也是美国黑人的生存策略。黑人文学中的“坏黑鬼”(The Bad Nigger)这个喜剧人物形象总是用黑人俚语挑战白人权威。

20世纪60年代、70年代以来的美国黑人文艺复兴提倡黑人传统艺术和文化等价值观念。黑人作家兰斯顿·休斯(Langston Hughes)将幽默视为主题表现的主要手段,奥古斯特·威尔逊(August Wilson)用黑人幽默表达种族诉求,托妮·莫里森常用幽默揭示历史和表现种族问题。

四、本土印第安裔的喜剧模式

美国本土印第安裔文学中的喜剧人物在白人种族主义视角下屡见不鲜,本土裔作家路易斯·厄德里克、莱斯利·玛蒙·希尔科、詹姆斯·韦尔奇、谢尔曼·阿莱克西等刻画了不少印第安喜剧人物形象。早期白人作家的作品以嘲弄的笔调表现出对印第安人的种族偏见和种族歧视,1974年詹姆斯·韦尔奇的《血色冬天》(*Winter in the Blood*)改写了印第安裔美国人被嘲弄的这一刻板形象,韦尔奇的小说中充满悲伤的幽默,揭露了白人对印第安人的掠夺与戕害。

当代美国本土裔作家将印第安本土艰辛的生存情景杂糅在喜剧作品中。印第安作家往往设置郊狼等“恶作剧者”幽默形象,郊狼又笑又跳,用幽默来应对被灭绝的命运。美国本土喜剧小说中的“恶作剧者”是典型的喜剧式人物,本土裔小说家往往在小说中塑造一个“恶作剧者”形象,形成具有本土裔特色的喜剧风格。“恶作剧者”幽默、嬉笑、坚韧、玩世不恭、苦中作乐,以此来抵抗美国本土裔居民的艰辛生活和受到的不公正待遇,所以在本土裔文学中,幽默主要是一种抵抗策略。当然,作为北美土地上的原住民，幽默也是本土裔印第安人的性情所在。美国本土裔作家路易斯·厄德里克的《爱药》等小说，维兹诺、韦尔奇以及阿莱克西等作家的小说中往往突出一个“恶作剧者”的喜剧形象。

笑话常常是印第安裔作家采用的另一种幽默手法。在本土裔作家的写作中，隐忍是一种幽默，也是一种无奈的抵抗。厄德里克笔下的娜娜普什和阿莱克西笔下的复仇者郊狼都是喜剧人物。阿莱克西的《一个印第安少年的超真实的日记》(*The Absolutely True Diary of a Part-time Indian*, 2007)充分体现了印第安人悲伤的幽默。以讽刺幽默见长的美国本土裔作家谢尔曼·阿莱克西在小说《保留地布鲁斯》(*Reservation Blues*, 1995)中将印第安神话故事与白人历史传说杂糅，以纪实的方式展现印第安人身份以及被殖民的历史，书中充满冷峻的幽默，讽刺意味十分明显。

五、民间传统与女性喜剧角色

以女性为主的喜剧小说中，女性常常被刻画为悍妇的形象，男女两性争锋相对，女性为了在两性斗争中取胜，将其机智幽默发挥得淋漓尽致。当代美国小说中的喜剧人物也不乏白人男性落魄又幽默的角色。美国现代小说中的个人自述沿用口语叙事的方式表现幽默。盖瑞森·凯勒(Garrison Keillor)的《沃博艮湖的日子》(*Lake Wobegon Days*, 1985)就是一部集中了民间大众文化和幽默的小说。

民间传统在当代美国小说中经久不衰。我们在很多当代美国小说中都能找到哈克·贝恩似的大众人物形象和幽默叙事。第三人称叙事像纪录片似的纪实展现民众生活。以描写美国南方生活见长的短篇小说大师尤多拉·韦尔蒂和盖瑞森·凯勒在小说写作上继承了这种纪实风格。尤多拉·韦尔蒂《失败的战争》(*Losing Battle*, 1970)集中描写人物的滑稽可笑行为，运用方言，采用具有地方特色的朴实的比喻，并故意拼错单词以突出人物的幽默特性。

第三节　黑色幽默的盛行

当代美国喜剧小说呈现的总体特征是黑色幽默。自从马克·吐温的小说《镀金时代》(Gilded Age)于1873年问世以来，美国文坛对美国政治、民主等的讽刺从未间断。黑色幽默是二战后美国喜剧小说的一个新发展，尤其在60年代之后盛行。

当幽默滋生恐惧，黑色幽默便产生了。“黑色幽默”的概念由法国超现实主义创始人安德烈·布勒东(André Breton)于1939年在《黑色幽默选集》(*Anthologie de l'humour noir*)中首次提出。黑色幽默盛行却是在二战之后。冯内古特(Kurt Vonnegut)的《五号屠宰场》(*Slaughterhouse-Five*)用荒诞的手法强调战争给人带来的绝望感；约瑟夫·海勒(Joseph Heller)的《第二十二条军规》(*Catch-22*)运用黑色幽默极大地讽刺二战的残酷与荒谬。黑色幽默将严肃的思想用喜剧的方式呈现出来，从这点来讲，黑色幽默是一个矛盾的集合体，严肃的事件与喜剧风格在黑色幽默的写作中融合。黑色幽默虽然秉承了喜剧风格，可是在内涵上与喜剧大相径庭，传统的喜剧总是趋向欢喜的场面和结局，而黑色幽默却用喜剧风格彰显痛苦与悲愤，以嬉笑的方式给人的心灵带来冲击与震荡。

重写与改写成为黑色幽默新的生成力量。重写与改写打破了原作的叙事思想，人物角色的设置也发生了极大变化，很多时候改写颠倒了原作中的正反人物角色，从而产生幽默效果。黑色幽默对政治和社会极具讽刺力量。黑色幽默重新审视现实和历史事件，在文学中充当反抗的力量。因此，族裔文学、历史小说中总能出现黑色幽默的影子。黑色幽默这股解构的力量为后现代文学注入了活力。托马斯·品钦的《万有引力之虹》讽刺并揭露了二战的侵略本性，是典型的黑色幽默小说。

黑色幽默用极其夸张、嘲笑、怪诞的笔调反映西方现代社会的混乱、荒谬和非理性。在某种程度上，黑色幽默是表现现代西方人的异化感和虚无感以及迷茫心理的一种方式。就表现荒谬和虚无而言，黑色幽默当属现代主义文学流派。黑色幽默集喜剧和悲剧于一体，将幽默作为一种抵抗虚无、荒诞、无奈的手段，达到一种特殊的讽刺艺术效果。黑色幽默多采用反讽的叙事策略，具有喜剧元素的同时也体现出较强的悲剧感。

较之传统的喜剧小说，黑色幽默小说呈现的主题与风格更加复杂，将悲与喜、苦与乐夹杂在一起，有种悲喜交加的无奈。黑色幽默以幽默为策略面对现实的荒诞，用笑声缓解生活的压力、荒谬与不公。20世纪60年代以来的美国黑色幽默比起传统的黑色幽默更多了辛辣的笔调和荒诞的处境描写，黑色幽默用幽默的语词语调揭露现实，锋芒毕露，其本质是绝望的。黑色幽默在“已经失去内在价值的环境中强调人的生存价值”[①]。

黑色幽默模糊了悲喜的界限。黑色幽默小说的叙述语调冷静，在苦笑中批判社会，反讽自嘲，释放绝望的情绪。黑色幽默小说家的思想观念和艺术观念包含了“黑色”的现实感受、“荒诞”的哲学认知以及“喜剧”艺术观[②]。

20世纪60年代存在主义思潮对黑色幽默影响深刻。以萨特为代表的存在主义思想认为存在是荒谬的，人生是痛苦的。人生在一个充满矛盾的世界里，承受着痛苦与不幸。黑色幽默作家在创作主题上表现出存在主义强调的悲观绝望等末世荒诞基调。

60年代嬉皮士等反理性反文化行径风行一时，折射出60年代美国社会的荒诞现实。荒诞是黑色幽默的核心内涵[③]。黑色幽默小说和荒诞派戏剧是20世纪60年代小说和戏剧领域两个重要的文学流派。黑色幽默小说家运用幽默的方式、喜剧的艺术形式表现荒诞绝望的现实世界。

20世纪60年代和70年代以来，美国黑色幽默作家主要有约瑟夫·海勒、库尔特·冯内古特、托马斯·品钦、约翰·巴斯、詹姆斯·珀迪、布鲁斯·杰伊·弗里德曼、唐纳德·巴赛尔姆、弗拉杰米·纳博科夫、爱德华·阿尔比(Edward Albee)、菲利普·罗斯等。以战争为背景的黑色幽默小说主要有约瑟夫·海勒的《第二十二条军规》(1961)，库尔特·冯内古特的《五号屠宰场》(1969)，托马斯·品钦的《万有引力之虹》(1973)。政治主题的黑色幽默小说主要有罗伯特·库弗(Robert Coover)的《公众的怒火》(*The Public Burning*, 1977)，冯内古特的《茫茫黑夜》(*Mother Night*, 1979)。财富主题的黑色幽默小说有冯内古特的《上帝保佑你，罗斯瓦特先生》(*God Bless You Mr Rosewater*, 1965)，品钦的《拍卖第四十九批》(*The Crying of Lot* 49, 1966)。科技主题的黑色幽默小说包括冯内古特的《猫的摇篮》(*Cat's Cradle*, 1963)、《时震》(*Time Quake*, 1997)；托马斯·品钦的《熵》(*Entropy*, 1960)、《V》(*V*, 1963)。

---

① 王守义：《美国文学变革的二十世纪——〈美国文学选读〉下册序言》，载《求是学刊》1988年第5期，第57－60页。
② 景虹梅：《黑色幽默经典小说主题研究与文本细读》，济南：山东人民出版社，2017，第57页。
③ 张和龙：《幽默缘何染黑色》，载《外国文学》2003年第01期，第90页。

宗教主题的黑色幽默小说有约瑟夫·海勒的《上帝知道》(*God Knows*, 1984),约翰·巴斯的《羊童贾尔斯》(*Giles Goat-Boy*, 1966)。精神病患者主题的黑色幽默小说包括海勒的《出事了》(*Something Happened*, 1974),冯内古特的《冠军早餐》(*Breakfast of Champions*, 1973)等。

第四节　主要作家介绍与代表作品选读

一、尤朵拉·韦尔蒂

(一) 尤朵拉·韦尔蒂简介

尤朵拉·韦尔蒂(Eudora Welty, 1909—2001)是20世纪美国南方的一位拥有极高赞誉的女作家,也是南方文艺复兴的代表作家。她出生于美国密西西比河西部三角洲杰克逊城的一个中产阶级家庭,父亲是俄亥俄州人,母亲是西弗吉尼亚人。韦尔蒂的母亲热爱文学,父亲酷爱摄影,父亲曾是南方一家保险公司的经理。在殷实又温馨的中产家庭中,韦尔蒂受到良好的教育和美满的家庭生活熏陶。韦尔蒂于1929年从威斯康星大学毕业,1930年进纽约哥伦比亚大学商学院学习广告设计,1931年回到家乡在当地电台、报刊等行业从事过不同的职业,这些工作经历为她后来的写作累积了素材。20世纪30年代末期韦尔蒂辞去工作回到杰克逊城,在父亲留下的哥特式住宅从事写作,终身未婚。

1936年韦尔蒂发表第一部短篇小说《一个旅行推销员之死》(*Death of a Traveling Salesman*),之后陆续发表短篇小说和长篇小说。韦尔蒂获得过普利策奖、国家图书奖、国家文学艺术奖章、亨利·詹姆斯奖、欧·亨利奖等多种文学大奖。

韦尔蒂的写作风格风趣幽默,满含哲理。韦尔蒂曾说:"契科夫那种俄罗斯式幽默感与我们南方人如出一辙"[①]。韦尔蒂生动描写美国南方的风土人情,她的作品中处处可见民间语言和美国南方女性特有的口语等语言特色。韦尔蒂写作的故事背景多是美国南方小城镇,她的笔触细腻、语言生动,一个个南方的故事透露出作者对生活的理解和思考。韦尔蒂的叙述句法紧凑,语言简练有力,笔调冷静轻松,语义却深刻。韦尔蒂用朴素幽默的笔调记录着美国南方的人情世故和历史变迁。

韦尔蒂的早期作品集中在20世纪40年代,她在70年代完成了两部长篇小说,在八十年代发表了最后一部短篇故事集《月亮湖》(*Moon Lake and Other Stories*, 1980),1984年发表《一个作家的起步》(*One Writer's Beginnings*)。在人生的最后20年,韦尔蒂写的更多的是散文和书评。韦尔蒂有名的短篇小说集有《绿帘》(*A Curtain of Green and Other Stories*, 1941),其中包括17个短篇故事。《僵化的人》(*Petrified Man*, 1941)是韦尔蒂的第二部短篇故事集,收取8个短篇故事。此外,韦尔蒂的短篇小说集有《大网》(*The Wide Net and Other Stories*, 1943),《西班牙音乐》(*Music from Spain*, 1948),《金苹果》(*The Golden Apples*, 1949),《伊尼斯弗伦的新娘》(*The Bride of the Innisfallen and Other Stories*, 1955),《十三个故事》(*Thirteen Stories*, 1965),《月亮湖》(*Moon Lake and Other Stories*,

① 尤朵拉·韦尔蒂:《尤朵拉·韦尔蒂访谈》,杨向荣译,原载《巴黎评论》一九七二年号,《书城》2013年9月,第118页。

1980)等;长篇小说有《强盗新郎》(*The Robber Bridegroom*, 1942),《三角洲婚礼》(*Delta Wedding*, 1946),《庞德的心》(*The Ponder Heart*, 1954),《失败的战争》(*Losing Battles*, 1970),《乐观者的女儿》(*The Optimist's Daughter*, 1972)等。

韦尔蒂是天生的作家,家乡就是她写作的全部题材,凯瑟琳・安・波特(Katherine Anne Porter)在韦尔蒂《绿帘》的序言中指出,韦尔蒂扎根在家乡①。韦尔蒂的故事饱含热情和想象,也时常采用神话典故。她的小说充满讽刺的笔调和悲喜的基调,很重视细节,富有地方特色。在接受《巴黎评论》采访时,韦尔蒂坦言,"我只把自己当作一个描写人类的作家,我写的是我熟悉的事物,我也正好喜欢自己独特的一隅。"②

密西西比是韦尔蒂熟悉的地方,也是韦尔蒂写作的源泉,家乡滋养了韦尔蒂的想象力。韦尔蒂写地方小镇的故事,但故事的内涵并不囿于某个地方而是对全部生活的理解。密西西比也为韦尔蒂送上无上荣耀,1973 年,密西西比州宣布 5 月 2 日为"尤朵拉・韦尔蒂日"。

《绿帘》中,主人公拉舍夫人的丈夫意外去世,拉舍夫人沉浸在无限悲痛中断绝与世人交往。园中绿色植物藤蔓像是一堵墙隔开了墙外的世俗生活与拉舍夫人内心沉闷的孤寂世界。家中干活的黑人男孩天真无邪,拉舍夫人在男孩身上看到旺盛的生命力,突然萌发出想要毁灭男孩的冲动。然而就在拉舍邪念触发之时,大雨倾盆而下阻止了拉舍夫人这一念头。

《失败的战争》讴歌大萧条时期密西西比一带穷苦农民的坚强品质。这部小说运用复调小说的对话性表现不同人物思想的交流与矛盾。作品人物形象饱满,隐喻意味深远。诚如小说之名所蕴含的反讽意味,小说在人物设置上体现出戏仿、反讽等技巧,揭露南方的衰落与家族内部的温情。

(二)《乐观者的女儿》简介

《乐观者的女儿》是韦尔蒂在母亲去世后写的带有自传色彩的长篇小说。《乐观者的女儿》于 1973 年获得普利策文学奖,被认为是韦尔蒂最好的小说。

《乐观者的女儿》分为四部。在第一部中,劳雷尔赶回新奥尔良探望卧病在床的父亲迈凯尔瓦,并和父亲商量去看考特兰医生。在父亲病床边,劳雷尔看出人人敬仰的法官父亲面对疾病的无力感以及父亲的第二任妻子——来自乡下的费伊在父亲病床前飞扬跋扈、自私自利的情形。劳雷尔在父亲病床前悉心陪伴并鼓励父亲,但是父亲没能摆脱疾病的折磨,最终病逝,劳雷尔和继母费伊护柩回家。在第二部中,小镇众人迎接迈凯尔瓦法官的棺木回家,瞻仰法官遗容,缅怀法官的种种善良与英勇,其中夹杂着继母费伊及其母亲一行在葬礼现场的吵闹。葬礼结束,劳雷尔和继母费伊回到家。第三部,葬礼过后,小镇邻居对法官第一任妻子、劳雷尔的生母贝基无限缅怀,对继母费伊则满是非议。劳雷尔整理父亲母亲的信件等遗物,陷入对父母爱情生活的回忆。第四部,劳雷尔回忆与丈夫菲尔生前美满的幸福时光,劳雷尔与继母费伊争夺母亲生前用的揉面板并最终因感受到记忆的承载放弃争夺,离家远行。

作者从葬礼上探望逝者的切面展现南方小镇人情世态,无比幽默地表现出人物的种种心思和阶级偏见,不乏讽刺。劳雷尔的父亲迈凯尔瓦法官是这座小镇的头面人物,父亲心地善良、德高望重,全镇为父亲举行葬礼,小镇居民将辞世的迈凯尔瓦法官视为代表小镇荣耀的英雄人物,而葬礼上继母费伊及其

---

① Welty, Eudora. *A Curtain of Green and Other Stories*. New York: A Harvest Book, Harcourt. Inc., 1941, p 6.

② 尤朵拉・韦尔蒂:《尤朵拉・韦尔蒂访谈》,杨向荣译,原载《巴黎评论》一九七二年号,《书城》2013 年 9 月,第 121 页。

母亲却吵闹不休，葬礼仪式中各种力量的交锋蠢蠢欲动。

《乐观者的女儿》隐喻南方向现代过渡的社会转型时期小镇人的应对状态。南方过去与现在的碰撞冲突处处可见。以费伊为主的外来破坏性力量瓦解着南方的价值观和秩序，怀旧的南方无处躲避，无力应对。费伊是很糟糕的外来者形象，虽然代表单个的力量，可是这个冲击却让包括法官在内的小镇人措手不及，可见老南方的衰退势不可挡，小说展现的正是南方历史与现实的碰撞。

从女性主义视角来阅读这部小说，有评论家认为母亲贝基是第一次女权运动时期的南方淑女，温柔顺从、体面矜持；而劳雷尔作为70年代第二次女性主义浪潮之后的女性，代表了有思想有见地、头脑冷静、经济独立的新女性；继母费伊是从北方来到南方的闯入者，粗俗贫穷却又大胆，张扬舞爪，无视南方传统与秩序。父亲经历了两个完全不同的妻子，对此也可以读出作者对父权制的商榷。

韦尔蒂叙事技艺高超，在日常的叙事中展露出南方的历史变迁和社会风貌，也夹杂着作者对女性生活状态与婚姻的思考。如果南方象征着历史荣耀、秩序和体系，那么北方相对是物质、趋利和世俗的代表。南方对来自北方的外部世界十分抗拒。南方的集体观念和北方个人主义的价值观之间的张力也表现得十分明显。

(三) 作品选读:《乐观者的女儿》①

"And under the cloak of modesty he wore, a fearless man! Fearless man!" Major Bullock suddenly burst into speech, standing at the foot of the coffin. "Remember the day, everybody, when Clint McKelva stood up and faced the White Caps?" The floor creaked agonizingly as he rocked back and forth on his feet and all but shouted, filling the room, perhaps the house, with his voice. "The time Clint sentenced that fellow for willful murder and the White Caps let it be known they were coming to town out of all their holes and nooks and crannies to take that man from the jail! And Clint just as quick sent out word of his own: he was going to ring that jail and Courthouse of ours with Mount Salus volunteers, and we'd be armed and ready. And the White Caps came, too-came a little bit earlier than they promised, little bit earlier than the rest of us got on hand. But Clint, Clint all by himself, he walked out on the front steps ofthe Courthouse and stood there and he said, 'Come right on in! The jail is upstairs, on the second floor!'"

"I don't think that was Father," Laurel said low to Tish, who had come up beside her.

Major Bullock was going irrepressibly on. "'Come in!' says he. 'But before you enter, you take those damn white hoods off, and every last one of you give me a look at who you are!'"

"He hadn't any use for what he called theatrics," Laurel was saying. "In the courtroom or anywhere else. He had no patience for show."

"He says, 'Back to your holes, rats!' And they were armed!" cried Major Bullock, lifting an imaginary gun in his hands.

"He's trying to make Father into something he wanted to be himself," said Laurel.

---

① Welty, Eudora. *The Optimist's Daughter*. New York: A Division of Random House, Vintage Books, 1978, pp. 83-106.

"Bless his heart," mourned Tish beside her. "Don't spoil it for Daddy."

"But I don't think it's fair now," said Laurel.

"Well, that backed 'em right out of there, the whole pack, right on out of town and back into the woods they came from. Cooked their goose for a while!" declared Major Bullock. "Oh, under that cloak of modesty he wore—"

"Father really was modest," Laurel said to him.

"Honey, what do you mean? Honey, you were away. You were sitting up yonder in Chicago, drawing pictures," Major Bullock told her. "I saw him! He stood up and dared those rascals to shoot him! Baring his breast!"

"He would have thought of my mother," said Laurel. And with it came the thought: It was my mother who might have done that! She's the only one I know who had it in her.

"Remains a mystery to me how he ever stayed alive," said Major Bullock stiffly. He lowered the imaginary gun. His feelings had been hurt.

The mystery in how little we know of other people is no greater than the mystery of how much, Laurel thought.

"But who do you call the man, Dad?" asked Wendell, plucking at his father's sleeve.

"Shut up. Or I'll carry you on home without letting you see the rest of it."

"It's my father," Laurel said.

The little boy lookedat her, and his mouth opened. She thought he disbelieved her.

The crowd of men were still at it behind the screen. "Clint's hunting a witness, some of the usual trouble, and this Negro girl says, 'It's him and me that saw it. He's a witness, and I's a got-shot witness.'"

They laughed.

"'There's two kinds, all right,' says Clint. 'And I know which to take. She's the got-shot witness: I'll take her.' He could see the funny side to everything."

"He brought her here afterwards and kept her safe under his own roof," Laurel said under her breath to Miss Adele, who had come in from the door now; it would be too late for any more callers before the funeral. "I don't know what the funny side was."

"It was Missouri, wasn't it?" said Miss Adele.

"And listening," said Laurel, for Missouri herself was just then lit up by a shower of sparks; down on her knees before the fire, she was poking the big log.

"I always pray people won't recognize them-selves in the speech of others," Miss Adele murmured. "And I don't think very often they do."

The log shifted like a sleeper in bed, and light flared all over in the room. Mr. Pitts was revealed in their midst as though by a spotlight, in the act of consulting his wristwatch.

"What's happening isn't real," Laurel said, low.

"The ending of a man's life on earth is very real indeed," Miss Adele said.

"But what people are saying."

"They're trying to say for a man that his life is over. Do you know a good way?"

Here, helpless in his own house among the people he'd known, and who'd known him, since the beginning, her father seemed to Laurel to have reached at this moment the danger point of his life.

"Did you listen to their words?" she asked.

"They're being clumsy. Often because they were thinking of you."

"They said he was a humorist. Anda crusader. And an angel on the face of the earth," Laurel said.

Miss Adele, looking into the fire, smiled. "It isn't easy for them, either. And they're being egged on a little bit, you know, Laurel, by the rivalry that's going on here in the room," she said. "After all, when the Chisoms walked in on us, they thought they had their side, too—"

"Rivalry? With Father where he lies?"

"Yes, but people being what they are, Laurel."

"This is still his house. After all, they're still his guests. They're misrepresenting him falsifying, that's what Mother would call it." Laurel might have been trying to testify now for her father's sake, as though he were in process of being put on trial in here instead of being viewed in his casket. "He never would have stood for lies being told about him. Not at any time. Not ever."

"Yes, he would," said Miss Adele. "If the truth might hurt the wrong person."

"I'm his daughter. I want what people say now to be the truth."

Laurel slowly turned her back to the parlor, and stood a little apart from Miss Adele too. She let her eyes travel out over the coffin into the other room, her father's "library". The bank of greenery hid the sight of his desk. She could see only the two loaded bookcases behind it, like a pair of old, patched, velvety cloaks hung up there on the wall. The shelf-load of Gibbon stretched like a sagging sash across one of them. She had not read her father the book he'd wanted after all. The wrong book! The wrong book! She was looking at her own mistake, and its long shadow reaching back to join the others.

"The least anybody can do for him is remember right," she said.

"I believe to my soul it's the most, too," said Miss Adele. And then warningly, "Polly—"

Fay at that moment burst from the hall into the parlor. She glistened in black satin. Eyes straight ahead, she came running a path through all of them toward the coffin.

Miss Adele, with a light quick move from behind her, pulled Laurel out of the way.

"No. Stop—stop her," Laurel said.

Fay brought herself short and hung over the pillow. "Oh, he looks so good with those mean old sandbags taken away and that mean old bandage pulled off of his eye!" she said fiercely.

"She's wasting no time, she's fixing to break aloose right now," said Mrs. Chisom. "Didn't even stop to speak to me."

Fay cried out, and looked around.

Sis stood up, enormous, and said, "Here I am, Wanda Fay. Cry on me."

Laurel closed her eyes, in the recognition of what had made the Chisoms seem familiar to her. They might have come out of that night in the hospital waiting room—out of all times of trouble, past or future—the great, interrelated family of those who never know the meaning of what has happened to them.

"Get back!—Who told them to come?" cried Fay.

"I did!" said Major Bullock, his face nothing but delight. "Found'em without a bit of trouble! Clint scribbled 'em all down for me in the office, day before he left for New Orleans."

But Fay showed him her back. She leaned forward over the coffin. "Oh, hon, get up, get out of there," she said.

"Stop her," Laurel said to the room.

"There now," said Miss Tennyson to all of them around the coffin.

"Can't you hear me, hon?" called Fay.

"She's cracking," said Mrs. Chisom. "Just like me. Poor little Wanda Fay."

"Oh, Judge, how could you be so unfair to me?" Fay cried, while Mr. Pitts emerged from behind the greens and poised his hand on the lid. "Oh, Judge, how could you go off and leave me this way? Why did you want to treat me so unfair?"

"I can tell you're going to be a little soldier," Major Bullock said, marching to Fay's side.

"Wanda Fay needed that husband of hers. That's why he ought to lived. He was a care, took all her time, but you'd go through it again, wouldn't you, honey?" asked Mrs. Chisom, pulling herself to her feet. She put out her arms, walking heavily toward her daughter. If you could have your husband back this minute.

"No," Laurel whispered.

Fay cried into the coffin, "Judge! You cheated on me!"

"Just tell him goodbye, sugar," said Major Bullock as he tried to put his arm around her shoulders, staggering a little. "That's best, just plant him a kiss—"

Fay struck out with her hands, hitting at Major Bullock and Mr. Pitts and Sis, fighting her mother, too, for a moment. She showed her claws at Laurel, and broke from the preacher's last-minute arms and threw herself forward across the coffin onto the pillow, driving her lips without aim against the face under hers. She was dragged back into the library, screaming, by Miss Tennyson Bullock, out of sight behind the bank of greenery. Judge McKelva's smoking chair lay behind them, overturned.

Laurel stood gazing down at the unchanged face of the dead, while Mrs. Chisom's voice came through the sounds of confusion in the library.

"Like mother, like daughter. Though when I had to give up her dad, they couldn't hold me half so easy. I tore up the whole house, I did."

思考与讨论

(1) 布洛克少校对迈凯尔瓦法官的夸赞引来劳雷尔的轻声违和,这暗示了什么?

(2) 在本该是安静肃穆的葬礼上听到如此多的嘈杂声音,作者用意何为?

(3) 作者如何用讽刺的手法描摹葬礼上的众生相?

(4) 南方口语在叙事中如何展示幽默的特性?

拓展阅读

[1] Akins, Adrienne V. "'We weren't laughing at them... We're grieving with you': Empathy and Comic Vision in Welty's The Optimist's Daughter". *The Southern Literary Journal*, 2011(2): 87-104.

[2] Welty, Eudora. *The Optimist's Daughter*. New York: Vintage Books, 1978.

[3] Welty, Eudora. *A Curtain of Green and Other Stories*. New York: A Harvest Book, Harcourt. Inc., 1941.

[4] 曹莉.尤朵拉·韦尔蒂和她的短篇小说[J].外国文学,1998(2):41-46.

[5] (美)尤朵拉·韦尔蒂.乐观者的女儿[M].杨向荣译.南京:译林出版社,2013.

二、菲利普·罗斯

(一) 菲利普·罗斯简介

菲利普·罗斯(Philip Roth, 1933—2018)是当代美国最有影响力的犹太裔作家。菲利普·罗斯出生于美国新泽西州纽瓦克市的一个犹太家庭,父亲从加利西亚移居美国,信仰正统犹太教,母亲是传统的家庭妇女。罗斯在攻读博士学位期间于1957年放弃学业,专门从事写作。1959年菲利普·罗斯发表第一部短篇小说《再见,哥伦布》(*Goodbye, Columbus*),获得美国国家图书奖,1962年出版第一部长篇小说《随波逐流》(*Letting Go*)。罗斯一生笔耕不辍卷帙浩繁,共出版30部长篇小说,一部评论集《阅读自己和他人》(*Reading Myself and Others*, 1975),发表多篇短篇小说。

按照时间顺序,罗斯的作品大致可分为三个阶段:20世纪60年代是早期创作阶段,这一时期的代表作品有中短篇小说集《再见,哥伦布》、小说《狂热者伊莱》(*Eli, the Fanatic*, 1957)、《波特诺的抱怨》(*Portnoy's Complaint*, 1969),集中表现了犹太移民个人和家庭的现实困境。第二阶段是20世纪70年代,罗斯于1971年发表政治讽刺长篇小说《我们这一伙》(*Our Gang*, 1971),讽刺批评美国社会,之后出版“欲望系列”第一部《乳房》(*The Breast*, 1972),反映现代人的处境与内心矛盾。第三阶段是从70年代末期至2000年,罗斯的“朱克曼系列”陆续发表,《鬼作家》(*The Ghost Writer*)于1979年出版,讲述文学创作与犹太文化的内部关联问题。

1986年罗斯创作长篇小说《反生活》(*The Counter Life*),反映美国犹太人和非犹太人的关系。就在这一年,美国文学批评家莱斯利·费德勒指出,美国犹太人与非犹太人的“同化”平息了美国犹太文学这一“类型”①,罗斯十分关注当下美国犹太人的生活状况。

罗斯在艾奥瓦大学、普林斯顿大学和宾夕法尼亚大学都曾执教,于1992年退休后,依然坚持写作。《遗产》(*Patrimony*, 1991)获美国国家书评人协会奖,《夏洛克战役》(*Operation Shylock*, 1993)获福克纳奖,《萨巴斯剧院》(*Sabbath's Theater*, 1995)获美国国家图书奖,《美国牧歌》(*American Pastoral*, 1997)获普利策小说奖。

1997年到2000年,罗斯创作了“美国三部曲”,其中第一部《美国牧歌》为罗斯赢得普利策奖。这部小说中,罗斯反思历史与社会现实,小说反映两代犹太人对待生活和犹太价值观的分歧,展示出传统的价值观念今非昔比的现实情境。第二部《背叛》(*I Married a Communist*, 1998)和第三部《人性的污点》(*The Human Stain*, 2000)重新考量犹太身份,对美国梦进行了极大的嘲讽。他在2001年发表《垂死的肉身》(*The Dying Animal*),在2004年发表《反美阴谋》(*The Plot Against America*),从一个犹太青年的视角思考重构二战。2005年,罗斯出版《凡人》(*Everyman*),无名的主人公是美国普通人中的一员,这部作品依然保持罗斯一贯的轻松幽默的笔调。《凡人》为罗斯赢得了第三个美国国家书评人协会奖。2010年最后一部小说《复仇女神》(*Namesis*)问世,这部小说旨在展现当代美国人的众生相。菲利普·罗斯讽刺美国政治的腐败和用棒球隐喻美国梦的虚幻。菲利普·罗斯不仅是美国犹太裔作家也是美国主流作家的代表。菲利普·罗斯比起辛格和马拉默德等犹太裔作家更具美国化,但罗斯在小说中写出犹太传统中虚伪和不光彩的一面,或许这也是其备受争议的原因之一。

(二)《鬼作家》简介

《鬼作家》是菲利普·罗斯的力作,也是罗斯“朱克曼系列”作品之一。作品讲述文坛新锐朱克曼拜访仰慕的大作家洛诺夫,并视之为精神之父的历程。小说主人公朱克曼寻求文学创作上的精神之父,探寻文学与人生的交集,小说通过两代作家写作的两难境地反映了现实与虚构、文学与人生的关系和矛盾冲突。

《鬼作家》共分为四部分。第一部分“大师”,讲述文学新锐朱克曼受邀前往文学大师洛诺夫家做客,在仰慕拘谨的言行中处处透露着严肃。第二部分“内森·代达罗斯”,朱克曼同洛诺夫谈起自己即将发表的一部小说引起父亲和犹太社区的争议,希望从精神之父洛诺夫身上得到精神支持。晚上,朱克曼住在洛诺夫家的书房偷听到文学大师洛诺夫与学生兼情人艾米·贝莱特之间的暧昧。第三部分“冤家命定”,朱克曼将艾米·贝莱特虚构为犹太苦难精神之魂安妮·弗兰克,并想象和安妮结婚以后得到了父亲和犹太社区对他的重新认可。第四部分“嫁给了托尔斯泰”,朱克曼从想象世界回到现实世界,目睹洛诺夫和妻子霍普以及情人艾米之间的家庭纠纷和情感纠葛,讽刺揭示作家真实生活的一面。

---

① 乔国强:《美国犹太文学》,上海:上海外语教育出版社,2019年,第516页。

(三) 作品选读:《鬼作家》[1]

Lonoff and I sat talking together in the living room after dinner, each sipping with admirable temperance at the tablespoonful of cognac he had divided between two large snifters. I had so far experienced brandy only as a stopgap household remedy for toothache: a piece of absorbent cotton, soaked in the stuff, would be pressed against my throbbing gum until my parents could get me to the dentist. I accepted Lonoff's offer, however, as though it accorded with my oldest post-prandial custom. The comedy thickened when my host, another big drinker, went to look for the right glasses. After a systematic search he finally found them at the rear of the bottom cabinet in the foyer breakfront. "A gift," he explained, "I thought they were still in the box," and took two into the kitchen to wash away dust that seemed to have been accumulating since the time of Napoleon, whose name was on the sealed brandy bottle. While he was at it he decided to wash the four other glasses in the set, and put them back in hiding in the breakfront before rejoining me to begin our merrymaking at the hearth.

Not much later—in all, maybe twenty minutes after he had refused to respond in any way to her plea to be replaced by Amy Bellette—Hope could be heard in the kitchen, washing the dishes that Lonoff and I had silently cleared from the table following her departure. She seemed to have gotten down from their bedroom by a back stairway—probably so as not to disturb our conversation.

While helping him to clear up, I had not known what to do about her broken wineglass or about the saucer she inadvertently had knocked to the floor when she rushed from the table. My duty as ingenue was clearly to spare the stout man in the business suit from bending over, especially as he was E. I. Lonoff; on the other hand, I was still trying to get through by pretending that nothing shocking had happened in my presence. To keep the tantrum in perspective, he might even prefer that the broken bits be left where they were for Hope to clean up later, provided she did not first commit suicide in their room.

Even as my sense of moral niceties and my youthful cowardice battled it out with my naïveté, Lonoff, groaning slightly from the effort, brushed the glass into a dustpan and retrieved the saucer from beneath the dining table. It had broken neatly in two, and after inspecting the edges he observed, "She can glue it."

In the kitchen he left the dish for her to repair on a long wooden counter where pink and white geraniums were growing in clay pots beneath the windows. The kitchen was a bright, pretty room, a little cheerier and livelier looking than the rest of the house. Besides the geraniums flowering abundantly here even in winter, tall reeds and dried flowers were stuck all about in pitchers and vases and little odd-shaped bottles. The windowed wall cupboards were bright and homey and

---

[1] Roth, Philip. *The Ghost Writer*. Toronto: McGraw-Hill Ryerson Ltd., 1979, pp. 34 - 44.

reassuring: food staples labeled with unimpeachable brand names—enough Bumble Bee tuna for an Eskimo family to survive on in their igloo till spring—and jars of tomatoes, beans, pears, crabapples, and the like, which seemed to have been put up by Hope herself. Pots and pans with shining copper bottoms hung in rows from a pegboard beside the stove, and along the wall above the breakfast table were half a dozen pictures in plain wooden frames, which turned out to be short nature poems signed "H. L.," copied in delicate calligraphy and decorated with watercolor designs. It did indeed look to be the headquarters of a woman who, in her own unostentatious way, could glue anything and do anything, except figure out how to make her husband happy.

We talked about literature and I was in heaven—also in a sweat from the spotlight he was giving me to bask in. Every book new to me I was sure he must have annotated with his reading pen long ago, yet his interest was pointedly in hearing my thoughts, not his own. The effect of his concentrated attention was to make me heap insight onto precocious insight, and then to hang upon his every sigh and grimace, investing what was only a little bout of after-dinner dyspepsia with the direst implications about my taste and my intelligence. Though I worried that I was trying too hard to sound like the kind of deep thinker for whom he had no love, I still couldn't stop myself, under the spell now not just of the man and his accomplishment but of the warm wood fire, of the brandy snifter balanced in my hand (if not yet the brandy), and of the snow falling heavily beyond the cushioned window-seats, as dependably beautiful and mystifying as ever. Then there were the great novelists, whose spellbinding names I chanted as I laid my cross-cultural comparisons and brand-new eclectic enthusiasms at his feet—Zuckerman, with Lonoff, discussing Kafka: I couldn't quite get it, let alone get over it. And then there was his dinner-table toast. It still gave me a temperature of a hundred and five each time I remembered it. To myself I swore that I would struggle for the rest of my life to deserve it. And wasn't that why he'd proposed it, this pitiless new master of mine?

"I've just finished reading Isaac Babel," I told him.

He considered this, impassively.

I was thinking, for sport more or less, that he is the missing link; those stories are what connect you, if you don't mind my mentioning your work—"

He crossed his hands on his belly and rested them there, movement enough to make me say, "I'm sorry."

"Go ahead. Connected to Babel. How?"

"Well, 'connected' of course isn't the right word. Neither is 'influence.' It's family resemblance that I'm talking about. It's as though, as I see it, you are Babel's American cousin—and Felix Abravanel is the other. You through 'The Sin of Jesus' and something in Red Cavalry, through the ironical dreaming and the blunt reporting, and, of course, through the writing itself. Do you see what I mean? There's a sentence in one of his war stories: 'Voroshilov combed his horse's mane with his Mauser.' Well, that's just the kind of thing that you do, a stunning little picture in every line.

Babel said that if he ever wrote his autobiography he'd call it The Story of an Adjective. Well, if it were possible to imagine you writing your autobiography—if such a thing were even imaginable—you might come up with that title too. No?"

"And Abravanel?"

"Oh, with Abravanel it's Benya Krik and the Odessa mob: the gloating, the gangsters, all those gigantic types. It isn't that he throws in his sympathy with the brutes—it isn't that in Babel, either. It's their awe of them. Even when they're appalled, they're in awe. Deep reflective Jews a little lovesick at the sound of all that un-Talmudic bone crunching. Sensitive Jewish sages, as Babel says, dying to climb trees."

"'In my childhood I led the life of a sage, when I grew up I started climbing trees.'"

"Yes, that's the line," said I, expecting no less but still impressed. On I went. "Look at Abravanel's Properly Scalded. Movie moguls, union moguls, racketeer moguls, women who are moguls just with their breasts—even the down and out bums who used to be moguls, talking like moguls of the down and out. It's Babel's fascination with big-time Jews, with conscienceless Cossacks, with everybody who has it his own way. The Will as the Big Idea. Except Babel doesn't come off so lovable and enormous himself. That's not how he sees things. He is a sort of Abravanel with the self-absorption drained away. And if you drain away enough, well, in the end you arrive at Lonoff."

"And what about you?"

"Me?"

"Yes. You haven't finished. Aren't you a New World cousin in the Babel clan, too? What is Zuckerman in all of this?"

"Why—nothing. I've only published the four stories that I sent you. My relationship is nonexistent. I think I'm still at the point where my relationship to my own work is practically nonexistent."

So I said, and quickly reached for my glass so as to duck my disingenuous face and take a bitter drop of brandy on my tongue. But Lonoff had read my designing mind, all right; for when I came upon Babel's description of the Jewish writer as a man with autumn in his heart and spectacles on his nose, I had been inspired to add, "and blood in his penis," and had then recorded the words like a challenge—a flaming Dedalian formula to ignite my soul's smithy.

"What else?" Lonoff asked. "Come on, don't get bashful. This is enjoyable. Talk, please."

"About—?"

"All these books you read."

"Your books included or excluded?" I asked him.

"Suit yourself."

I said, "I think of you as the Jew who got away."

"And does that help?"

"There's some truth in it, isn't there? You got away from Russia and the pogroms. You got away from the purges—and Babel didn't. You got away from Palestine and the homeland. You got away from Brookline and the relatives. You got away from New York—"

"And all of this is recorded where? Hedda Hopper?"

"Some there. The rest I pieced together myself."

"To what end?"

"When you admire a writer you become curious. You look for his secret. The clues to his puzzle."

"But New York—I was there for three months over twenty years ago. Who told you I got away from New York?"

"Some of the Jews down there you got away from."

"I was there for three months and I think I got a word in only once. What word I don't remember, but suddenly I belonged to a faction."

"That's why you left?"

"Also, there was the girl I'd fallen in love with and married. She wasn't happy."

"Why not?"

"Same as me. Those were terrifying intellectual personalities even back then. Real ideological Benya Kriks, even in their diapers. I didn't have enough strong opinions to last me down there through a year. My Hope had even fewer."

"So you came back here, you got away for good."

"From Jews? Not altogether. The game warden tells me there are some more up in these woods besides me. But you're more or less right. It's the deer in their fields that drive the farmers crazy, not the few of us they see around here in caftans. But where's the secret, Nathan? What's the puzzle?"

"Away from all the Jews, and a story by you without a Jew in it is unthinkable. The deer, the farmers, the game warden—"

"And don't forget Hope. And my fair-haired children."

"And still all you write about are Jews."

"Proving what?"

"That," I said, cautiously, "is what I'd like to ask you."

He thought about it for a moment. "It proves why the young rabbi in Pittsfield can't live with the idea that I won't be 'active'."

I waited for more, but in vain.

"Do you know Abravanel?" I asked.

"Nathan, surely by now you get the picture."

"What picture?"

"I don't know anybody. I turn sentences around, and that's it. Why would Abravanel want to know me? I put him to sleep. He spoke at Amherst last spring. An invitation arrived so we drove over to hear him. But that's the only time we've ever met. Before the lecture he came down the aisle to where I was sitting and introduced himself. He was very flattering. My respectful younger colleague. Afterward we had a drink with him and his actress. A very polished fellow. The satirist you don't really see till you catch the commedia dell'arte profile. There's where the derision lives. Head-on he's something of a heartthrob. Bombay black eyes, and so on. And the young Israeli wife is like lava. The Gentile dream of the melon-breasted Jewess. And the black head of coarse, curly hair—the long female version of his. You could polish a pot with it. They tell me that when she played in the big movie of the Bible she stole the show from the Creation. So there were those two, and there was I with Hope. And with this," he said, once more lightly laying his hands on his belly. "I understand he does a humorous imitation of me for his friends. No harm intended. One of my former students ran into him in Paris. He'd just addressed a full house at the Sorbonne. I'm told that upon hearing my name he referred to me as 'the complete man—as unimpressive as he is unimpressed.'"

"You don't like him much."

"I'm not in the business. 'Liking people' is often just another racket. But you're right to think well of his books. Not up my alley maybe, all that vanity face to face, but when he writes he's not just a little Houyhnhnm tapping out his superiority with his hooves. More like a Dr. Johnson eating opium—the disease of his life makes Abravanel fly. I admire the man, actually. I admire what he puts his nervous system through. I admire his passion for the front-row seat. Beautiful wives, beautiful mistresses, alimony the size of the national debt, polar expeditions, war-front reportage, famous friends, famous enemies, breakdowns, public lectures, five-hundred-page novels every third year, and still, as you said before, time and energy left over for all that self-absorption. The gigantic types in the books have to be that big to give him something to think about to rival himself. Like him? No. But impressed, oh yes. Absolutely. It's no picnic up there in the egosphere. I don't know when the man sleeps, or if he has ever slept, aside from those few minutes when he had that drink with me."

思考与讨论

(1)《鬼作家》是如何表达犹太性的?

(2) 犹太作家在创作犹太人故事的时候面临怎样的困境?

(3) 菲利普·罗斯如何借助年轻作家朱克曼拜访文学大师洛诺夫的事件阐释文学艺术与生活之间

的关系？

(4) 小说题目“鬼作家”的幽默讽刺意义体现在哪里？通过比较文学大师洛诺夫和青年作家朱克曼，你认为谁是犹太民族的“鬼作家”？

拓展阅读

[1] Parrish, Timothy, ed.. *The Cambridge Companion to Philip Roth*, Cambridge: Cambridge University Press, 2007.

[2] Roth, Philip. *The Ghost Writer*, Toronto: McGraw-Hill Ryerson Ltd., 1979.

[3] 菲利普·罗斯.鬼作家[M].董乐山译.上海:上海译文出版社,2011.

[4] 杨金才、朱云.中国菲利普罗斯研究现状论析[J].当代外国文学,2012(04):151－163.

[5] 张生庭、张真.自我身份的悖论——菲利普罗斯创作中的身份问题探究[J].外语教学,2012(04):78－81+93.

三、谢尔曼·阿莱克西

(一) 谢尔曼·阿莱克西简介

谢尔曼·阿莱克西(Sherman Alexie, 1966—　)是美国文学界的新秀作家。1992 年阿莱克西的第一部诗集《盛装舞蹈业》(*The Business of Fancydancing: Stories and Poems*)出版，之后他创作了 4 部长篇小说，4 部短篇故事集，11 部诗集和 2 部剧本，2007 年阿莱克西的小说《一个印第安少年的超真实日记》获美国国家图书奖。

阿莱克西生长在华盛顿州斯波坎印第安保留地上的威尔皮尼特镇，父亲是斯波坎印第安人，母亲是科达伦人。阿莱克西于 1991 年获得华盛顿州立大学学士学位。正如所有美国本土裔作家一样，阿莱克西关注印第安传统，关注身份、种族等主题，但是阿莱克西同时也关注印第安青少年成长的主题，他笔下的青少年追寻传统也向往成长。阿莱克西强调纯正的印第安部落形象和印第安文化，在作品中极力维护纯正的印第安文化，并以此作为抵抗基督教白人中心的策略。

阿莱克西运用幽默改写了白人作家笔下将印第安人消除的宿命安排。阿莱克西刻画的印第安人物往往是小说的中心，而白人只是没有话语权的小人物，是边缘化的他者，借此修正印第安人被白人歪曲想象的刻板印象。阿莱克西作品非常典型的特色是幽默讽刺。通过幽默，读者在大笑之余重新认识印第安人的真诚和白人的伪善。幽默是印第安人在以美国白人为中心的社会的生存之道，幽默也是吸引白人读者阅读并重新考量印第安作家作品，消除对印第安刻板印象的途径，幽默是“清理最深的情感伤口的消毒剂”①。幽默在阿莱克西的作品中不仅仅是修辞和策略，更是保卫印第安文化和历史的武器。

阿莱克西在接受艾斯·麦格伦的访谈中坦言，印第安作家内心深处有着被盎格鲁白人殖民之前的

① Alexie, Sherman. *The Lone Ranger and Tonto Fistfight in Heaven*. New York: Atlantic Monthly Press, 1993, p.164.转引自刘克东:《趋于融合——谢尔曼·阿莱克西小说研究》,北京:光明日报出版社,2011 年,第 16 页。

印第安怀旧之情。阿莱克西对印第安人生活的期望并不仅仅停留在生存之层面,他更想要表现超越生存的理想生活,所以我们在阿莱克西的作品里总能读出越界的理想生活状态。盎格鲁白人给印第安人带来的灾难和创伤是一种永久性的集体伤痛,面对伤痛的记忆、困顿的现实和迷茫的未来,幽默是阿莱克西选择抵抗白人霸权的方式,也是消除偏见与白人交流的策略。阿莱克西曾在访谈中说,"我笔下的幽默是有政治意味的"①。幽默或许是消除障碍、增进理解、打破僵局的前奏。

评论家对阿莱克西的幽默手法评论不一。有评论家认为阿莱克西的幽默巧妙地与白人读者对话,幽默的"陌生化"表现力在吸引白人读者的同时可以让白人读者重新思考曾经对印第安人的迫害历史,进而反省并重新认识印第安文化和价值。也有评论家认为阿莱克西的幽默策略和"泛印第安"写作弱化了印第安人对白人的抵抗。

阿莱克西创作了10余部诗集,包括《盛装舞蹈业:故事和诗歌》(*The Business of Fancydancing: Stories and Poems*, 1992)、《我会去偷马》(*I Would Steal Horses*, 1993)、《旧衬衫,新皮肤》(*Old Shirts and New Skins*, 1993)、《黑寡妇的夏天》(*The Summer of Black Widows*, 1996)、《喜欢三文鱼的男人》(*The Man Who Loves Salmon*, 1998)、《危险的天文学》(*Dangerous Astronomy*, 2005)、《脸》(*Face*, 2009)。阿莱克西的短篇小说集最有名的当属《独行侠森警和唐托在天堂的赤拳搏斗》(*The Lone Ranger and Tonto Fistfight in Heaven*, 1993)、《十个小印第安人》(*The Little Indians*, 2003)、《战舞》(*War Dances*, 2009)。长篇小说主要有4部:《保留地布鲁斯》、《印第安杀手》(*Indian Killer*, 1996)、《飞逸》(*Flight*, 2007)、《一个印第安少年的超真实日记》。阿莱克西还创作了颠覆盎格鲁白人中心的剧本《狼烟》(*Smoke Signals*, 1998)和《盛装舞蹈业》(*The Business of Fancydacing*, 2003)。

《保留地布鲁斯》讲述斯波坎印第安保留地上,不同族群的几位青年男女组成布鲁斯摇滚乐队的故事,乐队名称叫"郊狼跳跃",他们的演出在保留地很受欢迎,可是乐队在纽约演唱公司试唱时却因为失误受到重创,乐队队员或自杀或从此萎靡消沉,但也有成员在坚守。小说表达了印第安青年与白人合作的愿望,但是最终受挫。评论家认为《保留地布鲁斯》有泛印第安的倾向,并没有表现出印第安各个部落的独特性,但不同族群联盟组成一个乐队的构思或许是阿莱克西印第安族群整体观念的体现。乐队中还体现出本土裔印第安青年和非裔青年组合的设想,以及接受两位白人女伴唱的想法,各个种族平等相处的思想在此可见一斑。

《印第安杀手》的故事发生在城市西雅图。这部小说可以看出印第安人和白人的各种对抗。白人学者、媒体等权威阶层对印第安文化带有歧视的言论激起了寻求文化之根的印第安青年的愤怒。白人对印第安人的不尊重与印第安青年极力维护民族文化的对峙是小说的焦点。印第安青年是弱势的一方,但却发出了抵抗的声音,抵抗白人的恶劣行径。白人媒体广播员掌握话语权,大肆歪曲报道、篡改历史与事实,激起白人社区对印第安的仇恨,也激发了印第安青年对白人的对抗。媒体对待白人与对待印第安人的态度大相径庭,一个白人被杀媒体随即大肆报道,而印第安青年玛丽死在立交桥下白人警察却无动于衷。《印第安杀手》写出了白人和印第安人之间各种二元对立的矛盾与冲突,也表现出印第安人面对白人的诬蔑和偏见却无力抗争的事实。

《飞逸》的主人公是一位青少年,小说具有魔幻色彩,主人公思考并尝试了种种与白人相处的方式,

① Nygren, Ase. "A World of Story-Smoke: A Conversation with Sherman Alexie." *MELUS*, vol. 30, no. 4, 2005, p. 160.

进而探寻人类共存于地球的方式，尊重是印第安人和白人相处的关键点。《飞逸》有明显的理想色彩，也是一部体现“精神顿悟”的成长小说。但《飞逸》区别于一般成长小说，其主人公更多的是要面对身份认同和处理与白人相处的种族关系。这部小说构想了一个比较理想的结尾，印第安青少年最终融入美国主流社会。

《一个印第安少年的超真实日记》比《飞逸》更具有理想主义色彩。小说主人公朱尼尔得到印第安部落的谅解，同时也得到了白人的友谊。这部作品呈现出的印第安青年具有勇敢的品行和幽默的性情，是一个既能传承印第安传统精神又安于现代生活的理想人物，是一个处于印第安社会进入现代转型时期的人物，具有印第安人的果敢、智慧和现代人的探索追寻精神。

（二）《一个印第安少年的超真实日记》简介

《一个印第安少年的超真实日记》是阿莱克西半自传性质的小说。小说主人公阿诺·朱尼尔·祖灵（Arnold Junior Spirit）是一个从贫苦保留地走出来的印第安青年。朱尼尔在少年时代就发现保留地无比贫困，不愿一辈子待在保留地，于是鼓起勇气转学到白人社区的学校。

进入白人学校后，朱尼尔受到白人同学对印第安人的言语侮辱和歧视，朱尼尔不堪侮辱，但没有因此而消沉，反而迎难而上，勇敢地及时反击，为自己也为印第安人赢得了最基本的尊严。朱尼尔在课堂上敢于质疑老师的错误，在篮球场上表现突出，平日与其他白人同学平等融洽相处，最终赢得白人友谊的同时也得到了部落族人的谅解。

朱尼尔是一个积极勇敢的印第安青年，这为保留地很多沉迷于酒精麻醉、消极怠世的贫困印第安人树立了积极勇敢的榜样。朱尼尔以一己之力试图跨越白人与印第安人之间的种族界限，充当了改变印第安人生活现状的先锋英雄，他的正能量似乎给印第安困顿不前的生活注入了一股新的能量，带来新的希望。

这部小说对保留地印第安人的贫困生活进行了细致的描写，对保留地印第安人的生活状态和心理也有细腻的呈现，白人殖民者一次次瓜分印第安人的土地，留下贫瘠的保留地使得印第安人很难维持生计。小说中充满幽默的笔调，不乏自嘲的语气。书中的插画更是给小说增添了幽默轻松的色彩。

（三）作品选读：《一个印第安少年的超真实日记》[①]

I was born with water on the brain.

Okay, so that’s not exactly true. I was actually born with too much cerebral spinal fluid inside my skull. But cerebral spinal fluid is just the doctors’ fancy way of saying brain grease. And brain grease works inside the lobes like car grease works inside an engine. It keeps things running smooth and fast. But weirdo me, I was born with too much grease inside my skull, and it got all thick and muddy and disgusting, and it only mucked up the works. My thinking and breathing and living engine slowed down and flooded.

My brain was drowning in grease.

---

① Alexie, Sherman. *The Absolutely True Diary of a Part-time Indian*. New York Boston: Little, Brown and Company, 2007, pp.1－12.

But that makes the whole thing sound weirdo and funny, like my brain was a giant French fry, so it seems more serious and poetic and accurate to say, "I was born with water on the brain."

Okay, so maybe that's not a very serious way to say it, either. Maybe the whole thing is weird and funny.

But jeez, did my mother and father and big sister and grandma and cousins and aunts and uncles think it was funny when the doctors cut open my little skull and sucked out all that extra water with some tiny vacuum?

I was only six months old and I was supposed to croak during the surgery. And even if I somehow survived the mini-Hoover, I was supposed to suffer serious brain damage during the procedure and live the rest of my life as a vegetable.

Well, I obviously survived the surgery. I wouldn't be writing this if I didn't, but I have all sorts of physical problems that are directly the result of my brain damage.

First of all, I ended up having forty-two teeth. The typical human has thirty-two, right? But I had forty-two.

Ten more than usual. Ten more than normal. Ten teeth past human.

My teeth got so crowded that I could barely close my mouth. I went to Indian Health Service to get some teeth pulled so I could eat normally, not like some slobbering vulture. But the Indian Health Service funded major dental work only once a year, so I had to have all ten extra teeth pulled in one day.

And what's more, our white dentist believed that Indians only felt half as much pain as white people did, so he only gave us half the Novocain.

What a bastard, huh?

Indian Health Service also funded eyeglass purchases only once a year and offered one style: those ugly, thick, black plastic ones.

My brain damage left me nearsighted in one eye and farsighted in the other, so my ugly glasses were all lopsided because my eyes were so lopsided.

I get headaches because my eyes are, like, enemies, you know, like they used to be married to each other but now hate each other's guts.

And I started wearing glasses when I was three, so I ran around the rez looking like a three-year-old Indian grandpa.

And, oh, I was skinny. I'd turn sideways and disappear.

But my hands and feet were huge. My feet were a size eleven in third grade! With my big feet and pencil body, I looked like a capital L walking down the road. And my skull was enormous.

Epic.

My head was so big that little Indian skulls orbited around it. Some of the kids called me Orbit. And other kids just called me Globe. The bullies would pick me up, spin me in circles, put their finger down on my skull, and say, "I want to go there."

So obviously, I looked goofy on the outside, but it was the inside stuff that was the worst.

First of all, I had seizures. At least two a week. So I was damaging my brain on a regular basis. But the thing is, I was having those seizures because I already had brain damage, so I was reopening wounds each time I seized.

Yep, whenever I had a seizure, I was damaging my damage. I haven't had a seizure in seven years, but the doctors tell me that I am "susceptible to seizure activity."

Susceptible to seizure activity.

Doesn't that just roll off the tongue like poetry?

I also had a stutter and a lisp. Or maybe I should say I had a st-st-st-st-stutter and a lisssssssththththp.

You wouldn't think there is anything life threatening about speech impediments, but let me tell you, there is nothing more dangerous than being a kid with a stutter and a lisp.

A five-year-old is cute when he lisps and stutters. Heck, most of the big-time kid actors stuttered and lisped their way to stardom.

And jeez, you're still fairly cute when you're a stuttering and lisping six-, seven-, and eight-year-old, but it's all over when you turn nine and ten.

After that, your stutter and lisp turn you into a retard.

And if you're fourteen years old, like me, and you're still stuttering and lisping, then you become the biggest retard in the world.

Everybody on the rez calls me a retard about twice a day. They call me retard when they are pantsing me or stuffing my head in the toilet or just smacking me upside the head.

I'm not even writing down this story the way I actually talk, because I'd have to fill it with stutters and lisps, and then you'd be wondering why you're reading a story written by such a retard.

Do you know what happens to retards on the rez?

We get beat up.

At least once a month.

Yep, I belong to the Black-Eye-of-the-Month Club.

Sure I want to go outside. Every kid wants to go outside. But it's safer to stay at home.

So I mostly hang out alone in my bedroom and read books and draw cartoons.

Here's one of me:

I draw all the time.

I draw cartoons of my mother and father; my sister and grandmother; my best friend, Rowdy; and everybody else on the rez.

I draw because words are too unpredictable.

I draw because words are too limited.

If you speak and write in English, or Spanish, or Chinese, or any other language, then only a certain percentage of human beings will get your meaning.

But when you draw a picture, everybody can understand it.

If I draw a cartoon of a flower, then every man, woman, and child in the world can look at it and say, "That's a flower."

So I draw because I want to talk to the world. And I want the world to pay attention to me.

I feel important with a pen in my hand. I feel like I might grow up to be somebody important. An artist. Maybe a famous artist. Maybe a rich artist.

That's the only way I can become rich and famous.

Just take a look at the world. Almost all of the rich and famous brown people are artists.

They're singers and actors and writers and dancers and directors and poets.

So I draw because I feel like it might be my only real chance to escape the reservation.

I think the world is a series of broken dams and floods, and my cartoons are tiny little lifeboats.

思考与讨论

(1) 小说开篇朱尼尔怎样自嘲自己的长相？这样的自嘲与主题有什么关联？

(2) 白人牙医对印第安人有什么样的刻板印象？为什么？

(3) 这部小说以一个十四岁男孩的口吻叙事，这样的叙事视角对深化主题有怎样的用意？

(4) 重复的修辞手法起到怎样的讽刺效果？

拓展阅读

[1] Alexie, Sherman. *The Absolutely True Diary of a Part-time Indian*. New York & Boston: Little, Brown and Company, 2007.

[2] Bird, Gloria. The Exaggeration of Despair in Sherman Alexie's Reservation Blues. *Wicazo Sa Review*, vol.11, no.2, 1993, p.51.

[3] 刘克东.重塑印第安新形象——美国当代印第安作家谢尔曼·阿莱克西述评[J].天津外国语学院学报,2010(3):59-64.

[4] 王守仁.新编美国文学史[M].上海:上海外语教育出版社,2019.

[5] 虞建华.美国文学词典[M].上海:复旦大学出版社,2005.

第八章 当代美国哥特小说

自英国作家霍勒斯·沃波尔(Horace Walpole)于1764年发表小说《奥特兰托堡》(*The Castle of Otranto*),哥特小说开始登上文学舞台。这种虚构的中世纪小说营造出浓郁的神秘与恐怖氛围:幽暗的古堡、破旧的老宅、暗藏机关的密室、白衣飘飘的疯女子、遁世神秘的修士。哥特小说迎合了当时逐渐兴起的浪漫主义,注重在作品中表现情感的审美趣味,挑战启蒙运动倡导文学作品应"理性"(reason)和"得体"(decorum)的观念,它将读者熟知的景象作为叙述对象,密集地刻画情感冲突,颠覆读者的认知经验,扰动和刺激读者的情感,令其沉浸在小说营造的冲突中,时而困惑、时而惊恐。哥特小说在题材上专注于对"怪怖"(uncanny)的刻画,通过惊悚的情节调动并释放个体的强烈情感,有别于当时的文学传统,故被贴上了"另类"的标签,这恰恰体现出哥特小说与主流叙事的区别与其自身的价值。哥特小说游弋在熟悉与陌生的缝隙中,游走在善与恶的灰色地带,它让超自然或非理性的事物出入我们的日常生活,重塑我们对熟悉事物的认知经验和情感纽带。由此,恐惧、陌生与杂糅成了哥特小说的叙事特点,其叙事内容与手法也在不断突破传统。

美国哥特文学最初从欧洲大陆流行的吸血鬼和鬼怪故事中取材,但因美国缺少欧洲古老漫长的历史,故无法复制欧洲大陆的哥特文学,因此早期的美国作家意识到应将哥特文学置于美国自身的民族叙事中。查尔斯·布罗克登·布朗(Charles Brockden Brown)发表的《维兰德》(*Wieland*, 1798)、《奥蒙德》(*Ormond*, 1799)、《亚瑟·莫文》(*Arthur Mervyn*, 1799)和《埃德加·亨特利》(*Edgar Huntly*, 1799)都与美国的民族叙事紧密联系,并尝试从深度和广度上探索美国哥特小说的潜能。自此以后,美国哥特小说经久不衰,直到现在依然历久弥新,畅销作品屡见不鲜。

美国哥特小说历久弥新的原因有三:第一,哥特小说挑战了理性秩序和惯常的认知,这符合美国文学发展的需求。整体而言,美国文学追求日新月异,讴歌平民化与商业化,它有意疏离欧洲所代表的旧世界的文学传统,形成了关于自身独特的种族、宗教、历史、家族和性别叙事。美国哥特小说自然不能置身事外,不仅如此,它还在美国文学的叙事发展中找到了自身的叙事特点,它将不被理性法则和主流观念接纳的边缘事物引入读者的观测、认知和理解中,开拓文学的探索领域,丰富文学主题,突破审美藩篱。第二,美国哥特小说从颠覆美国文学的传统中寻找发展的力量。传统的美国文学旨在构建一个幸福且健康的国家,一座耸立的"山巅之城",它崇尚征服与改造自然,是生机勃勃的、现代化的、白人主导的民族叙事。美国哥特小说打破传统,寻找颠覆的契机并从中汲取力量,质疑主流文学呈现的愿景。它展望了一个失败的乌托邦,一个无论从文字层面还是隐喻层面都病态的当代美国社会。第三,美国哥特小说，因其能动地关注个体的独特情感和精神状态以及人性的脆弱和现实的怪诞，适合表现被主流叙事所掩盖、压制和遗忘的主题。它表达对权力话语的不适、焦虑、怀疑甚至厌恶，而这一特征符合当代美国多元文化角力的现状。因此，在当代美国文学中，哥特小说虽不显赫，但却有一席之地。

第二次世界大战后，美国小说叙事受现实主义、后现代主义、荒诞主义、女权主义、元小说、自传体、意识流等因素的影响而异彩纷呈，这让当代美国哥特小说不再拘泥于单一化、类型化的形式，呈现出杂糅的特征。“冷战”的疑云和对核战争的恐怖心理、结构主义和后现代文学的兴盛、民权运动与女性主义运动的高潮、少数族裔文化和主流白人权力话语间的角力，使得一些美国作家对传统的文学叙事产生怀疑和焦虑：如何面对隐匿在美国边疆开拓史背后的野蛮及对其他族裔的恐怖镇压？人与非人的界限在哪里？女性与边缘群体如何表达被权力话语压制的现状与自身的焦虑？如何应对都市的扩张带来的犯罪、堕落和疾病的肆虐？这些问题都在美国当代哥特文学中得以探讨，具体体现在以下三个方面：第一，边疆历史的遗产。疆域的开拓成就了美利坚民族，对荒野的征服不仅拓展了美国的版图，也造就了社会的繁荣，而淹没在主流叙事之下的残暴与杀戮却也给文明蒙上一层阴影。当代美国哥特小说重新审视边疆开拓进程中的血腥与杀戮，反思边疆历史带给美国当代社会的遗产。第二，族裔问题。民权运动的兴起及其取得的成果，使得族裔问题不仅成为主流文学无法回避的主题，也成为哥特小说新的焦点。哥特文学颠覆认知经验的特征与少数族裔特异性的表达需求不谋而合，因此，它往往能突破传统叙事的藩篱，凸显甚至深化少数族裔特有的叙事主题。当代美国哥特小说不仅以新的叙事角度审视少数族裔的身份与权力问题，更表达了对自身族裔信仰、宗教和文化何去何从的焦虑。第三，吸血鬼小说。作为哥特文学里历史悠久的一种类型小说，吸血鬼小说不囿于一隅，而是突破自身壁垒，积极谋求与当今美国多元文化的杂糅，让当代美国文学里的吸血鬼具备多重隐喻，表现现代社会里人们的焦虑与恐惧、欲望与挣扎。虽然它们中不乏娱乐化、商业化的应景之作，但吸血鬼小说为当代美国哥特小说继续前进提供了潜能与动力。

第一节　边疆历史的哥特小说

美国的边疆随着“西进运动”(westward movement)不断拓展，“边疆”是“商人、猎人、矿工、农场主、伐木工人和各种各样的冒险家松散的定居地”，是“不断扩展的社会的临时边界”，是“一种社会形式”“一种意识状态”，是“未被开发的边缘地带”，是“简单的蛮荒形态向复杂的现代社会转变的第一阶段”，它常与“西部”通用，用以指称特定时期特定的地理方位[①]。边疆的扩展历程亦可看作是美国社会的拓殖过程，“在使这个国家的人民及制度‘美国化’方面，没有任何力量比占领美洲大陆所必需的三百年间沿西部边缘的定居地而反复再生的文明所起的作用更大”[②]。边疆给美国文学提供了丰富的素材，传统美国文学作品里的西部与爱默生笔下的自然异曲同工——广袤的自然对于人有着重要的涤荡胸怀、抚慰心

① 参见〈https://www.britannica.com/topic/American-frontier〉。
② 雷·艾伦·比林顿：《向西部扩张：美国边疆史》，周小松等译，北京：商务印书馆，1991年，第9页。

灵、启示美感的作用[①]。因此，当提及美国西部时，一幅人在广阔天地间无拘无束、恣意驰骋的欢快画面不禁会浮现在脑中。然而，当代美国哥特小说审视边疆历史的遗产时，聚焦隐匿在边疆历史里的残暴与血腥(这些都有意或无意地被之前的主流文学压制和掩埋)，反思边疆历史。

《埃德加·亨特利》是第一部有价值的涉及美国边疆历史的哥特小说。小说的背景设定在18世纪80年代至90年代的美国边境，当时新生的美国并不稳定，紧张与混乱随处可见。新移民的涌入带来了不同的宗教和政治信仰，刚建立的定居地又受到印第安人的袭击。无论移民还是本土裔，在殖民地后裔眼中都是“他者”，主人公亨特利的经历就反映了这种不同族群间的不信任和相互排斥的紧张关系。随着亨特利调查的推进，他逐渐发现一个令其不安的事实：“他者”的野蛮也存在于自身，亨特利在内外冲突中表现出一种情感转移(displacement)，他将对野蛮的恐惧变作对荒野的恐惧——参差不齐的山脉、幽深的峡谷、回响声不断的洞穴都暗示着这片土地的敌意。这种恐惧源自亨特利内心的不安与焦虑：找寻他人的罪恶最终发现罪恶在自身。

查尔斯·布朗为后期的边疆哥特小说提供了很好的范例。首先，边疆不仅是故事的背景，它还象征着一个民族在崇高理想与无法无天、黑暗和不安的潜流之间分裂的现实。正如麦尔维尔认为，邪恶并不是因为良善缺席，而是因为邪恶本身就是一种积极主动的力量[②]。荒原和森林构成了熟知的隐喻(如莎士比亚的《仲夏夜之梦》)，在边疆哥特小说里，进入荒野象征着从文明进入野蛮，从有意识的状态进入无意识的状态，从清醒进入梦魇。这种二元对立的冲突不断撩拨、挑战、颠覆人对外部世界和自身的认知，人的精神逐渐变得错乱，边疆成为小说角色发泄恐惧和欲望的地方。其次，反思边疆的历史成为边疆哥特小说叙事的焦点。当代美国哥特小说通过多重视角发掘拓荒历史，重新思考边疆历史对美国社会的影响。在边疆开拓进程中，长期的混乱和危机没有因为边疆历史的远去而消散；暴行和罪恶层出不穷，但却被刻意地掩埋。边疆的开拓并未带来臆想中的进步，反而成为了堕落的开始——边疆既能使人实现理想与信仰，也能使人堕落退化成野蛮状态——这成为了边疆哥特小说里挥之不去的恐惧之源：恐惧自身成为那个野蛮的“他者”。最后，美国疆域的拓展与推进不是一步到位的，边疆的扩展几乎贯穿了整个美国历史。它不是简单的物理层面的扩展，也不是一种生活方式在新土地上复制的过程，而是伴随着城镇化和社会生态构建的演进过程。因此，当代美国边疆哥特小说主题范围也变得多样且广泛，不局限于暴力、宗教、种族冲突，也辐射到家庭关系、性别关系以及人的内在精神机制等。

詹姆斯·拉斐特·迪基(James Lafayette Dickey)的第一部小说《拯救》(*Deliverance*, 1970)讲述了四位城市居民在阿巴拉契亚南部崎岖的荒野中进行为期三天的独木舟之旅，其间他们遭受来自种种自然力量的磋磨，经历了暴力堕落的山民对他们的摧残。《拯救》营造出神秘与恐怖的氛围：让人烦躁不安的潮湿闷热的气候、永远无法摆脱的蚊群、力量惊人且无法预测的水流，还有神出鬼没的、猎杀主人公们的山民。诡异的场景与大量暴力场面和直白的性描写交织在一起，让整部作品呈现出复杂、含混的意义。小说运用的反讽手法凸显出文明与野蛮之间的含混界限。山民是边疆开拓者遗留在此的后代，他们未与周围的文明世界同步，行为暴力野蛮。在目睹同伴被山民残忍地强暴后，艾德(主人公之一)在迷狂状态下与山峰“交媾”。主人公们脱逃追杀，再次进入文明世界后，却对自己的杀戮行经闭口不言，并

① 张冲：《新编美国文学史(第一卷)》，上海：上海外语教育出版社，2000年，第278页。

② Matthiessen, Francis Otto. *American Renaissance: Art and Expression in the Age of Emerson and Whitman*. New York: Oxford University Press, 1941, pp.24-25.

庆幸即将建好的水坝会将一切痕迹掩埋。迪基试图让读者理解:潜藏在人类基因里的兽性,就来自过去某个阴暗的角落[①]。

彼得·马西森(Peter Matthiessen)的《杀死沃森》(*Killing Mister Watson*, 1990)、《迷失者之河》(*Lost Man's River*, 1997)和《骨中骨》(*Bone by Bone*, 1999)三部小说取材于真实历史事件,讲述了一位凶残的种植园主埃德加·沃森(Edgar J. Watson)的生活、命运和不幸,呈现出佛罗里达西南部万岛地区(The Ten Thousand Islands)从荒野到边疆到定居地的丰富且复杂的历史。马西森后来将这三本著作改编成一部小说《影子乡村》(*Shadow Country*, 2008),获得了当年的美国国家图书奖。

小说以一个嗜酒如命的甘蔗种植园主沃森遭遇20人的伏击并被击毙的事件开场,而他的故事也随着他女儿的调查、周围人的回忆、报纸剪报、杂志、信件、日记摘录以及邻居和亲属的证词拼贴组合完整。小说的背景是19世纪末20世纪初,沃森于19世纪90年代来到万岛地区。当时的南佛罗里达是一个荒凉的地区,居住着塞米诺尔印第安人(Seminole Indians)、逃跑的奴隶、内战逃兵、其他离经叛道者和亡命之徒。沃森是一个复杂多变的人物,他是逃亡者、拓荒者、种地的好手、谋杀犯、受害者、家长、族长以及当地的元老。最初,沃森在周围人眼中是一个安静而友好的人。随着10个人用方言回忆沃森的生平故事或复述他们所知的沃森的故事,他的危险性、破坏性和恐怖逐渐累积。他的生平俨然成为了当地的民间传说,他传奇、罪恶的一生成为佛罗里达边疆这一动荡地区最具代表性的叙事。可以这样说,小说对沃森传奇人生的调查也是对该地区在1890至1910年间的历史、社会、自然和生态的研究。

小说在探寻沃森生平的过程中,充分刻画了当地的各色人物。他们既是沃森生平的讲述者,亦是他暴力一生的见证者,有些甚至是其罪恶行径的合谋者与参与者。这里面有私酒贩子、鳄鱼偷猎者、军火走私犯;有深受种族主义伤害的女性;有酒鬼、暴徒和残疾人;还有黑人。在这恶劣的环境里,这些人是被孤立的族群,是原生世界里的叛徒、逃亡者,也是荒野的开拓者,他们靠着莽撞、本能和"传统"来对抗外部世界而偏安一隅。随着铁路不断在周边地区修建,外部文明逐渐渗透并影响着这块边疆之地,沃森和他所秉持的那套边疆生存之道——无论对其本身还是对其追随者而言——都显得不合时宜。因此,杀死沃森成为了当地第一次由众人投票决定的民主行为,这种做法具有强烈的讽刺意味——为对抗私人的暴行而诉诸集体的暴行。这种"民主"行为终结的不仅是沃森的生命,也是佛罗里达的边疆历史。

隐没在边疆历史进程里的种族主义也能在《影子乡村》里觅得踪迹。在对沃森生平的多重叙事里,所有的叙事者都对那些针对印第安人、黑人和混血人种的野蛮行径和暴行习以为常。所以,"沃森的故事本质上是讲述美国边疆的故事,讲述征服荒野、剥削弱势群体的故事,讲述这个国家为此付出代价的故事"[②]。佛罗里达边疆史是美国历史的一个缩影。这个时期对自然和对弱势群体的暴力行径已成为美国构建民族意识形态和民族身份"最重要的神话"[③]。马西森谈及《影子乡村》这部小说时也表明:"在沃森传奇的隐喻中,我想我是在写山姆大叔(Uncle Sam),写种族歧视和社会不公正,写正在摧毁他们希望的美国生活"[④]。

---

① Butterworth, Keen. "The Savage Mind: James Dickey's Deliverance." *The Southern Literary Journal*, vol. 28, no. 2, Spring 1996, pp. 69-78.

② Matthiessen, Peter. *Shadow Country*. New York: The Modern Library, 2008, p. 1.

③ Wood, Amy L. ed. *The New Encyclopedia of Southern Culture (Vol. 19): Violence*. Chapel Hill: University of North Carolina Press, 2011, p. 1.

④ Norman, Howard. "Peter Matthiessen, The Art of Fiction No. 157." *The Paris Review*, no. 150, Spring 1999, pp. 187-215.

第二节　族裔问题的哥特小说

我们在美国历史里不难发现对少数族裔的罪恶暴行，如对黑人的奴隶制度、对印第安人的驱逐与屠杀、对墨西哥裔和华裔的压迫等等。时至今日，种族问题依然是美国社会生活中的一个核心议题，美国人不愿意承认美国生活背后的“残酷事实”①，然而，无论怎样回避或者粉饰，历史中存在的奴隶制和种族灭绝的残酷现实都无法一直被隐藏和压制，它们的影响力并未随着时间的流逝而减弱，因此，“那些想要讲述自己国家辉煌成就的小说家发现奴隶制更加棘手”②。哥特文学善于发掘被主流叙事所掩盖、压制和遗忘的主题，种族主义就成为当代美国哥特小说发掘的对象，并以此表达对权力话语的不适、焦虑、怀疑甚至厌恶。

奴隶制、黑人和南方是无法回避的，也是当代族裔哥特小说中常见的要素。这类作品有两个特征：第一，重述奴隶制的罪恶和黑人遭受的苦难。南北战争以后，关于南方的很多通俗文学都以伤感和怀旧的面目示人，描述种植园主的贵族风范和黑人奴隶安于现状的景象，体现出美化内战前的南方的意图。非洲裔作家以及一些有良知的白人作家敏感地意识到这种美化南方和淡化奴隶制带来的危害，他们或创作哥特小说，或将哥特元素加入到自己的作品中，以直白的恐怖场景展现黑人奴隶遭受的非人待遇，书写对奴隶制和种族主义的控诉。第二，美国南方作为历史上奴隶制盛行的地区，成为众多哥特小说的创作背景。这类作品以战后南方的社会风貌为背景，展现破败的种植园庄园、贵族式的传统南方家族的衰落，通过探寻隐匿在家族历史中的骇人秘密，探讨历史上南方社会一系列不合理的制度和思想，以及它们带来的毁灭性影响。

白人基督教文学常将魔法、巫术和原生信仰视为原始的、异端的和另类的，进而常对其贬损，而当代美国族裔哥特小说从族裔文化的因子里发掘这些怪怖的、越界的、非理性的元素，丰富其叙事内容，在小说内部构建起虚拟的逻辑世界。文学作品是现实生活的反照，其本质就是陌生化（defamiliarization），哥特小说不一定对有关魔法、巫术和原生信仰的超自然现象给出合理的解释，它们将现实世界的因果法则暂时搁置，以陌生化的叙事唤起读者对有别于理性和逻辑的事物的关注与思考，通过陌生化效应，丰富了读者对世界的感知，增强叙事内容与现实事实的张力，强化小说主题。

托妮·莫里森的《宠儿》以毫不退缩的笔触描绘出奴隶制带来的难以想象的残酷景象，同时颠覆了南方哥特小说的固有模式。闹鬼的房屋不再是种植园主的庄园，而是曾为奴隶的黑人简陋的家；隐匿家族黑暗秘密的不是白人，而是黑人。小说里，随着宠儿鬼魂一再的逼迫和追问，日常的景物和生活琐事时刻警醒着读者，使之对恐怖真相的压迫感久久不能释怀。故事里最骇人的一幕是塞斯杀子，这一幕看似符合对黑人“他者”形象的描述——野蛮且愚昧，然而当其背后的动机——为避免自己的孩子再次堕入被奴役的地狱而杀死她——被揭示后，奴隶遭受的苦难和奴隶制造成的贻害激起了读者的共情和反思，彻底颠覆了对黑人的刻板印象。同时，面对宠儿一再追问家族往事，塞斯挣扎抗拒，家人逃离回避。

① Fisher, Philip. *Hard Facts: Setting and Form in the American Novel*. New York: Oxford University Press, 1987, p.5.

② Bendixen, Alfred. "The Development of the American Novel: The Transformations of Genre." Alfred Bendixen. ed., *A Company to the American Novel*. Chichester: Wiley-Blackwell, 2012, p.9.

莫里森用鬼魂的歇斯底里与塞斯等人的茫然无措表达出一种深层隐喻:非洲裔族群的文化和身份之根在哪里?非洲裔族群与故土非洲的联系因为罪恶的奴隶贸易被强行割断,而在新土地上又因种族主义无法融入、培育和发展新的精神家园,莫里森将定义身份的矛盾与焦虑转移到自己族群中,也让读者重新审视非洲裔美国人的精神、文化和现实困境。

同美国黑人文学一样,美国本土裔作家的小说也对美国文学传统中印第安人的刻板印象作出回应。自欧洲殖民者踏上美洲土地的那一刻起,美洲印第安人就符合他们对"他者"的一切想象,印第安人顺理成章地成为"魔鬼""野兽""怪物"的具象化载体。本土裔美国人成了美国哥特文学里的常客,他们的习俗、信仰、仪式都成为了白人文学作品里恐怖的发源地。然而,当代美国印第安小说以后殖民的视角颠覆美国白人文学的传统,在哥特小说里将邪恶的源头重新分配。

莱斯利·马蒙·西尔科(Leslie Marmon Silko)的《典仪》(*Ceremony*, 1977)就表明印第安人的"典仪"不是"巫术"(witchery),而是治愈主人公塔尤(Tayo)肉体与精神创伤、重构自我与自然和谐关系的重要方式。西尔科运用了碎片化、非线性的情节构建整个故事,乍一看显得混乱且复杂,但当我们遵循主人公塔尤的心理恢复历程,就会发现这是一个从混乱走向和谐、由无序变成有序的过程,而在其中起到重要作用的就是塔尤用来修复自己心灵创伤的典仪。塔尤是一名二战老兵,也是混血印第安人,他的心理创伤不仅来自其在战俘营中的恐怖遭遇,还与其童年遭受的种族主义伤害密不可分。因此,他的康复过程是漫长且复杂的,族人为他进行的传统的治疗仪式也不能立竿见影地起效果。塔尤意识到真正的"巫术"是白人精神世界里为遏制邪恶和杀戮而变得更邪恶,制造更多杀戮的做法,因此,塔尤在有能力杀死艾莫(Emo)的时候却没有那样做,因为他不想屈从于白人的巫术。当塔尤遵循治疗师的指示,走向自己母亲曾经生活过的保留地找寻到三个标志(星光、牛群和女人)后,他完成了治愈心理创伤的典仪,这三种事物象征着本土裔美国人质朴的精神内核:与自然亲近、与万物休戚与共、与人和谐相处。

第三节　吸血鬼小说

当代美国哥特小说麾下的鬼怪小说、吸血鬼小说、僵尸小说等诸多类型小说,都以杂糅的方式与其他门类的小说结合,以异彩纷呈的形式呈现。其中,吸血鬼小说受到大众的追捧,在各种媒介都出现过名噪一时的作品,如斯蒂芬妮·摩根·梅尔(Stephenie Morgan Meyer)的《暮光》(*Twilight*)系列小说[①],电视剧《真爱如血》(*True Blood*, 2008—2014),电影《刀锋战士》(*Blade*, 1998、2002、2004)等,它们主题复杂且多样,在学术界甚至有专门的"吸血鬼研究"(vampire studies)。

吸血鬼起源于中世纪的欧洲大陆的传说,在众多传说的拼贴下,吸血鬼成为一种邪恶恐怖、具备超自然能力、似人又非人的生物。他们要么因为生前背叛上帝,要么因为犯下不可饶恕的罪恶行径,要么是被其他吸血鬼转化,从而变成似人又不是人的一种存在。在最初的文学作品中,吸血鬼是嗜血者,是邪恶的异端,是肮脏不洁的"他者",他们的唯一结局是被毁灭。自布莱姆·斯托克(Bram Stoker)的《德

① 按:这个系列小说是指《暮光》(*Twilight*, 2005)、《新月》(*New Moon*, 2006)、《月食》(*Eclipse*, 2007)和《破晓》(*Breaking Down*, 2008)。

古拉》(*Dracula*, 1897)面世后,吸血鬼不再仅仅是虚构的角色,他成为了文化产业的中心,他成为了一种风格的代表,一种文化的标签①。在斯托克之后,吸血鬼一改丑陋、恐怖的形象,成为举止优雅得体,衣着讲究,具备超自然的能力,且极具诱惑性和挑逗性的形象。

当代美国吸血鬼小说明显的特征是杂糅和多样性。首先是吸血鬼形象的多样化。吸血鬼可以是精英,也可以粗鄙肮脏;有女性,有男性;有白人,也有非洲裔和拉美裔;有底层流浪者,也有政客;有男同性恋者,也有女同性恋者。吸血鬼身份与阶层的多样性,一方面是当代美国社会多元性的体现,文学作品呼应了多元文化的表达需求;另一方面也是对传统吸血鬼叙事的解构,它消解了以往文学作品中吸血鬼承载的宗教与道德批评功能,让吸血鬼走向多元,走向大众,当然也不可避免地走向娱乐化。

其次是吸血鬼小说背景的多样化。吸血鬼可以浮现于历史事件里,如黛博拉·哈克尼斯(Deborah Harkness)的《女巫现身》(*A Discovery of Witches*, 2011),也可以挣扎在现实的日常生活里,如安德鲁·福克斯(Andrew Fox)的《白胖吸血鬼的蓝调生活》(*Fat White Vampire Blues*, 2003),甚至可以是未来世界里新的物种,如奥克塔维娅·巴特勒(Octavia Butler)的《雏鸟》(*Fledgling*, 2005)。这些小说或探寻一段隐秘的历史,或以幽默反讽的笔触展示现实社会生活的荒诞,或以后人类(post-humanism)的视角探寻人的存在意义与价值。吸血鬼不死的特性让其能自由穿梭于过去、现在和未来,带领读者重新发现、解读和反思自身的经验和对周围世界的认知。同时,叙事背景的多元化与吸血鬼形象正邪混杂的不确定性丰富了对作品意义的解读。

还有,吸血鬼小说可以与其他多种类型小说结合,有吸血鬼浪漫爱情小说、吸血鬼科幻小说、吸血鬼悬疑惊悚小说等等。吸血鬼小说与其他类型小说的多样化结合,一方面体现了现代主义与后现代主义对当代美国文学的影响,另一方面也体现了吸血鬼小说的可塑性。虽然这类小说良莠不齐,但它们对人性、自我身份和权力话语的探索却从未止歇。总之,作为哥特小说的类型小说之一,当代吸血鬼小说在体现哥特小说的杂糅性的同时,也反映出人们面对多元性社会生活产生的不适与焦虑。

当代美国吸血鬼小说在后现代主义与多元文化的共同影响下,不断探索和突破作为类型小说的禁锢,无论其叙事、风格还是主题都呈现出杂糅特征。然而,它身上具备的哥特文学的颠覆特质使其依然能继续对两性关系、人的生存与挑战以及现代化社会的隐忧进行持续的书写与思考。

第一,表现女性对两性关系的焦虑。如前文所言,斯托克之后的吸血鬼形象已不再是肮脏、恐怖的形象,而化身成为极度性感的角色,并满足女性对男性的期待,但吸血鬼嗜血残暴的本性,也能使其成为表达女性对两性关系不安与焦虑的隐喻。

斯蒂芬妮·摩根·梅尔的《暮光》系列小说讲述了孤独少女贝拉(Bella Swan)与迷人的吸血鬼爱德华(Edward Cullen)突破禁忌相恋的故事。这部作品杂糅了吸血鬼、狼人、校园文学、恐怖悬疑等多种元素,受到读者欢迎。但透过大众娱乐的表象,《暮光》系列小说蕴含着女性对婚恋、生育的焦虑与不安。小说里的贝拉心智成熟、聪慧冷静、独立决断,面对"异类"爱德华可以抛下世俗约束而勇敢接纳。然而,当外表迷人、一向沉稳的爱德华展示出嗜血残暴的一面后,贝拉也会惊惧、迷惘和退缩。面对一个在生理上、心理上还有社会权力上都异于甚至优于自己的异性时,作为女性的贝拉在其内心的防备与恐惧是无法消除的。同时,书中对贝拉孕育后代的过程描写不仅没有一般文学作品中的温馨与柔情,反而透着

① Gelder, Ken. *Reading the Vampire*. London: Routledge, 1994, p.65.

血腥与恐怖。胎儿生长的速度惊人，并持续消耗着贝拉的生命力，胎儿在母体中就具有了巨大的破坏力（踢断了贝拉的肋骨和胯骨），更让贝拉在分娩时命悬一线。在梅尔笔下，生育不再被罩上美丽、温情的光环，生育对女性是一项生死挑战。生育后的贝拉生命岌岌可危，而拯救她的方法只有将其转化成为吸血鬼。这样的隐喻暗示女性在经历生育后将会变成一个"异类"——一个生理、心理甚至社会层面的"异类"。用女性视角审视性别焦虑的吸血鬼小说还有莎莲·哈里斯（Charlaine Harris）的《至夜将死》（*Dead Until Dark*, 2001）和黛博拉·哈克尼斯的《女巫现身》。前者讲述了女主人公从依恋男性，到挣扎抗争，最后认识并肯定自身价值的心路历程；后者则讲述了女主人公在得知自己隐秘的身份后，回探历史事件，发现无论是猎杀吸血鬼，还是猎杀女巫，都是男性对女性施加的权力暴力这一真相。

第二，表达现代人对灾难的焦虑。文学作品从不缺乏灭世灾难的主题，从现代医学角度而言，吸血鬼吸食血液的特殊进食方式，使其成为传播疾病的媒介，吸血鬼在当代文学作品中也成为了流行病的隐喻。肖沃尔特（Elaine Showalter）就指出，19 世纪末吸血鬼小说的涌现与当时作为不治之症的梅毒具有一定的联系[①]。性传播疾病隐匿在两性关系的隐私领域，当对疾病的恐惧和臆想无法通过开诚布公的方式消除时，疑虑和焦虑便无法化解。诚然，梅毒现在已不再是威胁人类的主要疾病，然而现代社会由于分工的细化使得人与人之间的联系与交流比以往更加紧密，但人与人之间的心理壁垒却未能同步消除，因此，现代社会并未从流行病的阴影中摆脱出来。现代社会生活节奏迅速，人员流动频繁，人与人之间隔阂加剧，这一系列因素让流行病的爆发与传播更加迅速且更加难以应对。

史蒂芬·金（Stephen King）的《塞勒姆镇》（*Salem's Lot*, 1975）讲述了作家本·米尔斯（Ben Mears）在阔别 25 年后重回家乡小镇，却发现镇上的居民逐渐变得诡异，原因竟是小镇的居民正一个个变成吸血鬼。小镇上第一个变成吸血鬼的是男孩丹尼（Danny Glick），他虽已死亡，但在死前已经感染了他的母亲和其他亲友。本和其他几个未感染者联合起来，试图遏制病毒的传播。然而，吸血鬼的数量还是在不断增加。当一家有吸血鬼后，首先是家人，之后亲友也会相继变成吸血鬼。面对庞大的吸血鬼群体和几近沦陷的小镇，本和幸存者们无力应对，最终他们选择逃离。史蒂芬·金用吸血鬼隐喻流行病，以恐怖、悬疑的笔触刻画人在应对流行病爆发时的无力、无助与矛盾心理。小说里，人们面对吸血鬼这种古老生物的威胁时，无法从现代医学里找到治愈的途径，只能依靠迷信和宗教传说找寻破解之法。然而，根除的方法是要将病人灭杀，这显然与人的情感和伦理相冲突。正因为此，当一个家庭出现病人时，家人出于正常的伦理情感并没有灭杀他们，这不仅将自己置于危险中，也将公众置于危险中。《塞勒姆镇》以吸血鬼为隐喻，展现出现代社会人们对流行病的焦虑与困境，它以小见大，以一场小镇面临的灭顶之灾刻画众生百态，展现出群体利益与个体伦理选择之间的冲突，以及二者在人性抉择中的角力。在这样的灾难语境下，以本为代表的传统文学里的个人英雄也显得无力且徒劳，最终只能落荒而逃。

第三，表达现代生活的焦虑情感。现代化、都市化和科技发展给人们的生活带来便捷，却没有将人们带向安全、富足与自由的乌托邦，原有的道德伦理、生活观念受到巨大的挑战并引发了新一轮对生活和生命意义探寻的焦虑。当代吸血鬼小说以更具个性化的叙事方式书写荒诞的生活带给现代人的焦虑。

安德鲁·福克斯的《白胖吸血鬼的蓝调生活》以生活化的语言刻画了一个与现代生活格格不入的吸

① Showalter, Elaine. "Syphilis, Sexuality, and the Fiction of the Fin de Siècle." Lyn Pykett. ed., *Reading Fin de Siècle Fictions*. London: Routledge, 1996, pp. 166 - 183.

血鬼故事。朱尔斯·达钦(Jules Duchon)是生活在新奥尔良的吸血鬼,因为现代人从饮食中摄取的营养过于丰富,连累朱尔斯体重达到450磅。他思维守旧,在他的同类与时俱进,通过各种营销手段骗取人们定期、自愿地供给血液时,他依然坚持自食其力,通过街头猎杀的方式获取赖以为生的血液,而他肥胖的外形无疑影响了他成功的机率。他无法认同和理解同为吸血鬼的好友成为变装者的做法,故与之疏远;他更无法理解为何与他同样肥胖的吸血鬼女友会嫌弃自己。作为一个存在了400多年的吸血鬼,他见证了自己的邻居正在被他们津津乐道的现代生活带向地狱。他遭到一个内心邪恶、衣着光鲜的黑人吸血鬼马利切(Malice X)的挑衅与威胁,理由是他竟然吸食黑人女性的血液,这让马利切觉得遭受了种族主义迫害,誓要将朱尔斯杀死。面对生活里种种荒诞现实,朱尔斯发现自己400多年的阅历与经验毫无用武之地。福克斯借着这个另类生物的口吻,用黑色幽默的笔触对当代生活的荒诞性进行了巧妙的讽刺。

当代吸血鬼小说不再拘泥于单一的类型,采用越界的叙事手法,杂糅其他类型小说的元素,展现更多元、更多样的叙事主题。我们不能否认诸多吸血鬼小说娱乐化的现实,正如我们也不能轻视当代吸血鬼小说所蕴含的颠覆话语权力的意义。

第四节　主要作家介绍与代表作品选读

一、科马克·麦卡锡

(一)科马克·麦卡锡简介

科马克·麦卡锡(Cormac McCarthy, 1933—　)是美国当代著名的小说家,文学批评家哈罗德·布鲁姆把他和托马斯·品钦、唐·德里罗和菲利普·罗斯一起列为当代美国最重要的四大小说家[①]。麦卡锡因其作品风格和南方文学的代表人物福克纳、奥康纳有某种关联,被认为是南方哥特文学的代表人物,也因其成名作《血色子午线》和"边境三部曲"等作品描写美国西南边疆的原因,被认为是西部作家[②]。麦卡锡所有小说最明显的特征是过度、直白的暴力场景,这使得他的作品呈现出黑暗压抑的氛围,同时,他在叙事过程中往往回避对人物内心的刻画,使得读者无法明辨其对暴力的态度,因此,他作品的价值导向常引起争议。

麦卡锡早期的作品有《果园守护人》(*The Orchard Keeper*, 1965)、《暗夜幽灵》(*Outer Dark*, 1968)和《神之子》(*Child of God*, 1974)。《果园守护人》讲述主人公和他的两位人生导师发生在田纳西乡间的纠葛,他们三个人的命运因一具被丢弃在泥坑里的尸体而巧妙地联系在一起,主人公最终发现把他逐出美好安宁生活的恰是那些他认为值得托付爱与忠诚的人。《暗夜幽灵》讲述一对兄妹遗弃他们因乱伦

① Bloom, Harold. *How to Read and Why*. New York: Simon and Schuster, 2001, pp.254-255.

② 参见 Philips, Dana. "History and Ugly Facts of Cormac McCarthy's Blood Meridian." *American Literature*, vol.68, no.2, Jun., 1996, pp. 433-460.; Kollin, Susan. "Genre and the Geographies of Violence: Cormac McCarthy and the Contemporary Western." *Contemporary Literature*, vol.42, no.3, 2001, pp.557-588.

而生的孩子之后又各自寻找孩子的经历。《神之子》取材自发生在田纳西州的真实案件，以悬疑、简洁、引人入胜的文字讲述了莱斯特·巴拉德被人类大家庭抛弃而走向堕落，成为杀人犯和恋尸癖者的过程。在早期的作品里，麦卡锡延续了美国南方哥特文学的暴力、荒诞和黑色幽默。

创作完上述作品之后，麦卡锡将目光转向美国的边疆地区，先后创作了《血色子午线》、“边境三部曲”和《老无所依》(*No Country for Old Men*, 2005)。其中，为麦卡锡赢得声名的是由《天下骏马》(*All the Pretty Horses*, 1992)、《穿越》(*The Crossing*, 1994)和《平原都市》(*Cities of the Plain*, 1998)组成的“边境三部曲”。

《天下骏马》讲述了得克萨斯州青年约翰·格雷迪·科尔的成长故事。主人公踏上一段前往未知地区的旅程，他的游历与回忆及梦魇交叠在一起。在遭受种种邪恶行径后，他意识到邪恶既由他的无知和傲慢引发，又是宇宙中无法逃离的力量。《穿越》的故事发生在二战前和二战中，讲述主人公比利·帕汉姆(Billy Parham)和其弟博伊德(Boyd Parham)三次穿越新墨西哥州和墨西哥边境线的故事。故事以反讽和黑色幽默的笔触描写主人公每次穿越边境后都遭遇与最初目标背离的意外、灾难与失望。《平原都市》将前两部中约翰·格雷迪·科尔和比利·帕汉姆的故事结合在一起。他们成为密友，同在新墨西哥州的农场打工。科尔邂逅妓女玛格达莱娜(Magdalena)，两人热恋，但他们决意结婚的举动触怒了妓院老板。玛格达莱娜在结婚前夕被残忍杀害，而科尔也在复仇中身受重伤而死。比利离开牧场，终生流浪。麦卡锡在故事最后安排一位神秘女子出场，当她听完比利抱怨无法理解他的身份与目的后，她如同一位熟悉这漫长故事的读者一般，和蔼地告诉比尔她对这二者很了解。

《老无所依》以一场失控和血腥的毒品交易作为开场，展现了一出现代社会里的西部片场景。贝尔警长(Sheriff Bell)发现他所管辖的平静社区正面临着一场由冷血、癫狂、狡诈且自负的安东·齐格(Anton Chigurh)带来的暴力浪潮。麦卡锡在犯罪惊悚小说的叙事中审视当下唯利是图的社会，以暴力和血腥的笔触描述贪婪对人性的腐蚀作用以及由此产生的灾难性后果。

在麦卡锡的小说里，暴力不是偶发的、冲动的行为，它成为了人们生活中某种必然的、常态的存在，他用直白的文字描写暴力的残酷，使得这些场景极具冲击力和震撼效果，同时也让人重新思考暴力与人性的关系，反思暴力的本质，审视现代社会的人性。

（二）《血色子午线》简介

《血色子午线》与麦卡锡早期的风格有明显的变化，他突破南方哥特小说阴暗、封闭的地域场景，将叙事推向更广袤的西部，讲述了一个发生在西部边疆荒野里的充满暴力的故事。

《血色子午线》的主人公无名无姓，作者在小说里只用少年(kid)称呼他。故事发生在19世纪40年代，少年自幼丧母，离家游荡在美墨边境地带，先加入美国的军事阻挠武装组织，后加入“格兰顿帮”(Glanton Gang)。该帮以退伍老兵格兰顿为首，由一群来自美国的亡命徒组成。在格兰顿和帮派二号灵魂人物、绰号“法官”的霍顿(Holden)带领下，他们专门猎杀印第安人并剥取头皮换奖金谋生。这支队伍在墨西哥边境地区四处游荡，不加区分地屠杀不同部落的印第安人，甚至深入墨西哥境内屠杀墨西哥人，老幼妇孺均不放过。他们的残忍行径遭到印第安人的报复，终因恶行而遭覆灭，少年侥幸逃生。小说最后跨越到二十八年后，已成为成年男人的主人公在酒馆偶遇“法官”霍顿，被其杀害，小说随着霍顿在篝火旁的舞蹈结束。

《血色子午线》是一部重要的哥特文学作品，哥特小说“越界性”（transgression）和“过度性”（excessive）的特点在其中充分展现。它以粗粝的语言、刻意复古的句式，毫不避讳地再现了发生在 19 世纪美墨边境历史中的暴力、野蛮和苦难，其浓郁的血腥场景展现出一幅幽暗的人性前景。小说突破幽暗封闭的南方哥特文学的限制，在广袤的荒野里恣意挥洒恐怖与血腥，用直白的语言渲染人性的残暴，探寻语言刻画暴力的边界，颠覆了有关旧西部和边疆叙事的神话。哈罗德·布鲁姆对这部小说推崇备至，认为它是 20 世纪最伟大的小说之一，当代美国小说家中只有麦卡锡能够写出“如此令人震撼、令人难忘的作品”，他也承认他“最初两次想读完《血色子午线》的努力都以失败告终，因为麦卡锡所描绘的铺天盖地的杀戮令人生畏”①。

《血色子午线》有别于传统文学中以暴制暴、除暴安良式的男性叙事。暴力不是男性实现自身价值与理想的手段，它成了终极目的。在极致的暴力背后，透露着施暴者复杂焦虑的精神现实。故事中，施暴者的暴力与其内心的恐惧犹如一对双生子，纠缠折磨着他们。格兰顿一次次的屠杀是为了逃避来自被屠杀部落幸存者的报复，他的恐惧让他越来越疯狂，进而做出更恐怖的行径。“恐惧的文化将对信任产生破坏，而这种破坏会进一步扩大恐惧的范围”②，从这个层面讲，格兰顿及其手下的暴力行为已然不是男性气质的反映，而是男性内心极度不安全感的非理性宣泄，它不是“豪迈”与“不羁”，只是抚慰自己内心恐惧的非理性挣扎，其结果是触发更加强大的精神反噬。《血色子午线》里的边疆不再是恣意驰骋、追寻理想、寻找希望、获取宁静的乌托邦，它让广袤的、空旷的、无遮蔽的边疆地带成了男性的精神炼狱。

《血色子午线》中的霍顿是小说中最让人难忘的角色之一。他秃顶、魁梧、身强力壮，凶暴如恶魔；他学识渊博，天文地理知识信手拈来，还能用蝙蝠粪和人尿制造火药；他通晓多种语言，能言善辩，在人类学、博物学、生物进化论和法学等多个领域都能侃侃而谈；他是一位小提琴手和敏捷的舞者；他还是一个骗子，一个虐待狂杀手。他将战争本身称为终极交易，而人类则是战争的终极实践者。他认为战争本质上是一场意志之战，结果由“更大的意志”（命运）决定。他认为是战争决定了宇宙的进程，所以“战争就是上帝”。在他眼中，所有那些没有真正为战争服务的人都将消失、被人遗忘。在小说的结尾，霍顿是格兰顿帮唯一的幸存者，似乎命运注定只有他能永远活着，跳着战争的舞蹈。

（三）作品选读：《血色子午线》③

XVII

...

They began to come upon chains and packsaddles, singletrees, dead mules, wagons. Saddletrees eaten bare of their rawhide coverings and weathered white as bone, a light chamfering of miceteeth along the edges of the wood. They rode through a region where iron will not rust nor tin tarnish. The ribbed frames of dead cattle under their patches of dried hide lay like the ruins of primitive boats upturned upon that shoreless void and they passed lurid and austere the black and desiccated shapes of horses and mules that travelers had stood afoot. These parched beasts had died with their

① Bloom, Harold. *How to Read and Why*. New York: Simon and Schuster, 2001, p.255.

② Svendsen, Lars. *A Philosophy of Fear* (2nd Edition). John Irons, trans., London: Reaktion Books, 2008, p.8.

③ McCarthy, Cormac. *Blood Meridian: Or the Evening Redness in the West* (25th Anniversary Edition). New York: Modern Library, 2001, pp.275 - 279.

necks stretched in agony in the sand and now upright and blind and lurching askew with scraps of blackened leather hanging from the fretwork of their ribs they leaned with their long mouths howling after the endless tandem suns that passed above them. The riders rode on. They crossed a vast dry lake with rows of dead volcanoes ranged beyond it like the works of enormous insects. To the south lay broken shapes of scoria in a lava bed as far as the eye could see. Under the hooves of the horses the alabaster sand shaped itself in whorls strangely symmetric like iron filings in a field and these shapes flared and drew back again, resonating upon that harmonic ground and then turning to swirl away over the playa. As if the very sediment of things contained yet some residue of sentience. As if in the transit of those riders were a thing so profoundly terrible as to register even to the uttermost granulation of reality.

On a rise at the western edge of the playa they passed a crude wooden cross where Maricopas had crucified an Apache. The mummied corpse hung from the crosstree with its mouth gaped in a raw hole, a thing of leather and bone scoured by the pumice winds off the lake and the pale tree of the ribs showing through the scraps of hide that hung from the breast. They rode on. The horses trudged sullenly the alien ground and the round earth rolled beneath them silently milling the greater void wherein they were contained. In the neuter austerity of that terrain all phenomena were bequeathed a strange equality and no one thing nor spider nor stone nor blade of grass could put forth claim to precedence. The very clarity of these articles belied their familiarity, for the eye predicates the whole on some feature or part and here was nothing more luminous than another and nothing more enshadowed and in the optical democracy of such landscapes all preference is made whimsical and a man and a rock become endowed with unguessed kinships.

They grew gaunted and lank under the white suns of those days and their hollow burnedout eyes were like those of noctambulants surprised by day. Crouched under their hats they seemed fugitives on some grander scale, like beings for whom the sun hungered. Even the judge grew silent and speculative. He'd spoke of purging oneself of those things that lay claim to a man but that body receiving his remarks counted themselves well done with any claims at all. They rode on and the wind drove the fine gray dust before them and they rode an army of gray-beards, gray men, gray horses. The mountains to the north lay sunwise in corrugated folds and the days were cool and the nights were cold and they sat about the fire each in his round of darkness in that round of dark while the idiot watched from his cage at the edge of the light. The judge cracked with the back of an axe the shinbone on an antelope and the hot marrow dripped smoking on the stones. They watched him. The subject was war.

The good book says that he that lives by the sword shall perish by the sword, said the black.

The judge smiled, his face shining with grease. What right man would have it any other way? he said.

The good book does indeed count war an evil, said Irving. Yet there's many a bloody tale of war inside it.

It makes no difference what men think of war, said the judge. War endures. As well ask men what they think of stone. War was always here. Before man was, war waited for him. The ultimate trade awaiting its ultimate practitioner. That is the way it was and will be. That way and not some other way.

He turned to Brown, from whom he'd heard some whispered slur or demurrer. Ah Davy, he said. It's your own trade we honor here. Why not rather take a small bow. Let each acknowledge each.

My trade?

Certainly.

What is my trade?

War. War is your trade. Is it not?

And it aint yours? Mine too. Very much so.

What about all them notebooks and bones and stuff?

All other trades are contained in that of war.

Is that why war endures?

No. It endures because young men love it and old men love it in them. Those that fought, those that did not.

That's your notion.

The judge smiled. Men are born for games. Nothing else. Every child knows that play is nobler than work. He knows too that the worth or merit of a game is not inherent in the game itself but rather in the value of that which is put at hazard. Games of chance require a wager to have meaning at all. Games of sport involve the skill and strength of the opponents and the humiliation of defeat and the pride of victory are in themselves sufficient stake because they inhere in the worth of the principals and define them. But trial of chance or trial of worth all games aspire to the condition of war for here that which is wagered swallows up game, player, all.

Suppose two men at cards with nothing to wager save their lives. Who has not heard such a tale? A turn of the card. The whole universe for such a player has labored clanking to this moment which will tell if he is to die at that man's hand or that man at his. What more certain validation of a man's worth could there be? This enhancement of the game to its ultimate state admits no argument concerning the notion of fate. The selection of one man over another is a preference absolute and irrevocable and it is a dull man indeed who could reckon so profound a decision without agency or significance either one. In such games as have for their stake the annihilation of the defeated the decisions are quite clear. This man holding this particular arrangement of cards in his hand is thereby removed from existence. This is the nature of war, whose stake is at once the game and the authority and the justification. Seen so, war is the truest form of divination. It is the testing of one's will and the will of another within that larger will which because it binds them is therefore forced to select. War is the ultimate game because war is at last a forcing of the unity of existence. War is god.

Brown studied the judge. You're crazy Holden. Crazy at last.

The judge smiled.

Might does not make right, said living. The man that wins in some combat is not vindicated morally.

Moral law is an invention of mankind for the disenfranchisement of the powerful in favor of the weak. Historical law subverts it at every turn. A moral view can never be proven right or wrong by any ultimate test. A man falling dead in a duel is not thought thereby to be proven in error as to his views. His very involvement in such a trial gives evidence of a new and broader view. The willingness of the principals to forgo further argument as the triviality which it in fact is and to petition directly the chambers of the historical absolute clearly indicates of how little moment are the opinions and of what great moment the divergences thereof. For the argument is indeed trivial, but not so the separate wills thereby made manifest. Man's vanity may well approach the infinite in capacity but his knowledge remains imperfect and however much he comes to value his judgements ultimately he must submit them before a higher court. Here there can be no special pleading. Here are considerations of equity and rectitude and moral right rendered void and without warrant and here are the views of the litigants despised. Decisions of life and death, of what shall be and what shall not, beggar all question of right. In elections of these magnitudes are all lesser ones subsumed, moral, spiritual, natural.

The judge searched out the circle for disputants. But what says the priest? he said.

Tobin looked up. The priest does not say.

The priest does not say, said the judge. Nihil dicit. But the priest has said. For the priest has put by the robes of his craft and taken up the tools of that higher calling which all men honor. The priest also would be no godserver but a god himself.

Tobin shook his head. You've a blasphemous tongue, Holden. And in truth I was never a priest but only a novitiate to the order.

Journeyman priest or apprentice priest, said the judge. Men of god and men of war have strange affinities.

I'll not secondsay you in your notions, said Tobin. Dont ask it.

Ah Priest, said the judge. What could I ask of you that you've not already given?

...

思考与讨论

(1) 霍顿对战争持什么观点？其他人对霍顿的战争观持什么态度？

(2) 选文中的场景描写起到什么作用？为什么？

(3) 选文的语言风格是怎样的？这样的语言风格对主题有什么作用？

拓展阅读

[1] Bell, Vereen M. *The Achievement of Cormac McCarthy* (1st Edition). Los Angeles: Louisiana State Univ Press, 1988.

[2] Goddu, Teresa A. *Gothic America: Narrative, History, and the Nation*. New York: Columbia University Press, 1997.

[3] Turner, Frederick Jackson. *The Frontier in American History*. Los Angeles: Create Space Independent Publishing Platform, 2014.

二、鲁道夫·安纳亚及其代表作简介

(一) 鲁道夫·安纳亚简介

鲁道夫·安纳亚(Rudolfo Anaya, 1937—2020),生活在新墨西哥州,是小说家和教育家,著有多部小说、诗歌和戏剧。其作品充分体现了他的墨西哥裔美国血统,正如他所言:"我不想离开新墨西哥州。在这里,我环顾四周时会有一种感觉,这些山、这条河、这片土地、这片天空都是我的"①。他继承西班牙语民间传说和口头文学的传统,开拓了奇卡诺文学的新天地,产生了巨大影响。2015 年,因其开拓性的美国西南部故事,同时,作为一名教育家,他把对文学的热爱传给了新一代,他获得了美国国家人文基金会国家人文奖章(National Endowment for the Humanities National Humanities Medal)。

安纳亚的第一部小说《祝福我,乌蒂玛》出版后广受好评,这让安纳亚踏上了长期且多产的文学创作道路,继续创作了《阿兹特兰之心》(*Heart of Aztlán*, 1976)和《托吐加岛》(*Tortuga*, 1979),这三部小说构成了叙述美国拉美裔儿童成长的文学三部曲。小说《阿兹特兰之心》的背景是 20 世纪 60 年代美墨边境的卡奇诺运动,描写了一个家庭从农村走向城市的过程,直面墨西哥劳工遭遇的一系列问题。小说《祝福我,乌蒂玛》从流传在美墨边境的故事、诗歌及戏剧中找寻突破,讲述了 20 世纪 40 年代末在新墨西哥州长大的一个小男孩在奇卡诺治疗师影响下成长的故事。小说《托吐加岛》以作者自身经历为蓝本,刻画了因伤而困在石膏里的男孩的情感,探寻墨西哥裔如何在更大的社会层面确定身份与归属感。

安纳亚后来的小说《尤罗娜传说》(*The Legend of La Llorona*, 1984)、《胡安·奇卡斯帕塔斯历险记》(*The Adventures of Juan Chicaspatas*, 1985)、《阿尔比凯克城》(*Alburquerque*, 1992)和《洛佩斯回家》(*Randy Lopez Goes Home*, 2011)以及中篇小说《黄昏恋曲》(*The Old Man's Love Story*, 2013)突破族裔叙事的框架,虽深深植根于美国西南部和墨西哥裔的生活,但却超越了地域和文化的界限,表现出具备普遍意义的伦理价值和道德观。他还以墨西哥私家侦探桑尼·巴卡(Sonny Baca)为主角创作了系列悬疑侦探小说,包括《齐亚的夏天》(*Zia Summer*, 1995)、《格兰德河的秋天》(*Rio Grande Fall*,

① Dick, Bruce & Sirias, Silvio, eds. *Conversations with Rudolfo Anaya*. Jackson: University of Mississippi Press, 1998, p.13.

1996)、《萨满的冬天》(*Shaman Winter*, 1999)和《赫美斯山的春天》(*Jemez Spring*, 2005)。桑尼·巴卡系列小说在风格上明显转变,但依然延续着他早期作品中确立的主题,依然在寻找与土地、族群和祖先智慧的精神联系。

(二)《祝福我,乌蒂玛》简介

作为多元文化主义和双语主义的倡导者,安纳亚谈及《祝福我,乌蒂玛》里独特的双语特征和魔幻现实主义时强调,"这种文化在西南部已有400年左右的历史,它与西班牙裔、墨西哥裔、本土裔美国人的传统、宗教和世界观是相通的。所以当你谈论奇卡诺文学时,你会有一种非常独特的混合感"①。

《祝福我,乌蒂玛》讲述了20世纪40年代新墨西哥州的奇卡诺人在社会变革的大背景下找寻身份的历程。故事围绕着男孩安东尼奥(Antonio)的经历展开。安东尼奥是一个六岁的奇卡诺男孩,有着敏锐的洞察力和爱质疑的天性,常常会做一些生动且具备预言性质的梦。他以孩童的好奇心和探知方式试图理解周围的世界,与此同时,他也在内心调和着来自父母双方对立的期望。乌蒂玛(Ultima)是一个年老的奇卡诺治疗师(curandera),她来到安东尼奥的家准备度过她的余生。当安东尼奥在试图理解自己与周围事物的冲突和矛盾时,她便给予建议。小说透过安东尼奥的探寻历程将社会变化、宗教与文化冲突、民族认同以及主人公心理和认知的发展展现在读者面前。书中神秘且富有动感的场景变换、预言性的梦境以及暴力与死亡的情节使整个故事有很强的可读性。

《祝福我,乌蒂玛》最具地域特色的部分就是对巫术的描写。巫术植根于美国西南地区的西班牙裔和本土裔文化中,有关这一地区的历史和叙述中不乏有关于药剂、魔法石、玩偶、邪眼、黑色仪式和其他巫术的记录。少数族裔普遍存在泛神论的世界观,宇宙间的善恶是并存的,善恶不仅体现在凡人身上,神祇也有善恶之分。巫师的黑暗力量出自神的安排,因此他们通常享有很高的地位。当然,如果他们滥用魔法而有损巫师声誉,也会遭到惩罚(如特伦门蒂娜三姐妹因施黑魔法而遭反噬)。小说中有关巫术的刻画主要集中在以乌蒂玛为代表的治疗师和以特伦门蒂娜三姐妹(three Trementina sisters)为代表的邪恶女巫(brujas)的斗法场景。另外,小说还有意在人物和情节的设置上巧妙地暗合了命理学,比如特伦门蒂娜三姐妹、三个带有预言性质的梦、三次关于乌蒂玛身份的揭示、乌蒂玛三次干预别人的命运等等。小说还通过"对立"暗喻墨西哥裔与白人在多个层面的冲突,比如安东尼奥父母的宗教观以及他们对生活和安东尼奥的愿景是对立的;当地人的信仰是对立的(天主教和巫术);宇宙的力量是以善与恶的形式对立的;自然也是以各种形式对立的(如干燥与清凉,贫瘠与肥沃)。这些对立不仅反映出安东尼奥内心的冲突和对自我身份认识的挣扎,也反映了该地区社会和文化的冲突。

(三)作品选读:《祝福我,乌蒂玛》②

Once

Hey Toni-eeeeee. Hulooooo Antonioforous!

A voice called.

At first I thought I was dreaming. I was fishing, and sitting on a rock; the sun beating on my

① Dick, Bruce & Sirias, Silvio, eds. *Conversations with Rudolfo Anaya*. Jackson: University of Mississippi Press, 1998, p.99.

② Anaya, Rudolfo. *Bless Me, Ultima*. Berkeley: TQS Publications, 1972, pp.106-121.

back had made me sleepy. I had been thinking how Ultima's medicine had cured my uncle and how he was well and could work again. I had been thinking how the medicine of the doctors and of the priest had failed. In my mind I could not understand how the power of God could fail. But it had.

"Toni-eeeeee!" the voice called again.

I opened my eyes and peered into the green brush of the river. Silently, like a deer, the figure of Cico① emerged. He was barefoot, he made no noise. He moved to the rock and squatted in front of me. I guess it was then that he decided to trust me with the secret of the golden carp.

"Cico?" I said. He nodded his dark, freckled face.

"Samuel told you about the golden carp," he said.

"Yes," I replied.

"Have you ever fished for carp?" he asked. "Here in the river, or anywhere?"

"No," I shook my head. I felt as if I was making a solemn oath.

"Do you want to see the golden carp?" he whispered.

"I have hoped to see him all summer," I said breathlessly.

"Do you believe the golden carp is a god?" he asked.

The commandment of the Lord said, Thou shalt have no other gods before me...

I could not lie. I knew he would find the lie in my eyes if I did. But maybe there were other gods? Why had the power of God failed to cure my uncle?

"I am a Catholic," I stuttered, "I can believe only in the God of the church—" I looked down. I was sorry because now he would not take me to see the golden carp. For a long time Cico did not speak.

"At least you are truthful, Tony," he said. He stood up. The quiet waters of the river washed gently southward. "We have never taken a non-believer to see him," he said solemnly.

"But I want to believe," I looked up and pleaded, "it's just that I have to believe in Him?" I pointed across the river to where the cross of the church showed above the tree tops.

"Perhaps—" he mused for a long time. "Will you make an oath?" he asked.

"Yes," I answered. But the commandment said, Thou shalt not take the Lord's name in vain.

"Swear by the cross of the church that you will never hunt or kill a carp." He pointed to the cross. I had never sworn on the cross before. I knew that if you broke your oath it was the biggest sin a man could commit, because God was witness to the swearing on his name. But I would keep my promise! I would never break my oath!

"I swear," I said.

"Come!" Cico was off, wading across the river. I followed. I had waded across that river many times, but I never felt an urgency like today. I was excited about seeing the magical golden carp.

...

---

① 按:奇科是安东尼的朋友,他带安东尼奥去看金鲤鱼并给他讲述洪水摧毁城镇的预言。

We sat for a long time, waiting for the golden carp. It was very pleasant to sit in the warm sunshine and watch the pure waters drift by. The drone of the summer insects and grasshoppers made me sleepy. The lush green of the grass was cool, and beneath the grass was the dark earth, patient, waiting...

To the northeast two hawks circled endlessly in the clear sky. There must be something dead on the road to Tucumcari, I thought. Then the golden carp came. Cico pointed and I turned to where the stream came out of the dark grotto of overhanging tree branches. At first I thought I must be dreaming. I had expected to see a carp the size of a river carp, perhaps a little bigger and slightly orange instead of brown. I rubbed my eyes and watched in astonishment.

"Behold the golden carp, Lord of the waters—" I turned and saw Cico standing, his spear held across his chest as if in acknowledgment of the presence of a ruler.

The huge, beautiful form glided through the blue waters. I could not believe its size. It was bigger than me! And bright orange! The sunlight glistened off his golden scales. He glided down the creek with a couple of small carp following, but they were like minnows compared to him.

"The golden carp," I whispered in awe. I could not have been more entranced if I had seen the Virgin, or God Himself. The golden carp had seen me. It made a wide sweep, its back making ripples in the dark water. I could have reached out into the water and touched the holy fish!

"He knows you are a friend," Cico whispered.

Then the golden carp swam by Cico and disappeared into the darkness of the pond. I felt my body trembling as I saw the bright golden form disappear. I knew I had witnessed a miraculous thing, the appearance of a pagan god, a thing as miraculous as the curing of my uncle Lucas. And I thought, the power of God failed where Ultima's worked; and then a sudden illumination of beauty and understanding flashed through my mind. This is what I had expected God to do at my first holy communion! If God was witness to my beholding of the golden carp then I had sinned! I clasped my hands and was about to pray to the heavens when the waters of the pond exploded.

I turned in time to see Cico hurl his spear at the monstrous black bass that had broken the surface of the waters. The evil mouth of the black bass was open and red. Its eyes were glazed with hate as it hung in the air surrounded by churning water and a million diamond droplets of water. The spear whistled through the air, but the aim was low. The huge tail swished and contemptuously flipped it aside. Then the black form dropped into the foaming waters.

...

The orange of the golden carp appeared at the edge of the pond. As he came out of the darkness of the pond the sun caught his shiny scales and the light reflected orange and yellow and red. He swam very close to our feet. His body was round and smooth in the clear water. We watched in silence at the beauty and grandeur of the great fish. Out of the corners of my eyes I saw Cico hold his hand to his breast as the golden carp glided by. Then with a switch of his powerful tail the golden carp disappeared into the shadowy water under the thicket.

...①

I went home and thought about what I had seen and the story Cico told. I went to Ultima and told her the story. She said nothing. She only smiled. It was as if she knew the story and found nothing fantastic or impending in it. "I would have told you the story myself," she nodded wisely, "but it is better that you hear the legend from someone your own age..."

"Am I to believe the story?" I asked. I was worried.

"Antonio," she said calmly and placed her hand on my shoulder, "I cannot tell you what to believe. Your father and your mother can tell you, because you are their blood, but I cannot. As you grow into manhood you must find your own truths—"

That night in my dreams I walked by the shore of a great lake. A bewitching melody filled the air. It was the song of the mer-woman! I looked into the dark depths of the lake and saw the golden carp, and all around him were the people he had saved. On the bleached shores of the lake the carcasses of sinners rotted. ②

Then a huge golden moon came down from the heavens and settled on the surface of the calm waters. I looked towards the enchanting light, expecting to see the Virgin of Guadalupe, but in her place I saw my mother!

Mother, I cried, you are saved! We are all saved!

Yes, my Antonio, she smiled, we who were baptized in the water of the moon which was made holy by our Holy Mother the Church are saved.

Lies! my father shouted, Antonio was not baptized in the holy water of the moon, but in the salt water of the sea!

I turned and saw him standing on the corpse-strewn shore.

I felt a searing pain spread through my body.

Oh please tell me which is the water that runs through my veins, I moaned; oh please tell me which is the water that washes my burning eyes!

It is the sweet water of the moon, my mother crooned softly, it is the water the Church chooses to make holy and place in its font. It is the water of your baptism.

Lies, lies, my father laughed, through your body runs the salt water of the oceans. It is that water which makes you Márez and not Luna. It is the water that binds you to the pagan god of Cico, the golden carp!

Oh, I cried, please tell me. The agony of pain was more than I could bear. The excruciating pain broke and I sweated blood.

There was a howling wind as the moon rose and its powers pulled at the still waters of the lake.

---

① 按：此处省略奇科给安东尼奥讲述的预言：如果人类继续犯罪，大地将会沉入水中，所有人都会淹死。

② 按：原著从此处开始用斜体表示安东尼奥的梦境。

Thunder split the air and the lightning bursts illuminated the churning, frothy tempest. The ghosts stood and walked upon the shore.

The lake seemed to respond with rage and fury. It cracked with the laughter of madness as it inflicted death upon the people. I thought the end had come to everything. The cosmic struggle of the two forces would destroy everything!

The doom which Cico had predicted was upon us! I clasped my hands and knelt to pray. The terrifying end was near. Then I heard a voice speak above the sound of the storm. I looked up and saw Ultima.

Cease! she cried to the raging powers, and the power from the heavens and the power from the earth obeyed her. The storm abated.

Stand, Antonio, she commanded, and I stood. You both know, she spoke to my father and my mother, that the sweet water of the moon which falls as rain is the same water that gathers into rivers and flows to fill the seas. Without the waters of the moon to replenish the oceans there would be no oceans. And the same salt waters of the oceans are drawn by the sun to the heavens, and in turn become again the waters of the moon. Without the sun there would be no waters formed to slake the dark earth's thirst.

The waters are one, Antonio. I looked into her bright, clear eyes and understood her truth.

You have been seeing only parts, she finished, and not looking beyond into the great cycle that binds us all.

Then there was peace in my dreams and I could rest.

思考与讨论

(1) 为什么安东尼奥在寻找金鲤鱼的路上会想到天主教的教义？这反映了他什么样的心理活动？

(2) 安东尼奥看到金鲤鱼时的心理活动是什么样的？与之前相比，他的心理发生了怎样的转变？

(3) 在安东尼奥的梦境中，他父母争执的焦点是什么？安东尼奥的反应是什么样的？乌蒂玛如何看待这场争执？

拓展阅读

[1] Geary, Robert. *The Supernatural in Gothic Fiction: Horror, Belief, and Literary Change*. Lewiston: Edwin Mellon, 1992.

[2] Robinson, Cecil. *No Short Journeys: The Interplay of Cultures in the History and Literature of the Borderlands*. Tucson: University of Arizona Press, 1992.

[3] Rosales, Jesús & Fonseca, Vanessa, eds. *Spanish Perspectives on Chicano Literature: Literary and Cultural Essays*. Columbus: Ohio State University Press, 2017.

三、安妮·赖斯及其代表作简介

（一）安妮·赖斯简介

安妮·赖斯（Anne Rice，1941—2021）出生于新奥尔良市的一个爱尔兰天主教家庭，但她在少年时期就放弃了天主教，20岁时与诗人斯坦·赖斯成婚。他们的第一个女儿米歇尔（Michelle）在五岁时死于白血病，这让她深受打击。因此，她在作品《夜访吸血鬼》里创作了一个孩童吸血鬼克劳迪娅（Claudia）的形象，以寄托自己的情感。

赖斯的第一部小说《夜访吸血鬼》（*Interview with the Vampire*，1976）的意外成功，促使她以吸血鬼为题材创作出一系列小说，包括《吸血鬼莱斯特》（*The Vampire Lestat*，1985）、《吸血鬼女王》（*The Queen of the Damned*，1988）、《盗尸贼》（*The Tale of the Body Thief*，1992）、《恶魔迈诺克》（*Memnoch the Devil*，1995）、《吸血鬼阿曼德》（*The Vampire Armand*，1998））、《梅瑞克》（*Merrick*，2000）、《血和黄金》（*Blood and Gold*，2001）、《布莱克伍德庄园》（*Blackwood Farm*，2002）、《血之颂歌》（*Blood Canticle*，2003）、《莱斯特王子》（*Prince Lestat*，2014）、《莱斯特王子和亚特兰蒂斯王国》（*Prince Lestat and the Realms of Atlantis*，2016）和《血之圣餐》（*Blood Communion*，2018），构建了一个庞大的吸血鬼帝国，形成了一部吸血鬼编年史（Vampire Chronicles）。

安妮·赖斯笔下的吸血鬼都有自己独特的个性和对生命及存在的独特思考，正如她自己所言："在幻想的领域内，我可以接触到真实的自己……这给予我一个通道——吸血鬼可以和我谈论生与死，至爱与遗憾，还有悲伤与痛苦以及恶与恨"①。她笔下的吸血鬼不再是人的对立面，虽然他们像传统文学作品里的吸血鬼一样保留了恐怖的能力，但他们更像是一群"局外人"（outsider），"他们身处所有事件之中，然而所有的一切都与他们无关"②，他们忍受孤独，追寻生存的意义和人性的本质，在兽性本能和人性渴望中挣扎。安妮·赖斯的吸血鬼小说拒绝二元化的对立，模糊界限与分歧，她笔下的吸血鬼不能简单以善与恶、天使与魔鬼进行定义和区分。她的作品从《夜访吸血鬼》开始就体现出解构与破坏的力量，促使我们重新审视对吸血鬼的恐惧与厌恶，并提供了一种审美的可能性。

（二）《夜访吸血鬼》简介

《夜访吸血鬼》是安妮·赖斯于1976年出版的小说，以吸血鬼路易（Louis）和采访者丹尼尔·莫洛伊（Daniel Molloy）的对话开场，讲述了路易200年的心路历程。1791年，生活在路易斯安那州的种植园主路易因家庭变故悲痛欲绝，试图自杀。吸血鬼莱斯特（Lestat）找到他并将他转化成了吸血鬼后，两人便在一起生活。莱斯特继续以猎杀人类为生，而路易发现自己无法摆脱世俗道德的约束，只肯猎杀动物。当两人的身份暴露后，他们逃到了新奥尔良。路易最终在莱斯特的影响下开始吸食人血，但他内心对莱斯特毫无怜悯的猎杀举动日渐反感。

一天晚上，路易吸食了一个感染瘟疫的女孩，在女孩濒死之际，莱斯特将她转化为吸血鬼，给她取名

① Riley, Michael. *Interview with Anne Rice*. London: Chatto and Windus, 1996, p.14.

② Ibid., p.3.

为克劳迪娅(Claudia),成了他们二人的“女儿”。尽管克劳迪娅很快学会像莱斯特一般肆意杀人捕食,路易却对克劳迪娅非常宠溺。随着岁月的增长,克劳迪娅已是一个思想成熟、聪明自信的女人,但她的身体却永远是6岁孩童的模样。她开始憎恨始作俑者莱斯特。克劳迪娅用计给莱斯特下毒,割开他的喉咙,并和路易一起把他的尸体扔进了沼泽地。随后他们一起去了欧洲,想在“旧世界”寻找自己的同类。出乎意料的是,他们在途中遭到莱斯特的伏击,路易放火烧了房子,困住莱斯特,与克劳迪娅一起侥幸逃生。

在巴黎,他们遇到了同类——400岁的阿曼德(Armand)和他的“吸血鬼剧院”(Théâtre des vampires)。阿曼德和他的吸血鬼剧团成员在舞台上上演吸食真人的表演,而观众们则认为这些杀戮只是表演。克劳迪娅内心厌恶这种做法,但路易很快就对阿曼德着迷,克劳迪娅担心路易会为了阿曼德而离开她,要求路易把玩偶制造商玛德琳(Madeleine)变成吸血鬼,以便她离开路易后有人能继续陪伴她。路易最初拒绝,意识到克劳迪娅的困境后,他屈服了。

三人平静地生活了一段时间,莱斯特又找到了他们。在他的指控下,路易被阿曼德剧团的吸血鬼锁进棺材,而卡劳迪娅和玛德琳则被他们扔进一间没有屋顶的牢房。等阿曼德从棺材里救出路易之后,路易发现克劳迪娅和玛德琳都已化成灰烬。路易一怒之下烧了剧院,杀光里面所有的吸血鬼后,和阿曼德一起离开。路易和阿曼德一起在欧洲旅行,但路易一直没有从克劳迪娅的死亡中完全恢复。最终,他和阿曼德分道扬镳。

厌倦了“旧世界”的路易最终返回新奥尔良,他孤独一人,厌倦了作为吸血鬼的永生和由此带来的各种痛苦与折磨。故事最后,采访者丹尼尔着迷吸血鬼的力量,请求路易把他转化为吸血鬼,路易生气地拒绝并消失。

安妮·赖斯用悲悯的语调展现了吸血鬼路易迷惘而困惑的生命体验,永生对路易而言更像是一种诅咒与惩罚,颇具讽刺意味的是采访者丹尼尔只惊叹于吸血鬼的神奇力量,却未能体会到路易的痛苦与绝望,竟要求路易将他转化为吸血鬼。丹尼尔对永生的迷恋反映出人性的偏狭,他没能意识到路易迷惘与痛苦的永生之路是浮士德式悲剧的另一种注解。不仅如此,赖斯更是通过克劳迪娅从“死—生—死”的历程让这一悲剧以更强烈的形式呈现。克劳迪娅最初因感染瘟疫而被遗弃街头,濒临死亡,路易的捕食和莱斯特的转化让她陷入到一种悖论里,她既是“死的”又是“活的”(从人类变成吸血鬼而存在于世间),她“活着”又“已死”(以非人类的形式存在却被禁锢在死去那一刻的躯壳内)。这样的存在形式让她遭受了深刻且痛苦的禁锢——不仅是生理的、心理的、社会的,还有文化的。历经岁月的克劳迪娅在心理上已是一个成熟的女性,在身体上她却无法摆脱6岁孩童的形象;她和路易与莱斯特是一样的存在,论智谋与胆识有过之而无不及,但她在世人眼中只能以“女儿”的身份(一种低等的、服从者、被照顾者的身份)出现在他们身边;她憎恨她的创造者和“父亲”莱斯特,因为是他阻碍了她的成长,她杀死莱斯特的举动,是一起文化层面的“弑父”行为。在这之后,她并未获得理想中的自由。作为“女孩”,她无法独自社交、生活,她不得不继续依附路易;正当她为自己谋划出一条独自生活的道路时,那个阴魂不散的“父亲”莱斯特再次站在她面前,指控她的“弑父”行为,这让她彻底地灭亡了。安妮·赖斯通过克劳蒂娅的悲剧,以女性作家特有的洞察力展现了女性在男权社会破除自身神话的困境。

另外,《夜访吸血鬼》舍弃了传统吸血鬼叙事中双性别主角模式,毫不避讳地呈现同性关系。小说中细致地刻画了莱斯特与路易之间以及路易与阿曼德之间的复杂的情感纠葛,这种对禁忌欲望的书写也成为后来诸多吸血鬼小说中常见的叙事内容。赖斯巧妙地利用了吸血鬼"另类"的特征，把当时同样作为"另类"的同性恋禁忌叠加上去，使得这部吸血鬼小说更具颠覆性。

（三）作品选读：《夜访吸血鬼》[1]

Part III

...

Entering the rooms of the Hôtel Saint-Gabriel, I set the picture on the mantel above the fire and looked at it a long time. Claudia was somewhere in the rooms, and some other presence intruded, as though on one of the balconies above a woman or a man stood near, giving off an unmistakable personal perfume. And then, as if in a mist, I[2] saw a woman there.

She was seated calmly at that lavish table where Claudia attended to her hair; and so still she sat, so utterly without fear, her green taffeta sleeves reflected in the tilted mirrors, her skirts reflected, that she was not one still woman but a gathering of women. Her dark-red hair was parted in the middle and drawn back to her ears, though a dozen little ringlets escaped to make a frame for her pale face. And she was looking at me with two calm, violet eyes and a child's mouth that seemed almost obdurately soft, obdurately the Cupid's bow unsullied by paint or personality; and the mouth smiled now and said, as those eyes seemed to fire: "Yes, he's as you said he would be, and I love him already. He's as you said." She rose now, gently lifting that abundance of dark taffeta, and the three small mirrors emptied at once.

And utterly baffled and almost incapable of speech, I turned to see Claudia far off on the immense bed, her small face rigidly calm, though she clung to the silk curtain with a tight fist. "Madeleine," she said under her breath, "Louis is shy." And she watched with cold eyes as Madeleine only smiled when she said this and, drawing closer to me, put both of her hands to the lace fringe around her throat, moving it back so I could see the two small marks there. Then the smile died on her lips, and they became at once sullen and sensual as her eyes narrowed and she breathed the word, "Drink."

I turned away from her, my fist rising in a consternation for which I couldn't find words. But then Claudia had hold of that fist and was looking up at me with relentless eyes. "Do it, Louis," she commanded. "Because I cannot do it." Her voice was painfully calm, all the emotion under the hard, measured tone. "I haven't the size, I haven't the strength! You saw to that when you made me! Do it!"

I broke away from her, clutching my wrist as if she'd burned it. I could see the door, and it seemed to me the better part of wisdom to leave by it at once. I could feel Claudia's strength, her will, and the mortal woman's eyes seemed afire with that same will. But Claudia held me, not with

---

① Rice, Anne. *Interview with the Vampire*. New York: Ballantine Books, 1976, pp. 270 - 278.

② 按：这里是路易的回忆，所以都以第一人称视角讲述。

a gentle pleading, a miserable coaxing that would have dissipated that power, making me feel pity for her as I gathered my own forces. She held me with the emotion her eyes had evinced even through her coldness and the way that she turned away from me now, almost as if she'd been instantly defeated. I did not understand the manner in which she sank back on the bed, her head bowed, her lips moving feverishly, her eyes rising only to scan the walls. I wanted to touch her and say to her that what she asked was impossible; I wanted to soothe that fire that seemed to be consuming her from within.

And the soft, mortal woman had settled into one of the velvet chairs by the fire, with the rustling and iridescence of her taffeta dress surrounding her like part of the mystery of her, of her dispassionate eyes which watched us now, the fever of her pale face. I remember turning to her, spurred on by that childish, pouting mouth set against the fragile face. The vampire kiss had left no visible trace except the wound, no inalterable change on the pale-pink flesh. "How do we appear to you?" I asked, seeing her eyes on Claudia. She seemed excited by the diminutive beauty, the awful woman's-passion knotted in the small dimpled hands.

She broke her gaze and looked up at me. "I ask you … how do we appear? Do you think us beautiful, magical, our white skin, our fierce eyes? Oh, I remember perfectly what mortal vision was, the dimness of it, and how the vampire's beauty burned through that veil, so powerfully alluring, so utterly deceiving! Drink, you tell me. You haven't the vaguest conception under God of what you ask!"

But Claudia rose from the bed and came towards me. "How dare you!" she whispered. "How dare you make this decision for both of us! Do you know how I despise you! Do you know that I despise you with a passion that eats at me like a canker!" Her small form trembled, her hands hovering over the pleated bodice of her yellow gown. "Don't you look away from me! I am sick at heart with your looking away, with your suffering. You understand nothing. Your evil is that you cannot be evil, and I must suffer for it. I tell you, I will suffer no longer!" Her fingers bit into the flesh of my wrist; I twisted, stepping back from her, foundering in the face of the hatred, the rage rising like some dormant beast in her, looking out through her eyes. "Snatching me from mortal hands like two grim monsters in a nightmare fairy tale, you idle, blind parents! Fathers!" She spat the word. "Let tears gather in your eyes. You haven't tears enough for what you've done to me. Six more mortal years, seven, eight … I might have had that shape!" Her pointed finger flew at Madeleine, whose hands had risen to her face, whose eyes were clouded over. Her moan was almost Claudia's name. But Claudia did not hear her. "Yes, that shape, I might have known what it was to walk at your side. Monsters! To give me immortality in this hopeless guise, this helpless form!" The tears stood in her eyes. The words had died away, drawn in, as it were, on her breast.

"Now, you give her to me!" she said, her head bowing, her curls tumbling down to make a concealing veil. "You give her to me. You do this, or you finish what you did to me that night in the hotel in New Orleans. I will not live with this hatred any longer, I will not live with this rage! I cannot. I will not abide it!" And tossing her hair, she put her hands to her ears as if to stop the sound of her own words, her breath drawn in rapid gasps, the tears seeming to scald her cheeks.

I had sunk to my knees at her side, and my arms were outstretched as if to enfold her. Yet I dared not touch her, dared not even say her name, lest my own pain break from me with the first syllable in a monstrous outpouring of hopelessly inarticulate cries.

"Oooh." She shook her head now, squeezing the tears out onto her cheeks, her teeth clenched tight together. "I love you still, that's the torment of it. The measure of my hatred is that love. They are the same! Do you know now how much I hate you!" She flashed at me through the red film that covered her eyes.

"Yes," I whispered. I bowed my head. But she was gone from me into the arms of Madeleine, who enfolded her desperately, as if she might protect Claudia from me—the irony of it, the pathetic irony—protect Claudia from herself. She was whispering to Claudia, "Don't cry, don't cry!" her hands stroking Claudia's face and hair with a fierceness that would have bruised a human child.

...

And there they were together, a tender mortal crying unstintingly now, her warm arms holding what she could not possibly understand, this white and fierce and unnatural child thing she believed she loved. And if I had not felt for her, this mad and reckless woman flirting with the damned, if I had not felt all the sorrow for her I felt for my mortal self, I would have wrested the demon thing from her arms, held it tight to me, denying over and over the words I'd just heard. But I knelt there still, thinking only. The love is equal to the hatred; gathering that selfishly to my own breast, holding onto that as I sank back against the bed.

...

"All you've said to me is true," I said to her. "I deserve your hatred. I've deserved it from those first moments when Lestat put you in my arms."

She seemed unaware of me, and her eyes were infused with a soft light, and then she said, wondering, "You could have killed me then, despite him. You could have done it." Then her eyes rested on me calmly. "Do you wish to do it now?"

"Do it now!" I put my arm around her, moved her close to me, warmed by her softened voice. "Are you mad, to say such things to me? Do I want to do it now!"

"I want you to do it," she said. "Bend down now as you did then, draw the blood out of me drop by drop, all you have the strength for; push my heart to the brink. I am small, you can take me. I won't resist you, I am something frail you can crush like a flower."

"You mean these things? You mean what you say to me?"

"Would you die with me?" she asked, with a sly, mocking smile. "Would you in fact die with me?" she pressed. "Don't you understand what is happening to me? That he's killing me, that master vampire who has you in thrall, that he won't share your love with me, not a drop of it? I'm fighting for my life! Give her to me so she can care for me, complete the guise I must have to live! And he can have you then! I am fighting for my life!"

I all but shoved her off. "No, no, it's madness, it's witchery," I said, trying to defy her.

Oh, if she could only have understood! But that was nothing to me now; something far more terrible than I could grasp was happening, something I was only beginning to understand, against which my anger was nothing but a mockery, a hollow attempt to oppose her tenacious will. She hated me, she loathed me, as she herself had confessed, and my heart shriveled inside me, as if, in depriving me of that love which had sustained me a lifetime, she had dealt me a mortal blow.

...

But it went beyond that, in some region from which I was shrinking as I strode back and forth, back and forth, my hands opening and closing at my sides, feeling not only that hatred in her liquid eyes: It was her pain. She had shown me her pain! *To give me immortality in this hopeless guise, this helpless form.* I put my hands to my ears, as if she spoke the words yet, and the tears flowed. For all these years I had depended utterly upon her cruelty, her absolute lack of pain! And pain was what she showed to me, undeniable pain.

...

The urgent pain of Claudia's loss pressed in on me, behind me, like a shape gathered from the corners of this cluttered and oddly alien room. But outside, even as the night seemed to dissolve in a fierce driving wind, I could feel something calling to me, something inanimate which I'd never known. And a power within me seemed to answer that power, not with resistance but with an inscrutable, chilling strength.

思考与讨论

(1) 克劳迪娅向路易提出了什么要求？为什么？

(2) 路易对克劳迪娅的要求有什么反应？他最后的决定是什么？

(3) 为什么克劳迪娅说路易给了她一具“糟糕的伪装”和“无助的形体”？

拓展阅读

[1] Auerbach, Nina. *Our Vampires, Ourselves.* Chicago: University of Chicago Press, 1995.

[2] Botting, Fred. *Sex, Machines, and Navels: Fiction, Fantasy, and History in the Future Present.* Manchester: Manchester University Press, 1999.

[3] Day, William Patrick. *In the Circles of Fear and Desire: a Study of Gothic Fantasy.* Chicago: University of Chicago Press, 1985.